# ROBBI RENEE

# Somebody's HUSBAND

BLACK ODYSSEY MEDIA

WWW.BLACKODYSSEY.NET

Published by
BLACK ODYSSEY MEDIA

www.blackodyssey.net
Email: info@blackodyssey.net

SOMEBODY'S HUSBAND. Copyright © 2025 by ROBBI RENEE

Library of Congress Control Number: 2023919239

First Trade Paperback Printing: January 2025
ISBN: 978-1-957950-57-0
ISBN: 978-1-957950-58-7 (e-book)

10 9 8 7 6 5 4 3 2 1

Manufactured in the United States of America

Distributed by Kensington Publishing Corp.

Dear Reader,

I want to thank you immensely for supporting Black Odyssey Media and our ongoing efforts to spotlight the diverse narratives of blossoming and seasoned storytellers. With every manuscript we acquire, we believe that it took talent, discipline, and remarkable courage to construct that story, flesh out those characters, and prepare it for the world. Debut or seasoned, our authors are the real heroes and heroines in *OUR* story. For them, we are eternally grateful.

Whether you are new to Robbi Renee or Black Odyssey Media, we hope that you are here to stay. Our goal is to make a lasting impact in the publishing landscape, one step at a time and one book at a time. We also welcome your feedback and kindly ask that you leave a review. For upcoming releases, announcements, submission guidelines, etc., please be sure to visit our website at www.blackodyssey.net or scan the QR code below. And remember, no matter where you are in your journey, the best of both worlds begins now!

Joyfully,

Shawanda Williams

Shawanda "N'Tyse" Williams
Founder & CEO, Black Odyssey Media

# AUTHOR'S NOTE

"And the day came when the risk to remain tight in a bud
was more painful than the risk it took to blossom."
— *Anais Nin*

*Somebody's Husband* is not a story of infidelity but a story of
second chances. It's the story of a man who loved a woman immensely,
believing that she would be his one and only true love ... until he was
faced with a season of suffering, causing a loss so monumental, he
could hardly stand to take a breath.

But then one day, the man was able to breathe without effort.
A familiar feeling returned, a sensation he'd become numb to years
ago ... a thunderous *thud* in the center of his chest. A spark that
set his soul aflame. But he was in his head, allowing the wounds of
his past to direct his path instead of following the beat of his heart.
Then one day, this man realized that it was acceptable to mourn a
lost love *and* reach for a new day to laugh and love again.

# Chapter one

"Dres, you don't think this house is too big? Too expensive? And it needs a ton of work, babe," Nina said, looking over her shoulder at her husband as they toured the dated 1970s home in Upper Marlboro, Maryland.

Dresden gazed at his wife with the same dreamy eyes that landed on her pretty face across the yard at Howard University when they were college freshmen.

Dr. Dresden Xavier and Nina Rose Hanover married three years ago after graduating from Howard University. Dresden was premed, and Nina was an education major.

Dresden continued his studies at Howard University Medical School, where he recently graduated after completing his residency at the University of Maryland Medical Center. Nina joined Teach For America and worked as a middle school math teacher for two years.

The Xaviers decided to make Maryland their permanent home after Dresden was offered a coveted position as a lead researcher in the university's Comprehensive Cancer Center.

*"No, it's not too big, and yes, it's too expensive, and yes . . . It's a diamond in the rough," Dresden said, chuckling as he shortened the distance between them.*

*Gliding his hand around her swollen pregnant belly, he pulled her into his body.*

*"Rosie, we deserve this. Sweetheart, you deserve this," he uttered the words against her neck before kissing her there.*

*Nina rested in his protective embrace and smiled.*

*"Baby, you've been my rock since the day we met. You've supported my dreams even when it meant postponing yours. I owe you this, Mrs. Xavier."*

*Dresden spun her around to face him. Leaning into the kiss, they chuckled at how her protruding belly blocked their intimacy. He cupped her face, drew her lips closer, and kissed her softly.*

*"I guess we're moving on up," she sang sarcastically, mocking the classic television show's theme song.*

An audible sigh echoed through the empty space. Dresden stood in the middle of his living room, slowly circling, digesting all the memories that resided in the walls and crevices of his family's home.

He recalled the night he carried his wife, Nina, over the threshold of their new home, although they'd already been married for a few years. And the day they brought home their identical twin girls, Bella and Bryn, from the hospital. He reminisced on the nights he and his wife, who he lovingly called *Rosie*, would slow dance to Teddy Pendergrass in the sunroom after the girls were asleep.

After nineteen marvelous years in the four-bedroom home nestled on a cul-de-sac, much had changed in just two short years. Dr. Dresden Xavier was a forty-four-year-old single dad to his now-nineteen-year-old twins . . . and a widower.

Two years ago, in the very home that they eventually made their dream home, his wife of twenty-two years peacefully passed away. She was surrounded by her family and close friends after a valiant eighteen-month battle with ovarian cancer.

"Daddy, you ready?" Bryn asked.

Dresden slowly spun around to view his beautiful baby girl. Both Bryn and Bella carried so many features of their mother, but Bryn . . . Bryn was Nina's clone. Gorgeous cinnamon skin was speckled with freckles, and auburn-brown curly hair grew back after she shaved her head alongside her mother. Bryn had the widest smile that could brighten the foggiest day, just like his Rosie.

He nodded, opening his arms to receive her. Bryn hadn't said she needed comforting, but the reddened gloss in her eyes told all her secrets. She quickly diminished the gap between them, burrowing her face into her daddy's chest. Bryn tried her best to compose the brewing emotions, but something about her dad's caress allowed her to release them. A deafening wail whirled through the space entwined with the family memories. She was a daddy's girl, but her mother's death crippled her. It disabled the entire family.

Nina was the bedrock, . . . the foundation of the Xavier clan. She always had been. Postponing her desire to attend graduate school, she worked tirelessly as a schoolteacher while Dresden completed medical school and then his residency. She dreamed of starting an education nonprofit serving Black kids in the Baltimore area. Nina's dream was further deferred when she became pregnant. Raising twins who quickly transitioned into rambunctious toddlers became her full-time job.

Dresden kissed the top of his daughter's head as she settled. Although they were surviving, the grief was often unpredictable and overwhelming. The decision to leave the only home his daughters had known revived so many unexpected emotions that they'd vainly attempted to erase.

"We're going to be OK, sweetie. Leaving the house doesn't mean we're leaving Mom because she's—"

"The sun, the moon, and the stars. Mommy is everywhere we are," Bryn said, sniffing and swiping away her tears.

He nodded.

Dresden covered her cheeks with kisses until his daughter reluctantly released a boisterous giggle.

"Dad," Bryn groaned, playfully pushing him away.

"Is Daddy giving sloppy kisses again, B?" An identical voice to Bryn's rang from the front door.

Bella crossed the threshold into the house and joined in on the embrace. Where Bryn was feisty and fearless like her mother, Bella was somewhat timid and cautious, similar to her dad. She had to calculate and forecast every possibility before making any decisions. The one choice that she was absolutely resolute about was delaying college to stay home to care for her mother.

Nina and Bella were always a close-knit unit, but during those final months, they were inseparable. Their moments were sometimes filled with lively chatter, and other instances overflowed with tearful yet silent exchanges. They'd document family recipes, journal, paint, and even select a design for Bella's wedding dress so that Nina could participate in the process whenever that day came.

When her mother died, Dresden expected Bella to be the most devastated, given the numerous hours they spent together over the last several months of Nina's life. Surprisingly, Bella had been the most grounded throughout the entire ordeal. She managed her grief in what her mother would consider an "appropriate way."

Bella allowed herself to feel ... *everything*. She cried, screamed, laughed, and braved the woe whenever and wherever she needed to, whereas Dresden and Bryn went numb, suffering in silence and solitude. They busied themselves with school and work.

Bella's eyes surveyed the only home she'd known and mouthed, "*Wow*," stunned and saddened by the emptiness. The space that used to be filled with beautiful paintings and artifacts that Nina personally selected was now bare, mirroring the void in the Xavier family.

Dresden rested his arms on his daughters' shoulders as they took one last look around the house. A sconce light on the wall flickered, and a soft gush of air prickled their skin. Bryn and Bella chuckled in unison, sounding so much like their mother. Their melodic chords discharged a pang through Dresden's chest.

Twin eyes gazed at their dad, and then Bella uttered, "Mom said you were never going to fix that light," she quipped.

Dresden lifted the corner of his mouth in a sorrow-filled smile.

"Yeah, I guess that was her reminding me," he said, hugging his daughters tighter before they walked toward the door.

Bella and Bryn walked to the truck, leaving Dresden to bid his final farewell alone. He closed his eyes and inhaled the familiar scent of the home for the last time. Whimpering, he faintly whispered, "*I love you, Nina Rose.*"

A second breeze drifted by, tickling his nose. He closed his eyes, allowing the gust to dry his tears. Dresden smiled, seeing visions of Nina as he recalled one of their last conversations.

"*Who the hell am I going to be without you, Rosie? You were supposed to love me forever. We were supposed to do this thing for forever, remember?*" *Dresden allowed himself to cry in front of his wife for the first time since her diagnosis.*

*Nina rubbed the thick carpet of hair on his head while he wept, but there was no sound, just muted tears.*

"*You can love me forever, Dres, and still have room in your heart to love again. I don't want you to finish this race alone. Our girls will need a strong woman to guide them through life's decisions, heartbreak, and love.*" *Nina swallowed hard, taking a moment to catch her breath.*

"You give the best kisses and hugs and have the biggest heart, Dresden Xavier," she said, cupping his chin. "It would be a disgrace to keep all that goodness to yourself."

Nina kissed his cheek, taking another deep breath. As of late, she relied heavily on oxygen to sustain her energy.

"And while it pains me to say this, you can't keep all that good dick stored away," she said as her laugh turned into a cough.

"Nina," Dresden groaned but couldn't quell the faint laughter.

He stroked a finger down her face, which was thinner than usual but still gorgeous. Dresden admired how his wife maintained her sense of humor through their tragedy.

"What, babe? You know you had me under a spell, sprinkling all that ding-dong dust over me the first time we had sex."

Dresden howled, burying his face into her lap as she giggled, kissing the top of his head.

"And it's OK if she's pretty, but not too damn pretty, OK?" she teased, cupping the powerful curves of his face in her hands to lift his head.

"Promise me you'll try, Dresden. The way you love is too good not to share it with the world. Promise me," Nina pleaded, gazing directly into his misty eyes.

"I promise, baby," Dresden declared as his voice broke.

He climbed into bed with his wife. His big body shielded her like a coat of armor.

"Touch me, Dres," Nina whispered, stroking her fingers through his beard.

She traced her fingertip down the slope of his neck, across his firm chest and stomach, finally landing on his growing manhood. Nina caressed his shaft through the thin fabric of his shorts. He moaned because even in her condition, his wife was the cause and cure of his need. He would never deny her the desires of her heart. Nina's wish was always his command.

*Dresden showered gentle kisses all over her face before reaching her lips. After a few soft pecks, he parted the seam of her mouth with his tongue. Even in her delicate state, the kiss was wild and reckless. Their hands explored each other boldly . . . lustfully. He lifted her nightgown, wandering his fingers up her thighs, lightly caressing her center. Nina's head collapsed back onto the bed, moaning in pure bliss. It had been too long since they'd shared a passion-filled moment like that.*

*The chemo and other treatments wreaked havoc on her body but, unfortunately, did nothing to fight the aggressive disease. Three weeks earlier, Nina decided that she was done and opted to discontinue all treatments. Without the debilitating medication, she gained bursts of energy that allowed for brief instances of the insatiable connection they always shared.*

*Dresden knew she was nearing the end, so he cherished every opportunity to demonstrate his desire and adoration for her. That night, he made fervent, yet gentle, passionate love to his Rosie for the very last time.*

"Dad, you ready?" Bella muttered from the doorway.

He nodded. "Yeah, baby girl, I'm coming."

Dresden exhaled an exasperated breath as he walked out of the house and locked the door. Life without Nina had been excruciating, crippling to the point that he thought he was going insane. But after two years of battling grief, he believed that he was finally ready to partake in a new journey.

While his Rosie would never grace his presence again in this earthly life, the best of her resided in his girls. Her soul would forever dwell in his heart.

# Chapter two

A month ago, when Dresden and the twins decided to drive from Maryland to Missouri, they were elated by the adventure. Now that they were two days into their four-day journey, the Xavier family was already exhausted.

Bryn and Bella were bickering more than usual for some unknown reason, while bouts with unexpected traffic due to construction slowed them down. And a botched hotel reservation caused the trio to pile into one room, more than any of them could bear for even one night. Dresden had an achy back from sleeping in a chair the night before and a migraine from the high-pitched squabbling from his daughters.

"Girls, that is enough!" he shouted aggressively, maneuvering the SUV off the highway and into a rest area.

The twins' eyes widened because their father rarely raised his voice, let alone directed toward them.

"Dad—" Bryn tried to speak, but Dresden abruptly tossed up his hand.

"Please. Don't. I just need a minute," he said, annoyance deepening the bass in his voice.

He exited the truck, rubbing a hand down the back of his newly bald head to massage the nape of his neck. Bella and Bryn stared at his back until his stately frame disappeared in the wooded area. Twin orbs stared at each other, a bit panicked and perplexed.

"Do you think he's going to survive this?" Bryn's angst couldn't be denied as she spoke.

Bella nodded. "Daddy is strong. The first few weeks will be tough, but he'll be fine."

"Yeah, but Mom's love for him is what made him strong. Without her ... and in a new place," Bryn countered questioningly. "I don't know. Maybe we shouldn't have left. Daddy is a creature of habit."

"True, but it's time for him to find a new habitat, B. Daddy is a natural nurturer, and pretty soon, he won't have us there to dote over. Being closer to Granny, PopPop, Auntie, and the rest of the family will be good for him. Trust me."

"You really think you're the daddy whisperer, huh?" Bryn uttered, rolling her eyes.

"Because I am," Bella smirked.

"Seriously, B, how can you be so certain that this move is what he needs?" Bryn inquired.

Bella paused, turning to look out the window at her father seated at a table under a large tree. She really didn't believe that she was the *dad whisperer*, as Bella called it, but their mother was. Nina had a unique ability to know what Dresden was thinking even before he spoke any words. During those late-night chats, her mom willed some of that savviness on to her daughter.

"Mom told me," Bella said with the utmost confidence.

Dresden gulped down the cold water before he released a bothered breath. When they planned this trip, he envisioned spending quality time with his girls, visiting landmarks, and making new memories. He had no dream the adventure would be filled with disorderly arguing and gloomy silence. His girls either disagreed over what to eat or buried their heads in their phones.

Dresden was ready to ditch his truck *and* his daughters to find the nearest airport headed anywhere. They'd just left Ohio and were driving into Indiana, so there was still a ways to go before reaching their destination. While he hated admitting it, he understood that his testiness was not all about his teenage daughters. He was surrounded by so much love, but he still felt alone. The farther he traveled away from the place where he became a man, fell in love, nurtured his family, and lost the love of his life, Dresden felt more disconnected from his anchor, his cornerstone.

A kaleidoscope of butterflies fluttered around Dresden as Nina's lyrical tone echoed in his psyche. Lately, he'd been seeing her face more vividly than ever. The reminiscence of moments during her final days played continually in his mind.

*"Why would I sell the house, Rosie?" he asked while they played cards on the balcony attached to their bedroom.*

*Nina was in good spirits and wanted some fresh air, to play games, and to drink wine. Dresden obliged. The twins were gone with their friends, and it was a rare night that they had the house to themselves. Their home had become somewhat like an open house. Friends, family, and health-care providers circled in and out daily.*

*"Because it's our house, Dres. It's my house. We picked every speckle of paint, cabinet fixture, and piece of furniture. I would rather know that another family is enjoying what we built instead of you and whoever her ugly ass will be living in here," Nina said, laughing.*

*"But I thought you said she could be pretty," Dresden cackled, teasing her.*

*"I changed my mind."* Nina rolled her eyes, feigning annoyance. *"She better be ugly as hell with even uglier feet,"* she giggled.

*"But seriously, babe, I want you to explore. Go back home to Monroe like you've always wanted to. We've both been so engrossed in these girls and our careers that we became comfortable in our cushy suburban lifestyle. That is not what we originally planned, but it's the cards that God dealt us . . . And it's been beautiful."*

Dresden frowned. Considering their current situation, he would not describe it as *"beautiful."*

*"Yes, even now. It's probably more beautiful right now,"* she spoke as if she could read his mind.

*"How so?"* Dresden scoffed. He could not comprehend how losing the love of his life was beautiful.

*"Because we have no other choice but to live life richly, fully, and meaningfully. If I weren't sick, we'd be stressing about the girls going to college or your next research project. But now, under the circumstances, every single second counts, and each and every one has been breathtaking with you, my love."*

Dresden stood from his chair and repositioned to squat in front of her. Nina rested her head against his and shared one of those beautiful moments she spoke about.

*"Discover a new world, Dres. Don't get comfortable. Live . . . for me, babe,"* she whispered against his lips. *"Promise me."*

*"I promise."*


"Dad," Bryn whispered, carefully approaching him.

Bella wasn't too far behind her big sister, who was older by seventeen minutes.

Dresden stirred, wiping the traces of memories from his face. He turned to face his girls, who were joined by locked arms. At that moment, they'd reverted back to little girls who always seemed to unify when they were in trouble. He chuckled a little at the bashful expressions on their faces, contradicting their demeanor less than an hour ago.

"B is going to drive while I find us a nice restaurant near the hotel in Indianapolis so you can get some rest," Bryn said.

"And we promise only to fight maybe once more until we get to Monroe City," Bella bantered, and they both lifted their hands for a pinkie swear, unsuccessfully holding in their matching smiles.

Dresden shook his head, unable to suppress his grin. Bryn and Bella leaned in to place a kiss on each cheek before wrapping their arms around their dad. Dresden acted unfazed for about half a second before he wrapped his girls in so much love. They happily headed back to the truck to complete the final leg of their journey.

*Welcome to Monroe City!*

Dresden flashed a closed-mouth smile as he gazed at the sign leading him into his hometown. Monroe City had been home from three years old until he left for college. Moving from a small town to a big city like Washington, D.C., was a significant transition. While he would return several times a year to visit his parents when they weren't living their best-retired life traveling around the world, Dresden was confident he would never return to the town permanently.

*Never say never*, Dresden thought as he drove by what used to be Mr. Carson's meat shop. It was now a large grocery store. His head was on a swivel as he navigated some familiar streets, noticing that the city had drastically changed since his last visit almost three years ago. When Nina was diagnosed with cancer, Dresden's family from Monroe City would visit Maryland as much as possible.

Monroe City had definitely matured, offering chain stores, restaurants, and even a mall with high-end boutiques. Family-owned establishments once occupied downtown, but now bars and fancy restaurants owned by young entrepreneurs lined the streets.

Monroe University was still the center of attraction for the city. But even with all the upgrades, the Midwest pace would take some getting used to for the Xavier family.

Turning in the driveway of his parents' blue and white ranch-style home, he honked the horn to get their attention. They'd downsized in recent years, but the quaint, regal home was just as luxurious as his childhood dwelling.

Dresden's mother, Marcella, was sitting on the wraparound porch enjoying the light breeze offered by the spring afternoon. He shook his head, hearing his mother give his father instructions as she watched her husband, Dresden Sr., plant flowers in the yard.

Dresden laughed when his mother yelled, "Hey, Junior," while she waved. Marcella was the only person in his life that called him *Junior*. His father usually called him son, while his sister, niece, and nephews called him D and Uncle D, respectively.

The twins quickly exited the truck to greet their grandparents. Similar to the connection with her dad, Bryn had a special relationship with her PopPop, while Bella was a granny's girl.

"Hello, my rays of sunshine," his father greeted the twins.

"PopPop! You lookin' good, young man," Bryn teased, repeatedly kissing against his bearded cheek that bore more salt than pepper.

Bella joined in on the other side.

Their grandmother descended the steps with open arms. She was wordless and emotional. Every time she laid eyes on the twins, she saw the best of her daughter-in-law in the chocolate marble eyes of her granddaughters.

Whenever Marcella allowed herself to think about the family's loss, she was affected. Nina was more than a daughter-in-law; she was her friend. Bryn and Bella fell into the comforting embrace of their grandmother and held on until their own sensitivities were quelled.

"Pop, you look great. How are you feeling?" Dresden said, drawing his father into a hug.

"I'm good, son. Walking every day and enjoying this garden your mother started but didn't finish," he chuckled, saying the last part loud enough for his wife to hear.

"Move, Senior," Marcella said, playfully shoving her husband.

"Ma," Dresden drawled. "It's so good to see you."

It had been several months since his parents visited, and he was thankful to see them in good health and spirits. The more he gazed at them, the more the loneliness faded.

Cupping the curves of his face, his mother cooed, "It's wonderful to see you, Junior. You lookin' just as handsome as your daddy."

Dresden smiled, cradling his arm around her shoulders. They slowly ambled up the steps and into the house, making a fuss over each other.

After dinner, Bella and Bryn were in the house with their Aunt Adriana and their cousins while Dresden rocked in the chair alongside his parents on the patio. He'd almost forgotten how beautiful Monroe City was when the sun retreated to make room for the moon.

Watching the sunset was a regular routine for his parents. After many years of marriage, his father still looked at his mother like a precious gemstone. Dresden smiled, blessed to have an amazing example of lifelong love and respect in his parents.

Dresden Sr. and Marcella were married for forty-six years and still behaved like newlyweds. At sixty-nine years old, thankfully, they were both in excellent health, financially stable, and enjoyed life together while maintaining their separate identities and activities.

At forty-four years old, Dresden had no dream that this would not be him and Nina in another twenty years.

"Glad you survived the drive with the girls," his dad said, chuckling.

"Barely," Dresden countered, shaking his head. "They got it together near the end, though."

"When will the moving truck get here?" his mom asked, sipping her iced tea.

"A few days if they don't run into any problems. I'll sign the papers and get the keys to the house tomorrow."

"Rodney and his team will be ready to paint as soon as you say the word," Dresden Sr. announced, referring to his nephew who took over the family's painting business.

Dresden nodded.

The breeze on the beautiful spring evening was relaxing. He rested in leisurely silence, enjoying the company of his parents.

"How are you feeling about all of this? Are you ready?" Marcella probed, interrupting the serene reverie.

Dresden sucked in a breath before taking a sip of the beer he'd been babysitting. "I'm not sure how to answer that. Are you ever really ready for a change like this?" he spoke but wasn't focused on anyone in particular.

"Are you regretting the decision? You've been away from here for a long time," his dad asked.

Dresden shook his head. "No. Nina wanted me to do this, so, no regrets."

"But what do *you* want, Junior?" his mother continued her interrogation, leaning over to rest a hand on his knee.

*I want my old life back. I want my wife back*, he mused. Dresden's leisurely rock in the chair became more labored.

"Again, how do I answer that?" Dresden paused, processing. "When you ask me what I want . . . My answer will always be that I want *her* back, but I know that's unrealistic. When you ask, am

I ready . . . I guess I'm never ready because then, I have to face the fact that she's gone, which is a daily feat."

He stalled for a long minute, deliberating on his hard truth.

"Neither of those scenarios is practical because my Rosie is gone, no matter how I try to rationalize it. I'm learning that it will never get easier to accept because the loss has required me to let go of my old routine. Nina was my old routine, so she is at the root and embedded in the thread of the old stuff," he sighed, shifting his eyes between his parents.

"But one day at a time, one foot in front of the other. I've created a new routine, a new normal, and this move is a critical part of that. For me. For my girls."

Sympathy and compassion flooded his parents' eyes as they nodded.

"We are proud of you, son. I truly wish it was under different circumstances, but I'm happy to have you close by," Dresden Sr. said, patting his son on the shoulder.

"I'm glad you are looking at this as a new beginning, honey," Marcella chimed.

Dresden nodded, lifting his beer bottle in the air. "To new beginnings."

# Chapter three

"Here's the bucket. Here's the bucket. Shit!" Harper shouted, running across the room, but it was too late.

She irritably huffed, watching as he spewed vomit all over the floor.

"I'm sorry," Terrance slurred, wiping his mouth before he buried his head into the empty bucket.

"No need to apologize. I will learn my lesson one day. Keep a bucket on *both* sides of the bed," she said, more irritated than she wanted to be.

Quickly striding down the hallway and into the kitchen, Harper grabbed paper towels, a trash bag, and the mop to clean up the second mess of the morning. It had already been a tough day for Terrance, and it was only a little after eight.

The new medicine he started yesterday was causing a commotion in his stomach. The little food he'd eaten in the past fifteen hours ended up all over him or on the floor. Rarely had he made it to the bucket.

Before crossing the threshold into his bedroom, Harper paused to deeply inhale understanding and exhale frustration. He was not to blame, but she was exhausted. Being a caretaker, mom, and full-time professor was grueling. Harper was physically and mentally drained, but she had to be strong for him . . . for her family.

Entering the room, she groaned as she spotted Terrance trying to get out of bed. She rolled her eyes.

"Terrance Damien Kingsley, why can't you sit your ass down," Harper fussed, catching him right as he stumbled.

"Harper, I'm just trying to help," he whispered, his voice weak.

"I don't need your help. What I need is for you to keep that bucket near the bed and drink water like I asked you to. The nurse should be here in a few, and I need to get ready for work."

Terrance settled on the edge of the bed and reluctantly drank hot lemon water that was probably cold by now. His eyes followed Harper while she cleaned up the mess he'd made. He could see the irritation and fatigue darkening the whites of her pretty caramel-hued eyes. Terrance loved this woman. He loved how she cared for him even under their unorthodox conditions.

When Terrance Kingsley met Harper Moore over twenty years ago, he knew that he should have walked away immediately, but her energy was so potent that he couldn't ignore the magnetic connection.

Beautiful brown-sugar skin, braids pulled into a high bun, and narrowed eyes focused on the computer screen caught his attention as soon as he walked into the 24-hour Denny's restaurant during a stop in Monroe City.

Terrance was an over-the-road truck driver who often ate and rested in the restaurant near the truck stop where he parked his rig. That night was his first time seeing Harper, who only worked on the weekends.

Three weekends passed by before he mustered up enough courage to approach her. When Terrance slid into the booth across from her, she peered up over her dark-rimmed glasses with no intention of masking the scowl.

"*May I help you? I'm on my break. Someone else can take your order,*" *she announced, immediately returning her focus to the textbook.*

"*What are you so focused on, beautiful?*" *Terrance asked, ignoring her instructions.*

"*My business,*" *she snarkily uttered, then lifted a brow as if to say,* "*Please leave me alone.*"

"*Something seems to have you stumped. Maybe I can help,*" *he pressed, refusing to walk away as her glare suggested.*

*Harper rolled her eyes before pulling off her glasses. She leaned back and crossed her arms over her chest, surveying him.* "*I doubt it. I'm studying for my economics class.*"

"*Try me,*" *he uttered with confidence.*

*Harper's head reared back. She wasn't expecting* that *response. Nibbling her bottom lip, she tried to suppress the blush forming on her cheeks. She paused, eyeing his monstrous frame from the low-cut fade and chubby cheeks to his thickset thighs and big feet. He was stout but not fat by any means. She immediately thought that he likely played football in the past.*

*Flipping the page in her textbook, Harper failed miserably to maintain her annoyed glower. Terrance's espresso skin was as smooth as silk, and the matching dark brown orbs glistened like marbles. She blinked, unable to stare too long; otherwise, she would get lost in those whirlpools he called eyes. But it was his sparkling smile that made her want him to stick around for just a minute longer.*

"*OK . . . What is the Invisible Hand Theory?*" *she asked with a smirk forming at the corner of her mouth.*

*Terrance rubbed his fingers through his beard, which was as dark as his skin. He took a beat to consider her question. Harper started to adjust her position in the booth to continue studying since it appeared he had no clue what she was referring to.*

"*The Invisible Hand Theory created by economist Adam Smith?*" Terrance said questioningly.

Harper gasped, shocked that he was familiar with the construct. She nodded once her surprise faintly diminished.

"*The theory states that there are unseen forces that guide a free market economy to give us the best possible market outcomes,*" Terrance blurted.

"*Speak English, please,*" Harper teased, but she was dead serious.

He chuckled, blessing her with that beautiful smile again. "*Think about it this way. Steve Jobs had an idea to create great products and make money, right?*"

She nodded.

"*Steve set the price based on what he thought his products were worth, and people bought them at that price. Then came competitors like Samsung and Google, who priced their products higher, forcing Apple to do the same. The theory states that the more money people make, the better off they are.*"

"*Uh ... Megamind ... How do you know that? Why do you know that?*" she probed.

Terrance chuckled. "*I'm in my last semester at the University of Phoenix online program, but I'm a business major, so I've taken a few economics classes.*"

He eyed her, admiring the gorgeous wide smile that caused her eyes to narrow to slits.

"*I'm Terrance. Terrance Kingsley,*" he said, reaching across the table to shake her hand.

"*Harper. Harper Moore,*" she retorted, cradling her tiny hand in his, then quickly pulled away.

"*Nice to meet you, Harper Moore.*" Terrance licked his plump lips, and Harper knew it was time to leave. She closed her computer and gathered her things as she scooted out of the booth.

*"Well, wish me luck on my exam tomorrow," she said with a little giggle. Harper stood, giving him a glimpse of her petite yet thick frame. His smile slightly fell when his eyes landed on her swollen belly. Her pregnant, swollen belly.*

"Dad," Trae yelped from the bedroom doorway, disrupting Terrance's reminiscing.

"Yeah, son?" he responded, repositioning to get comfortable on the bed.

"I asked if you needed anything before I left. Mom is in her room getting dressed, and the nurse just got here," Trae said.

"Nah, man, I'm good. Have a good day at school. I love you, son," Terrance muttered through his discomfort.

Trae nodded. He stared at his dad, trying to suppress his brewing emotions. He swallowed hard to clear what felt like a brick stuck in his throat.

"I love you too, Dad. Try to get some rest." Trae quickly spun around, shuffled down the hallway, and ran into his mom. She cupped his cheeks, lifting his lowered head to face her.

"You OK, my sunshine?" Harper asked, already knowing the answer to her question.

Terrance Damian Kingsley III was Harper and Terrance's seventeen-year-old son. He was a senior in high school and was headed to Monroe University in the fall on a track scholarship. Their son was both a mama's baby and a daddy's boy, but Trae and his father had a special bond.

Since the day Trae was born, Terrance carted him around everywhere like his Doublemint twin. Terrance was determined to give his son the father he didn't have. Unfortunately, Terrance Kingsley Sr. was killed during a freak accident while serving in the military when Terrance was four years old.

Terrance was his namesake's first baseball and track coach. They shared a love for watching soccer in other languages and Bruce Lee movies while eating the stinky pizza Harper despised: pepperoni with extra onion and jalapeños.

His father's diagnosis and the recent aggressive nature of the disease practically debilitated Trae. He wanted to quit track and adjust his schedule to care for his dad, but Terrance insisted that his son enjoy the last semester of his senior year.

"He's getting weaker. Smaller. He's losing so much weight," Trae said. The tremble of his tenor broke Harper's heart.

A little over a year ago, Terrance started to retain fluid in his abdomen and experienced shortness of breath and vomiting. One night, the symptoms were so bad he drove himself to the hospital. What the doctors initially thought was a hernia was quickly elevated to a colon cancer diagnosis.

Early on, surgery coupled with experimental and traditional treatments worked wonders. Terrance returned to his role as the CEO of Kingsley Trucking, the company he built from one truck to a fleet of twenty. Resuming a normal life, the entire family was hopeful that Terrance had overcome the worst.

Unfortunately, three months ago, Terrance's symptoms returned with a vengeance. This time around, his body was resistant to chemotherapy but thankfully responded to radiation and cryotherapy. But the anemia, fatigue, and appetite loss were devastating and just plain sad to witness. The once-two-hundred-and-fifty-pound monster of a man was now often so feeble that he required a wheelchair to get around.

"I know it's tough, Trae, and getting emotional is all right. It's all right to cry, baby boy. Your dad is a fighter, and he promised you and your brother that he wouldn't quit until when?" Harper encouraged.

"Until God said so," Trae whispered, wiping the stray tear from his face.

"God is in control of this situation, and we will make sure your dad lives every minute of his life filled with love and laughs. That's what we promised, right?"

He nodded.

"OK. Now, get going before you're late. Are you OK to drive?" Harper asked, quickly switching to drill sergeant mom.

"Yeah, Ma, I'm good. I love you," Trae's baritone tenor that still shocked Harper boomed.

"I love you more, Trae."

Harper watched her baby boy disappear down the hall and around the corner. She halted before returning to Terrance's room, holding her breath until she heard the front door close. Releasing a painful gasp, she collapsed her head against the wall. Deep inhales through the nose and cleansing exhales through the mouth . . . *Get it together, Harper. Get it together*, she repeated until she heard footsteps approaching.

"Mrs. Kingsley, is everything all right with Mr. Kingsley?" Nurse Shelly asked.

She was the full-time nurse caring for Terrance during the day while Harper worked.

"Ma, what's wrong?" another voice sounded from behind Shelly.

The handsome face of her oldest son, Hasan, appeared. He came over every morning to help his dad shower before he went to work at the family's trucking company. Although Terrance was not Hasan's biological father, he was the only dad he'd ever known.

The way Terrance tells the story, he fell in love at first sight with a pretty, pregnant college freshman.

*"Um . . . oh," Terrance stuttered, staring at Harper's protruding stomach in the burgundy polo shirt.*

*"Oh," she parroted, rubbing circles across her belly.*

"You're pregnant," he continued, unsure of what to say.

"I am," Harper said, shrugging.

"But you're so young. And you're working here and going to school," he said but was stating the obvious.

She nodded. "This li'l peanut was a surprise, so I have to work to save money to take care of him. But I also can't lose my scholarship," she said, shrugging again. "So I gotta do what I gotta do, ya know?"

Terrance stared at her, admiring her strength and adoring her beauty.

"What about the baby's father? Is he working as hard as you are?" Terrance asked, and his tone was laced with a bit of indignation.

The creepy titter she released was borderline sinister. "No. No, he's not. It's just me and peanut," Harper whispered. The hint of melancholy couldn't be ignored.

Over the next several weeks, Harper and Terrance's relationship blossomed over watered-down coffee, Grand Slam breakfast specials, and endless discussions about nothing and everything. He tutored her in economics, and she helped him build a business plan to support his dream of owning a trucking company.

Terrance was utterly enamored with her. And she absolutely adored him. He admired her tenacity while she appreciated his tenderness. But most importantly, they cherished their friendship.

When Harper was scheduled for an induction at forty weeks, Terrance was right by her side. After twenty hours of labor, Hasan Terrance Moore was born. Terrance cried. He bawled real tears like he was the father.

As far as he was concerned, he was. Terrance adjusted his schedule to ensure he could attend doctors' appointments and birthing classes. During overnight stays in Monroe City, he rubbed her swollen feet and made midnight runs to the donut shop to appease her cravings. Terrance even helped furnish the baby's side of Harper's studio apartment.

"I can take care of you, Harper. I want you and Hasan to be my family. Can I take care of you?" Terrance sobbed at her bedside.

*Harper deliberated on the good, bad, pros, and cons. The craziness of this proposal. But how could she say no when she glanced down at her baby boy and then up into the compassionate, misty eyes of a man who appeared to want to give her the world?*

*"Yes," she whispered.*

"Ma," Hasan repeated, jolting Harper from her musing. "What's wrong?"

Harper shook her head, allowing a faux smile to creep across her cheeks. "Nothing. Nothing's wrong, San. Your dad had a rough morning. He's resting now but will need a shower," she said, turning her focus to the nurse.

"Shelly, he has not kept anything on his stomach since yesterday evening, around five, other than ice chips and broth. The doctor wanted to monitor for forty-eight hours before discontinuing the new medicine, but it hasn't been good so far," Harper continued, walking toward the bedroom.

They all peeked into the room where Terrance was resting. He cut his eyes over to the door and flashed a faint smile, motioning for them to enter.

"I'm heading out. You're in good hands as always," Harper said, closing the distance between them. "Call me if you need anything."

"Have a good day, Harp. Thank you, and I appreciate everything," Terrance uttered the same sentiments to her every day before she left the house.

She nodded and smiled.

"San, did you bring the contracts for me to review?" he asked their son.

Hasan nodded. "Yeah, Dad."

"Terrance, maybe today is not the best day for you to try to work. You need rest with that medicine," Harper fussed but knew it was in vain.

"Have a good day, Harper," he said dismissively, but the smile on his face indicated facetiousness.

She shook her head, lightly chuckling. "Have a good day."

It was really a disgrace to stroll into work already completely drained with no relief in sight, Harper thought as she walked into the Regina M. Benjamin School of Nursing on the campus of Monroe University. Her class was scheduled to begin in just a few minutes, and she was already exhausted.

As a veteran professor in the nursing program, Harper instructed advanced clinical research and decision-making courses, so *burnout* was not an option. Her students shuffled into the classroom, and she immediately transformed from a sleepy caregiver to a dedicated educator.

Professor Kingsley was known for her no-nonsense yet pragmatic approach to teaching. The students loved her, and her fellow administrators admired her diligence, so much so that she was being considered for tenure.

Harper persevered through her last class, although she was practically sleepwalking. Hiding away in her office, she leaned back in the chair and kicked up her feet to relax for just a few minutes.

Thankfully, she had no meetings with her teaching assistants or students begging to retake the most recent exam. Taking a second to enjoy a moment of silence, she sipped her iced latte and savored the beautiful view from her office.

It was early May, and Monroe's campus's rolling hills were vibrant emerald green. Swarms of students filled the quad as early commencement preparations were underway.

"Professor Kingsley."

Harper jerked from her daydreaming, almost choking on the final sip of her latte. Spinning around to see who the hell was disturbing her peace, she quickly stood to greet the unexpected guest.

"Dr. Hurts. Hello," Harper said, clearing her throat.

Dr. Olivia Hurts was the Distinguished Chair of the nursing school and one of the longest-tenured professors at the university. Her lineage at Monroe University extended back to her great-great-grandfather, with a building named in his honor. To make it plain, an endorsement—*or denial*—from Dr. Hurts could make or completely demolish one's career at the university. *Shit, in Monroe City*, Harper thought.

"Do you have a minute?" Dr. Hurts asked but continued to proceed into Harper's office.

"Yes, of course. Please, have a seat." Harper motioned toward the leather guest chair on the opposite side of her desk.

"How is Terrance?" Dr. Hurts asked, sympathy softening her usually stern gaze.

"He's fighting. Doing the best that he can under the circumstances."

Dr. Hurts nodded. "And how are *you*, Harper?"

Harper snickered, leaning back in the oversized chair. "Surviving. I'm doing the best that I can as well . . . *under the circumstances*." She shrugged.

"I know that this is a tough time for your family. You all are in my prayers," Dr. Hurts said.

Ironically, her tone always seemed caring, yet dismissive as if asking the questions was simply a formality, lacking genuine concern.

"Thank you. I appreciate that. What can I do for you, Dr. Hurts?" Harper said, wanting to move this conversation along.

"This may not be the best timing, but I wanted to discuss a specialty clinical trial in the hospital's cancer center that we have been asked to proctor. One professor will be offered the esteemed privilege of working on this assignment," she exclaimed.

"Dr. Hurts, I hate to cut you off, but as you said, this is a tough time for my family, so the timing isn't right—"

"It's for colon cancer research," she blurted, interrupting Harper's looming objection. "A trial specifically for Black men. New technology and targeted therapy will be tested."

Harper momentarily perked up but was quickly dejected when she considered what Dr. Hurts said.

"Why does this sound like the Tuskegee experiment?" Harper was being flippant, but there was some seriousness to her question.

"Now, you know better than that, Professor Kingsley," Olivia scoffed. "We are a historically Black institution that seeks to impact change for Black people. Black men are 40 percent more likely to die from colon cancer than white men, and they are dying younger and—"

Harper raised a finger, taking the opportunity to interject. "Dr. Hurts, with all due respect, I do not need a lecture on the data. I am *very* familiar with the odds for Black men," Harper said, neglecting to conceal the glower forming at the corner of her mouth.

Dr. Hurts nodded in understanding. "My apologies. You are right," she said, standing from her seat. "I wanted to offer you the opportunity before anyone else since a tenure vote is coming soon. As your sponsor, I want to ensure you have met all the requirements. A project like this will guarantee a unanimous vote. But take a few days—"

"I'll do it," Harper quickly announced. "There's no time like the present, right?"

Dr. Hurts mutedly surveyed her, seemingly to determine if this was something Harper was ready to take on, given all her other responsibilities.

"Yes. Yes, of course," Dr. Hurts muttered skeptically. "And who knows. Maybe this experience will yield success for you all around."

Harper nodded, understanding what Dr. Hurts was referring to. With this trial, she would satisfy her tenure nomination requisite and possibly give Terrance a fighting chance to beat this disease.

"Dr. Dresden Xavier has been hired to lead the trial. I will share your information, and someone from his team will send you the details. Congratulations, Professor Kingsley. I do believe you are one step closer to tenure. Please do not disappoint me," Dr. Hurts uttered snootily.

Harper rose from her seat to shake her hand. While Dr. Hurts wore a minuscule smile, Harper could not revel in the moment. It was truly bittersweet.

"Thank you, Dr. Hurts. Your advocacy is greatly appreciated," she said, expelling an anxious breath. "I will not let you down."

Harper watched as Dr. Hurts walked out of her office before she plopped down in her seat. Nervously clattering her teeth, she wondered if she may have bitten off more than she could chew.

"Shit, Harp," she whispered.

# Chapter four

"Welcome, welcome. Please, come in and find a seat. We will get started promptly at the beginning of the hour," Dresden said, greeting the doctors and nurses comprising his research team.

He checked his watch, patiently waiting for the clock to strike nine in the morning. Today was his first meeting as head of the specialty cancer trial. Dresden organized a dynamic team that ranged from seasoned professionals to second-year residents with experience in various specialties.

This particular research project was extremely risky for the hospital because it was the first of its kind that would leverage both prescription medications, unconventional herbal methods, and innovative technology to fight colon cancer in Black men between the ages of thirty-five and fifty years old. Even considering the risks, Dresden was enthusiastic that the results could be transformational for Black men stricken with the disease in the prime of their lives.

At the exact stroke of nine, he said, "Good morning, everyone. I am Dr. Dresden Xavier, and I'm pleased to work with each of you on what I believe is going to be a life-changing solution for the countless number of Black men who are receiving a diagnosis of this horrific disease right now as we speak." Dresden paused, slowly dragging his eyes across the room to ensure each person understood the gravity of his words.

"My experience as head of specialized research at the University Cancer Center in the Maryland area and some work in other countries have allowed me to research and mitigate various strains of this disease. I plan to bring many of the lessons I've—"

Dresden's words were abruptly interrupted when a petite, brown-skinned woman came plowing into the conference room. The door loudly clanked behind her as embarrassment and fatigue marred the beauty of her face. She whispered her apologies while her eyes darted around the room, searching for a seat at the packed conference table.

Dresden stared at her, but he couldn't bring himself to stop. It was as if the air evacuated from the room. While eyes were focused back on him, he was engrossed with her. An infrequent yet familiar boom thundered through the center of his chest. The same boom he experienced the first time he saw Nina. He shook his head, endeavoring to shun the electrifying sensations.

Extending his hand, he offered her the seat occupied by his backpack. She smiled, and the rumble in the center of his chest resumed. Dresden cleared his throat and gulped down half of the bottled water, attempting to get his bearings. *Am I having a damn heart attack?* he mused.

Unconsciously eyeballing her, he followed the smooth motion of her curvy body while she tiptoed through the room. The nameless woman had rendered him speechless. Smooth skin the color of brown sugar with almond eyes a shade or two lighter graced a gorgeously crafted face. Her chocolate brown hair with streaks of auburn-blond highlights swayed in a center-part feathered bob that tickled her shoulders.

While her beauty was intricate and sophisticated, her demeanor was friendly and uncomplicated. An action as simple as how she landed her eyes on each person while smiling to greet them personally caused the pounding in his chest to roar. Dresden tried . . . God, how he tried, but he couldn't take his eyes off her.

The room remained hushed while the woman took her seat. Ignoring the multiple sets of eyes staring, she removed a spiral notebook and a pen from her tote before settling into the chair. She looked up at Dresden and nodded, seemingly signaling for him to continue.

The dreamy smile that lifted the corner of his mouth could not be prevented. He ogled her for just a second longer. She outwardly appeared self-assured, but he immediately noticed a tug-of-war between confidence and coyness residing in her eyes. Dresden tried to ignore the twinkle in those gorgeous oceans she called eyes. Another bashful smile made him completely lose his train of thought.

With eager eyes trained on him, Dresden kneaded the back of his neck, looking toward his colleague, Priscilla, for a save. She pursed her lips, shooting him a questioning look.

"Um . . . Where was I?" he whispered more to himself than the group.

"The lessons you've learned, Doctor," Priscilla drawled, raising a brow.

"Oh, um . . . Yes, as I was saying. I plan to bring the lessons I've learned over the years, but we are a team, and I expect each of you to share your recommendations and opinions. Constructive feedback, healthy debate, and radical candor are welcomed around here. The one time you hold back could be a matter of life or death."

Dresden nodded, slowly pacing the room to confirm understanding from all ten core team members.

"We will operate with a sense of urgency, yet thoughtfulness and respect, while challenging each other. Now, I would love to get to know a little something about each of you. Tell us who you are, what you've been doing with your career, and why you wanted to join this trial," he said, then opened the floor for his chief of staff, Priscilla, to introduce herself.

Leaning against the wall at the front of the room, Dresden smiled and nodded as introductions popcorned around the room. The imaginary microphone finally landed on the effortless beauty seated to his right. Dresden was giddy with anticipation because he still did not know her name. For the past ten minutes, he daydreamed, desiring the melody of her mysterious voice.

"Hello, everyone. My name is Harper Kingsley, and I am a professor in the nursing school at Monroe University. I am a two-time Monroe alum and a Doctor of Nursing Practice. I'm originally from Kansas City but have lived in Monroe for over twenty years. I joined this trial to continue to expand my knowledge of innovative research methods to teach my students," she said, pausing momentarily to reflect on the two main reasons.

One was her opportunity to secure tenure at the university; the other, she had not disclosed to anyone. When she paused, Dresden was about to proceed with the meeting's agenda, but Harper continued to speak.

"And . . . because I have two sons, and I want to play a part in finding a solution that could prevent them and other Black men from dying too soon from this disease," she uttered, shrugging dismissively but blinked rapidly to quell the mist forming in her eyes.

She never admitted that to anyone, but Harper had spent many sleepless nights thinking about her sons' fate, especially Trae, given his father's history with cancer.

"I believe those are excellent reasons. Thank you for your transparency, Professor Kingsley."

Dresden was practically blushing because his guess was accurate. The tone of her voice was just as breathtaking as the visual.

*Boom. Boom.*

That thump was becoming a nuisance, but he had a feeling that it would not be the last time he experienced it.

"Thank you, everyone. I greatly appreciate you taking the time to meet this morning. I will see you all next week. The trial will start in two weeks after the trial participant list is finalized. We'll spend time next week ensuring that we're all following protocol before patient data is shared. Priscilla, anything else we need to know before we end the meeting?"

Priscilla strolled to the front of the room dressed in a pretty purple suit.

"Yes, Dr. Xavier, thank you. We are grateful to have many volunteers ranging from healthy, meaning no signs of the disease but a family history, up to stage three localized cancer, and the placebo group. Since our trial is a segment of a larger trial, we cannot accept patients at metastatic stage four. We will get into more details next week, so please review your materials before we reconvene. Welcome to the team, and thank you, Dr. Xavier, for your leadership," Priscilla said with a wide smile, and the audience clapped.

"There are light refreshments and coffee in the next room. Feel free to stick around and mingle," she chimed as the small crowd began to scatter.

Dresden tossed back the rest of his water before some participants inundated him with questions. He nodded, smiled, and engaged with each of his team members. Periodically, he would glimpse Harper's profile across the room. She was magnificent.

The simple black slacks hugged her minimal yet perfect curves, while the nominal cleavage peeking from the white-and-black polka-dot blouse offered a preview of plump, desirable breasts. Studded diamond earrings indicated her modesty, while red patent stilettos signified boldness.

"Dr. Xavier, hello. Hi, I'm Harper. Harper Kingsley. I'm so sorry that I was late. I assure you that it will not happen again," she said, shaking his hand.

Dresden attempted to speak, but the words were lost in the gold speckles dancing in Harper's eyes. He quickly closed his eyes and shook his head, trying to release the momentary shackles that held him hostage. Clearing his throat, he coupled his hands with hers, finally able to comment.

"No problem, Mrs. Kingsley. Life happens to us all," he said, giving her a wide smile.

"Indeed, it does. Thank you for understanding. And please, call me Professor Kingsley," she uttered, pausing momentarily.

"If your schedule allows, I would like to talk to you about something before we start next week. Should I reach out to Priscilla to schedule a meeting?" Harper asked.

"I have time to talk right now," Dresden said, motioning toward the hallway for privacy. "Is everything OK?"

"Oh, yes. Everything is fine, but I can't stay right now. I have a class in an hour, and I need to run an errand beforehand." Harper eyed the clock on the wall.

"I understand. How about Thursday? I believe I'm pretty open all day. Honestly, I'm still trying to find an assistant, so I don't have a good handle on my calendar," he chuckled.

Harper smiled. "No worries. Thursday around noon works for me."

"Great. It's a date. I mean . . . I'll see you then," Dresden stammered.

They settled in seconds of agreeable silence, their hands still clasped together. Harper unconsciously nibbled on her bottom lip because the man was delicious. Dresden riled, jerking his hand away from hers like a bolt of electricity suddenly charged through his body.

"I look forward to working with you, Harper, um, Professor Kingsley," he muttered, stumbling over his words like a horny teenage boy.

"You as well, Dr. Xavier. I'll see you on Thursday. Priscilla has my information if you need to reschedule."

He nodded, internally kicking himself for acting like a complete weirdo.

Dresden watched Harper extend goodbyes to the rest of the team before exiting the room. He continued to ogle her through the glass-front space as she strolled down the hall. She momentarily paused, turning her head to glance back into the room.

Smiling, their eyes connected, and she nodded. She waved goodbye, and he tapped his fingers against his temple, then released into a salute. Dresden concentrated on Harper's graceful, sexy sway until she was finally out of his sight.

"Happy first day at work, Daddy," Bryn and Bella happily chimed when their dad walked through the door.

Dresden cackled, observing the round cake with chocolate icing on the kitchen counter. He closed his eyes, inhaling the delectable aroma simmering from the oven.

"Is that your mom's shepherd's pie recipe I smell?" He grinned, playfully rubbing his stomach.

"Mm-hmm," the twins sang in unison, beaming excitedly as if they were toddlers.

"And is this her famous Oreo cookie chocolate cake?" he inquired excitedly.

"Mm-hmm," they repeated with the same level of enthusiasm.

"Every time you'd start a new trial, we always helped Mom prepare your favorite meal," Bella sang, matching her dad's excitement.

"It's tradition," Bryn declared, shrugging her shoulders.

Dresden kissed each daughter on the forehead before pulling them into a hug. His earlier brooding immediately vanished in their presence. When he awakened this morning, Dresden felt Nina's absence in the depths of his soul. His grief was like a wildfire: contained in one instance and then suddenly spreading uncontrollably, consuming any and everything in its path.

The first day of a new trial always started with Nina expressing her pride in him, followed by a much-needed pep talk.

*You are Dresden mutherfucking Xavier, babe.* He chuckled at the thought because his angelic Nina cursed like a sailor. Her pride was further demonstrated during a morning filled with passionate lovemaking.

Bryn grabbed his backpack from his shoulder, shaking him from his musing. His girls doted over him as if he created the moon and stars. They were the best reminders of his late wife, and he was grateful that the memoirs no longer presented as his worst nightmare.

Nina raised the twins to be independent, thoughtful, and respectable young women, and this demonstration of kindness was just a snapshot of how Bella and Bryn brightened his world, especially in those moments when he felt helpless . . . hopeless without Nina.

The Xavier family had become accustomed to their new normal: a dining room table set for three instead of four and talks of their Nina in the past tense. They prayed over their food and enjoyed joyful laughter, a great meal, and a delicious bottle of wine . . . Another

Nina tradition. Since taking the twins to France when they were sixteen, their mother allowed them one glass of wine on special occasions.

"So, how was it, Dad? Are you going to like the hospital?" Bryn asked.

He nodded. "I think so. They were very accommodating. My chief of staff, Priscilla, runs a tight ship, so I believe we will accomplish a ton," he said, scooping a heap of potatoes into his mouth.

"And the team?" Bella said curiously.

Dresden chewed as he drifted back to the memory of the brown-sugar beauty that had inundated his thoughts since she stormed into his world just hours ago. A faint smile decorated his face as he swallowed.

"I have a team of ten dynamic, smart, and driven folks. I'm pretty happy with the selections," he declared, unable to contain the half-suppressed titter.

"Daddy, why are you blushing?" Bryn asked matter-of-factly.

"Blushing? Your daddy doesn't blush, baby girl," Dresden exclaimed dismissively.

But he was indeed blushing.

"Hmm . . . Blushing could only mean *one* thing," Bella sang. "Is there a pretty woman on this team of *dynamic people*?" she teased, smiling wide as she searched his face.

Dresden tried his damnedest, but the peaks of his cheeks reddened as the corners of his lips curved into a closed-mouth grin.

"That's it, isn't it? What's her name?" Bella squealed with an animated beam.

"Shut up, Bella," Bryn fussed, her brow furrowed at the notion.

"Why would you jump to *that* conclusion?" She rolled her eyes. While Bryn and Bella were twin wonders, their one topic of contention was . . . *Daddy dating*. Bella was in the affirmative. She wanted her dad to at least start dating since he was a bit "rusty."

He and Nina had been together since their sophomore year in college. While love and marriage were not necessarily what Bella desired for him right away, he, at least, deserved companionship.

On the other hand, Bryn could not fathom her father with anyone other than her mother. She despised the thought. Dresden dating was a hard no for her. *It's only been two years*, she'd profess, when she and her sister would argue about the subject. Bryn was daddy's girl and a bit stingy with him. It was bad enough that she had to split his attention with her sister. She *definitely* did *not* want to share him with a woman who was *not* her mother.

Deep down, she knew it was selfish but did not care. In Bryn's opinion, her parents' love could never be duplicated. *He can get a li'l plaything to satisfy his needs, but that's it*, Bryn privately ruminated.

The girls knew that their dad was a very handsome man. After Nina died, they had to calm the libidos of their hot-to-trot friends in the presence of their dad. But their friends' moms were the worst. Nina wasn't even settled in her grave, and these women were preparing meals and dropping off cakes to gain the attention of the attractive, successful, and now-single doctor.

Even when their mother was alive, women often showed Dresden attention in her presence. Nina knew exactly how fine her husband was and loved toting him around as her eye candy.

"Bryn," Dresden said, eyeing her harshly. "Respect," he uttered slowly.

The bass of his baritone was enough to make her sit up straight and apologize. "Sorry, Daddy. I'm sorry, B," she whispered.

The crinkle in his brow slowly faded while they ate in silence. Parenting two outspoken teenagers alone caused some permanent wrinkles on his forehead and even more gray hairs.

"For the record, I did not meet anyone. You both know how I nerd-out about a new project. I am just excited about the work and delighted with the team," he said dryly, but the faint flutter in his stomach at the thought of Harper Kingsley conflicted his words.

"It's OK, Daddy. We'll talk later," Bella declared, winking as she waved her hand dismissively at her sister. A sly smirk painted her face as she took another bite of the casserole.

Bryn rolled her eyes, aggressively stabbing the lettuce with her fork.

Hours later, Dresden was showered and relaxing in the small sitting room connected to his master suite. He'd intended to continue unpacking boxes but found himself sifting through old pictures on Facebook instead.

One memory from years ago turned into hours of navigating various moments in time with Nina and the girls: Their visit to Disney World, pictures from Bella's dance recitals, and Bryn's science fairs. He laughed at images from the time they left the twins with Nina's mother and hopped on a flight to New Orleans to enjoy a drunken, sex-filled weekend.

His phone chimed, and a red indicator popped up on Facebook Messenger with the number four next to it. Dresden shook his head, already prepared to see a random person asking for money or some other virus-inducing scam. He clicked on the indicator to delete the messages but was surprised by the familiar names in bold on his screen.

> **Teresa McDaniels:** Hi, Dresden. Welcome back to Monroe. My number hasn't changed. Call me.

> **Maurice Miles:** Dres! What up, boy? Chatty Cathy said you were back in town. Hey, man, I was sorry to hear about your wife. Let's grab a beer when you get settled. Hit me.

**Cathy Billups:** Hey, Dresden. Since you're back, I thought it would be cool to have a happy hour with the old crew. Does Thursday or Friday night work for you?

**Vanessa Franklin:** Hey, stranger. Long time no see. How are you? I heard through the grapevine known as Chatty Cathy Billups that you are back in town. Let's grab coffee or a drink. My treat. 593-222-7787.

Dresden chuckled at the *Chatty Cathy* references. Catherine Billups was the editor of his high school newspaper, which doubled as a gossip column. If you wanted to know who the star football player was creeping with after hours, somehow, Cathy figured out a way to incorporate it into the *Seminole Star*.

He bumped into Cathy in the hospital hallway just a few days ago. She has worked in finance for the past ten years. When Cathy said she would have to tell our classmates that Dresden had moved back to Monroe, he didn't realize that the news would travel at warp speed.

Rereading the last message, Dresden mouthed, "*Vanessa Franklin.*" She was his next-door neighbor throughout middle and high school. Their parents were still friends and travel buddies.

In middle school, Vanessa was the girl that none of the boys paid much attention to. She was taller than most of the guys and maybe one hundred pounds soaking wet. Dresden walked with her to school as a favor to her mother because Vanessa was bullied. To his dismay, during those short walks, she would fantasize about him as her "boyfriend."

But the summer before their freshman year of high school, milk had done her body good. Vanessa grew into her five-foot-eight-inch frame and sprouted out in all the right places. Her crush on Dresden was quickly replaced with multiple infatuations with the popular jocks. They remained close friends while in school, but he was never interested.

Scrolling through a few pics on her page, it was clear she was still drinking her milk. Dresden decided to reply to Maurice's message and share his contact information. He noted Vanessa's phone number, *just in case.*

His phone rang, indicating an incoming video call. He smiled, seeing *Li'l Bit* on the screen.

"Well, hello, my favorite niece," Dresden greeted.

"Uncle D, I'm your *only* niece," Sasha, his thirteen-year-old niece, giggled.

"What's up, Li'l Bit?"

"Can you please tell your sister I am old enough to go to a skating party without her chaperoning?" Sasha whined, rolling her eyes.

"Sasha Octavia Norman, give me that phone before I hurt you," Dresden's sister, Adriana, fussed.

Dresden laughed at the momentary commotion happening on the phone.

"Hello," his sister said, irritation wrinkling her meticulously arched brows. "I can't believe that girl called you. She talked to her dad, and he said it was my decision. And my damn decision is that she *does not* need to go to this skating party from eight to midnight without me," Adriana said, her tone growing increasingly frustrated.

Adriana was Dresden's only sibling and was four years younger. She had three children, Sasha being the youngest and the only girl. Her husband, Rashad, was a senior officer in the navy who traveled for extended periods several times within a year. This was one of those times.

"Dri, calm down."

"Yes, Mom. Calm down." Sasha's voice echoed in the background. "Daddy said RJ can take me. RJ has already agreed to drop me and Laura off *and* pick us up. What's the big deal?" she continued her negotiation.

Adriana rolled her eyes and sternly pointed, signaling her daughter to leave the room.

"But you're on *my* phone," Sasha sassed.

"Well, it's mine now," Adriana retorted with just as much sass as her daughter.

Dresden laughed as he listened to the mother-daughter exchange. He heard the door close, and his sister's face appeared in the camera.

"Sis, what's the problem?"

"Have you seen that girl, D? She has blossomed overnight, and she's feeling herself. I found eyeliner in her book bag, and she wants lashes. Fake eyelashes," Adriana spat. "I told her she will not walk around my house looking like Snuffleupagus."

Dresden hollered once a visual of The Muppets character popped into his head. Secretly, he enjoyed watching his baby sister spiral out of control. It reminded him of Nina and the twins when they were thirteen.

Adriana was the epitome of a boy mom, so when she found out that she was pregnant again when her youngest son was eight years old, she cried. Then she wailed uncontrollably when she discovered that she was having a girl.

"That's nothing. Do you recall the shit Bryn would get into? I'm still pissed about that tattoo on her leg." Dresden shook his head.

Adriana rested a fist against the side of her head, chuckling.

"Nina called me crying after she claimed she put Bryn out of the house. Bryn-Bryn's li'l butt was in the backyard chilling in the treehouse," she cackled.

They shared a laugh recalling Bryn's rebellious phase.

"So, you see, they all go through it. Has Sasha given you any reason not to trust her, Dri? Well, other than the eyeliner," Dresden said teasingly.

"No," Adriana whimpered.

"She's an honor roll student, a talented volleyball player, and she murders everybody on the drums in the band. And besides, RJ thinks she's his child anyway so he will make sure his sister is safe just like I did with you," Dresden assured.

"I'm sending her to live with you since you're back home," Adriana laughed. "You're right. I'm just not ready for my baby to grow up," she said, leaning against the headboard.

"I know. But trust me, kids will rebel harder if you don't loosen the reins a little. Especially these girls."

She nodded.

"So, how was your first official day?" Adriana asked, sipping on a well-deserved glass of wine.

"Good," he answered blankly.

"Good? That's it?" she probed.

"The hospital staff is very accommodating to how I prefer to conduct my research, and my team is great. A very talented group of people," Dresden said dryly.

"And?" Adriana pressed.

"And what?"

"Why do you sound rehearsed?" she probed, squinting her eyes curiously. "You usually can't stop talking about a new trial."

He remained silent, staring into eyes that mirrored his mother's.

"I know you, big brother. Something's up with you. I see it in your eyes," Adriana said.

Dresden shook his head, but his sister was right. Something *was* up, but he could not explain it. When he first met Nina, he spotted her sitting alone in the grass on Howard's campus from a mile away. Walking with his friends, he felt a pull, like a magnetic me the space to process whatever was circulating through his mind.

force that whispered, "*Yo, D, check out the honey with the big curls and denim overalls.*"

A similar sensation plagued him as soon as Harper walked through the door. That boom. That same force muttered, "*Yo, D, check out the honey with the wavy hair and pretty eyes.*" The connection he felt was kindred—a shared aura of hopeful sadness.

"During the meeting with my team, something strange happened today," Dresden mumbled, struggling to articulate his thoughts.

"OK . . ." Adriana's voice faded, but her focus remained on her brother.

She immediately saw a shift in his demeanor. He became serious . . . stoic.

Dresden paused for an extended heartbeat, and his sister gave him the space to process whatever was circulating through his mind.

"I . . . I experienced something today that I haven't in a very long time, and it scared the shit out of me. This woman . . . Harper. When she walked into the room, I-I felt . . ." he stammered.

"What?" Adriana blurted, practically hanging onto the edge of her seat.

"Feelings. Attraction. *Shit*, butterflies," he whispered, almost ashamed of his admission.

Adriana smiled. "You say that like it's a bad thing."

Dresden released an exasperating breath. Sinking farther down into his seat, he brushed a hand down his face, mumbling, "Because it is."

"Why?" she uttered as her smile faded.

Dresden tossed his head back on the love seat, repositioning the phone to see the sympathy lacing his sister's pretty face.

"Rosie," he barked, clearing his throat as an unexpected traitorous tear traveled down his face. "I miss her so fucking much, Dri," Dresden cried.

"I know you do," Adriana said, her dewy eyes matching her brother's.

Dresden blurted out an audible breath. "I wasn't supposed to do this without her. All of my damn butterflies are supposed to be reserved for only her," he declared.

He went mute again, and Adriana silently supported him through the anguished episode. Over the past three-plus years since Nina's diagnosis and her untimely death, Dresden's sister would quietly sit on the phone with him for hours, prepared to provide whatever nurturing her big brother required. Sometimes, silence was all that he needed.

"Do you want to talk about Nina?" Adriana's voice was soft as she gently inquired.

He stared at the ceiling fan but shook his head.

"Soo ... Do you want to talk about Harper?" Adriana questioned.

Dresden darted his eyes to his sister, pausing to consider what he would say about a woman he met for less than two hours.

*She's beautiful. She's smart. Sexy as hell. There was unhappiness in her eyes but delighted determination in her smile*, he mused, finding so many things he could say. He focused his eyes back on the ceiling and shook his head.

"Nah, sis, there's nothing to talk about."

# Chapter five

T he breezy May night afforded the perfect opportunity for Harper to enjoy a quiet evening on the patio. A half-empty bottle of red wine was the only companion she desired tonight. The semester ended, and she was on a deadline to submit final grades. She intently reviewed the last few electronic exam submissions with her computer on her lap. Once she logged off, she was technically on summer break, aside from her involvement in the medical trial.

Harper reviewed the trial proposal and was very impressed with Dr. Xavier's philosophy on transformational medical research. In his document, he wrote about his travels to various parts of Africa and other countries early in his career. Harper was amazed by his methodology to step outside the norm and go beyond what he'd been taught in medical school.

As much as she tried to only focus on his résumé, she could not negate his sexiness. Something about an educated Black man with an edge made her kitty purr. Snickering, Harper shook her head in a vain attempt to dodge the images of Dr. Xavier that played on repeat in her head.

Sighing, she took another sip of wine before sifting through the remaining pages of the preparation resources. The trial schedule was a bit hectic, but it still allowed her to possibly plan a brief getaway during her summer break. *I wonder if the boys can take care of their dad for a few days alone*, she pondered while navigating to her travel agent's website.

"Hey," Terrance said, leaning on a cane in the doorway.

A little surprised, Harper quickly glanced away from her task to eye him. "Hey."

She lifted her clear-rimmed glasses to the top of her head, preparing to get up from the couch to assist him in maneuvering onto the patio.

"Let me help you," Harper continued. She began shifting the papers and removing the computer from her lap when he shook his head.

"I'm good, Harper. I got it," he said, then pointed to the empty side of the outdoor couch. "Can I join you?" he asked, slowly moving toward the couch before she could answer.

"Of course."

Harper watched his slow amble. Lately, the slight effort would have taken his breath away. But he'd had a few good days of increased energy, so seeing that Terrance desired fresh air was good.

"It's a beautiful night," he uttered, staring at the moon.

She nodded.

"You look like you have a lot going on," he said, motioning to the computer and papers scattered around her.

She nodded again, flashing a one-cheek smile.

"Are you ready for the research trial?" he asked, making small talk.

Harper and Terrance's communication had been tense lately. They had not talked much beyond confirming doctors' appointments and Trae's schedule. When malaise and gloom temporarily depleted both of their wills to battle his disease, their preferred weapon was vicious words spewed at each other. Even before his illness, arguments between the Kingsleys could get brutal, both going for the jugular to win a battle where there would be no victors.

Once more, she nodded, recognizing his attempt to engage. "Yeah, that's what I was just reviewing. Almost a hundred pages of research, medical terms, and confidentiality policies," she said, resting her head against a balled fist. "And this is just the beginning."

He lifted a brow. "You sound overwhelmed," he said, observing the stress line wrinkling her brow.

Harper looked at him and shrugged. "A little bit," she admitted.

"I'm sorry, Harper." Terrance faintly whispered. His voice was thick with regret and sprinkled with sorrow. Both emotions burdened him, hanging heavy on his heart.

She shook her head. "No need to apologize. I signed up for this, so it's on me. But school's out so that relieves some of the stress."

"Is there anything I can do?"

She shook her head again. "No. Just keep getting stronger." Harper's smile widened to assure him that she was sincere.

Terrance tittered, knowing damn well that this composed version of Harper was fake. She had a lot on her plate, and he was a major portion. For a moment, he battled with addressing the tension or letting it go.

"You got a chance to meet the team, right? What do you think about this doctor?" Terrance asked, opting for the latter.

"I think he's brilliant," she sang, blurting her thoughts faster and dreamier than she intended.

Harper's body language was more perky than it had been since their conversation began. The hint of something in her voice and a slight shimmer in those honey eyes couldn't be ignored. Was it excitement? Curiosity? Intrigue? Terrance scanned her for an extended heartbeat.

"Brilliant, huh?" he jeered.

"I just mean that Dr. Xavier's research approach is unconventional, unlike anything I've seen in my career. It will raise questions, but I believe the outcome will be pioneering for Black men at earlier stages of this disease," she explained, regaining her poise.

Terrance nodded mutedly.

"I hear that. I'm glad you get a chance to participate in this, Harp, not just for your tenure but because you thrive in *unconventional* situations. The *brilliant* Dr. Xavier is lucky to have you," he joked, but Harper didn't miss the inkling of sarcasm lacing his tone.

"Um, what are your thoughts about volunteering? For the trial, I mean . . ." she mumbled the words, unsure of how he would respond.

"What? I honestly hadn't thought about it," he shrugged.

"Well, I think you should know that Trae is going to ask you to join," Harper confessed.

He whipped his head to face her.

"What? How do you know? He said that?"

Terrance flooded her with questions.

She nodded.

"He asked me about what I was going to be working on, and I shared some of the research with him," Harper explained.

Terrance shook his head, dropping it back to absently stare at the oscillating ceiling fan. "I'm really tired of being poked and prodded, Harper," Terrance finally admitted.

"I know," she whimpered.

Lately, Harper noticed Terrance's desire to battle the disease was waning. While she could never comprehend what he was dealing with, she understood that he was more exhausted than anyone in this situation. She would completely understand if he decided to stop any treatments to live the rest of his days under his terms. But their boys, conversely, wouldn't comprehend that decision.

"When is this conversation supposed to happen?" Terrance irritably probed.

"After his graduation. He said he wants it to be his gift," Harper shared, rubbing her eyes to prevent the impending emotional response.

Terrance audibly exhaled, pursing his lips. "My baby boy," he whispered.

His uneasiness and apprehension were apparent for more reasons than he'd dare disclose to Harper. Shaking away the angst, he lifted a brow, delivering a faux smile.

"Well, I guess we can return his new car then?"

Terrance released an uncomfortable laugh, and Harper joined in. Their attempt to stifle their anxiety was futile.

"Since you think this doctor is *brilliant*, what's your opinion?" he snickered, rolling his eyes.

"Why do you keep saying it like that?" Harper scoffed.

"I'm just using your description. Saying it like you said it," he muttered, tossing his hands up, feigning innocence.

"Whatever," she whispered, shifting to crisscross her legs to get more comfortable. "The new chemo pill seems to be giving you more energy after it gave you hell at first. Your symptoms have been manageable, and the diagnosis is still stable, right?"

She didn't wait for a response.

"There are levels to the clinical trial, so I am unsure if you would qualify. The drug being tested is not a cure, but extended remission is the initial goal. More time . . . It could be worth a shot," she said, shrugging.

Terrance's eyes faltered a bit as he blankly gazed into the darkness. He repeatedly nodded but was wordless until he uttered, "Is there a conflict with you being involved?"

She shook her head. "I don't think so. From what I've read, all patient information is concealed and confidential from even the trial team. Dr. Xavier and his primary assistant will only be privy to patient records."

Terrance returned to his hushed, vacant stare.

Harper observed as he mentally processed the pros and cons. She'd always told Terrance that she and the boys would be his soldiers, but this was his battle to fight. Anytime he wanted to surrender, Harper promised him that she would console and nurture their children through it all.

"If I'm accepted, I'll do everything in my power to fight this. For Hasan, Trae . . . *you*. I'll do anything." Terrance fixed his dark brown eyes on her for reassurance.

"Are you sure, Terrance?" Harper said, raising her brow, seeking confirmation.

"I'm sure, Harp. Set it up," he retorted.

She nodded. "OK. I'll see what I can do."

Harper roused from her sleep, squinting as she peered at the clock. "*Shit!*" she groaned, feeling the impact of a whole bottle of wine. Tomorrow was Trae's high school graduation, and the big party was in two days. Today was not the day to oversleep since she had a list of things to do before the ceremony.

Slowly but surely, Harper climbed out of bed and began trotting to her bathroom. She halted her advance. The scent of bacon and coffee delighted her nose. Her brow creased, wondering who the hell was cooking breakfast in her house because she was confident that Trae was sleeping in. Hasan was at his apartment, and Terrance was usually still asleep or watching television at this time of morning. And he had no business in the kitchen.

Harper grabbed her robe to cover her barely clad body before she journeyed to find the source of the smell. She peeked around the corner, and her eyes landed on a tall, now-lanky figure clothed in a white tank top and black pajama pants. Bobbing the bald head that used to be covered in thick coils to the sounds of Jay-Z, Terrance anchored himself to the edge of the kitchen counters as he slowly crept around the space.

Waffles, bacon, and scrambled eggs were arranged on a platter. He stretched to reach for the cabinet holding the plates and almost lost his balance.

"Terrance," she exclaimed but not too loud to prevent from startling him.

"Hey, Harp. Good morning," Terrance said, continuing to rap the words to the music.

"What are you doing?" Harper minimized their distance to collect the plates he was trying to retrieve.

"What does it look like? Fixing breakfast. It's a special time for the family."

"I understand that, but you need to rest for the *special day*. We are going to have a long night with the ceremony and dinner. That's a lot for you—"

"Harper. Please. I'm good," he shouted, then sighed deeply. "I'm sorry. But, please . . . Let me do this."

Their eyes locked in a silent altercation. Harper tossed up her hand, submitting to his silent scolding. Reluctantly, she took a seat at the kitchen island. Muted avoidance loomed over them like an unidentified spacecraft. Harper had grown accustomed to doing and being everything to everybody. Even before his illness, Terrance never willingly prepared a meal for their family.

Harper finally shifted her glare away from him to focus on her phone. Terrance chuckled, knowing he'd only won the battle but not the war.

"I know you have a mile-long list for Trae's graduation party. What do you need me to do?" Terrance asked, setting the plate of steaming food in front of her.

"Thank you," she mouthed, shaking her head. "Nothing. I got it," Harper said, never disjoining her eyes from her phone.

"You got it," he whispered, scoffing.

"What is that supposed to mean? Why that tone?" She stared at him for what seemed like a lifetime until he answered her.

"Nothing, Harper. Like you said, you got it."

Terrance sat at the kitchen table across from the island and began to eat his food with his back to her.

"Is that a problem? If I say I got it, you know I got it," she said, stabbing her fork into the fluffy scrambled eggs.

"Yeah, you always got it. Always want to do things yourself," he uttered over his shoulder.

Harper cocked her head back in disbelief. Rising from the barstool, she grabbed her plate and crossed the room, adjusting her robe to close it tighter before she plopped in the chair across the table from him. They were seated at the heads of the table in a standoff.

"Do I always *want* to do things by myself, or do I *have* to do them so that they actually get done?" she asked but wasn't really seeking his response. "I think the latter."

"How you figure that?" he smirked.

"Terrance, I am not about to do this with you. My mood is bad, and my patience is nonexistent today, so let's drop it," she spoke sternly, emphasizing every syllable.

"Nah, let's do it. Let's talk, Harper, because you've been wanting to get this shit off your chest for a minute. Me being sick don't change how you feel."

"No, it doesn't change how I feel, but it changes how I respond to my feelings," she countered.

"So, instead of communicating like a grown adult, you would rather hold it in or bitch to your li'l friends when you don't think I can hear you," Terrance spat.

*He's really choosing violence on this beautiful morning*, she thought, gearing up for the inevitable *Clash of the Kingsleys*.

Her eyes widened, then narrowed into slits because it was clear Terrance's intention this morning was to disturb her peace. What started with his acknowledgment of a special day was quickly transitioning into one of their customary disagreements.

In their marriage, Harper was never one to bite her tongue or sugarcoat her feelings about the issues they faced. During the last five years of their marriage, the relationship had been much like the concept of oil and water.

The oil molecules are attracted to oil, and the water molecules behave the same. For Terrance and Harper, he'd do his thing, and she did hers. Even when they would shake up things a bit in an attempt to comingle by exploring their undeniable sexual attraction, eventually, they would separate again. But since his diagnosis and treatment, she treaded lightly with Terrance. But today, he was water, and she was oil.

"You have the nerve to talk about communicating like a grown-up," she snickered. "This is from the person who would be isolated in his man cave when he didn't get his way. The person who would volunteer to take an overnight delivery just to avoid *grown-up* conversations with his *wife*," Harper scoffed.

"So, please don't talk to me about doing things on my own. Trust me, that was *not* my desire as a married woman, but my hand was forced." Harper stood, prepared to walk away, but his words stopped her advance.

"How, Harper? Who forced you? I worked every fucking day to make a very good life for this family," he countered.

"And so did I," she muttered dismissively.

"I provided for this household and nurtured those boys," he continued, pointing toward the upstairs bedrooms.

"And so did I," she said drably.

Terrance cut his eyes at her, pissed by her nonchalant nature. "You never trusted me to do shit, Harp. You *never* gave me the benefit of the doubt," Terrance fussed.

Snickering, she mouthed, "*Benefit of the doubt?*"

"I was empty, Terrance. Bankrupt. I had no more benefit of the doubt to give," she shouted.

With each word, her voice trembled with agitation. The painful memories bled from every syllable uttered.

Terrance leered at her with fire and remorse blazing in his eyes. Harper's hostile attitude and compassionate guise were his ruin and reconstruction at the same damn time. She could speak with so much loathing yet adoration, and he hated it. And she knew it, but she didn't care. And he knew that he deserved every ounce of her wrath.

"You want to know what else I did, Terrance? I cleaned and organized this house whenever you destroyed it with your gadgets. I took the kids to every doctor's appointment. Made sure they had supplies for school and lunch money in their accounts when you volunteered to be gone. I disciplined them while you were able to be the fun coach and Xbox friend. When the patio light was broken for months, I practically begged you to take care of it so I wouldn't have to walk from my car in the dark. But what happened? *I* called the electrician. Terrance, I did *everything*."

Suddenly, the space was still. Harper and Terrance watchfully stared in opposite directions to avoid each other's penetrating glare. Terrance considered her words, and for the first time in over five years, he may have finally heard her.

Harper couldn't even cry anymore. She'd become numb to the environment and simply did what she needed to do to sustain her family—*shit*—her sanity.

They frolicked in uneasy stillness for several lengthy, languid heartbeats. Harper was waiting for Terrance while Terrance waited for Harper. They engaged in this brutal song and dance for far too long. Harper tried to liberate, disengage from it all, but their circumstances took the lead.

Footsteps sounded above their heads. Trae was awake. Harper cleared their plates, dumping the remnants in the trash before she rinsed the dishes. She walked by Terrance, who was still seated at the table when he fingered the belt loop on her robe, pulling her closer to him.

"Harp," he whispered, his voice barely audible.

"Terrance, you are an amazing dad to our sons. A great businessman. A great provider. And you've always been my best friend. But as a husband, you didn't always show up for me in the way that I needed you to. The way I *begged* you to. So, when you see me just getting things done without asking for your assistance, it's because that is how your lack conditioned me to be."

She pulled away from his weak hold. "Thank you for breakfast," she mumbled.

Terrance watched her walk away. Her exit left him feeling hollow. Emptier than the illness ever could. Her departure, even just to her bedroom, was a stark reminder of everything he was losing.

# Chapter six

"What's up, Harp?" Terrance growled sleepily.

"Terrance, where are you?" Harper shouted.

"At the crib. What's wrong?"

"What the hell do you mean what's wrong? You're supposed to pick me up for dinner at Dr. Hammond's house. Remember?"

"Oh shit. I completely forgot. What time is it?" Terrance yelped. The commotion in his background indicated that he was shuffling around.

"Did you think that Trae went to Joya's house just to give you a break?" Harper fussed.

"I'm sorry, Harp. Let me shower and get dressed, and I'll be on my way."

"Don't bother. We're already thirty minutes late. I've called you a million times."

"This is not the time for your exaggerating, Harper. I said I'm sorry."

"You always say you're sorry," Harper barked.

"Babe, I'll make it up to you. I promise," Terrance declared.

"*You're always going to make shit up to me, Terrance. And please, stop making promises we both know you won't keep,*" she said, gritting through clenched teeth.

Terrance rubbed a hand down his wavy coils, clutching the nape of his neck. He shook his head, hearing the saddened symphony of Harper's cries.

"*Harp, I'm sorry. I fucked up. Baby, I'm on my way.*"

"*No. Thanks, but no thanks, Terrance. I'll figure it out . . . like always.*"

*Click.*

*Harper was gone.*

Harper blinked away tears, reminiscing on the day she realized that her marriage was on life support with no resuscitation plan . . . the night she told Terrance that she wanted a divorce.

Tapping on his shoulder, she awakened Terrance from his nap. He'd fallen asleep in the living room.

"You should get some rest in bed," she said almost inaudibly.

He nodded, blinking as he stared into her reddened, puffy eyes.

With a hand pressed to the middle of his back, Harper slowly walked behind Terrance toward his bedroom. He was exhausted, and so was she. The heated discussion from earlier and the daylong silent treatment drained all of their reserves.

They quietly lumbered through their night routine. She documented his vitals, ensured he took his medication, and positioned a bucket on each side of the bed. Harper stared at him after adding extra blankets to the bed for occasional night chills. Sleep was burdening his dark eyes. Preparing to leave the room, she whispered the same prayer she had elevated every night.

*Dear God, thank you for another day. Please comfort and relieve your sick servant. Bless him with your healing power and grant us strength where he is weak. Amen.*

"Harp," Terrance drawled languidly.

She paused, not bothering to turn around. Peering over her shoulder, she hummed questioningly, "Hmm?"

"I'm sorry," he whimpered through an exasperated breath.

She nodded. "I know. Good night."

Harper turned off his light and closed the door before hurriedly traipsing down the hallway to her bedroom on the opposite end of the house . . . The master bedroom they previously shared. She slammed the door and collapsed against it as if she were being chased. With her back pressed against the door, she practiced her breathing.

*Inhale positivity. Exhale bullshit. Inhale positivity. Exhale bullshit.*

Heated conversations with Terrance were always stressful, but since he'd been sick, they were even more laborious. Harper would try her best to refrain, but he knew exactly what buttons to push to take her from zero to one hundred. And, as always, she felt like shit afterward. She never regretted her honesty because it was their ugly truth, but her approach definitely disappointed her.

Harper was lethal when she was provoked. Her dismissiveness and piercing words cut like a blade . . . a defense mechanism erected from a lifetime of disappointments.

She advanced farther into the massive master suite, circling around the space. Terrance and Harper designed their home about fifteen years ago to accommodate their family of four, which included two rambunctious little boys.

They carefully selected every piece of furniture and color palette to make their bedroom a retreat from the hustle of their busy lives. Now, the room seemed too big for Harper alone, but she still appreciated the oasis on nights like this. Shades of gray and blue with hints of rose gold were splayed across the space. A plush pale yellow duvet covered the king-size bed she once shared with Terrance.

*Oh my, how the tables have turned*, she thought. Harper shook her head at the *very brief* memory of the love that was made in that bedroom. She could draft an exhaustive list of his flaws during their marriage, but Terrance's sexual abilities were not one of them. That was during better days and happier times.

In the beginning, she looked forward to the makeup sex after a heated argument. Terrance atoned for his mishaps with every wanton kiss and salacious slurp of Harper's essence. The following day, the error of his ways was completely erased from her memory as if she starred in *50 First Dates*. But his pardon would be short-lived after multiple offenses that could no longer be ignored.

Harper pressed a hand to her forehead and deeply exhaled. Ambling into the bathroom, she adjusted the shower temperature to as hot as she could stand it. Weighty, teardrop breasts, a little midsection pudge, and shapely thighs stared back at her in the mirror. She pin-curled the week-old silk press to hopefully stave off her natural curls for a few more days. After applying the charcoal facial mask, she stepped onto the marble tile, allowing the steam to soothe away the day's angst.

After the steam shower, Harper footed into black pajama shorts that cradled her ass and a matching tank top barely concealing her pebbled nipples. The way she smothered her skin with scented oils and body spray, one would think she was preparing to climb into bed to mount a man.

But after yet another demanding day, she would end her night alone. Black Girl Magic Riesling and a good book would be her companions for the night.

Harper cuddled into her body pillow and thumbed through her audiobook catalog to find the perfect narrator to rock her to sleep.

"I think it's a *Shu* type of night," Harper quipped, referring to Alexandria House's *Them Boys*, Book 3.

"Jakobi as Shu Shu is going to get me right tonight," she quietly squealed.

Harper instructed Google to turn off the lights, leaving only a glare from the television. Securing her earbuds, she sipped wine before closing her eyes to drift off into book-bae land.

The bass-filled tenor echoing through her ears and the lust-filled words so eloquently delivered had her kitty at the brink of eruption. Harper hadn't experienced the fleshy girth of a man in over a year.

After the divorce was final, curiosity was literally killing the cat. Hasan's biological father and Terrance were her only partners, so she desired to explore the anatomy of another man . . . stat— particularly the thirty-four-year-old, Michael Ealy-looking doctoral student who'd been flirting with her for months. The prospect of being labeled a cougar excited her. But the thought of that young tender penetrating her walls had her downright salivating. But, unfortunately, the light-skinned, green-eyed bandit was a disappointment. All that length, and he had no idea what to do with it. And sadly, he was unwilling to be coached.

Harper did not know what these young girls were requiring sexually these days, but she had no desire for her pussy to be gnawed at haphazardly or pounded on for an hour with no climax in sight. *Where the hell they do that at?*

She grinned at the brown leather box tucked away in her nightstand. It housed all of her favorite bedside boyfriends. Tonight, she wanted the lifelike, sculpted details of the vibrating chocolate penis she affectionately named "Midnight."

Harper longed to be touched . . . desired . . . fucked. While Midnight took her on the best excursions, she craved a set of warm, imposing, manly hands to stroke her breasts and somebody's heated tongue to pay close attention to her hardened nipples. She wanted thick, heavy fingers to impale her inner walls, gliding in and out and in and out while he tongue-kissed her affectionately.

Gliding Midnight up and down her swollen lips until he was completely lubricated, Harper mimicked the movements of her yearning. Her back arched as she vainly attempted to suppress a moan.

Tossing her head back, she smiled while slowly gliding the girth into her moist center one inch at a time. She was drenched. Closing her eyes, visions of a brown, six-foot, bulky, bald god of a man pranced behind her lids.

*Doctor Xavier*, she mutedly pondered, too embarrassed to narrate her inner musings. Harper's moans grew lustier while Midnight's penetration rocked harder, deeper, and faster at her command.

*In, out, in, out, click. In, out, in, out, click.* She groaned through the sluggish cadence, increasing the intensity of the vibrator after every stroke. Biting her bottom lip, she expelled a breath through her nose, trying her damnedest not to scream. The sound of his voice, coupled with the shimmering smile, dispatched a hammering through her center.

*In, out, in, out, click*—all the way to the maximum speed.

"Shit, shit, mmm, shit," she groaned, bucking her ass up and down, urging the pinnacle to the surface.

"Ahh," Harper sang lustfully, the ferocious climax ripping through her core.

An intimate moment with Dr. Xavier was nothing but a dream, a figment of her imagination, but the breathless panting and quivering limbs were evidence that her orgasm was a delicious reality.

The chime of her cell phone broke through the audio in her ear and tucked up her euphoria. She jerked, spent from the most alluring orgasm she'd experienced in a very long time. Harper couldn't move as the call ended, and the phone immediately rang again.

She rolled her eyes, seeing her friend's name on the screen.

"What the hell does Joya want?" she mumbled, clicking her earbud to answer the phone.

"What?" Harper groaned.

"Hey, girl. You busy?" Joya happily uttered.

"Mm-hmm." She hummed, blankly staring at the ceiling.

Joya Fletcher was Harper's neighbor and friend. They'd moved into the neighborhood when there were just a few houses on the street years ago. They became fast friends as working moms with kids around the same age.

"Um, friend, you sound like you just got some good dick. And since I know that ain't the case, which bedside bae blew your mind?" Joya quipped, laughing at her own silliness.

"Shut up, Joy," Harper chuckled. "We all don't have a husband who serves it to us morning, noon, and night. So I gotta do what I gotta do until my situation changes."

Harper schlepped out of bed and walked into her bathroom. Hitting the mute button, she peed while listening to her chatty friend complain about how often her husband wanted to have sex.

"I wonder if *Dr. Feelgood* has good dick," Joy blurted.

Harper jerked her neck back in confusion, staring at the phone. How did the conversation shift to Dresden? She quickly wiped herself clean and washed her hands before unmuting the phone.

"Where the hell did *that* come from?" she questioned.

"I'm just saying. Maybe Dr. Feelgood can *change* your situation," Joya giggled. "The way you described him, I bet he's slanging that brainiac Steve Urkel and Ur'kel kinda D."

Harper hollered, laughing.

"I wouldn't know. Maybe you can ask *Mrs. Feelgood*."

"He's married?" Joya yelped loudly.

Harper sipped the rest of the wine while simultaneously nodding her head. "According to his wedding ring . . . yes."

"You didn't say nothing about a wedding ring. Damn. I really want to know if Dr. Feelgood has good dick," Joya spat nonchalantly.

"Joya," Harper screeched but released a resounding laugh. "Can you stop saying that? I have to work with this man," she said, climbing back into bed.

"What? Don't try to act like you weren't bragging about how fine that man is after a couple of hours with him. And don't try to act like you ain't glance at his dick print."

"Heffa, no, I did not," Harper kinda lied.

"Lies," Joya spat.

"OK, fine. Maybe once," Harper laughed.

But how could she *not* glance at least once at that man's . . . *manhood?* Dr. Xavier strolled around that conference room, all manly and fine. The tailored white shirt and slim-fit slacks clung to his stately frame. He practically flaunted his mystery monster dick in her face.

"*And?*" Joya asked.

"And . . . I'd put money on the quality . . . *and* quantity of his dick," she cackled, repositioning in bed.

"Well, Dr. Xavier is out of the running, but let's think about who you can bet on. You deserve to have a little fun . . . to have a life, Harper," Joya fussed.

"And how do you suggest I do that? Huh? Where am I supposed to bring a man? To my house . . . Where my sick ex-husband sleeps down the hall. What would I say?" she paused, snickering. "Sorry, Terrance, I can't take care of you tonight because my new man is here." Harper rolled her eyes.

While she was flippant, a storm of emotions began wreaking havoc. Swiping a runaway tear, she continued. "And besides, Terrance requires—"

Joya interrupted before she could finish her statement.

"I know, Harper . . . Terrance requires a lot of assistance, but that's why you hire a night nurse or call Kelvin to sit with his friend. And the boys are old enough to look after their dad for a night. You have options."

"Yeah, I hear you," Harper said dismissively.

"Do you really? Seriously? Friend, I'm worried about you. You need a moment to breathe before you break, Harper," Joya said, her tone laced with worry.

"Joy . . . friend . . . I hear you."

"Well, hear this too. You don't have to bring a man home. Go on a date, have a few laughs, and then get a room so he can knock a few cobwebs off that kitty," Joya cackled, lessening the previous tension.

A deep sigh escaped from Harper, and then they lingered in a moment of silence.

While they were bantering about Dr. Xavier and Harper's cobwebbed kitty, Joya heard the exhausted heaves from her best friend.

"Harp, you OK?"

Harper swallowed hard, staring absently at the wall.

"I'm tired, Joy," she cried.

"I know, sis. I know."

"As much as I have going on, as busy as I am, why do I feel so alone?" she admitted.

"Just because you're booked and busy doesn't mean you're happy. You are dealing with a ton, Harper. Being a caretaker to your very ill ex-husband is enough to drive any woman crazy. Add Trae's confusion and Hasan's withdrawal, plus the stress of your job . . ." Joya paused.

"Whew. Sis, I'm worn out just thinking about it, so I can only imagine what you're going through."

"I thought God wasn't supposed to give you more than you can bear. I don't want to be on the strong warrior list anymore," Harper murmured.

"He doesn't. But he never said being strong was easy. And you are one of the strongest women I know, but even the strong need a break."

*A break. What's that?* Harper mused.

"Do you need to come to the she-shed?" Joya quipped but was dead serious.

Harper giggled, knowing all too well what would happen in the shed. Joya had an actual she-shed in her backyard equipped with a television, plush chairs, surround sound, and a stash of weed. Blunts, edibles, vape pens . . . Shit, she even had some infused teas and coffee.

"Girl, no. I need to be coherent all weekend. I want to make sure Trae's graduation is perfect."

"OK, girl. Well, how about dinner soon . . . and *then* a trip to the she-shed?" Joya said, hollering in laughter.

"It's a date. Thank you, friend."

"Terrance Damien Kingsley the Third," Principal Ward announced as Trae crossed the stage.

He was so handsome in the royal blue graduation gown draped with various color ropes, recognizing his academic and sports honors. The splitting image of his father, his smile stretched ear to ear as he shook the principal's hand and then struck a pose for the cameras.

Trae lifted his degree cover in the air and pointed in his family's direction. He pounded a fist to his chest three times, and Terrance mimicked the action.

Harper couldn't contain her tears. Nobody could. Everyone understood the deep connection that Terrance and Trae shared. More importantly, family and friends knew how significant this day was, far beyond Trae graduating from high school.

Over the past few months, there were moments when they did not know if Terrance would be strong enough to attend the ceremony. But Terrance's determination outweighed the doctors' expectations.

Harper rested her hand atop Terrance's and smiled. He nudged his shoulder against hers and winked.

"We did it," he said.

"We did it," she repeated.

And just like that, the discontentment and bickering from earlier was replaced with the Kingsley family mantra.

# Chapter seven

"Daddy, we're going to be late," Bella shouted from the kitchen.

"I'm coming. I'm coming," Dresden said, fiddling with his watch as he strode down the hallway from his bedroom.

"Is *that* what you're wearing?" she frowned, eyeing her father from head to toe.

Dresden followed her gaze with a furrow of his own. He thought he looked pretty good. He was dressed in meticulously pressed navy slacks, a crisp pale yellow dress shirt opened at the collar, and peanut butter brown Tom Ford loafers with a matching belt. His bald head and thick onyx beard added to his stately splendor.

"What's wrong with what I'm wearing?" he asked, observing his appearance.

"You look like . . . a husband," Bella said, ogling the glistening platinum ring on his left finger.

Once again, he followed her eyes and landed on his left hand. Nervously fondling the ring, Dresden shrugged dismissively.

"I *am* a husband. *Nina Xavier's* husband," he declared with the utmost confidence.

Bella casually strolled toward her father, condensing their breach. She rested a hand on his shoulder and gasped before speaking. "Daddy, but you're not anymore. Not the way you were, anyway. I know that Mom will always be your number one girl, but . . ." Bella's serene voice faded before continuing. "Don't you think it's time you met some people? Some *women*-type people?" she said teasingly.

Dresden shook his head. "Thank you, but I don't need dating advice from my nineteen-year-old daughter. I'm goochie, Bell," he quipped, pinching the tip of her nose.

"Nobody says goochie anymore, Daddy," Bella scowled, rolling her eyes.

Snaking her arm around her father's, she chuckled, uttering, "Come on, old man."

Dresden and Bella were headed to Monroe University for her freshman orientation. He'd forgotten entirely about the all-day commitment since he was still vetting assistants. Priscilla, his chief of staff, made it crystal clear that she was responsible for overseeing the trial, *not* his calendar. Today was his lunch meeting with Harper, and contrary to his daughter's belief, he carefully selected his attire for *her*. But, unfortunately, he'd have to cancel.

"Monroe University is going to be a bit of a culture shock for you, no?" Dresden asked, darting his eyes to Bella seated in the passenger seat.

"Culture shock? Say more," she requested, her brows lifted curiously.

"Bell, you were one of what, twenty Black kids in your high school. Your friends drove Benzes and Range Rovers. Monroe is an HBCU, hella woke, and for the culture. I'm talking blackity-black-black."

"You say that like it's bad, Mr. Howard U himself," Bella teased.

"Not bad at all. I'm excited about this experience for you. I just want to make sure you're ready."

"Daddy, just because most of my friends were white—"

"*All*," Dresden chortled through a cough before he laughed.

"Fine. Just because *all* of my friends were white doesn't mean I am not down with the culture," she uttered. Her attempt at mocking a bgirl was an epic fail.

Dresden shook his head.

"Baby girl, you're wearing a Metallica T-shirt and checkerboard Vans sneakers."

Bella smirked, looking down at her vintage T-shirt, distressed mini-shorts, and high-top shoes.

"Metallica is *amazing*, and my shoes are comfy," she shrugged.

"Seriously, though. Why Monroe? You had offers from Howard, Hampton, and Penn. You never even visited the campus."

Bella considered disclosing her reasoning to her father, but she didn't believe that now was the time. While staying on the East Coast was originally her preference, she was happy to be close to family and see how her dad grew up in Monroe City.

"Monroe had the best of both worlds for me. The HBCU experience and I get to spend time with Grammy, Pop, Auntie, and my cousins."

Honestly, he was ecstatic that Bella chose an HBCU for her post-high school matriculation. His baby girl could sometimes be a bit removed from Black culture. The twins had attended private, predominately white schools until Bryn decided she wanted to attend the neighborhood public school, which was a melting pot. On the other hand, Bella opted to stay with her friends at Belmont Academy. So, when she darted into her dad's bedroom one Saturday afternoon to celebrate her acceptance to Monroe University, he was shocked yet pleased with her decision.

Dresden nodded at Bella's reasoning, but he knew his daughter and that there was more to the story. Once the massive golden gates marking the entry to Monroe University appeared, he decided not to press.

Bella beamed, eyeing the beautiful campus's rolling greens and historic buildings.

"It's no Howard University, but I guess it will suffice," Dresden teased.

As her dad navigated the campus, Bella's head was on a swivel, observing the myriad hues of melanin.

Braided bombshells, kinky-curly divas, loc'd ladies and men, and weavy-wonders proudly traversed the grounds in all of their power-to-the-people glory. Sorority girls and frat boys decorated in their respective colors paraded the auditorium parking lot, directing the incoming freshmen and their parents.

Dresden peeped Bella's fascination with the young ladies in crimson and cream. He smiled, elated that his daughter seemed happy with her decision.

As they entered the auditorium, a crowd of scholars chanted, "Monroe," while another group responded with, "You know."

They loudly repeated the mantra, to Dresden's dismay.

"Daddy, please don't shout out whatever you all said at Howard. *Please*," she whined whisperingly.

Dresden cupped his hands around his mouth, inhaling a deep breath as if he were about to belt out Howard University's fight song.

"Daddy, no." Bella swatted his hands from his face.

The pair chuckled as they proceeded to the check-in table.

An hour into the orientation, the incoming freshmen were separated into groups. Bella bade her dad goodbye when the parents were asked to remain seated.

Music that Dresden refused to claim as hip-hop blared through the auditorium speakers. Incoming scholars danced and twerked their way out of the space. When the last student exited, the deejay immediately switched the music to some good old nineties R&B. Now, it was the parents' opportunity to prance and celebrate their pending empty nest.

Dresden tapped on his phone, bopping his head to the music until a beautiful, familiar, raspy voice roared through the microphone—*that boom*. The cluttering in his chest returned. He lifted his head to see who had the power to transmit a chill through his spine at the mere sound of their voice.

"Parents, can I get your attention, please?" She tapped on the microphone to settle the rowdy crowd.

"Thank you." She smiled, looping her eyes over the faces of happy and disheartened parents.

"My name is Harper Kingsley, and I am a professor in the nursing program and the director of student wellness programs here at Monroe University. We are so pleased to welcome your scholars to Monroe, where we nurture and cultivate young minds into dynamic leaders."

She was stunning. Harper recited an entire monologue of other shit about the school, but he didn't hear a word. Dresden couldn't take his eyes off her.

Draped in a tan dress that professionally fit her thick curves like a glove, she unhurriedly paced across the stage in leopard print stilettos that imprinted red flames on the hardwood floor every time she stepped. The prettiest face was framed by auburn curls draped across her shoulders, and tortoiseshell glasses rested on her button nose. *Damn.*

"Our scholars and your babies will be leaving you for a few hours to tour the campus and get to know some new faces," she continued. "You will spend the next hour with me and a few of my colleagues to walk you through how we ensure your scholars' success here at Monroe University. After that, you are free to have lunch in the cafe or enjoy Old Town Monroe, which is walkable from campus. You can attend various sessions throughout the afternoon, but please return to the main auditorium by four o'clock for our closeout celebration."

Dresden tried his best to pay attention to each presentation, but his eyes remained set on Harper. The hour felt more like a lifetime and was pure torture for him.

*But why?* he thought.

"Your ass is only going to stutter in her presence anyway," he mumbled begrudgingly, then flashed a manufactured smile to the woman staring from a few seats over from him.

It had been far too long since Dresden was so attracted to a woman that he became speechless. *No woman since Nina.* But it was more than just attraction with Harper; he was captivated. Her beauty transcended her physical attributes. Her smile, style, and excitement illuminated her eyes every time she said, "Our scholars." Even her deep, introspective gaze when he spoke about his travels abroad was sexy.

For as long as he can remember, Dresden's heart and head were only drawn to one type of woman . . . Nina. Tall, thick, tawny-colored skin with short, auburn coils and hazel eyes . . . *the woman of my dreams.* But the stark differences between Nina and Harper in looks and personality boggled his brain. The petite, brown sugar-hued, zealous beauty with the shoulder-length curls had left him dumbfounded yet hella curious.

When Dresden's eyes dashed back toward Harper, she was now observing him. He was actually giggling internally but opted to smile and nod his head in recognition. Her blush could not be missed as she returned the sentiment.

The slew of parents rushed out of the auditorium while Dresden hung back. He leisurely sauntered down the steps like a panther stalking its prey. Random women would stop and stare, almost tripping up the steps at the sight of the effortlessly handsome man.

Dresden was often clueless about the type of commotion his presence caused. Nina and his daughters would tease him about his cute naivety. Lust-filled ogles unapologetically surveyed the length of his stocky, athletic frame. He politely nodded and proceeded toward his target.

Harper eyed Dresden coming her way, looking like a piece of Godiva chocolate wrapped in edible gold. His six-foot frame packed a punch with an extended neck, broad chest, muscular arms, and slightly bowed legs. The man walked like he was carrying precious cargo between his legs.

*He's somebody's husband, Harper. Don't look down, Harper. Don't. Look. Down.*

Clearing her throat, she focused back on her colleague, but he may as well have been speaking Portuguese because she could not comprehend his words. The only thing registering for her in that instance was the scent of Creed cologne and Dr. Dresden *mutherfucking* Xavier.

The group of university administrators began to disperse, allowing Dresden to part through the flock. The ladies gossiped as they walked away, gawking at him from the crown of his bald head to the gleam of his expensive shoes.

Harper shook her head, but she fully understood the reaction. This man was good enough to eat . . . Simply delectable. And fine. Like, *fine fine*. Not in a supermodel type of way, but a muted self-assurance that amplified his sexiness.

The fact that he was a highly-educated Black man with a gentle yet dominating presence, a steely-nerved god at the helm of a risky yet potentially transformational medical trial, didn't hurt either. What woman didn't admire a man with a little bit of power?

Harper flashed him a closed-mouth smile as he approached her.

"Professor Kingsley. Hello. I wasn't expecting to see you here today," Dresden greeted with his hands stuffed in his pockets.

"Hello, Dr. Xavier. This is why you ditched me for lunch, huh?" she chuckled, reaching to shake his hand.

Dresden stared at her hand as if it were a snake snapping to bite him. The amorous sensation he felt the last time he touched her had him terrified. Harper revived the resounding thunder in his center.

With squinted eyes, she cocked her head to the side, then asked, "Not a fan of handshakes, Doctor?" she teased, thinking about how he hesitated to shake her hand the first time they met.

He faintly stirred. Her raspy voice disrupted his haze. "Oh no. My apologies. Handshakes are welcomed," he chortled.

Her satiny, small hand collided with his smooth, imposing one. The tenderhearted gazes dancing between them were a combination of fear and familiarity. Dresden retreated, immediately stuffing his hand back into his pants pocket as if it were on fire.

"I know that I asked to reschedule for early next week, but if you're available now . . ." he said, his voice trailing off. "Maybe we can grab lunch if you haven't eaten."

Dresden planted his eyes on the wooden and muted gold watch that added to his unassuming swag.

"Actually, I haven't eaten all day, so your timing is perfect," Harper shared, wrinkling her nose seemingly trying to recall her last meal.

"Well, would you like to join me, Professor?" he proposed with a smile.

Harper tried her best not to nibble on her bottom lip. She wanted to scream, *"Yes, boy, I would love to join you."* But she calmly nodded instead as she squealed, "Sure."

"Any recommendations?" Dresden asked.

"The cafeteria is going to be insane with students and parents. I know a good place nearby if you're up for a short walk."

Dresden smiled, motioning his hand before he said, "Show me the way."

July in Missouri was scorching hot, but neither Dresden nor Harper seemed to mind the short trek across campus to a quaint bistro in Old Town Monroe. The vintage wooden door with the stained-glass window with *Bourbon Bistro* etched in the material squeaked as he opened the door, allowing her to proceed him.

Dresden immediately noticed the floor-to-ceiling wall cabinet filled with a catalog of bourbons. Harper must've seen the gleam in his eyes because she smiled.

"The best bourbon in town. They have a smoked old fashioned to die for," she said, walking across the stained floor without waiting to be seated.

Harper slid into the middle booth near the circular bar, smiling at a few patrons scattered throughout the space.

"You come here often?" Dresden asked, taking a seat on the opposite side of the booth.

She nodded. "I used to," was her only response.

Dresden lifted his brows, noticing the brevity of her answer. They sat in silence for a brief moment until—

"Is that my pudge?" sounded loudly from across the room.

A petite, caramel-skinned woman with more salt-than-pepper hair grinned as she hurriedly approached the booth. Dresden cocked his head banteringly as he mouthed, *"Pudge?"*

"Don't ask," she whispered, her eyes wide with embarrassment.

He chuckled.

Harper snickered, then rolled her eyes, allowing a faint blush to brighten her cheeks.

"Hi, Auntie," she said lowly, puckering her lips to meet her aunt's cheek.

"You've been ignoring your old auntie, huh? Sending your hellos through Hasan," the woman scoffed.

Harper shook her head. "You know I've been a little busy, Auntie," she explained.

"I know, baby. How's our boy?" her aunt asked, the bright grin morphing into a concerned expression.

Harper didn't need to question who her aunt was referring to. When asked about Terrance, she always said, "Our boy."

"Good days and bad. Just keep praying," Harper exclaimed.

Auntie nodded.

"Now, who is this handsome thang here? You must be new in town, baby," Auntie sang, thrusting her ample hip a bit farther into Dresden's direction.

Harper chuckled. "Auntie, stop. This is my boss, Dr. Dresden Xavier," she said, swinging her eyes over to him.

*Auntie ain't wrong, though. This man is fine*, she thought before continuing.

"Dr. Xavier, this is my aunt Herlon. She and my uncle have owned this place for what, twenty years, Auntie?" Harper's gaze returned to her aunt for clarification.

"Yes, ma'am. Our sons have recently upgraded to keep up with you young folks around here, but yep, twenty-two years."

Aunt Herlon paused, circling her head around the place, her face decorated with pride.

"It's nice to meet you, Doctor . . ." her voice trailed off, attempting to remember his name.

"Xavier. But please, call me Dresden. Nice to meet you, Miss Herlon."

"Baby, call me Auntie. Everybody calls me Auntie around here," she declared.

Dresden nodded a silent *Yes, ma'am.*

"*Xavier,*" Auntie whispered. "Are you kin to Marcella Xavier?"

"Yes, ma'am. She's my mother," he said, his eyes darting back and forth between the two ladies with similar smiles.

"Oh, you're her boy from back East," Auntie said.

Dresden nodded.

"Marci and I are good church friends. Such a beautiful spirit, but a spitfire just like me," she cackled.

"Yes, she is," he laughed.

Her uttering took on a serious tone again when she patted him atop his hand and said, "We're still praying for you, baby. Prayers all around this table, it seems."

Dresden simply nodded again, understanding her statement. He was sure his mother had Nina's name on every prayer request list when she was ill.

Harper's eyes curiously danced between the two. She made a mental note to interrogate her aunt later about the mysterious Dr. Xavier.

They settled for a moment in silence while Aunt Herlon loitered, shifting her eyes between them. Harper was a little uneasy, so she disrupted the hush.

"I think we're ready to order, right?"

She looked at Dresden, hiking her brows for agreement. He lifted his hand, permitting her to order first.

"I'll have the salmon Caesar salad and a ginger ale, please," Harper requested.

"Let me try the grilled chicken club sandwich, soup of the day, and water, please," he ordered.

"Coming right up."

Aunt Herlon strolled away, belting out the order to the cook once she entered the kitchen.

Dresden noticed that Harper would fall into bouts of silence as if she were nervous about something. He vainly attempted not to stare but couldn't ignore the slope of her button nose or the mole resting right at the corner of her right eye.

Even through the glasses, her umber eyes glistened like crystal balls that he desperately wished could tell his fortune. Shit, his future. He blinked several times to prevent the trance he was certain she would put him under.

"So," she croaked.

"So," he parroted with a smile. A *sexy-ass* smile.

"What's on your mind, Professor Kingsley?" Dresden rested his clasped hands on the table, prepared to listen to her every word intently.

Harper gulped down a few sips of water to lubricate the drought forming in her throat. "Yes, um. I would like to recommend someone who may qualify for the trial. Priscilla mentioned that the application wasn't closed yet."

Dresden's brow raised. He was unsure what he expected from this conversation, but that information wasn't it.

"Priscilla's the real boss," he chuckled. "She knows better than I would. Have them provide their information online as soon as possible, and she will request paperwork from their physician and schedule a preliminary exam."

Harper nodded, flitting her fork around in the half-eaten salad the waitress delivered while they were chatting.

"Is there something else, Professor Kingsley?" Dresden squinted, sensing that she was anxious about something.

"What if the person is a family member?" Harper stuttered.

Dresden lifted his eyes from his sandwich. "You have a family member with colon cancer?" His stare was dripping with sympathy.

She nodded. "Is there a conflict of interest since I'm on the trial team?"

"No. No conflict that I'm aware of, but Priscilla can confirm. All patients are assigned a trial number for anonymity, and the records are confidential and sealed. Even from me. So . . ." his voice waned as he hunched his shoulders. "No conflict."

"Thank you. I'll share the information and see if they are interested," she muttered, allowing a nervous smile to hike her cheeks.

What Harper did not say was that Terrance had already completed the paperwork and had an appointment scheduled for next week.

Talking to Dr. Xavier was necessary because she wanted to do her due diligence to ensure that the appointment would not be in vain if team members' families were prohibited from the trial.

Dresden's phone buzzed against the wooden table. "Excuse me," he said, holding one finger in the air.

He read the text message and shook his head, releasing an exaggerated huff.

"Is everything OK?" Harper inquired.

"Yes. This is an old friend of mine . . . He's pushing me to go to this happy hour tonight with some high school friends I haven't seen in years."

"That sounds fun, but I'm sensing you don't want to see these people," she chuckled.

"I think he's trying to play matchmaker and set me up on a date," Dresden admitted.

Harper's meticulously arched brows clashed together as her eyes momentarily fixated on the shiny platinum ring on his left hand and then back up to his face.

"Date?" she rasped incredulously. Scowling, Harper leered at him with an accusatory glare.

"Since when do married men . . . *date*, Dr. Xavier?" she said, leaning back in the booth with her arms crossed.

Yes, she'd imagined this man naked one too many times, but that would be the extent of her exploration of the good doctor since he was married.

Dresden's head jerked back, perplexed. He followed the trail of her eyes to his wedding ring. Realization softened his building frown. Instinctively, he fiddled with the platinum band.

"Oh, um . . . this," he smirked, lifting his finger to display the object in question.

"That," she said, pointing with a disgusted squint blazing her eyes.

"I-I'm not married. I mean, I was married. My wife . . . Nina . . . she . . . she died. A few years ago. I'm a widower," he stuttered through the admission.

A sigh escaped his lungs. Not a troubled exhale, but a cathartic one. He'd never been able to label himself as a widower.

"But . . . I can't seem to bring myself to take off this thing," Dresden smirked, shrugging his shoulders innocently.

Harper was mortified. Shit—embarrassed. She was two seconds from cursing him out on behalf of the unknown Mrs. Xavier. But she's . . . dead.

*Oh my God*, she thought.

Harper's heartstrings were being pulled all over the place. She blinked rapidly to cease the unexpected sob stirring in her stomach. Instinctively, she reached across the table and caressed his hand, still fingering the ring.

"Dr. Xavier, I am so sorry for your loss. I did not mean to assume. I was completely out of line."

He shook his head. "It's all good. What else were you supposed to think since I'm wearing this thing?" He lifted his hand, releasing an uneasy chuckle.

"My Rosie would've appreciated you having her back, though." Dresden laughed.

"Rosie," Harper whispered quizzically.

"Her name is . . . was Nina Rose Xavier. But I called her Rosie." His bleak, bass-filled timber sang like the saddest love song.

"And for the record, that's not the type of man I am. I was married for over twenty years, and I was *never* that man," Dresden declared in earnest.

The stare he fixed on Harper had her teetering between sympathy and seduction. This man is over here grieving his late wife while she endeavored to discreetly adjust in her seat to relieve the pressure building in her pussy.

His point was made crystal clear. But the hopeful yet defeatist guise on his face said Dr. Dresden Xavier was still somebody's husband.

*His Rosie*, Harper pondered.

Abruptly disconnecting from his alluring stare, she sipped her soda, thinking, *Whatever woman gets this man will be at war with a ghost.*

# Chapter eight

Initially unaffected by the blazing heat, Harper and Dresden trudged back to campus. They were hot and bothered by more than just the heat. The walk was quiet . . . yet a little tense.

"Professor Kingsley."

"Dr. Xavier."

They chimed simultaneously. "I'm sorry," they chuckled, continuing the harmonic unity.

Harper nodded for him to proceed.

"I didn't mean to come across brash, but I take my duties as a husb—" Dresden paused, shaking his head when he realized his declaration was delivered in the present tense.

"I *took* my responsibility as a husband very seriously," he said, baritone throaty.

"I respect that, Dr. Xavier," Harper chimed.

With her hands clutched behind her back, she fidgeted because this man was causing her to lose control of all faculties and common sense.

"You really should've cursed my ass out," Harper laughed, lightening the mood.

Dresden snickered. He thought Harper's meek demeanor was cute. "Never. You keep forgetting that I'm a gentleman," he said, winking. "Just don't assume I'm a trash-ass nigga again, and we cool," he continued, chuckling.

Harper's eyes danced, loving the humorous side of him. Dr. Dresden Xavier had a little hood swag tucked under that brainiac persona. And she kinda liked it.

"What? Do I have to be the astute doctor all the time?" he teased jokingly, adjusting his imaginary tie.

She shook her head. A heated tingle dashed across her face, signaling for her to go.

*Good Lord, this man*, she thought.

"No. I appreciate a good sense of humor," she said, pausing her stride.

Harper pointed a white-tipped fingernail in the opposite direction of where they were walking. "I'm actually heading this way. My orientation duties are done for the day."

He nodded.

"Well, thank you for lunch and for introducing me to a new spot, Professor Kingsley. I will definitely be returning to sample the bourbon."

"You should. Aunt Herlon will take good care of you," Harper said, blushing as she poked her tongue against the inside of her cheek.

They shared a slight smile while their joint coyness awkwardly lingered.

"Thanks for lunch. I'm looking forward to working with you, Dr. Xavier. I'll see you next week," Harper uttered, extending her hand to shake his.

Dresden eyed her outstretched hand for a brief second before retorting, "See you next week, Professor."

His eyes followed Harper's curvaceous physique until she disappeared behind the gleam of the sun.

Bella walked the campus, laughing with three other girls, before she spotted her dad across the grassy quad. She abruptly halted, watching him in awe. He was laughing. Playful . . . jovial, even. It had been years since she'd seen the leisurely, carefree expression on her father's face in the company of a woman, not since her mother.

A chill of emotions sprang through Bella's core as she thought about her mom.

*"You will have to help Daddy, Bella. He only has game with me,"* Nina laughed.

*"Daddy has zero game, Ma,"* Bella giggled.

*They were cuddled in bed after finishing the first season of* Insecure *for the hundredth time. Surrounded by pizza, wings, brownies, and soda, they shared their weekly mommy-daughter date.*

*Nina always made it a point to engage her twins individually and as a unit. Bella and Bryn couldn't have been more different than night and day, so what appealed to one didn't necessarily interest the other. So, the night before, she'd spent time painting with Bryn.*

*"Girl, your daddy has all of the game and swag. How do you think he got me?"*

*"Ma, stop it,"* Bella giggled. *"Daddy will probably not date for like ten years and will likely never marry again,"* Bella said, cleaning up their mess.

*"Bell, that's why I need you to help Daddy get out and meet people when he's ready. I'm not asking you to push him, but when he's ready, you'll know,"* Nina exclaimed.

*"How?"*

Nina blushed at just the thought of her one and only love. "*You know how Daddy puts on that fake smile when people come to visit me or if someone asks how I'm doing?*"

*Bella nodded.*

"*And you know how Daddy smiles every morning when he walks into the room to check on me?*"

"*Yes, like you're the sun reincarnated,*" Bella teased, rolling her eyes.

"*Well, when I leave, your dad is going to have a lot of days with an artificial smile. But the day you see his* real *smile, the one that brightens his eyes and releases that wrinkle in his forehead, you'll know he's ready.*"

"Bella, are you okay?" one of the girls called out, lightly tapping Bella's forearm to get her attention.

She jolted, nodding her head, quickly wiping the corner of her eyes.

"Yeah. Yes, I'm good. There's my dad. Come meet him," Bella requested, and the three young ladies followed.

"*That* is your daddy? Damn, Bella," the fair-skinned girl with the waist-length box braids squealed.

"More like *Zaddy*," the chocolate-hued girl with a halo of curls sang.

Bella rolled her eyes.

Dresden's already-wide smile expanded when he saw his daughter's pretty face.

"Bell, how was it?" Dresden uttered as she approached.

Bella couldn't refute the beam on his face. *Doesn't look artificial to me*, Bella thought.

"It was good. I wanted you to meet my suite-mates. This is Nadia, Mikayla, and Francesca. Roomies, this is my dad, Dr. Xavier."

The girls giggled their hellos, causing Bella to roll her eyes again.

"B, just meet us in the student center when you're done," Nadia instructed.

"Nice to meet you, Dr. Xavier," her friends sang, cackling as they walked down the brick walkway.

"Daddy, I'm gonna hang for a bit. We get to see our suites, and there's a welcome party at the student center."

"OK, B," Dresden joked, mocking her friends. "What time should I pick you up?"

"You shouldn't pick me up because you're meeting your high school friends tonight, remember?" Bella blushed, raising her brows.

"Bryn said she could pick me up. I invited her to the party."

"Still trying to convince your sister to attend Monroe full-time, huh?" Dresden quipped, tossing his arm around her shoulders as they walked.

"Yep," she said frankly. "When her little wacky idea falls apart, she'll be enrolled just in time for us to get an apartment next year."

"Bella," Dresden scolded, "your sister is serious about her business."

Nina and Dresden often wondered how they birthed identical twins who fought daily to be polar opposites. Both girls were honor roll students and athletically gifted in their own way. Bella excelled at dance, while Bryn shined at volleyball.

Both were interested in a career in health care but not exactly following in their father's footsteps. Bella was planning to study psychology with the hopes of counseling children who had lost a parent. Bryn, on the other hand, chose the most unconventional path.

Dresden snickered, thinking back on the conversation with Bryn about her future.

*"So, Dad, hear me out before you say no," Bryn pleaded, popping a potato chip into her mouth.*

*Dresden eyeballed her over the rim of his coffee cup. Sliding a bound booklet across the table with* The Rose Garden Business Plan *printed on the front, she continued. "As you know, medicinal and recreational use of marijuana is legal in Missouri now. When we move to Monroe, I would like to open a dispensary focused on health and wellness called The Rose Garden . . . after Mom."*

*After suppressing his emotions and staring at his daughter like she'd grown five heads, Dresden listened to the thoroughly researched plan. He knew firsthand how medicinal cannabis was proving to help some cancer patients in more ways than just pain management.*

*"Bryn, baby girl, this is a big step. Entrepreneurship is not for the faint of heart," Dresden exclaimed, flipping through the additional pages.*

*"I know, and I'm ready. Remember my lemonade stand when I was eight? I made almost two hundred dollars in one day," she giggled. "Look at Grandpop. Entrepreneurship is in my blood."*

*Dresden couldn't disagree with that logic. His father had managed a successful business for over thirty years. But, clearly, a dispensary was not what Dresden envisioned for his daughter's future. Both Bryn and Bella were smart, but Bryn . . . That young lady was brilliant.*

*After some negotiation, they agreed that he would be a silent partner only if Bryn enrolled in online business classes.*

"I know she's serious, Daddy. And I know it will be a success because Bryn doesn't lose. I just wanted to do this with her since . . ." Bella's voice dwindled, causing Dresden to dart his eyes in her direction.

"Since what, Bell?" he probed.

"Since my other partner in crime is gone," Bella whispered, shrugging while her eyes misted.

She tried her best to withhold it, but one lonely tear traversed her pretty face. Dresden swiped away the dew before cupping her chin.

"Your mom is the sun, moon, and stars, baby girl. She's always around. And you're not doing this alone. *We* are navigating this newness together. Okay?"

She nodded.

"I know. Days like today are just hard, ya know?" she croaked, wiping the remaining tears with the back of her hand.

Dresden nodded, pulling his daughter into a firm hug, then kissed against the puff of her curls.

"I'll see you tonight, okay? I won't be too late," Dresden assured her.

"In this case, late would be good," she chuckled, her arms still anchored around his waist. "Try to have fun, Daddy."

"I promise to try." He lifted his right hand, pledging a Scout's honor jokingly.

"Thank you." She curtsied playfully.

"Oh, Daddy?" she called, getting his attention before he walked away. "How do you know the professor from orientation?"

"Professor Kingsley?" he asked, raising a questioning brow.

Bella nodded.

"She's on my trial team."

Bella nodded again, recalling her dad's first day meeting the team. He wore a similar gleeful smile that day.

*Maybe Professor Kingsley is why* Bella pondered, staring at her dad while battling between the joy for her dad possibly feeling again and the constant, painful reminder that her mother was gone.

Downtown Monroe City was a far cry from what Dresden remembered as a teenager. Turning on Monroe Avenue, he admired the glistening sign hanging between two brick columns marking the area *Monroe on the Ave.*

Coffee shops, bars, salons, boutiques, and other small businesses lined the street. He made a mental note to talk to Bryn about this area. *I can definitely see The Rose Garden here*, he thought.

Dresden groaned, making a left into the parking lot adjacent to Ethos, the location of tonight's gathering. He wanted to go home and bury himself in a medical dictionary. Socializing hadn't had the same flavor since Nina became sick.

Like Bella, his wife was his partner in crime too. His dancing partner, drinking buddy—*his everything*. He could count on one hand the number of times he'd gone out since she died.

Dresden rested his head on the ivory leather headrest, contemplating an excuse to get out of this commitment. A familiar chill sprinted down his spine, causing him to chuckle. His Rosie's emphatic spirit always nudged him to step out of his comfort zone. He closed his eyes, meditating on her melodic voice frolicking in his head, singing, "*Come on, Dres*," encouraging him to put one foot in front of the other.

"OK, OK," he muttered.

Dresden stepped out of the black Escalade, tapping the door handle to secure the vehicle before he strolled to the entrance. Chocolate brown hardwood floors and gold-plated walls adorned with colorful paintings of different instruments greeted him before the hostess appeared.

"Hello, may I help you, handsome?" a gorgeous woman with skin as dark as hot fudge greeted him.

"Hello. Party for Maurice Miles," Dresden said, smiling.

"Yes, sir. Mr. Miles is in the private room. Please, follow me."

Dresden nodded and bobbed his head to the music piping through the space. Ethos was an intimate spot that clearly drew the after-work adult crowd. Jumbled hues of black and brown faces graced the melanated skin of professionals filling the place. Dresden was impressed. Ethos was a vibe.

"Here you are, handsome. Enjoy," the hostess said, winking as she pointed him toward the glass-front room.

Dresden coyly chuckled as his former classmates spotted him. Maurice Miles, the owner of Ethos and a childhood friend, was the first to approach him.

"D! What's up, man?" Maurice bantered, pulling him into a hug. "I was thinking you were going to bail on me."

"What's up, Rece? Good to see you, man," Dresden said, returning the gesture. "I'm a man of my word. I wouldn't do you like that."

"You find the place OK? Downtown Monroe is not what it used to be, huh?" Maurice uttered as they advanced farther into the private room.

"Yeah, man. It's definitely changed. Your spot is nice. Congrats."

Maurice nodded, circling his eyes around the small crowd.

"Uh-oh, D. I see you're still Mister Popular," Maurice announced while Dresden followed his sightline.

A swarm of vaguely familiar female faces began to gather around him. They were like vultures circling their prey. Nina was barely settled in her grave before women started vying to be the next Mrs. Xavier, so this reaction was no surprise.

Dresden greeted the ladies with head nods, handshakes, and some forced hugs before a sultry voice sang, parting the growing flock.

"Dresden Xavier. Aren't you a sight?" the voice teased.

Maurice's brows lifted in approval of the woman who accompanied the voice. Dresden digested her from the pointy-toed stilettos to the sleek-bobbed crown of hair.

"Vanessa Franklin," Dresden drawled.

"Hey, neighbor," she crooned sexily, nibbling the corner of her bottom lip.

Vanessa did not conceal her appreciation of the grown-man version of her childhood friend.

Dresden couldn't even try to lie. Time had treated Vanessa very well. Not only was she an established real estate investor in Monroe, but she was also the mother of Monroe University's football star, and Vanessa was sexy as hell.

Her mocha skin was always smooth as silk. She'd replaced her long hair with a sleek, short cut. The bright yellow pants hugged her curves in all the right places, and the sheer black top left nothing to the imagination.

Vanessa pulled him in for a taut hug before planting a kiss on his cheek.

"Are you back in Monroe to stay?" she asked, thumbing away the remnants of her red lipstick from his cheek.

"That's the plan," he said, taking a few steps back to create space between them, but Vanessa took a few steps forward, depleting the gap.

"Dre, let's get you a drink," Maurice said, saving him from Vanessa's domineering disposition.

If the sweaty brow was any indication of Dresden's discomfort, the sporadic stutter in his speech was, and Maurice noticed.

"I won't monopolize your time, but let's plan dinner soon," Vanessa uttered, retrieving his phone from his hand.

"Unlock, please," she said innocently, but the lust lingering in her narrowed eyes was nothing but the devil.

Dresden obeyed her directions, unlocking his phone just as she snatched it away again. Vanessa dialed her number from his phone.

"I'll be in touch, Dr. Xavier," she declared, slowly sauntering away.

"My nigga, you in trouble," Maurice sang, firmly placing his hands on Dresden's shoulders as they walked to the bar.

# Chapter nine

Dresden walked the halls of the medical center and turned heads with every step. The women working in the building, from the janitors to other physicians, could not take their eyes off him.

Priscilla and Harper stood at the front desk watching the staff openly ogle Dr. Xavier.

"You know what they call him, right?" Priscilla said but didn't remove her eyes from Dresden walking down the hall.

"What?" Harper asked, sipping coffee while she pretended not to peek at his goodness.

"*Dr. Feelgood,*" Priscilla chanted.

*Shit!* Harper coughed, choking on her coffee. She chuckled mutedly at his nickname, which was popular with her best friend, Joya, and among the staff.

His freshly shaved head and smooth line of the dark, ebony beard accented his beautiful Colgate smile. He swayed smoothly, dressed in cognac-colored slacks, a crisp white dress shirt, and dark chocolate loafers. Every stride exuded power, strength, and downright sexiness. Dresden glanced in their direction, causing Priscilla to fake like she was on the phone while Harper escaped to the staff lounge.

When he walked through the glass double doors etched with his name, marking his wing of the medical center, his chest was filled with gratitude and pride. Some men would allow the positional power to go to their heads, but Dresden was as humble as they came.

The hospital administrators entrusted him with this domicile for at least the following year. Hopeful fathers, sons, brothers, and friends would walk through those doors, wishing for a miracle, and Dresden would pray that his team could deliver.

Research of this magnitude came with highs and lows. Dresden always celebrated the positive, life-changing outcomes. However, he was often disheartened by the critical postmortem analysis necessary to conduct a thorough clinical trial. Medications and even cures for some of the most deadly diseases were not discovered until extensive research on the victims was conducted. Dresden considered them heroes.

"Good morning, Dr. Xavier. Your first appointment has arrived."

"Thank you, Priscilla," Dresden said, retrieving the tablet from her that housed his patient records.

Walking into exam room two, Dresden saw the back of a figure standing in front of the window overlooking the hospital grounds. A wheelchair was settled behind his tall yet lanky frame to aid him if he became unbalanced.

"Hello. Hello," Dresden spoke and knocked simultaneously to gain the man's attention.

"I'm Dr. Xavier," he said, extending his hand toward the patient.

The man turned around and nodded, clasping his hand in Dresden's.

"Terrance," he introduced.

"We only use initials for confidentiality during our visits, if that's OK," Dresden announced. "Inside these walls, you'll be assigned a number if you're accepted."

"Oh, yeah. I forgot. Miss Pricilla told me that. My apologies," Terrance uttered.

"No worries. Are you able to get on the exam table?" Dresden probed, preparing to begin the examination.

Terrance nodded.

"Let me apologize in advance. Your oncologist did not upload your files until early this morning, so I will review some information in real time. Is that okay?" Dresden asked, darting his eyes from the tablet back to Terrance. Dresden squinted skeptically, observing Terrance's lethargy.

"Yes, that's fine," Terrace responded, finally getting positioned on the table.

"But first, I want to ask you a few questions and conduct a simple exam."

Terrance nodded.

"What initial symptoms did you have that caused your concern?" Dresden inquired.

"A little over a year ago, I was having some stomach pain and constipation. One day, the pain was so bad I drove myself to the ER. At first, the doctors treated me for an ulcer. But after the pain persisted, more tests were done, confirming that it was colon cancer."

Dresden quickly typed notes into the computer mounted in the corner of the exam room.

"Before a year ago, had you ever had stomach pain or constipation issues? Even if they were minor?"

Terrance nodded. "Yeah. I guess. I would get this pain in my side when I ate certain foods. Constipation was normal for me in recent years."

"How recent?"

"Maybe five or six," Terrance shrugged.

"Any blood in the stools?"

He nodded again.

Terrance continued to narrate his medical history and journey with cancer. Surgeries, drugs, holistic options, you name it, he'd tried it.

"What was your weight at the time of your diagnosis?" Dresden continued his discovery.

"Two fifty," Terrance responded, lying on the exam table.

Dresden intently focused on the yellow highlighted vitals displayed on the tablet.

*One hundred pounds in a year*, he quietly calculated.

Dresden documented Terrance's other vitals before conducting simple mobility and pain level tests.

"I'm going to step out to review the X-rays from your last exam. I'll be back in a few. Do you need anything while you wait?"

"Water would be good," Terrance retorted.

Dresden nodded. "The nurse will be right in with the water and to help you get dressed. Sit tight."

Stepping into the hallway, Dresden heard her laughter before he could see her. Harper was leaning against Priscilla's desk but couldn't see him approaching.

"Good morning, Professor Kingsley," Dresden chimed.

She spun around midlaugh, bouncy curls falling into her eyes, which were not covered with glasses today. The white coat with her name and credentials stitched on the right lapel did not conceal her curves in the fitted pants and V-neck blouse.

"Good morning, Dr. Xavier."

"What's so funny? I might need a good laugh," he said, rounding the oversized desk.

"I brought coffee," Harper smiled, holding up a large paper bag.

"She bought a fancy coffee machine that requires several advanced degrees to operate," Priscilla bantered.

"I'm very serious about my coffee," Harper declared.

"I can see that. I don't believe I've ever heard of this coffee," Dresden chuckled, lifting the bag of specialty coffee beans. "I'm a Folgers or whatever's available kinda guy," he continued.

"Oh no, sir. I'm going to have to fix that for you. When I am done with you, you'll be begging for another cup," she announced.

"Is that so?"

Dresden's mind marched in an utterly inappropriate direction. He was glad Harper didn't notice the impassioned inflection of his tone. She continued ranting about her love for coffee; he thought it was the cutest thing.

"Trust me. You wouldn't want to work with me without coffee," she quipped. "And walking all the way into the hospital for Starbucks . . . It's a no for me."

Harper and Priscilla cackled while Dresden just shook his head.

"You do know we could've bought a coffee machine for the office," he said.

She shrugged but remained hushed.

"Make sure you get reimbursed, Professor Kingsley. And buzz me when that thing is ready to go," he quipped.

"Will do," Harper giggled, then sauntered away, leaving a fragrant trail of honey and orange blossoms.

Instinctively, Dresden's eyes lazily narrowed as he deeply inhaled. He dreaded the moment when he lost her aroma in the traitorous exhale. Just the scent of her had his manhood topsy-turvy.

He shook his head, mumbling lowly, "Why the fuck did I inhale?"

He turned to take a final glance at her. His head and heart struggled between passion and fake impassivity. He did not want to desire this woman, but the last thing Dresden was experiencing with Harper was a lack of interest.

"Dr. Xavier," Priscilla chimed, snapping her fingers to get his attention.

*Shit.* He'd completely forgotten that she was standing there. Dresden twitched, moving his head from side to side. He had to get his shit together.

"Are the files loaded on the big screen in my office?" he blurted harsher than he intended.

"Yes, sir. They're all ready to go."

"Thank you, Priscilla." Dresden bowed his head in appreciation before rushing away.

Terrance exited the restroom and found the nurse waiting with a wheelchair. The young nurse flashed him a sweet smile as he settled into the chair. He'd become accustomed to those sympathetic smiles from medical staff, but he returned the gesture anyway.

Eyes circling around the office space, Terrance admired the modern decor accented with soft hints of yellow, purple, and blue. For privacy, the medical trial offices were positioned on the opposite side of the cancer center. A hallway divided the two spaces, but the glass walls allowed visibility into the entryways.

Harper's bouncing curls danced down the hall, walking toward Dr. Xavier and the woman named Priscilla. He held up a finger for the pretty nurse to stop for a second. Terrance watched the exchange between his ex-wife and the doctor.

The reddened blush, the constant tug at her ear, and the nervous swipe across her brow were familiar. *She likes him*, he thought as an unexplained feeling overwhelmed him. It wasn't anger. Maybe regret, but he wasn't sure. Since their brief separation and then divorce, Terrance had never seen his wife in the presence of another man. He hadn't witnessed that beautiful, flirtatious smile in a very long time, and it broke his heart that he wasn't the cause.

Dr. Xavier's admiration couldn't be concealed either. Terrance had just met the doctor, but it was not hard to detect when a man was attracted to a woman. And what was there not to fancy about Harper? She was intelligent, charismatic, and beautiful.

Terrance was grateful for the privacy. He yanked his eyes away, instructing the nurse to proceed. Entering the empty exam room, the nurse wheeled him back to the window.

"Do you need anything else while you wait, sir?" the nurse asked.

He shook his head.

"Dr. Xavier will be right with you."

Antsy was the only way to describe his temperament. If he had the energy to pace the floor, he would. His medical records would tell a story Dr. Xavier would not want to read. *But he's a husband, a father. He'll understand my request*, Terrance mused, hoping that his declaration was true.

"It's a long shot and risky, but what do I have to lose?"

Stepping into his office, Dresden was happy to see that Priscilla had uploaded the most recent files and that the patient's complete history was ready for his review.

Priscilla was proving to be a rockstar. Her background as an oncology nurse and then office manager was the perfect combination of what he needed. He trusted her initial assessment of prospective volunteers' viability for the trial. Of course, Dresden did his due diligence to ensure that her assessment was correct, but for the most part, she'd been spot-on with her recommendations.

Immediately, he recognized the red highlight on the file labeled *TK-47218*, indicating her recommendation to deny entry for his current patient. As he swiped the screen to review the initial X-rays when Terrance was diagnosed compared to now, Dresden was perplexed.

"The cancer is everywhere. Why would his doctor recommend this?" he muttered quietly.

After carefully reviewing the records for another twenty minutes, Dresden returned to the exam room. Terrance was back at the window. Only this time, he was seated in the wheelchair.

"My apologies for the delay." Dresden paused to formulate his words. "Unfortunately—"

"I know, Doc. I already know," Terrance drawled slowly, interrupting Dresden but never releasing his stare from the window.

"Three to four months, right? I'll be lucky to see Thanksgiving," Terrance snickered eerily before adjusting the wheelchair to face the doctor.

Dresden nodded. "The referring physician should have told you that this trial is not for patients at your advanced metastatic stage. I'm sorry. I can recommend some holistic methods to keep you comfortable, but I cannot accept you into this trial. My nurse will get you squared away, and someone will transport you back—"

Terrance tossed up a frail hand, interrupting again.

"Dr. Xavier, I know you don't know me from a can of paint. But, man, I need you to do me this solid. I'm already dying, so what do you have to lose?"

Dresden looked at him like he was insane. Shit, maybe he was. A dying man can also be a desperate one.

"I don't understand what you are asking, T—"

"Terrance. Call me Terrance."

"OK, Terrance," he said, shrinking the distance between them.

"I'm asking from one father to another. As husbands . . . Wouldn't you do anything for *your* family?" Terrance questioned, desperate to relate to Dr. Xavier.

Dresden nodded.

"My wife . . . She's dead. But yes, I would do anything for my daughters . . . my family. Including telling them the truth," he stressed the last words.

When his mind was circulating, Dresden paced. He was moving so fast that he practically burned a hole in the tiled floor. Was this man asking Dresden to ignore his oath to do no harm?

"Again, Terrance, I am sorry your doctor wasted your time, but you do not qualify. There is no treatment to slow the progression of your disease at this phase. I cannot, in good faith, subject you to procedures that I know will not work," Dresden explained.

"What about the placebo?" Terrance asked, his tone pleading. "My wife told me that this trial might have a placebo group. Can't I do that?" The presumed desperation was evident.

Harper had not disclosed anything to Terrance, but he'd read through some of her files one night when she fell asleep in his room.

Dresden's pacing abruptly ceased. He crossed his arms over his chest with wrinkled brows, indicating confusion and frustration. While placebo groups weren't uncommon in clinical trials, the details of this particular trial were not readily available to the public. Interviews for that group hadn't even started yet.

"Your wife? Who?" he demanded.

"Harper. Harper Kingsley."

# Chapter ten

"Did Harper put you up to this?" Dresden said, gritting through his teeth.

"No. No. Harper only recommended the trial because she didn't know the disease had advanced. She-she doesn't know I'm terminal," Terrance whimpered his last words.

Dresden continued to pace the floor while wiping a hand down his face and clenching the back of his neck in aggravation.

"Mr. Kingsley, you have to tell your wife. Your family. The estimated weeks or months is just that . . . an estimate. This disease is unpredictable. It can stall in one moment and progress in the next. I can do nothing for you but suggest you talk to your wife. Again, I am sorry."

"I have two sons," Terrance blurted. "You said you have kids. Daughters, right? Wouldn't you do *anything* for your kids?" Terrance asked.

Dresden nodded, never halting his frantic motion. He would do anything for Bella and Bryn and give his life to his girls. He knew all too well what someone in this predicament would do to spare their family from the inevitable. His thoughts drifted back to Nina.

*"Rosie, hear me out. Research has come a long way. Let me introduce you to Dr. Marcia Rosen. She's the best oncologist for ovarian cancer in the States,"* Dresden pleaded as Nina rested in the lounge chair after another failed treatment and adverse prognosis.

*"Dres, baby, come here,"* Nina requested, holding out her feeble arms.

*He fell to his knees next to her, settling his face in the palms of her hands.*

*"For you, Bella, and Bryn, I will do anything to live even just a day longer."*

Dresden visibly trembled, tightly closing his eyes to erase the memory that he now regretted. *I was a damn bully. So fucking selfish. How could I put her through that?*

During the quiet moments when Nina didn't know he was watching, he saw her physical weakness and fatigue. While her mind remained strong, his Rosie was weary, but she would never relent to death until he and the twins unshackled her from the obligation of living.

"I am Superman to my boys. But this shit . . ." Terrance pointed to his stomach as if he knew exactly where the cancer was located. "This shit in my body is my fucking kryptonite. I can't win," he croaked, swallowing the emotions.

"But, I–I need to show my family that I did everything I could to live. I need them to know I fought. That I fought as hard as I could."

Terrance's eyes pooled with water, but he refused to allow the tears to fall. He bit into his bottom lip to stop the uncontrollable quiver.

"But, man, I'm tired. And I'm ready. But I need to use the time I have left to prepare my family. To fix what I fucked up with *her*." His last words were almost inaudible.

Dresden's head jerked to face him. They eye-warred for a long, dreadful minute. Terrance was never a man to beg for anything, but in that instant, squinted, anguished, tear-filled eyes silently pleaded.

"I could lose my damn license. I don't even know you, man," Dresden whispered, but his gruff tone was loud.

He resumed his pacing, aggressively massaging his temples.

"But you know *her*," Terrance said, watching the doctor for a reaction.

Dresden paused but did not turn around. He knew exactly who *her* was. Flashes of Harper at lunch danced in his psyche. Now he understood why she was so nervous. It's not only a family member with the disease but also her husband.

"I'll sign papers. Donate my body to your research after it's all over. Whatever I need to do to keep you protected. She'll never know. Nobody will ever know."

Dresden leaned against the wall, tossing a stress ball against the opposite wall in the empty hallway of the medical center. In a couple of weeks, these halls and examination rooms would be bustling with patients, but right now, the long corridor was his escape from reality.

Since his meeting with Terrance, he'd been hiding...brooding ...contemplating. What he was being asked to do could be career suicide. Shit, it could be illegal.

*Harper's husband is dying. And he wants me to keep that shit from her. From everybody.*

"I can't do this shit. He needs to spend this time with his family, not in this medical center with nothing but vitamins pumping through an IV," he mumbled to himself.

"Fuck," he yelped, hurling the ball one final time.

"Dr. Dresden. Are you OK?" Harper's voice was calm in the midst of his chaos.

He eyed the concerned expression on her face. The corners of his mouth slightly curved as he nodded.

"I'm fine. Just processing through some things."

"Coffee?" she asked.

"Pardon me?"

"You haven't had coffee. I can't process anything without a cup of coffee," she smiled, shoving the black thermos toward him.

Dresden hadn't noticed the two coffee cups in her hands. He chuckled, shaking his head while accepting the hot java.

"I pegged you as a black coffee with a couple of sugars kinda guy. I hope I'm right," she declared, propping one foot against the wall across from him, mimicking his stance.

He snickered, far too smitten by how damn adorable she was. "You are correct. Thank you."

Dresden sipped the coffee, and it was perfect. He lifted the cup to demonstrate his appreciation. Harper's grin beamed, excited to receive his approval. They lingered in a few moments of mental solitude other than the sporadic sips.

"Whatever it is, just know that you were built for this, and you'll make the right decision," Harper announced, raising a reassuring brow. "Enjoy your coffee, Dr. Xavier."

Dresden halted midsip, just staring at this . . . *marvel* of a woman. Her confidence in him was everything he didn't know he needed. *She's magnificent*, he thought. An impeccable soul that had him mesmerized and fucking mortified in the same breath. *I can see why Terrance is trying to live for her*, he thought, gazing at bouncing curls as she vanished down the hall.

While the warming sensation from the coffee helped soothe his agitation, the hopefulness in Harper's eyes solidified his stance.

For the rest of the day, Dresden operated on automatic. His day was filled with examinations so that he could finalize the trial list before the end of the day. Sitting in his office, he stared at the wall monitor displaying the records for *TK-47218*. The red highlighted word *denied* bled from the screen.

"Dr. Xavier," Priscilla said, knocking on the door as she entered. "I will leave soon, but I wanted to upload the final list. Is it ready?"

He stirred, startled by her sudden appearance. "Priscilla. Yes, um, I'll transfer the files to you right now."

The details on Dresden's laptop were visible on the big monitor. He clicked the green check mark on record *TK-47218*, switching the decision from denied to accepted.

"Um, Dr. Xavier, that patient is—" Priscilla frowned as she tried to continue speaking, but Dresden tossed up his hand to stop her.

"The list is final, Priscilla. Thank you, and have a good night."

# *Chapter eleven*

Harper glanced at the clock on the wall for the fifth time with a yellow highlighter lodged between her fingers. She was studying the research articles to prepare for the first round of analysis next week. She'd privately been concerned that her colleagues had a bit of an upper hand since they'd been actively practicing medicine, whereas she taught medicine for a living.

Although she could regurgitate the medical dictionary like her favorite poem, the study of medicine differed significantly from using the knowledge in practice.

Her sepia-brown eyes were exhausted as she glanced at the clock again. Jolting, she was stunned that four forty-seven had quickly ticked to almost eight o'clock on a Friday night.

"It's late."

Harper shrieked, throwing the highlighter toward the door in response to his bass-filled timbre. Dresden dodged the air-bound missile while chuckling.

"My apologies. I didn't mean to scare you."

Closing her eyes, she huffed an exaggerated exhale, releasing a chuckle of her own. "Oh my goodness. I'm so sorry. Did it hit you?"

He shook his head. "No, but you have a nice arm," he said, smiling as he entered the office with a black Gucci backpack draped across his shoulder.

Dresden was . . . delicious. Dress-down Friday did his body good. Lean yet athletic thighs filled dark denim jeans, while corded arms and rippled abs swelled in an ivory Henley. What she guessed were a pair of white and brown Jordan 1s dressed his feet to fit the six-foot-two-inch frame.

*Sweet baby Jesus.*

Harper leaned back in the chair, pleading with herself not to imagine this man naked. "*Focus on his eyes. Focus on his damn eyes,*" she muttered mutedly. *And what gorgeous eyes they are.*

He was across the room, lingering near the doorway, but the sensual aroma of amber and ginger whispered in the air, tickling her senses.

"Sexy—I mean, softball," she exclaimed, bucking her eyes, disgusted with herself.

"Pardon me?" Dresden said questioningly.

His woolly, thick brows creased in confusion as he closed the distance between them, bringing a note of citrus with him.

"My throw . . . I played softball in high school," she shrugged.

"Ahh, got it. I'll remember to pick you for my team during the next hospital fundraiser," he teased.

Making himself comfortable, Dresden sat at the round table, leaving two empty seats between them.

"Why are you still here, Harper?"

"I could ask you the same question, Dr. Xavier."

He peeked at his watch before speaking. "It's officially the weekend. Please call me Dresden."

"OK . . . Why are *you* still here, Dresden?" She flashed him a blushful smile.

"Well, my girls are at some festival, my sister is having girl time with my niece, and my parents are on a date," he said snarkily, but the grin decorating his face indicated playfulness.

"Honestly . . . My house is empty, and I don't want to be there right now," he uttered, then clasped his hand at his neck, rocking in the chair.

"Your turn," he said.

Harper eyed him, hesitant to admit that she didn't want to go home either. Not because her house was empty but quite the contrary. Terrance and his friends hosted a monthly fish fry for as long as she could remember. They rotated houses, and tonight was Terrance's turn to host.

Even when he became ill and moved back into their home, Harper tolerated the overdose of testosterone for one night. Usually, she and her best friend, Joya, would plan a girls' night out, but tonight was date night for the Fletchers.

"My house *is not* empty, so being here gives me a little alone time."

"A momentary escape from your husband and kids?" Dresden probed.

Harper snickered. "A momentary escape from my *ex-husband*, his friends, and my halfway-grown kids."

Dresden feigned unaffected, but he was affected like a mutherfucker. *Did she say ex . . . husband? Terrance . . . TK said Harper was his wife.*

"My mistake. I thought that you were married."

She shook her head. "No. Not anymore. We've been divorced for almost three years," she confirmed.

"Oh."

That one word didn't say much, but the perplexed expression on his face spoke volumes.

"Oh?" she mocked him, and they cackled.

"Ask me," Harper said, almost daring him.

Dresden studied her—bold, brown eyes with eyelashes like feathers. Unblemished nutmeg skin with a hint of clear gloss coating her pouty lips weakened him. Secretly, he'd admired her casual Friday attire all day. The denim shirt dress belted at the waist accentuated her ample hips and thighs while full breasts played peek-a-boo through the opened buttons. The hair sweeping her shoulders earlier was now pulled into a messy bun secured by two ink pens.

*Stop staring, nigga. Damn*, he scolded . . . but didn't obey.

"You mentioned that your *ex*-husband was at *home*. *Your* home?"

She nodded. "Well, it used to be *our* home before the divorce. He lives with me and our youngest son, Trae."

"So, you live together but are divorced," Dresden interrogated her carefully.

She nodded again.

He hiked a brow. *Wow*, he thought, but didn't realize the word actually escaped his mouth until—

"*Wow?* Why wow?" she chuckled. "So you think it's crazy for a divorced couple to live together too?" she said teasingly.

Dresden didn't respond, but his guise shouted a boisterous *Hell yeah*. "Maybe a little," he said, pinching his thumb and pointer finger together.

"Good, because I was starting to question my sanity," she joked.

Harper inhaled deeply while settling into the chair. She was used to the strange stares when people became aware of her and Terrance's unorthodox arrangement.

"Some years after we divorced, my ex, Terrance, got really sick and needed some help. So . . . I helped him," Harper whispered her last words, silently reliving the day her ex-husband moved back *home.*

*"Terrance. Terrance Kingsley," Harper spoke to the receptionist behind the desk at the hospital.*

*The woman couldn't state the floor number fast enough before Harper sprinted toward the elevator. She rushed down the halls on the seventh floor. The oncology floor.*

*"Room 212, room 212," she repeatedly mumbled to herself.*

*Harper lifted her hand to push open the door, but she hesitated, taking a moment to breathe and pray before entering the room. She walked into the cold, sterile room, circling her eyes around the space as multiple machines beeped in the background.*

Terrance lying in the hospital bed will forever be embedded in her memory. She hadn't seen Terrance in months because he had avoided her since the divorce. He'd come to pick up Trae but never entered the house or hid in the crowd during their son's track meets. So the sight before her was unfamiliar . . . heartbreaking.

*The big, strong beast of a man was frail and weak. Harper broke, allowing one thunderous sob to flee her lungs. She covered her mouth with both hands to conceal the weakening sound of her anguish, but it was too late.*

*"Harp," Terrance's baritone was coarse yet delicate . . . afraid.*

*Harper roughly wiped her tears away before rushing to his bedside. Clasping his hand in hers, she whispered, "Hey."*

*"I'm sick, Harp," he whimpered, shaking his head. "It ain't good. It's not good at all."*

*"Terrance, why didn't you tell me?"*

*"Because I was doing fine. The meds were working. I was good until . . ." His voice waned, fatigue forcing his eyes shut.*

*"It's OK. Just rest, Tee. We'll talk later. I got you, okay? I got you."*

"Wow," Dresden blurted this time. "That's . . . admirable, Harper," he said, not bothering to probe about her ex's sickness.

Harper's rosy cheeks hiked with a closed-mouth simper.

"We didn't part on bad terms. He's my sons' father and my friend, so . . ." Her shoulders hunched again. "Even though we were not *destined to be*, he'll always be my friend. And my friend needed my help."

Harper swallowed hard, hit with sudden emotions. She blinked back tears and coyly smiled.

She whispered, "Sorry," as she thumbed away a renegade tear.

Dresden shook his head, sliding his chair nearer to caress her hand. They eyed their conjoined fingers resting on the table before gazing back at each other. What should have been an awkward moment was actually friendly . . . comforting. Dresden's ogle was probing yet empathetic, but Harper didn't avoid his penetrating stare. She actually craved it.

"Don't apologize. That's grown-up shit, and as I said . . . admirable. Not many women could do what you're doing."

"I'm not going to pretend it's easy because it's hard as hell," she snickered, staring at a random mark on the wall.

"But Terrance saved me in ways he'll never know, so caring for him during this time is the least I can do."

Dresden faintly smiled at Harper's nonchalant shoulder shrug, but compassion and devotion radiated in her pretty brown eyes.

"You should tell him," Dresden uttered, causing her head to spin back in his direction.

"Tell him what?" Harper wore a bewildered smirk.

"How he saved you."

His stare was neither uncomfortable nor easy, but his gape caused Harper to squirm. She felt exposed as if he could see all of her lies and truths. Their eyes danced harmoniously—an akin connection rooted in sorrow and grief.

"When Nina decided to stop treatment and accept her fate, I was broken," he expressed, now gazing at that same mark on the wall. "Shit, destroyed." With pursed lips, he shook his head. "I didn't want to imagine living in a world where she didn't exist."

Dresden paused, allowing the story of Nina's last days to unfold in his head.

"But after she died, I realized how blessed I was to be able to express to her how she saved me. To share all the sentiments and words I needed to express how much I loved her."

Memories of his Nina always punctured old wounds, but he felt compelled . . . comfortable to share with Harper. Shifting his gaze to Harper, he offered a faint smile.

"I don't know your situation," he somewhat lied. "But what I do know is that circumstances with a loved one's health can change in an instant. Life is so short . . ." Dresden rose from his seat and took a few steps toward Harper.

He propped his body against the table, peering down at her. She unsuccessfully tried to evade his stare.

"Even if you're no longer in a marital relationship, it's clear that there's still love there. Tell him while you have time, Harper."

The bass-filled drawl of Dresden calling her name scattered a chill down her spine. Harper couldn't disagree with his declaration because she still loved Terrance. But in the midst of the love, hurt, abandonment, and weariness resided. She looked up at him and nodded in agreement.

"What if this *cleansing conversation* you're suggesting includes the good *and* the bad?" she said, disconnecting her eyes from him.

Instinctively, Dresden positioned a finger under her chin, lifting her face, forcing her to look at him.

"Say it anyway."

# Chapter twelve

Terrance and Harper pulled into the small parking lot of the blue and gray Victorian home that had been transformed into the family therapy offices of Dr. Morrison Ray and Dr. Avis Blanchard. Terrance circled his truck to open Harper's door, and they nervously walked to the midnight-blue double doors.

At Harper's request, the Kingsleys were scheduled for their first couples therapy appointment with Dr. Avis Blanchard. Harper was a little disappointed that Dr. Ray was not accepting new patients because he came highly recommended. But Dr. Ray assured Harper that she would be pleased with Dr. Blanchard.

Signing in at the receptionist's desk, they sat in the waiting area for about ten minutes.

"Dr. Blanchard is ready for you, Mr. and Mrs. Kingsley," the receptionist sang.

"Thank you," Terrance said, extending his arm for Harper to walk ahead of him.

*She tapped on the partially open door and was greeted by a smooth, raspy voice reminding them of Maya Angelou. Dr. Blanchard was a tall, dark-skinned woman, maybe in her fifties, with a short, tapered haircut. She wore a flowy African print dress with a flawlessly beat face and black-framed glasses. She was beautiful.*

*"Good afternoon. You must be Terrance and Harper," the doctor spoke softly with an even softer smile. "It's a pleasure to meet you."*

*"Nice to meet you as well," Harper said while Terrance nodded.*

*"Please, please, have a seat," she offered.*

*Unconsciously, Harper sat on one end of the plush leather sofa, and Terrance settled in the middle. Dr. Blanchard eyed the immediate distance between them as she sat across from them in a matching leather chair.*

*Her office was adorned with Afrocentric decor with bold yellow, orange, and ivory hues. Framed degrees from Spelman College and USC hung on the walls alongside pictures from her extensive travels.*

*Two candles burned on the cocktail table, with bottled waters, a box of tissues, two journals, and a cup of writing pens.*

*"Well, Mr. and Mrs. Kingsley, let me establish some house rules," the doctor said, crossing her legs to reveal the fire-engine red, sky-high stiletto heels.*

*"My role here is not to solve whatever you've identified as challenges in your marriage. My role is to help you find common ground. What does common ground mean, you may ask. Well, common ground means active listening, respect, and understanding instead of accusations—constructive feedback and, finally, accepting any decision from your partner. If you desire me to 'fix' your marriage, we should bid one another farewell right now. Any objections?" Dr. Blanchard declared candidly.*

*Harper and Terrance looked like deer caught in headlights. They were stuck and speechless. The reality of the doctor's disclosure hit them like a ton of bricks. For Harper, therapy was the final step before she toppled off the cliff. However, Terrance secretly wanted Dr. Blanchard to wave a magic wand and fix whatever Harper felt was wrong in the marriage. From his perspective, things were fine.*

*"No objections from me," Harper said, her eyes trained on Dr. Blanchard.*

*The doctor nodded, then shot her eyes over to Terrance.*

*"Same. No objections," he mumbled uncomfortably.*

*"Great," Dr. Blanchard smiled. "Now, which one of you initiated therapy?"*

*Harper raised her hand.*

*"Why?"*

*She swallowed, then released her breath before speaking. Harper opened her mouth, but no words surfaced. She cleared her throat, but again, she was voiceless.*

*"What is happening right now, Harper?" Dr. Blanchard asked, pointing her pen toward Harper's face.*

*"What?" Harper whispered.*

*"You're crying," Dr. Blanchard countered, then leaned over to pull a few tissues from the box.*

*Harper swiped her cheeks, surprised to see the traces of dampness on her fingertips.*

*"Were you aware that you were crying?" the doctor probed.*

*Harper shook her head.*

*"What are you feeling right now, Harper? Take a breath and release the first words that come up for you. Don't contemplate or formulate what you think your husband or I may want to hear."*

*Harper sucked in her cheeks before following the doctor's directions. Inhaling deeply, then exhaling slowly, she uttered, "Nothing. I don't feel anything. I'm a robot. Hollow."*

*"Why do you feel this way?" Dr. Blanchard continued her interrogation.*

Terrance sat silently, unable to look at his wife. He hated to see her cry. But he especially despised it when she accused him of being the cause.

"Because nobody sees me," she admitted, licking salty tears from the corners of her lips.

"Who is nobody?"

The hush was so heavy, as if the ceiling were collapsing and the walls were caving in.

"My husband," Harper breathily muttered. Placid, still tears streaked her face.

"Thank you, Harper. The first step is always the hardest." Dr. Blanchard confirmed with a gentle smile.

"Terrance, why do you think your wife wanted you all to come to therapy?" The doctor shifted her focus quickly.

"Because she's not happy," he blurted abruptly.

"Why do you think she's unhappy?"

Terrance shrugged. "I'm not sure. She's always upset about something, and usually, that wrath is directed toward me."

"Have you ever asked Harper why she's angry?"

"Yes." Terrance's left leg bounced uncontrollably.

"Can you share what she said?"

"She just complains. I can't do anything right, or she accuses me of doing nothing."

"Can you share an example of an accusation?" the doctor probed.

Terrance huffed, slightly rolling his eyes.

"What is happening, Terrance?" Dr. Blanchard asked him the same question, motioning her pen to signal the change in his demeanor.

"Honestly, this is stupid. No offense, Doc, but I don't really understand why we're even here. Harper gets mad over the smallest things."

Dr. Blanchard remained impassive, while Harper was livid. She'd practically gnawed her lip until she drew a little blood.

*"Can you share examples of these small things?" the doctor asked again.*

*"If I come in late or forget stuff sometimes, she's pissed."*

*"Sometimes," Harper shouted.*

*She was bursting at the seam and couldn't contain her angst anymore. Dr. Blanchard tossed up a finger to silence her. She nodded to Terrance, signaling for him to continue.*

*"Never mind, man. Like I said, this is stupid."*

Terrance's body spasmed suddenly when the nurse tapped him on the forearm. He was in a deep sleep during his massage. Lately, his relationship with Harper had been weighing heavily on his brain. When they went to therapy all of those years ago, Harper made it very clear that it was her final straw. They tried everything to avoid therapy: a date night schedule that Terrance did not abide by, a couples group at church, and a relationship workbook.

Harper read every book and listened to every audiobook to help find love in her spouse when all she really wanted was to walk away. She even talked to her primary care physician about her moods to determine if her estrogen levels were low. Terrance knew she had one foot out the door, and he disregarded her needs anyway.

*"Dammit, Terrance. If I have to do everything myself, why do I need you?" Harper shouted.*

*"What the hell are you saying, Harp? You don't want to be with me anymore?" Terrance asked, bracing for the answer because he knew that Harper would tell him the truth.*

*"No, Terrance, I don't. I'm spent. I'm done. I want a divorce."*

Terrance swiped a hand down his face to disrupt the wretched memory. The day his life changed forever. During that time, he and Harper were in a really bad place, unable to communicate without yelling. He preferred to maintain possession of the fun, loving, and friendly memories.

*I never thought she would leave*, he mused, thinking back on how clueless he was. *Nah, you weren't clueless. You were unwilling to listen. Fucking stubborn.*

It took him a minute to shake the fog from his nap. The cancer center was such a quiet and serene environment. It offered a community room for certain patients to get physical and occupational therapy and a nutritionist who prepared menus for specific dietary needs and protein shakes.

Terrance had been there all morning, and as crazy as it sounded, he was looking forward to the time at the center. On most days, he was stuck in the house with Nurse Shelly and limited interaction with anyone other than his family.

After the massage, he enjoyed a shake and physical therapy before he was wheeled to a private exam room. The nurse informed him that Dr. Dresden wanted to review some documents with him.

Honestly, Terrance was shocked when he received the notification that he'd been accepted into the trial. He was unsure of the doctor's stipulations, but whatever they were, he would yield to Dr. Xavier's demands.

"*Knock, knock*," Dresden said, pushing open the door to the exam room.

"Doc," Terrance greeted, slowly lifting his hand.

Dresden reached out to shake his hand and then nodded. "TK," Dresden started, but Terrance stopped him.

"I understand all of the confidentiality rules, but given our situation, can you please call me Terrance?"

Dresden nodded again.

He eyed Terrance for a long minute because he was wary about the *agreement*. Begrudgingly, Dresden accepted Terrance into the trial under the placebo group. He would be able to partake in the benefits of the clinic such as nutrition and exercise, but aside from his standard medications prescribed by his primary oncologist, Terrance would not be put on the trial's drug regimen.

"Terrance, against my better judgment, I am allowing you to be here. As a part of the placebo group, you will sign nondisclosure statements. Additionally, you will opt into the Willed Body Program to be researched for the advancement of medical science," Dresden said dryly, lacking any bedside manner.

"I'm a step ahead of you, Doc," Terrance announced, stunning Dresden to sit upright.

"I did some research. I already added it to my estate plans to eliminate any potential opposition from my family. Harper has oversight of the arrangements, but she cannot change any of my preestablished plans," Terrance said, a confident alertness laced his tone.

Dresden could not help but continue to gawk at Terrance. What he initially thought was insanity, he now realized was clarity . . . preparedness. Terrance was ready to die.

"I guess we're good, then," Dresden stuttered a bit, still stunned by what he was witnessing.

"Doc, can I ask you a question?"

Dresden nodded.

"Why'd you agree to this?" Terrance asked.

Dresden's mind immediately floated to his Rosie as he pondered the question. But surprisingly, Harper's pretty face capered in his peripheral.

"My wife. She had cancer. But she seized each day with passion and purpose right up to the very end," Dresden expressed with a subtle smile.

"During her fight, she taught me and my girls to celebrate every moment. She never allowed us to anguish in the inevitable. But she forced us to be glad in everything. Her legacy and memories are sustenance . . . They breathe life into me. I have no questions, or what-ifs, or regrets. Just gladness." Dresden's gaze was dreamy as the most beautiful beam decorated his face.

"So, I'm doing this for my Nina," he croaked, clearing the bubble of emotions in his throat.

Raising stern eyes to look at his patient, Dresden continued. "And you, Mr. Kingsley, you must do this for your sons. For Harper," Dresden encouraged forcefully.

Dresden finally made his way to the other side of the center to his primary office. The first day of any trial was hectic, and today was no different. Patient paperwork, vitals, and an informational session to ensure they understood the expectations of the trial were time-consuming.

It was already after two o'clock, and Dresden was running on nothing but coffee. Coffee that Harper made for him earlier. She was not playing when she said she was serious about her love for the java. The entire office looked forward to her morning experiments.

He chuckled, looking at the empty thermos. Suddenly, a familiar curvaceous image sneakily tiptoed down the hallway, passing his office door. With pinched brows, he hurried to the door to see what she was up to. A bewildered grin painted his cheeks as he observed her creep as if she had stolen something.

"And where are we sneaking off to, Professor?" Dresden whispered.

Harper suspended her pursuit, then slowly spun around. Those big, pretty eyes were cute and devious. She was holding a covered tray of sandwiches and a brown paper bag. The look on her face was laced with guilt and giddiness.

"Um," she squealed, "the administrators' luncheon ended, and they had a lot of food left over. I haven't eaten so . . . I snagged a few things."

"Did you snag enough for two?" His eyes perked in anticipation. She nodded.

"We can lie low in my office," he continued.

"I actually had another plan if you're down," Harper announced. Swirling her head, she quietly signaled for him to follow her.

"It's a date . . . I mean, I'm down," Dresden corrected.

Harper pretended she didn't hear him, but her blush said otherwise. "Let's go before Priscilla catches us," she whispered.

Dresden snickered, then covered his mouth before grabbing the bag from her hand. Harper guided them through the exit door at the end of the hallway. They trekked up several steps before reaching another door.

"The roof?" Dresden questioned.

She nodded. "This is one of the best places to see the city."

"How do you know that?" he probed, following behind her.

Harper pointed to a clean ledge for them to sit. "I did my internship hours here in college. And both of my boys had asthma as kids, so I spent a lot of sleepless nights in the ER."

He nodded.

Harper reached into the bag to reveal a bowl of pasta salad, chips, baguette bread, and the bottled water.

"What do we have here?" Dresden asked, opening the lid to the tray.

"I just grabbed some stuff in a hurry. It could be some crap I don't even eat," Harper laughed.

"Looks like you did good, Professor. Take your pick: turkey club croissant or roast beef on rye," he offered.

"Turkey, please."

They settled quietly, allowing the afternoon breeze to cool their simmering thoughts while streaks of sun rays illuminated the cityscape.

"Next time you plan a covert operation, send me a smoke signal or something. I would've helped you grab more stuff," Dresden laughed.

"I didn't plan it. I just happened to be walking by the empty conference room and saw the food. I snagged what I could just before the food service lady came to clean it up," she giggled, eating a forkful of salad. "What exactly does the bat signal look like," she giggled.

"Hmm . . . Maybe something like, *ca-ca, ca-ca*," Dresden crowed like a bird.

Their laughter mingled like music, filling the air with joy and light, everything the pair didn't know they needed.

"O . . . kay. Next time I need you, I'll definitely send out the signal," she chuckled.

"You do that, and I'll definitely be there," he announced.

# Chapter thirteen

Hasan squinted at the clock on the nightstand in his bedroom. *10:32 a.m.* He stretched his naked frame before clutching his hands to his head. The weed and Hennessy high caused his ears to ring. Lately, Hasan had been attempting to numb his woes in risky ways. He worked for his father's company during the day, practiced with his band, and drank all night . . . repeat.

While Terrance was doing everything he could to live, Hasan knew his father was dying. He could feel it, and the shit hurt like hell.

"San, are you up?" Harper asked, knocking on his bedroom door.

Hasan had been staying at his parents' house lately to help care for his dad. Usually, he would stay in the loft studio above the trucking company's office near Midtown.

"Yeah," he growled, barely able to lift his head from the pillow.

Harper opened the door and walked into his room without an invitation. In her house, she was only knocking once. *My house, my rules*, Harper would fuss.

"I brought you something," Harper said, holding a bottle of water and two Tylenol pills. Sitting on the edge of his bed, she shook her head, worried about her eldest son. Harper knew that Hasan had been drinking a lot lately and introduced weed as his drug of choice.

"Thanks," he mumbled, embarrassment streaking his handsome face. Hasan tossed back the pills and gulped down the water in seconds.

"You good, Ma? Dad okay?" he uttered, rubbing a hand down his face.

"Nah, I'm not good, Hasan, because I'm worried about you. This is the second time this week I've had to nurse you through a hangover. I can't keep doing this, San," Harper bellowed, vainly attempting to silence her emotions.

"I know you're concerned about your dad, but drinking and getting high won't change anything," she continued.

"I don't want to talk about it, Ma. I'm good," he mumbled, quickly rising from the bed.

He stumbled a bit before reaching for a T-shirt to cover himself.

"You're good . . . *really*?" Harper sarcastically probed because that was far from the truth.

"If you're good, why are Brian and your other band friends calling me and Trae looking for you?" Harper lifted her meticulously arched brows in question.

"Oh shit," Hasan screeched, then immediately realized what he'd said. "Sorry, Ma."

Hasan was the drummer in a band called Foreplay. They were performing at the Monroe City Festival tonight, and the band was supposed to have a sound check in twenty minutes.

He'd mastered multiple instruments since joining the band in grade school, but the drums were his first love. Foreplay was an R&B, neo-soul group that played their original music and remixed covers of popular songs. The band was always in high demand in Monroe and across the Midwest.

Harper grabbed his arm before he rushed into the restroom. Spinning him around, she clutched his face, staring into eyes mimicking hers.

"San, I need you to be strong for your brother. An example for him. He wants to do everything you do, and I know that you would be on Trae's ass if he were drinking and getting high all the time."

Hasan nodded.

"You're an adult and can make your own choices, but, baby, this ain't it. You are too smart and too talented to go down this road. Your dad's fate is in God's hands—not the doctors, not yours, or mine, but God's. And we have to honor His will, whatever it may be. You understand?"

Hasan was silent, but the tears dropping from his eyes were deafening . . . heartbreaking.

"I don't want him to die," Hasan whispered.

"I know, baby, I know."

Her son collapsed into her arms, releasing all the angst and despair he'd been taming for months.

"Dad can have three days, three months, three years . . . We don't know. But we should work to make the best of whatever time he has. And the only way you can do that, Hasan, is sober," Harper hummed, seeking reassurance.

He nodded. "I hear you, Ma. Let me get going. I love you," Hasan said, kissing her cheek.

"I love you more."

"Bryn, let's go," Bella shouted up the steps.

"I'm coming. Hold your horses," Bryn chimed, slowly walking down the steps. She paused, eyeing her sister weirdly.

"Is *that* what you're wearing?" Bryn questioned.

Bella reviewed her standard attire, from her favorite checkered Vans to the pleated denim miniskirt and Def Leppard vintage T-shirt.

"Yeah. What's wrong with what I'm wearing?"

"Nothing other than you look like you're in eighth grade," Bryn teased.

"Well, you look like . . . never mind," Bella said, ogling her sister.

Bryn sported a cropped haircut, large hoop earrings, Jordan's, denim booty shorts that didn't leave much to the imagination, and a cropped shirt with her *Rosie's Garden* logo.

"What? I look good, sis," Bryn said, popping her lips.

"Must your logo have a gigantic marijuana leaf on it?" Bella complained, rolling her eyes.

"It's called *marketing*, my dear. We'll see if you're talking all that shit when I make my first million," Bryn chuckled, pulling her sister into a hug.

"Um, language, Bryn," Dresden fussed, appearing from the hallway leading to his bedroom.

"Sorry, Dad,' Bryn whined playfully. "You sure you don't want to go to the festival with us?"

"Did you forget, Bryn? Daddy has a *date*," Bella beamed.

"A date? With whom?" Bryn bellowed, her cheerful mood speedily turned surly.

*Dad* and *dating* in the same sentence were like nails on a chalkboard.

"It's not a date. I'm meeting a childhood friend for dinner," Dresden tried to clarify.

"Is this childhood *friend* a woman?" Bryn asked.

Dresden nodded.

"Are you paying for her dinner?" she continued her interrogation.

"Of course," he said, his brows creased as if she'd asked the most asinine question.

Dresden was the true definition of a gentlemanly alpha man, so a woman paying the tab in his presence was out of the question.

"That sounds like a *date* to me, Daddy," Bella sang while Bryn growled.

"Vanessa's family lived across the street from us for years. I've known her since grade school, so we're just catching up," he explained. "But guess who doesn't have to explain himself to his daughters?" Dresden paused, although he'd already provided an explanation.

"Dear old Dad," he chortled, pinching their noses simultaneously.

That act still made them giggle, even if Bryn was pretending still to be annoyed.

"Girls, be safe. I'm going to the office for a bit before my . . . *dinner*. Keep your locations on. Just in case, OK?"

The twins nodded, hugging their dad as if everything good in the world resided in the center of his arms.

"Love you, Daddy," they cooed.

"Love you most," he countered.

Since Bryn was still pouting, Bella decided to drive. They hopped in their mom's old Lexus RX and headed to the festival in Midtown.

"Seriously, B, why the long face?" Bella asked.

Bryn remained hushed for a brief moment. Her dad's words, *Love you most*, danced around in her head. He'd only said those words to them and their mom. But Bryn couldn't help but wonder if her dad would ever feel that way about another woman.

"Do you really think he's ready? To date, I mean," Bryn finally croaked.

"He won't know until he tries," Bella shrugged. "Daddy doesn't deserve to live alone for the rest of his life, Bryn. Mom didn't want that," she whispered the last sentence.

"How do you know?" Bryn probed, shifting her body to stare at her sister in the driver's seat.

Bella would never tell her sister about how their dad behaved with Professor Kingsley that day during her orientation. The smile on his face and the joy in his baritone was genuinely cheerful. Borderline goofy. While she wasn't planning on playing matchmaker, she would give her dad time to date around and figure out what and who could bring delight into his life daily.

"Ma wasn't selfish like that. I believe she wants Daddy to be happy. And he has too much love to give not to share it with someone other than us," she said, repeating her mother's dying sentiment.

Bryn was silent, turning to look out of the window as the festival lights caught her attention.

Bella was scheduled to volunteer at the festival's community fair with the Hopeful Heart Counseling Center. She was in training to counsel teens who'd lost a parent. On the other hand, Bryn was there to network and promote her future business. They were meeting Bella's roommates to hang out and listen to the local band, Foreplay.

Bryn blew her sister a kiss as she sauntered off to be the life of the party as usual. Bella rolled her eyes, giggling at her twin. There was no wonder why their favorite karaoke song was Paula Abdul's "Opposites Attract."

"Bella, can you go to the truck and get the other boxes of brochures?" Rachel, the center's volunteer coordinator, asked.

"Sure, I'll be right back," Bella said, grabbing the keys from Rachel's hand.

She started toward the parking lot, observing the other tables and the growing crowd forming. Monroe City had definitely changed since they'd visited a year before her mom got sick.

It was your run-of-the-mill small college town back then. But now, it was becoming a flourishing city for young professionals but still treasured its rich heritage and small-town appeal. While Bella initially questioned her decision to attend Monroe City, she was becoming increasingly more satisfied with the choice.

"Shit," she shouted, bracing herself as she hit the concrete . . . ass first.

"Fuck. My bad," a husky figure a few inches taller than she yelped.

He extended his hand to help her up, but Bella quickly swatted him away.

"Watch where you're going next time," she fussed.

"My bad. I'm running late. I should've been more careful," the unknown man said, still hovering over her.

She squinted from the sun beaming over his head. Bella couldn't decipher his facial features, but the tattooed arm attached to the rugged hand was quite appealing to delicate Bella.

"Please, let me help you up," he pleaded, offering his hand again.

This time, Bella didn't hesitate to accept his help. She'd hit the ground pretty hard and was sure her ass was going to pay the price later.

"Thank you," she grumbled.

"I'm really sorry. Anything scratched or broken?" he said while still clutching her hand.

Bella shook her head. "More embarrassed than anything," she blushed. Pulling away from his grasp, she anchored her hand over her brow to block the sun.

*Ahhh!* she sang mutedly. He was like an angel. The most beautiful creature she'd ever seen.

"Let me make it up to you. Can I buy you a drink?" he said, pointing to the Budweiser-sponsored bar.

"I don't drink," Bella countered.

"Then maybe some lemonade. The frozen ones bang," he chuckled.

"No thanks. I have to get back to work."

"Well, my name is Hasan. Just in case you need to find me later to kiss your boo-boos," he teased, swiping his tongue across those plump lips.

"That won't be necessary. But thanks," she countered.

"You can't tell me your name?"

"You didn't ask."

"What's your name? Otherwise, I'll just call you 'Beautiful.'" Hasan flashed that dimpled smile passed down from his mother.

"Bella. My name is Bella," she responded coyly.

"Beautiful Bella. That won't be hard to remember."

Bella began to walk away, but Hasan touched her forearm gently, pausing her pursuit.

"I'll see you around," he said.

She nodded and quickly departed.

Hasan gawked at her as she disappeared behind the sun. She was absolutely stunning. He chuckled to himself because girls like her weren't usually his type. Bella appeared sweet and innocent. Lately, Hasan preferred the rugged and ready-for-whatever band groupies in every shade and shape.

But Beautiful Bella, with her smooth, sable skin tone, big puff of auburn curls, wide hazel eyes, and thick curves that she concealed in the oversized clothes, mesmerized all of his senses.

Hours later, Bella completed her volunteer hours, and Bryn had made some solid connections for her business. The twins were ready to enjoy the rides and games at the festival until it was time for the band.

They navigated through the thick crowd to get to the VIP area. Bella's boss gave her wristbands for seats near the front of the stage. The opening acts were pretty good, but Bella and Bryn were waiting to see what all of the fuss was about over this group, Foreplay. Bella invited her three roommates, and they could not stop talking about the guys in the band.

"Canon is the cutest by far," Nadia declared.

"No, ma'am. Rico is everything," Francesca rebutted.

"Everybody knows that the *drummer* is always the finest member of the band. San is *pressure*," Mikayla chimed, twerking her hip with her lips puckered.

"Um, I beg to differ. Have you seen Questlove from The Roots? No shade, but he's a no for me," Bryn announced sarcastically, but she was dead-ass serious.

"Facts," Bella agreed, nodding.

Lights flashed across the stage, displaying the word *Foreplay* in red lights. The white spotlight illuminated each position where the band members would stand once they appeared on the stage. When the DJ announced Hasan, the light beamed on his walnut skin, and Bella went breathless. She nibbled the corner of her lip when his eyes connected with hers.

Foreplay absolutely lived up to all of the hype. The twins were impressed and sweaty because they danced through every song. For the finale, each band member had a solo on their instrument. When it was time for Hasan, he spoke into the microphone.

"This is dedicated to the Beautiful Bella. I hope you accept my apology, baby girl," Hasan winked, then pointed a drumstick in her direction before he played a Kendrick Lamar beat.

"Who the hell is that, B?" Bryn yelped.

Bella smiled, growing happier about the move to Monroe City every day.

# Chapter fourteen

Harper stared at herself in the full-length mirror, leaning against a wall in her bedroom. Dinner and drinks with her girls were on the agenda for the night. Her wavy curls were straightened, with a middle part shaping her face.

Fitted denim jeans cloaked every curve of her ample thighs. The bright yellow blazer synched her waist and complemented her honey eyes. Simple gold hoops, bracelets, and nude heels completed the look. Harper swiped the Fenty gloss across her lips before taking another second to scrutinize herself.

"Approved," she sang, snapping her finger and pursing her lips.

Her giggle was disrupted by the loud roar of laughter from the living room. Terrance was having a good week, so Harper convinced him to invite some friends over to watch the boxing match. Surprisingly, he agreed.

Terrance hadn't wanted anyone to see him in his current state. He was accustomed to being the biggest, most imposing figure in the room, but the drastic weight loss caused him to isolate himself other than his visits to the clinic.

Harper shook her head as she walked into the living room, greeted by pizza boxes, beer bottles, and too much damn testosterone.

"Hey, fellas," she crooned, gaining everyone's attention.

Sounds of *"What's up?"* and *"Hey, Harper"* bounced around the room. She crossed the room and approached Terrance, who was perched in the reclining chair. Normally, he would attempt to quell the gladness burning his cheeks in her presence, but today, the fascination for his ex-wife was apparent.

Harper was gorgeous. Her graceful beauty was always Terrance's favorite trait. Eyeing her as she approached, he slightly shook his head, wondering what the hell could've been wrong with him to fuck up with a woman like her. Harper smiled as she closed the distance between them.

Softly brushing across his bald head, she whispered, "You good?"

He nodded. "You look amazing, Harp," Terrance exclaimed, placing his hand atop hers resting on his shoulder.

"Thanks."

"I couldn't agree more," a husky, annoying voice resounded behind her.

She rolled her eyes. *Kelvin.*

Terrance chuckled at her silent response. Kelvin had been Terrance's best friend since high school. He'd never been Harper's favorite person, but she appreciated his friendship, especially since Terrance's illness. But even with some commendable actions, the dude was grimy.

Harper turned around, forcing an artificial smile on her face. "Kelvin. How are you?"

"I'm good, *Harp*. Better now that I've seen you. It's been too long, beautiful," Kelvin said, examining her from head to toe.

He kissed her cheek, and she immediately wanted to wipe the remnants of him away.

"Nigga, what I tell you about that?" Terrance barked as loud as he was physically capable.

The nickname *Harp* was reserved for only Terrance. If anyone attempted to greet her with that sentiment, he quickly corrected them.

"My bad, bro. *Harper*. It's good to see you," Kelvin uttered, but his eyes were saying something else.

Kelvin had never been inappropriate with Harper, but she hated how his stare made her feel dirty . . . violated. His roaming eyes and the way he called her beautiful were always laced with a sprinkle of smut.

"Terrance, I'm riding with Joya. I shouldn't be too late. Trae is upstairs with Mariah. Please do not let her stay too late," she instructed, referring to Trae's best friend.

While Mariah was a pretty tomboy, she was quickly morphing into a young lady attracting her best friend's attention. Trae wouldn't admit it, but he was smitten with Mariah, and Harper wasn't trying to be a grandma any time soon.

"I got it, Ma. Go chill. Have fun," Hasan encouraged, kissing her on the cheek.

"Thank you, son," she said, returning the gesture.

Hasan draped his arm around her shoulder, walking her to the door.

"I love you, Ma," he murmured.

"I love you more," she retorted, thumbing away the lip gloss from his cheek.

Stepping onto her patio, Harper glanced across the street and saw that Joya was already in her car. She trotted down her driveway and hopped into the car.

"Hey, girl, hey."

"Hey, hey," Joya chimed. "You ready?"

"Yes, ma'am."

Dresden had run out of excuses and finally agreed to meet Vanessa for dinner. He suggested Ethos, hoping that Maurice would be there to save him again if necessary. Ironically, his friend called him earlier, inviting him to the restaurant to watch the fight.

While everyone else in his house spent their Saturday leisurely, Dresden worked all afternoon. He preferred the peace and quiet when he was buried in medical research books and patient files. Glancing at the clock, he committed to working another hour before meeting Maurice for a drink before Vanessa arrived for dinner.

The parking lot at Ethos was packed. I guess everyone had the same idea tonight. The sexy vibe, good food, great drinks, and an endless number of big-screen televisions made Ethos the perfect place for a fight night.

Dresden parked at a meter a block away. He was thankful for the light, cool breeze that gave him a sample of what would come in the fall. Dressed in dark jeans, an untucked button-down shirt, and a camel-colored blazer with matching Gucci loafers, his appeal was effortless. Women passersby swooned as he strode the sidewalk listlessly.

Entering Ethos, the same pretty hostess greeted him, this time by name.

"Dr. Xavier, Mr. Maurice is at the bar waiting for you."

Dresden nodded. "Thank you, Sierra."

Sierra's face lit up as bright as the sun, elated that he remembered her name. Dresden just had that effect on women.

He started in the direction of the bar, navigating through the crowd. The place was packed but wasn't unbearable. The medical doctor in him couldn't help his paranoid thoughts. *This is definitely a superspreader event.*

"Rece, what's up, bro?"

"D, it's good to see you, my man."

They exchanged a manly hug, then dapped before Dresden took a seat. Maurice motioned for the bartender.

"Whatever he wants is on me," Maurice announced.

"Angel's Envy neat. Thank you," Dresden said, then turned to his friend with a nod of appreciation.

"What've you been up to, man?" Maurice asked.

"Work. This trial is huge, so fifteen-, sixteen-hour workdays are becoming my norm."

"Damn. I'm proud of you, bro. You doing big things and changing lives."

"Yeah, man. It's all worth it." Dresden smiled.

"How are the girls? Or the young ladies, I should say," Maurice chuckled, but Dresden didn't respond.

His concentration was aimed across the restaurant.

"Yo, D., hello," Maurice snapped his finger to get Dresden's attention.

"Man, I'm sorry. I think I see someone I know."

"Vanessa's a little early, ain't she?" Maurice quipped questioningly.

"Nah, not Vanessa."

Dresden's gaze focused on the gorgeous smile of the honey-bronzed beauty seated in a booth near the windows. It was Harper. She was with two other women, and they appeared to be having a good time. Maurice followed his stare.

"You know them?" Maurice asked curiously.

"Just the one in the yellow. She works with me."

"You have a woman like that at your disposal, and you're meeting *Vanessa* for dinner?" he scoffed.

"It's not like that."

"By the look on your face . . . It's *exactly* like that." Maurice paused for a beat. "Well, a table of pretty women in my establishment requires a personal welcome from the owner," Maurice said, sliding out of the high bar chair with a sneaky grin plastered on his face.

He snapped his finger for the bartender again.

"Find out what the ladies are drinking at table nineteen and send over another round," Maurice instructed.

"Man, what are you doing?" Dresden gritted through clenched teeth.

"About to make their acquaintance. You should join me."

Maurice proceeded across the space, and Dresden casually followed. They approached the booth occupied by three cackling, gorgeous Black women. Maurice advanced first, while Dresden chose to hang back.

"Ladies, welcome to Ethos," Maurice said, flashing his Colgate-white smile.

The ladies paused as echoes of *Thank you* resounded.

"I am Maurice Miles, and this is my place," he announced, aimlessly motioning his hand around the space.

Just as he spoke, the waitress approached with another round of drinks for the table.

"Please have another round on me. If the accommodations are ever unsatisfactory, please ask for me, and I'll take care of you."

"Well, isn't that sweet of you, Maurice Miles," Joya sang.

"Very sweet," their friend Annette echoed, flirtation living in her chocolate-brown eyes.

"Dresden . . ." Harper blurted, disregarding the lustful exchange between her friend and the restaurant's owner.

"I mean, Dr. Xavier. Hi," she uttered, surprised by his presence.

It was becoming a habit for her to slowly drag her eyes from his head to his toes and back up again for good measure. *Why does he have to be so consistently sexy?* The man was simply irresistible.

Joya's eyes blossomed in recognition almost as wide as Harper's before she mouthed, "*That's Dr. Feelgood?*"

Annette followed up, breathily sighing, "Bitch," dragging her eyes over his massive frame.

"Hello, Professor Kingsley," Dresden greeted her.

Harper glanced at her watch and then said teasingly, "I think we're off the clock."

He coyly snickered. "I was just following your lead," he uttered, mimicking her playful demeanor.

Harper batted her eyes, focused on how he licked his lips, and smiled. She was privately ashamed that her unruly kitty started pulsing and dripping in his presence.

"Harper, can you introduce us to your friend?" Joya chimed.

"Oh, um . . . This is my *colleague*, Dr. Dresden Xavier. Dresden, these are my good friends Joya Fletcher and Annette Moore."

"It's girls' night, but we can make an exception for you, gentlemen. Would you like to join us?" Annette asked, scooting over to make room before they even answered.

"I wish we could, but I have to manage this growing crowd, and he's meeting someone for dinner soon," Maurice said.

Dresden begrudgingly shifted his eyes from admiring Harper's pretty face to leer at his friend. His muted glare said, "*What the fuck, bro?*" Maurice lifted his brows and shrugged dismissively as if he hadn't told all of his friend's business.

When Dresden's eyes darted back to Harper, she quickly looked away.

"Rain check?" Maurice asked, directing his attention to Annette. She nodded.

"Enjoy girls' night, ladies. Ron will take good care of you," Maurice announced before making his way to another table.

"Yes, ladies, enjoy your night," Dresden said, eyeing Harper once she finally reconnected her eyes with his.

The server, Ron, approached the booth, and Dresden placed a hand on his shoulder and declared, "The next round is on me for the ladies." Then Dresden nodded before journeying back to the bar.

Maurice leaned against the mahogany bar, sipping on his bourbon. He wore a devious smirk as he eyed his friend walking from the booth of gorgeous women. Dresden lifted a finger, motioning for the bartender to make him another drink.

"Sooo . . . Harper, huh?" Maurice said.

"Harper, what?"

"She's beautiful," Maurice announced.

"I know."

"So what's the problem?" he probed.

"There's no problem. We're colleagues . . . work friends."

"Hmm," Maurice hummed, nodding. "Work friends. That's what you're calling it?"

"Just say what you trying to say, nigga. Damn," Dresden thundered.

"What I just witnessed ain't 'work friends.' That googly-eyed, playing coy exchange . . . Seems to me, some feelings are mutual."

"Nah. Harper's cool and undeniably beautiful. But shit between us would be too complicated. I prefer not to mix work with pleasure." Dresden sipped his drink, vainly attempting not to stare in her direction.

"Shit . . . When work looks like that, mix away, my nigga," Maurice cackled. "Can I be real with you, though?" His friend paused, waiting for a response.

Dresden nodded.

"It kinda seems to me that *you're* the complication, bro."

Dresden crooked his neck, quietly begging his friend's pardon. "How so?"

"You had the love of a lifetime. There's no denying that. But if you're waiting for another Nina to fall into your lap, you'll be waiting forever," Maurice declared.

"There will never be another Nina," Dresden blurted harshly.

"Exactly. There *will never* be another Nina. But you're going to miss out on another something special if you don't let her go. Ain't no woman trying to fight a ghost," Maurice uttered.

If Dresden hadn't known Maurice for over twenty years, he would've probably punched him in the face. But his words were dripping with compassion . . . and truth. He sipped his drink with no rebuttal for his friend.

Darting his eyes over to Harper, he watched her undetected for several lengthy heartbeats . . . until her eyes connected with him. Their stare was penetrating . . . baffling. Dresden wanted to ignore the boom he felt thumping in his chest while Harper unsuccessfully endeavored to calm the butterflies in her stomach. The exchange was muted, but the clamorous yearnings were loud.

"Dresden, hey," Vanessa said, causing him to jolt when she rested a hand on his shoulder.

Vanessa pulled him into a taut hug that he awkwardly leaned into. He shot her a faux closed-mouth smile before turning back toward the bar. Glancing back at Harper, she delivered a smile that was just as fake as his before rejoining the conversation with her friends. And just like that, their moment was over.

"Did you see that heffa with all her tits hanging out?" Joya blurted.

"She was definitely doing the most," Annette said, taking a quick puff of the THC-laced vape pen.

After dinner, the ladies ended their night in Joya's she-shed in her backyard. Since Harper lived across the street and Annette's house was around the corner, it was the perfect end to girls' night.

"Dr. Feelgood looked like he didn't even want to be there. He kept darting those dark, sexy eyes over to our girl," Joya said, talking to Annette as if Harper weren't there.

Harper took a puff of the pen, then settled back in the chair before passing the pen to Joya.

"He was not looking at me. We are work friends. That's it. That's all," Harper sighed.

"Work friends, my ass. If that man wanted to prop you up on one of those exam tables, you mean to tell me you would say no?" Joya uttered loudly, sitting up in her chair to stare at her friend.

Harper attempted to maintain her composure, but she belted out a howl, shouting, "Hell no. My ass will have a fever ev-er-y-day." She clapped with each syllable.

They erupted in laughter.

"Honey, Dr. Xavier is about to be the new Midnight," Annette declared.

"Shit, Dr. Dresden looks like he might be better than Midnight," Harper announced.

"Well, it won't hurt to find out," Joya sang.

"It might hurt *real good*," Harper chanted.

Another round of cackles filled the she-shed. They were blissfully high.

"Shh, before Mason curses us out," Joya said, referencing her husband.

"I need to go anyway to check on Terrance," Harper announced as she eased out of the lounge chair.

The room instantly became quiet, transporting them back to reality.

"Annie, how are you getting home?" Harper asked.

"Junior is picking me up. He's on lockdown for having a li'l chick in my house, so he's my designated driver tonight."

Annette was the single mom of a twenty-year-old boy and a seventeen-year-old girl who'd been giving her the blues since her divorce a year ago.

"Serves his ass right. My godson betta not pop up with no babies," Joya griped.

"He ain't ready to die. Besides, I'm too sexy to be a granny," Annette bantered.

The ladies said their goodbyes once Annette's son pulled out of the driveway. Harper walked through her garage and into the house. She kicked off the flats that she'd transitioned into before leaving Ethos.

She trekked through the dim house and journeyed down the hallway toward Terrance's room. No matter how late she came home, she always checked on him before she lay down. The light from the television illuminated the bedroom. It was after one o'clock in the morning, so she was sure he was asleep.

Quietly, she peeked into the room. To her surprise, dark brown eyes peered at her with a faint smile.

"Hey," Terrance said, pulling the earbuds from his ears.

"Hey," she whispered. "You OK?"

He nodded. "Yeah. Couldn't sleep," he rasped, patting his hand on the bed, summoning her to come closer.

"Did you have a good time?" he asked.

She nodded. "I did. You know Joya and Annette guarantee a good time."

"Did y'all go to the she-shed?" Terrance chuckled.

Harper released a loud laugh that gave away what she was trying to conceal. She was tipsy and high.

She nodded again. "Yep. The she-shed for the win," she giggled.

Terrance laughed, shaking his head.

"Did Mason bring you anything from his stash?" she asked, referring to Joya's husband.

He nodded.

"So, we're both high," she cackled, and Terrance joined in on the banter.

"High as fuck," he drawled.

Harper lay flat on her back next to Terrance, and he mimicked her position. They stared at the ceiling in complete silence other than the soft sound of music coming from his earbuds.

"Where did y'all go?" he inquired.

"That new place in Midtown. Ethos."

"I heard about that place. How was it?"

"Good. *Very* good. The food was amazing, and the drinks were even better. The vibe was . . ." she paused. "Sexy."

Terrance shifted his head to look at her. Harper blushed while gliding her teeth across her bottom lip.

"We met the owner, Maurice Miles. He bought us drinks and paid for our food. Annette was trying to lock that down," Harper said, giggling.

"Annette be on the prowl," Terrance chortled, turning his head back to see the ceiling.

Harper nodded. "He's actually friends with Dr. Xavier."

"Who?" Terrance's voice was low and mellow.

"The owner. Maurice," she clarified.

"How do you know that?" Terrance probed.

"He was at Ethos," she uttered.

"Who?"

Harper snickered. The back and forth was comical in their condition.

"Dresden," she said, laughing. "I mean Dr. Xavier."

"Ah." That was the only response Terrance could find.

Harper's stare was absently focused on a piece of lint hanging from the ceiling fan while Terrance attentively surveyed her.

If this were a poker game, Harper would have to fold because her facial expressions revealed her hand every time. At just the mere mention of the doctor, his ex-wife was affected. Harper squirmed to calm the quiver between her thighs, and Terrance noticed. He was very familiar with Harper's tells when she was in need.

A tipsy Harper was a horny Harper. The lip-biting, squirming, and the sultry giggle had his dick hard. It had been a long time since he'd had sex and a hell of a long time since he'd experienced *her*.

She repositioned herself to lie on her side and face Terrance. He was already ogling her with a lust-filled smile. Harper didn't notice his arousal because he didn't cause the same reaction in her anymore. Her desire for Terrance waned years ago.

He kissed her forehead, then her nose. Terrance stroked his hand down the curve of her face. Harper immediately froze. She knew his tells too. The bedroom eyes, soft kisses, and delicate caress . . . Terrance's manliness was stimulated. He tilted his head closer, attempting to kiss her lips.

"Terrance," she whispered, pressing her hand against his chest to stop his pursuit.

"Harper," he sighed. "I just want to feel you."

She gasped warily. "Terrance, I can't."

He dropped his head back on the mattress, returning his eyes to the oscillating fan.

"I know."

Harper slowly sat up in the bed. Her eyes widened when she saw the tent in his jogging pants. Even in sickness, Terrance's manhood was long and wide. She shook her head, remembering the days when she would have mounted his monstrous frame and slid down on his pole to release the tension in her core.

But that wouldn't be fair to Terrance. He wasn't the cause or the cure for her anymore. The thump in her yoni had been throbbing since she laid eyes on *Dr. Feelgood* earlier.

# Chapter fifteen

Monroe University was lively on freshman move-in day. The band marched through the yard, playing all of the latest hip-hop hits. The sororities and fraternities assisted incoming students while student group tables lined the MLK Center.

It was a scorching August day, but the jovial students weren't fazed. The parents, on the other hand, were suffering. Dresden may have been the only parent beaming from ear to ear. He was elated to be moving his daughter into her dorm. And even more ecstatic that she would be surrounded by brilliant Black minds.

The day was bittersweet without Nina. Before she passed away, the family celebrated Bella's acceptance into Monroe University, but the day wasn't the same without her. Dresden transported boxes from the truck while Bella and Bryn decorated her bedroom, meticulously following their mother's decor design.

During one of Nina and Bella's girls' nights, they picked out her dorm colors and theme. Unsurprisingly, Bella's room was glammed out in various rose hues in honor of her mother. Dresden spared no expense to ensure that his baby girl was satisfied. Even in Nina's absence, he would make the best of the day.

Hasan and Trae play-fought like brothers do while moving the last few boxes into Trae's dorm room. Trae had already moved into his suite earlier in the summer before track camp but needed to move a few things from his mom's house.

Since their dad's diagnosis, Hasan tried to ensure that Trae was staying focused on school and track. His little brother struggled a bit like the entire family, but Trae could fall into a deep hole quickly, and Hasan would do anything to prevent that.

Trae was academically smart and athletically talented, whereas school did not come easy to Hasan. He wasn't dumb by any stretch; he just had some learning challenges requiring him to be more diligent about his studies. Music was his only motivation and working with his dad at the trucking company. Hasan had been Terrance's protégé since he was sixteen, so the family business was in his blood.

Terrance insisted that Hasan get an education if running the family business was what he desired. His father believed that he needed a business foundation to understand all aspects of entrepreneurship.

*"You need to understand a little bit of everything. Accounting, human resources, inventory . . . everything,"* Terrance would school him. Hasan finally folded and enrolled in classes online so that he would have time for his band and could continue working.

Hasan, his friend Canon, Trae, and a couple of his teammates perused the campus, flirting with every girl that crossed their path.

"Y'all dudes are gameless, man," Hasan cackled.

"Whatever, San. Those girls be on you because of Foreplay. Canon be singing them girls outta they panties, and y'all just take his leftovers," Trae joked.

Hasan tossed up his middle finger as the guys jested back and forth. He paused, squinting his eyes to better view the girl across the walkway in front of Betty Shabazz Hall. *Bella.* Quickly, Hasan shortened the distance between them with his crew watching behind him.

After the festival, Hasan found her on TikTok and messaged her. They exchanged phone numbers, but he never contacted her. The girl before him had changed her hair and was dressing differently, but her gorgeous face had not changed.

"What's up, beautiful?" Hasan said, caressing his fingers up and down her forearm.

She shot her eyes down, gawking at the place where his fingertips touched her. "Do I know you?" Bryn muttered mischievously.

She knew exactly who he was. Bella had only talked about *the fine drummer* every day since they met at the festival. He was also the guy that they talked shit about when he ghosted her sister.

As kids, Bryn and Bella could easily trick teachers and neighbors when they played switcheroo. Clearly, today was no different. Where Bella wore long curls in coils, Bryn's hair was tapered on the sides and back with big curls sprouting from the tops streaked with blond.

"You forgot about me already, Bella?" he questioned, flashing her a blushful smile.

Bryn was unaffected. "Oh yeah. It's the little drummer boy."

Hasan cocked his head, peering over his shoulder to ensure his boys didn't hear her. "Excuse me, sweetheart?" Hasan narrowed his eyes.

"You're the guy who did all that flirting just to ghost my sister."

"Your sister?" Hasan exclaimed, confused. "Bella, stop playing."

"Hey, Bryn, Dad said he's gone—" Bella ceased her conversation when she saw Hasan.

She rolled her eyes. "What are you doing here?" Bella said angrily, crossing her arms over her chest for extra effect.

"You're a twin?" he questioned, looking back and forth between the two girls.

"Yeah. Duh. What are *you* doing here?" she repeated.

"My little brother is a freshman. I was helping him move in," Hasan explained, pointing behind him toward Trae.

"I didn't know you go here," he continued.

"How *would* you know?" she fussed.

"Can I talk to you for a minute?" Hasan said, his eyes pleading.

Bella darted her eyes to Bryn, hoping her sister would let her borrow her terse tongue for a minute. But instead, Bryn was eye-fucking with Canon.

Bella angled her head to the side, silently signaling for him to talk. Hasan tenderly touched her elbow, pulling her away from his friends to speak privately.

"Listen, Bella. I'm sorry I didn't call. My dad is sick, and . . ." He paused, shaking his head. "It's been a lot."

She gazed at him, searching his expression for sincerity, but what she found was anguish . . . heartbreak. The tension stressing her brow softened because she understood his countenance all too well.

"I'm sorry to hear that. I'll be praying for him," she whispered.

Hasan nodded his thanks. "Are you finished moving in? Can I help you with anything?" he probed.

She shook her head.

"Well, can I take you somewhere?"

Bella shook her head again. Her thick curls bounced, and she may as well have been sprinkling magic dust because Hasan was under a spell.

"I have activities for Welcome Week. Maybe some other time."

"Soon. I promise," he said, pinching the tip of her nose.

Bella pursed her lips doubtfully, uttering, "Actions speak louder than words, Hasan."

# Chapter sixteen

The rainy September day draped the sky with bountiful clouds. Terrance reclined in the lounge chair, gazing out the window. The constant beep from the IV machine had him in a trance. His eyes danced, tracing imaginary images in the cloud puffs.

He had been nodding intermittently since the nurse left the room where he received his *treatment*. The clear saline drip was filled with nothing but a mix of vitamins and minerals. His time was short, but when he saw the expression on his family's face when he announced that he was accepted into the trial, he knew he'd done the right thing.

*When I die, they'll know that I did everything in my power to live*, he thought.

The faint knock on the door shook him from his daze. Dr. Dresden appeared in the doorway with what Terrance deemed was a permanent scowl in his presence.

"Doc," Terrance greeted, slowly lifting his hand.

Dresden reached out to shake his hand and then nodded. "Terrance," he responded.

"How are you feeling today?" he asked.

"Like shit."

Dresden lifted his head from the tablet in his hand to stare at Terrance. "Any pain? Fever?" he probed, immediately on alert for any signs of a potential emergency situation.

Terrance shook his head. "Nah, just dying," he chuckled, but Dresden found nothing funny.

"Have you talked to Harper . . . I mean, Mrs. Kingsley, about this?"

Terrance snickered, shaking his head again. "You were right the first time because we both know she's not my *Mrs.* anymore."

Dresden bobbed his head in understanding. "Yeah, but she's your friend. That's what you said, right?"

Terrance nodded. "My very best friend," he whispered.

"Best friends keep secrets?" Dresden pushed, a questioning inflection to his tone.

The men sat in silence for several minutes.

"I'm going to talk to her. I just have to find the right time."

"Time is not on your side, man," Dresden countered frankly.

Terrance remained stoic, knowing all too well that his time on this side of heaven was limited. Dresden expected some kind of retort or reaction, but Terrance laughed instead.

"What's funny?" Dresden asked, his forehead knitted in confusion.

"Harper is one of the most stubborn women I know. She's bullheaded, feisty, and won't take no for an answer. If I tell her I'm dying, she might call me a liar."

Dresden laughed.

"Her attitude would intimidate some men, but I loved that shit. When we first met, she cursed me out and accused me of stalking her." Terrance was blankly ranting. His face brightened with merriment.

Dresden sat on the stool across the room, debating if he should engage in this conversation, but he found himself intrigued by Terrance's walk down memory lane.

"How did you two meet?" Dresden acquiesced and asked the question against his better judgment.

"Denny's," Terrance chuckled.

"The restaurant?" Dresden asked.

Terrance nodded.

"She worked nights there while in school. I was a truck driver, and she'd always be there when I stopped in Monroe City. After several weeks, I'd ensure I got routes that would take me through Monroe just so I could see her. She was so damn pretty."

Terrance hummed as he lowered his eyes from reminiscing and fatigue.

*No lies told there*, Dresden thought.

There it was again . . . the silence. Dresden peeked at Terrance to determine if he'd drifted to sleep, but his glossy eyes stared out the window.

"Harp was just a girl when I met her. Eating waffle sandwiches while studying for an economics class," Terrance snickered. "But she grew up . . . Even when I didn't want her to."

"Why wouldn't you want her to grow up?" Dresden probed curiously.

Terrance gawked at him, contemplating his response. "Because I never wanted her to realize she didn't need me anymore."

Dresden raised a brow incredulously. What he'd observed of Harper Kingsley was a confident woman who had no qualms about speaking her mind.

*Maybe she was talking. Trying to tell him what she needed, and he wasn't listening*, Dresden thought.

"She doesn't strike me as the type of woman who would hang around just for the hell of it," Dresden exclaimed, sharing a condensed version of his pondering.

Terrance nodded. "Your observation is accurate. Harper was crystal clear about what she needed, but I didn't listen. I fumbled the first version of her: effervescent and carefree. I created the savage beast you see today."

Dresden pursed his lips, then nodded. He had not had the pleasure of being introduced to the beast living in Harper, but he was looking forward to an introduction one day.

"Harper needs somebody . . . a man who understands her need to both lead and follow. I didn't get that until it was too late," Terrance continued.

His tone was low and somber, wreaking with regret.

"Terrance, why are you telling me this? Seems like this may be what Harper needs to hear." He eyed Dresden and shrugged.

Terrance wouldn't dare tell him that he sees how he looks at her. How his face gleams every time he speaks her name. He could not admit that the glint of happiness in her pretty brown eyes no longer belonged to him. But worst of all, Terrance could never voice that Dr. Xavier may be Harper's next somebody.

"Just conversation, Doc," Terrance mumbled, fixing his eyes out the window again.

Dresden nodded, rising from his seat. "Get some rest, Terrance. Take care."

*Knock. Knock.*

Harper peeked around the door of Dresden's office. He always left his door partially ajar, so she was unsure if she should just walk in or knock, so she did both.

The deep creases in his brows indicated focus . . . stress. The trial was fully activated, and Dresden was working at least fourteen-hour days. Harper was aware because she wasn't far behind him. He would have to force her to leave many nights, jokingly threatening to fire her.

Harper knocked again, but his eyes remained locked on the laptop screen. She noticed the slight bob of his head and realized he was wearing earbuds. She closed the distance between them to stand in front of his desk. Knocking on the hardwood table, she finally caught his attention.

Dresden peered up and immediately awarded her with his smile. "Hey. Sorry. I was plowing through some work."

"No worries. Priscilla said you needed to see me," she uttered, standing at his desk.

"Yes, I wanted to talk to you about your trial assignment."

"OK, sure." Harper's mutter lacked confidence.

"Please, have a seat," he said, motioning his head to one of the two chairs.

Dresden closed the laptop and leaned back in his chair.

"Did I do something wrong, Dr. Xavier?"

"No. No. Quite the contrary," he uttered. "Your data analysis was spot-on. Very impressive, Professor Kingsley. I love the way you organized the information using a heat map. That will make things much easier for me to review moving forward."

"Thank you. I appreciate the feedback. I can't wait to start with patient contact. I have more ideas on how we can be more efficient with collecting patient diagnostics."

"About that . . . Professor Kingsley. I would like for you to lead the analysis team. I believe that is where you'll shine."

He halted, processing how he would explain his reasoning. Harper was right about Dresden being stressed. He was worried about how he would navigate the situation with Terrance. While it was true that Harper's analytical abilities were spectacular, Dresden could not have her in contact with patients or their disaggregated data.

The only way she would remain clueless and unattached to the situation was if she held a fully administrative role on the trial team. Anything else would be too risky because Harper was too smart and would eventually figure out the farce. While the cases were coded for confidentiality, Terrance's terminal diagnosis would soon become evident—*when he died.*

Harper assumed a similar position as Dresden, pacing his office and considering what he was offering. While having direct engagement with patients was important, leading the analysis for the entire trial was a critical role. Her name would be published in the final reports, giving visibility to prominent medical professionals nationwide. This was a great opportunity. *This would practically guarantee my tenure.*

"OK. I'll do it," she said, pausing her pace before resting her fists on his desk. "I trust your judgment and mentorship. Thank you for trusting me with this opportunity." The smile dashing across her face was so big that her eyes squinted.

*A shot to my fucking heart*, he mused.

Their eyes met across the table, and instantly, a silent exchange ensued. Gleaming gazes spoke words of professional appreciation, attraction . . . lust. Harper chewed the corner of her lip, then spun around to continue her leisurely pace. If he looked at her like that any longer, she wouldn't be responsible if her leg suddenly flung across his desk.

"Great. Great," Dresden said, clearing his throat because her ass perched on his desk was all that he was able to visualize for a moment.

"We'll . . . um . . . We'll discuss the details with the rest of the team tomorrow."

Harper started to giggle instead of engaging him in conversation.

"What's funny?" he asked, halting his rocking in the chair.

"Are your initials really DMX?" she tittered, fingering the framed degrees on the wall.

"Yep. Dresden Maxwell Xavier Jr. Why is that funny, though?"

"I don't know," she said, shaking her head through an uncontrollable chuckle. "I guess I instantly started reciting DMX songs in my head."

Dresden tossed his head back jovially. "You want to know something funny?" he asked.

She raised her brow, encouraging him to proceed.

"When I was pledging, every time my big brothers would see me in the yard, they made me recite the lyrics of 'What They Really Want,'" he laughed.

"You're kidding."

He shook his head, then blurted, "*There was Brenda, LaTisha, Linda, Felicia, Dawn, LeShaun, Ines, and Alicia. Theresa, Monica, Sharron, Nicki, Lisa, Veronica, Karen, Vicky.*"

Dresden regurgitated the lyrics flawlessly, and Harper hollered the entire time. Tears were misting her eyes as he cataloged the list of DMX's *bitches*. When he paused for a second to catch his breath, she seized the opportunity to jump in.

"*About three Kims, Latoya, and Tina. Shelley, Bridget, Cathy, Rasheeda,*" she pronounced, joining his chant.

Dresden's eyes brightened in surprise, but that didn't stop his flow. They harmoniously finished the song, boisterously cackling the entire way through the verses.

"OK, Professor Kingsley. Let me find out you got some bars," Dresden teased.

"I can do a li'l something," she quipped, nibbling her bottom lip again.

Dresden slid his top teeth over his bottom lip before gliding his thick tongue across the plump edges. His gaze was penetrating, causing Harper to become uncomfortable suddenly . . . moist between the thighs. *Thank God for these fitted pants.*

She recoiled, pinching her lips between her two fingers to prevent jumping over the desk and breaking the seam of his mouth with her tongue.

"*Knock, knock,*" a high-pitched female voice chimed.

Vanessa's flawlessly painted face peered around the door as she knocked, walking in without permission.

Both Dresden and Harper jerked, startled by the intrusion. They flitted bulged eyes at each other and then back to the doorway as if they'd been caught red-handed.

"Vanessa. What are you doing here?" Dresden asked, harsher than he intended.

"Surprise," she sang, holding up a large brown bag stained with grease.

"You said you'd be working late, so I brought you dinner," she continued, darting her eyes from him to Harper.

"I wish you would have called. I have a ton of work to do. I won't be good company," Dresden murmured, darting his eyes over to Harper.

Vanessa planted a skeptical gaze on Harper, dragging narrowed eyes from her halo of curls down to the soles of her Gucci sneakers. She was staring like Harper was an intruder invading *her* space. *Heffa, I was here first.*

Harper's brow hiked, begging her pardon. The eye-war was lethal between the two ladies, but Harper decided to do as the Forever First Lady instructed . . . *When they go low, you go high.*

The strain of her glare was immediately eased when her eyes settled on *him.*

"Dr. Xavier, is there anything else you need from me?" Harper inquired.

Dresden studied her, wondering if she realized how loaded her question was.

He shook his head, standing for the first time since they both entered his office.

"No. My apologies. I am being rude. Professor Kingsley, this is Vanessa, a friend from high school."

Harper and Vanessa nodded their heads simultaneously.

Clearing her throat, Harper swiped a curl from her face and headed toward the door. "I'm going to head out. Have a good night, Dresden," she said, emphasizing his name.

"Good night, Harper," Dresden snickered, recognizing what she just did.

*Petty ass.*

Harper never called him Dresden in the office and rarely in front of people, but he kinda liked it.

# Chapter seventeen

Halloween at the Kingsley house was a big deal, and this year was no different. All of the houses in the cul-de-sac welcomed the entire neighborhood to their *Fright on Featherton* extravaganza. Everything from meticulously decorated homes to hot dog and popcorn stands filled Featherton Street on the spooky night.

Terrance and the boys would usually transform the garage into one of the best-haunted houses on the street. Although he couldn't help much now, Terrance was still the mastermind behind their den of terror.

Harper shuffled through her kitchen dressed as Disco Barbie with a pink Afro wig and a pink and white sequined jumper. She cooked various dips, made Jell-O shots, and spiked apple cider to accompany the warm cinnamon donuts. Trae and Hasan were busy in the garage putting the final touches on the haunted house.

"Ms. Kingsley, I'm about to head out," Nurse Shelly said as she entered the great room.

"Thank you, Shelly. How's he been today? I think he pushed himself too hard trying to help the boys prepare for the party."

"Yeah, he definitely exhausted himself. His blood pressure was a little lower than usual throughout the day. If it stays that way tomorrow, I'll call the doctor. His appetite was good, though."

"It could be the trial medications," Harper offered, peering over her shoulder at the nurse while she washed her hands.

"That definitely could be it," Shelly nodded.

Harper closed the distance between them so that she could escort her to the door.

"Maybe check his vitals again after the party. If anything is concerning, call me," Shelly instructed.

"You sure you don't want to stay?" Harper asked.

"No, it's my godson's first Halloween, so I'm going to hang out with him and then get some rest."

"You deserve it. Thank you so much," Harper said, watching Shelly enter her car and drive away.

The sun was beginning to set, just in time to start the night's festivities. Her neighbors crowded the cul-de-sac, each preparing their driveways for the flood of kids in less than an hour.

Harper walked down the hall and then knocked on the bedroom door.

"You can come in," Terrance uttered lowly.

"Hey," she greeted, peeking around the door.

"Hey," he responded.

To her surprise, Terrance was fully dressed for the party. She expected him to be ready for bed after such a long day.

"I didn't think you'd feel up to coming out," she uttered, crossing the room to stand in front of him.

"It's Halloween. Why wouldn't I come out?"

"I just figured—"

"Well, you figured wrong, Harper!" Terrance shouted.

She cocked her head back as if his harsh tone slapped her in the face.

"*OK,*" she mouthed.

"Nurse Shelly wants me to check your vitals before you go to bed. She said your blood pressure was low."

He nodded. "No need. I feel fine."

"Terrance," Harper said sharply, finally causing him to look at her.

"What the hell are you wearing, Harp?" Terrance chuckled a bit, but his scowl was saying something else.

"I'm Barbie. Disco Barbie," she chuckled, twisting her hips playfully.

Terrance shook his head.

"Enough about me. Have you asked Dr. Xavier if the trial medications could cause your blood pressure to drop? We need to check into that—"

"They're assessing all of that shit, Harper. Damn," Terrance shouted, terminating the pleasant atmosphere.

Clutching his neck, he flinched a little before sitting in the chair by the window.

Harper glared at him. A mix of worry and outrage creased her face causing her eyes to narrow to slits.

"Fine," Harper said, gritting through clenched teeth. "I'll have Trae or San come and help you."

She spun on her three-inch platform heels, prepared to storm out of the room. Lately, Terrance's attitude had been unbearable. He'd been snapping at everybody and preferring to be alone in his room. So, the fact that he actually wanted to go outside was a shock.

"Harp," Terrance called out, halting her tracks. "I'm sorry."

Sluggish, her eyes lowered as she sighed.

"Today has been a rough day. I'm sorry for taking it out on you. I want to enjoy myself tonight."

Harper nodded, opting not to respond.

"Can you help me outside? I'd like to see everything before the swarm comes through."

She nodded again.

Harper strolled toward him, expecting to help him get to the wheelchair next to the bed. He waved her off. Slowly and carefully, Terrance made his way to the wheelchair. Harper blinked away the mist forming in her eyes. She admired his tenacity, his will to fight. But she'd noticed his increasing exhaustion, lack of appetite, and solitude. Harper had been a nurse for years and recognized the signs of surrender.

"You ready?" she croaked, swallowing the lump of emotions.

"Yeah. Let's show them how the Kingsleys do Halloween," he chuckled, lifting a frail fist toward her.

She connected her fist with his, smiling.

Bones and muscles were aching in places that Harper couldn't imagine. The Halloween party didn't shut down until after one o'clock in the morning.

"I knew I shouldn't have had that last Jell-O shot," Harper grumbled.

She schlepped out of bed, clutching her back and hip while gradually scooting across her bedroom. Today, the bathroom appeared a mile away. Evidence of a good time was plastered all over her face. Smeared pink lipstick and false eyelashes pressed against her cheeks. Thankfully, she remembered to remove the Afro wig before passing out last night.

Harper took a quick shower and dressed in some loungewear. It was almost noon, and she hadn't heard a peep from her sons or Terrance. He'd even had a good time last night. She fixed a cup of coffee for her and tea for Terrance before she sleepily meandered to his room.

The door was never completely closed, but Harper always knocked. She tapped on the door, but he didn't answer. Hearing the television, she decided to walk in. Terrance was still in the bed.

"You decided to sleep in too, huh?" Harper giggled, but her mirth was cut short.

The rise and fall of Terrance's chest was abnormal, as if he were in distress. He turned his head to look at her. Harper's breath hitched. His eyes were heavy and filled with tears.

The sound of glass shattering caused her to rile. Harper hadn't noticed that the tray had slipped from her hand.

"Terrance," she cried, rushing to his bedside.

Terrace lifted his hand, and she immediately grasped it, connecting them. He smiled at her.

"Get the boys," he rasped, struggling for every breath.

"No. No, no, no."

He nodded. "I'm good, Harp. I'm ready."

"But they're not ready, Terrance. The boys. Our babies—" Her voice broke as she wept into his chest.

Terrance rubbed her head with his other hand.

"I love you, Harper Kingsley. You are my best friend . . . my family. I should've said that shit every day, but I need you to know right now that I never stopped loving you. I want you to live, Harp. To love again. If not for you, then do it for me. Okay?"

She stared at him, wishing, praying that this was all a dream, but it wasn't.

"Can you do that for me?" he rasped.

She nodded against his chest before lifting her head. A waterfall of tears overwhelmed her face. Terrance surveyed her, admiring her beauty even in a moment like this.

"Pretty ass," he mumbled, pinching the tip of her nose.

She smiled, licking away the tears salting the corners of her mouth.

"If I could go back and change things, I would. There was so much shit I messed up in our marriage, and yet, you're still here . . . for better, for worse . . . sickness, health, until death. Thank you, Harper."

Clutching his hand tighter, Harper checked his pulse. It was steadily slowing. She stared at him because the words wouldn't come. The soft kisses to the back of his hand narrated her muted agony.

"Get the boys," he whispered again.

Harper hurried out of the room.

"Boys," she screamed.

"Hasan . . . Trae. Come now."

Groggily, the boys dragged their feet down the hallway toward their dad's room. Their demeanor instantly changed when they saw the distress and tears saturating their mother's face.

"Ma," Hasan blurted.

She shook her head, realizing there was no time for any explanations. "Go to your dad. Now," Harper instructed.

Hasan and Trae rushed into his room. They halted in their tracks once weak and leaden eyes slanted in their direction.

"Come here, Hasan," Terrance said, motioning for him to come closer.

Hasan swallowed hard. He'd had nightmares about this day. Kneeling next to the bed, he caressed his father's hand.

"I fell in love with you the same day I fell in love with your mother," he said, repeating the story he'd always told Hasan about the day he was born.

"You've always been mine. Don't let nobody tell you different, OK?"

Hasan nodded.

"Take care of your mama and your brother, okay? I'm tired, son. You're the man of the house, and I need you to tell me I can rest."

Terrance sobbed, finally allowing the tears to stream down the sides of his face, staining the pillow.

Hasan nodded again.

"Rest, Dad. I got it. I promise," Hasan uttered convincingly, but his voice was thick with emotions.

"Get Trae," Terrance mumbled in his ear.

Hasan motioned for his brother to come. Trae was buried in his mother's bosom, crying. He shook his head. "No," Trae yelled.

"Trae, your dad needs this, OK?" Harper spoke with the softest yet strongest voice. She cupped his face with both hands and swiped away his tears.

"He needs to hear your voice and see your face. It'll be OK," she said, nudging him to stand up.

Trae reluctantly walked to the bed. At first glance, it didn't appear that Terrance was dying. He looked similar to last night when he was laughing and having a good time. But as Trae crossed the room, he followed the erratic rise and fall of Terrance's chest with his eyes.

"Trae," Terrance whispered, lifting his hand to exchange their special handshake. It was slower than usual, but Terrance didn't miss a beat.

"I love you, son. You are the best part of me. Better than me. I'm so proud of you. I fought for you, your brother, and mama, but I'm tired, son. You gotta let me go."

Trae shook his head, resting it on his dad's chest.

"No," he cried. "What am I supposed to do without you?"

Terrance repeatedly stroked down his son's soft carpet of coils, allowing him to cry.

Trae crawled into bed with his dad while Hasan sat on the opposite side. Harper settled at the foot of the bed. She watched the clock slowly transition from one minute to the next, holding her breath as each second passed. Thirty minutes later, the room was utterly silent. Still.

Terrance opened his eyes, gazing directly at Harper. She lifted her head to see the corner of his mouth turned in a slight smile, which she returned.

Quickly, he shifted his eyes to Trae and Hasan, both snuggled on either side of him in the bed. But his eyes danced right back to Harper.

The silence was profound as she watched him begin to slip away. Harper was overwhelmed with emotions. While a crushing wave of grief crippled her, an odd sense of relief was present too. The pain ahead was going to be hard, but Harper found solace in knowing that her friend would suffer no more.

Terrance lifted his brows, then nodded, silently seeking her permission to go.

Harper swallowed hard, biting her quivering bottom lip. She swiped away a tear before heavily nodding her head.

Terrance's eyes lazily closed . . . *forever.*

The house was eerily quiet. Trae was locked in his room, and Hasan was in his dad's music room. Joya and her husband had been at the house since before the coroner came. Harper wanted to be alone and finally kicked them out around ten o'clock that night. The phone rang off the hook with family and friends calling with their condolences. Her parents were ready to hop on the highway from Kansas City, but she encouraged them to wait until they were rested.

Honestly, Harper just needed a minute. It felt as if she'd been holding her breath underwater since she watched Terrance take *his* last breath. While the grief was heavy, his transition was everything that any human could ask for. She never realized how priceless the opportunity to say goodbye was until now. Calling to inform Terrance's mother made Harper more aware of that fact.

He never had a close relationship with his mother. She was a young mom who left him to be raised by his grandparents. As she got older and battled cancer herself, she tried to build a relationship with her son, but it was filled with empty promises. Just like when he was a child, Juanita Kingsley would never show up for him, even during his sickness.

Although Harper had repeated the words, *Terrance passed away*, at least fifty times that day, each time felt like a new wound. Calling Juanita was her greatest test. No surprise to Harper, his mother made his death about her. Yes, she cried, but at the same time, she mumbled unnecessary gibberish about how she wished she could've been there and how *he* should've called.

The battle between Harper the angel and Harper the bitch was in a full-out war. This woman had the nerve to say he should have called her when *he* was fighting to live. Harper was all too familiar with the trauma he carried because of his mother. Terrance's mother was a master manipulator, but those tactics wouldn't work anymore. When Juanita rambled about not having any money to attend the services, Harper knew it was time for her to end the call.

It was after midnight, and the house seemed darker and more hushed than before. Harper ordered pizza that had been left untouched. She walked the house to ensure all doors were secured before grabbing a glass of wine and popcorn.

Walking from the kitchen toward her bedroom, she looked down the dim hallway, expecting to see the light on in his room. But everything was black. She glanced around the house. Terrance seemed to be everywhere: his pictures, his scent, and even his medical equipment were sprawled around the house. But he was nowhere.

"Here you are, handsome. Enjoy," the hostess said, winking as she pointed him toward the glass-front room.

Dresden coyly chuckled as his former classmates spotted him. Maurice Miles, the owner of Ethos and a childhood friend, was the first to approach him.

"D! What's up, man?" Maurice bantered, pulling him into a hug. "I was thinking you were going to bail on me."

"What's up, Rece? Good to see you, man," Dresden said, returning the gesture. "I'm a man of my word. I wouldn't do you like that."

"You find the place OK? Downtown Monroe is not what it used to be, huh?" Maurice uttered as they advanced farther into the private room.

"Yeah, man. It's definitely changed. Your spot is nice. Congrats."

Maurice nodded, circling his eyes around the small crowd.

"Uh-oh, D. I see you're still Mister Popular," Maurice announced while Dresden followed his sightline.

A swarm of vaguely familiar female faces began to gather around him. They were like vultures circling their prey. Nina was barely settled in her grave before women started vying to be the next Mrs. Xavier, so this reaction was no surprise.

Dresden greeted the ladies with head nods, handshakes, and some forced hugs before a sultry voice sang, parting the growing flock.

"Dresden Xavier. Aren't you a sight?" the voice teased.

Maurice's brows lifted in approval of the woman who accompanied the voice. Dresden digested her from the pointy-toed stilettos to the sleek-bobbed crown of hair.

"Vanessa Franklin," Dresden drawled.

"Hey, neighbor," she crooned sexily, nibbling the corner of her bottom lip.

Vanessa did not conceal her appreciation of the grown-man version of her childhood friend.

Coffee shops, bars, salons, boutiques, and other small businesses lined the street. He made a mental note to talk to Bryn about this area. *I can definitely see The Rose Garden here*, he thought.

Dresden groaned, making a left into the parking lot adjacent to Ethos, the location of tonight's gathering. He wanted to go home and bury himself in a medical dictionary. Socializing hadn't had the same flavor since Nina became sick.

Like Bella, his wife was his partner in crime too. His dancing partner, drinking buddy—*his everything*. He could count on one hand the number of times he'd gone out since she died.

Dresden rested his head on the ivory leather headrest, contemplating an excuse to get out of this commitment. A familiar chill sprinted down his spine, causing him to chuckle. His Rosie's emphatic spirit always nudged him to step out of his comfort zone. He closed his eyes, meditating on her melodic voice frolicking in his head, singing, "*Come on, Dres*," encouraging him to put one foot in front of the other.

"OK, OK," he muttered.

Dresden stepped out of the black Escalade, tapping the door handle to secure the vehicle before he strolled to the entrance. Chocolate brown hardwood floors and gold-plated walls adorned with colorful paintings of different instruments greeted him before the hostess appeared.

"Hello, may I help you, handsome?" a gorgeous woman with skin as dark as hot fudge greeted him.

"Hello. Party for Maurice Miles," Dresden said, smiling.

"Yes, sir. Mr. Miles is in the private room. Please, follow me."

Dresden nodded and bobbed his head to the music piping through the space. Ethos was an intimate spot that clearly drew the after-work adult crowd. Jumbled hues of black and brown faces graced the melanated skin of professionals filling the place. Dresden was impressed. Ethos was a vibe.

Harper hurried to her room as if she were running from a ghost. Putting the glass and bowl on the nightstand, she blankly stared, uncertain what to do with herself. She placed balled fists on her temples because she felt like she was going crazy.

Climbing into bed, Harper retrieved her phone from the table. Joya and Annette had been texting her nonstop. Other *thinking of you* or *do you need anything* messages flooded her inbox. She scrolled through the endless messages, leaving them unread until one message from an unknown number caught her attention.

> **573-222-0011:** Professor Kingsley, this is Dr. Xavier. I heard about Mr. Kingsley's passing. I am very sorry for your loss, and you have my deepest condolences. Please let me know what you need. Don't hesitate to call if you need a listening ear. The bat signal works every time.—DMX

Harper snickered at his closing, recalling him telling her to send the *bat signal* for help and their impromptu DMX karaoke in his office. She hovered over the keys, pondering on how she should respond.

*Thank you should suffice.* But for some reason, thank you wasn't enough. Dresden's offer of his listening ear played on repeat in her head. If anyone knew this feeling, it was him. He'd lost his wife under similar circumstances, so maybe a kindred friend would benefit them both.

After several extended moments of deliberation, Harper pressed the phone icon from his text message. *Oh shit!* she thought, realizing that it was almost one o'clock in the morning.

"Hello. Hello," he sang. His baritone was deep but didn't sound like he was asleep.

"Hi. Um, Dresden ... Um, this is Harper," she stuttered.

"Harper," he said, sighing as if he was relieved to hear her voice.

"I won't ask," he said.

"Ask what?" she whispered.

"The dumbest question anyone can ever ask after you've lost a loved one," Dresden continued and then paused for a heartbeat. "*How are you holding up?*" he said mockingly. "How the fuck do you think I'm doing?" Dresden blurted.

Harper couldn't quell the burst of laughter that shot from her. He chuckled too, but then the phone went silent. Her soft whimpering filled the air. Harper didn't utter a word. Dresden leaned against his headboard, listening to her symphony of tears. He secretly wished he knew her location so that he could physically comfort her, not because of the undeniable attraction to her, but because he understood what she was feeling.

Losing a spouse, even under Harper's and Terrance's circumstances, was life-altering. But losing a spouse so young and with children was debilitating at times. Dresden did not wish for anyone to be initiated into this fraternity of grief.

"Harper, you don't have to talk. You can cry all night, scream and shout if you need to, or be completely silent. I'll be here," Dresden exclaimed.

Harper's wails broke his heart.

"Thank you."

# Chapter eighteen

Gray suit, white shirt, purple tie, pocket square, socks and shoes. Harper plowed through the list of items she needed to take to the funeral home later that day. Terrance's service was in a few days, and she felt like a chicken without a head. Between managing the arrangements, worrying about her boys, filtering a million questions from family and friends, and dealing with her own distress, Harper was on the brink of a breakdown.

"Ma, someone is at the door with a plant," Trae said. His tone had been monotonal and distant all week.

"Did you answer the door, Trae?" Harper asked, her tone filled with annoyance.

"No. I saw somebody on the Ring camera," he said, holding up his phone.

Harper huffed, rolling her eyes.

"Can you answer the door, please?"

"Why do we need another plant? That's the dumbest shit. Giving people a plant when somebody dies. Why the hell would we want that?" Trae ranted.

"Hey! Hey! Cut it." Harper snapped her fingers, gritting through clenched teeth.

"Now, I know this is a tough time for us all, but you will not talk like that in my house, young man. I am *not* one of your friends," she fussed.

"Sorry, Ma."

"Go answer the door, Trae, and put the plant with all the others," she instructed.

Harper withdrew an exasperated exhale. Exhaustion could not describe what she was feeling. She was numb, operating on mere fumes.

After Trae responded to two more knocks at the door, he left to go to his friend Mariah's house. They all just needed a little space.

Harper paced the floor as she dialed Hasan again. She was waiting for her son to pick her up so that they could go to the funeral home. She tried him several times, and he was not answering the phone. She shook her head, and uncontrollable yet muted tears cascaded down her face. Harper swallowed her sorrows and grief and did what she'd always done . . . Take care of business.

After going to the funeral home, she stopped by the mall to pick up a dress she ordered and bought matching ties for Hasan and Trae. A stop at the post office and then a grocery store run concluded her errands. Finally, Harper plopped on her couch and cried. The distinctive chime from her phone indicated that someone was at her front door.

"Hey, friend," Joya and Annette's voices rang.

Their jovial expressions immediately deflated when they saw the desolated mask wrinkling her face.

"Hey, friends," Harper responded, then burst out crying.

"Harp. Sweetie, let us help," Joya said, wrapping her arms around her friend.

"You don't have to do this alone," Annette added.

Harper slowly nodded, mouthing, "OK, OK."

Joya and Annette stayed the night with Harper. While she slept, they answered calls, sent emails, and just simply helped their friend. They even hired a cleaning service to prepare the house for guests and secured a catering service for the repast. Harper awakened from a well-overdue slumber, and her girlfriends were still there, holding her down.

Three days later, Harper, Hasan, and Trae jointly marched into the church dressed in ivory with accents of Terrance's favorite color, purple. The service was a blur as dozens of family, friends, coworkers, and clients extended their condolences. Trae was completely destroyed, and Hasan was so withdrawn that he was practically emotionless. Harper smiled, shook hands, and accepted hugs from people known and unknown before sliding into the limousine.

Hasan and Trae decided they did not want to go to the cemetery. Harper was tired of arguing with her sons about protocol, so she relented. She honestly did not want to see Terrance lowered into the ground, but she promised to see him all the way to the end.

*"My plans are already made, Harp. I didn't want all of that to fall on you. I know you are not my wife anymore, but promise me you'll see this through . . . until death parts us."*

Harper clutched the purple flower in her hand as she watched the deep burgundy casket adorned with gold trim gradually descend into the earth.

"Rest peacefully, Tee. Until we meet again, my friend," she whispered, gently tossing the flower.

The groundskeepers hovered around as the first heap of dirt was tossed onto the casket. Harper was immobile, staring blankly up to the heavens. She closed her eyes, inhaling the crisp November air. The aged, soaring oak tree offered some protection from the wintry chill. The lavish greens soared for miles, decorated with floral arrangements, flags, pictures, and keepsakes honoring the final resting places.

A gust of wind blew through the spray of flowers, scattering purple buds around her feet. Harper gazed down, coaxing a smile to grace her face for the first time in twelve days. It was Terrance, a sign that he was okay.

The gentle hand that touched her shoulder caused her to stir.

"Harper," a baritone voice whispered, gazing directly into her cloudy eyes.

It was *him*. His eyes were pools of unwavering empathy; genuine compassion that felt like a warm embrace amid the winter's chill. She needed him and didn't even know it.

Dresden reached out to hug her, and Harper broke, collapsing into his arms. In that instant, his presence gave her permission to unleash the breath caught in her core. Harper cried intense, cleansing tears. This man satisfied a desire that she had no clue she craved. The jolt of energy that surged through them felt similar to the first time they met, but they did not uncouple this time.

"It's OK. It's OK. Let it out," he whispered.

Instinctively, he speckled kisses on her temple, cloaking her tighter in his corded arms.

"Dresden," she whimpered, reluctantly lifting from his chest.

Eyes were on her. Or maybe they were fixed on him because he was a fine, fetching stunner of a man.

Blotting her face with the silk handkerchief, she uttered, "I'm OK."

"It's OK *not* to be OK, Harper," he coached.

She nodded.

"I wasn't expecting you," Harper said, squinting as she smiled up at him.

"I just wanted to pay my respects. Check on you and your boys."

Dresden retrieved the cloth from her hand and dabbed it under each eye. Harper sucked in a whiff of air.

"Thank you. Hasan and Trae are doing the best they can. They didn't want to see this part," she said, shrugging. "I'm actually doing OK, though," she continued.

Dresden lifted a skeptical brow.

"Seriously, I am. Sleeping pills have helped," she chuckled. "But I just needed to get through today. Knowing he's at peace gives me peace, so I'll be good."

Dresden nodded.

Attending the services was a game-time decision for him. During his last interaction with Terrance, he knew that it would not be long. The cancer was everywhere, and miraculously, he was not unresponsive like other patients he'd seen at that stage.

Dresden could not stomach the funeral. He had not attended one since Nina's. But he wanted . . . *needed* . . . to lay his eyes on *her*. When he arrived at the cemetery, he immediately found Harper in the crowd. She was spectacular. Her beauty was undeniable, but it was her strength that he admired.

"Are you coming to the repast? It's at my house," she asked.

"I can't," he said, more blunt than he intended.

Dresden could not walk into her house where her ex-husband died. The ex that he knew was dying.

"Well, maybe just come by and get a plate. There's so much food, it's ridiculous," she laughed.

"Maybe," he countered.

"Harper," she heard Joya shout.

She was standing by the caravan of cars, motioning for her to come. The limousine driver was ready to leave.

"I have to go," she announced.

"Harper, if you need anything, like I said before . . . to talk, cry, shout, laugh. If you just need someone to sit on the roof with you, I'm here."

He nudged her chin and rested his lips on her forehead again. Harper nodded. "I just may take you up on that."

# Chapter nineteen

I *just want this fucking day to end*, Dresden mused, massaging his temples with his fingertips. Dr. Benjamin Oliver, chief of research, rambled on for what felt like hours with a dollop of sour cream from the burrito he ate during lunch lingering in the corner of his mouth.

They were meeting for the first quarterly review to get him up to speed on the trial's progress. While Dresden was prepared with the appropriate data and documentation, his mind was a blur. Today was not the day for this . . . for anything.

On December 31, Dresden usually intentionally isolated to submerge himself in memories of Nina. Today was his Rosie's forty-fifth birthday. In the past, his assistant of many years knew to block his calendar for that day, sometimes even the week, to give him space to grieve, process, and rebound.

Dresden had been so busy with an aggressive clinical calendar that he forgot to update his new assistant on his preferences during December and January.

"Dr. Xavier, does that work for you?" Dr. Oliver said, smirking a bit because it was clear that Dresden was on another planet.

"My apologies, Dr. Oliver. I have a lot on my mind. Will what work for me?"

"We've been invited to the Digital Health Summit in New Orleans, and I would love to recommend you as a speaker. Does that work for you?" he repeated.

"Yes. Yes, sir, that works for me. Um, when is it again?" he inquired, still not fully present in the conversation.

"In about a month. I'll have my assistant send you the details."

Dresden nodded as Dr. Oliver finally wiped away the cream stain from his face before retrieving his tray and walking away. Dresden shook his head, vainly attempting to diminish the fog plaguing him today.

Walking back to the medical center, Dresden toyed with taking the rest of the day off, but he quickly changed his mind once he remembered that they were short staffed. Harper was still unavailable after Terrance's passing. Dresden had periodically been in contact with her since attending the funeral service.

When he offered a listening ear, he honestly didn't think that Harper would call. What started with them talking about their shared grief morphed into casual conversations about their kids, work, and even what they were planning to cook for dinner. Dresden considered Harper a friend, and he hoped she would say the same.

Thankfully, the rest of the afternoon sped by. Dresden turned off the lights a little after three o'clock since the office closed early for the holiday. He hopped into his truck and headed home to spend the evening with his daughters.

The mood in the house was somber but celebratory. At Bella's request, the family attended a grief counseling meeting at the center where she'd been volunteering. After the meeting, Bella planned a celebration for her mother. She bought a lemon cream cake and French vanilla ice cream, her mom's favorite.

Dresden and Bryn usually preferred to wallow in sadness. Still, they had to admit that the opportunity to celebrate and reminisce as a family eased the pain a little every year, at least for a moment. Now that the house was quiet, Dresden was in his head about so many things.

He glanced at the clock. It was ten o'clock at night. He was already dressed as if he were going to exercise, so he tossed on his sneakers, grabbed his earbuds and a skull cap, then headed toward the front door. Bryn strolled through the foyer wrapped in a plush blanket. A wrinkly brow was her only communication.

"I'm going for a run," Dresden announced before she could ask.

"This late?"

He nodded. "Yeah. I need to clear my head," he said, closing the distance between them, then settled a soft kiss on her forehead. "Where's your sister?"

"On the couch asleep. We watched Mom's favorite."

"*Purple Rain*," they both whispered in unison.

"I'll be back. I have my phone if you need me."

"Be careful, Dad. Love you."

"Love you most," Dresden retorted with his usual sentiment.

Dresden already had Nina's favorite Prince playlist queued for his run. He stretched for a few minutes, then darted down the street on his regular trail. While Prince sang about diamonds and pearls, Dresden plodded the bend at the corner of his street headed toward the neighborhood park.

Long strides were accompanied by heavy breathing as he swiftly traversed darkened streets. Neighbors nodded as they walked their dogs, but he was in the zone. His tunnel vision flashed visions of Nina during birthday celebrations over the years. While mist cloaked his eyes, a slight smile decorated his face, reminiscing on how freaky his wife would get when *"Darling Nikki"* flooded the speakers. His dick was hard at the mere thought. Shit, his dick was aching at the thought of sex—period.

It had been a year since Dresden had been with a woman. One drunken night, while celebrating his birthday with some friends, he met a woman in an upscale lounge. They flirted most of the night, prompting Dresden to cover her tab. The woman strolled to his table to thank him, and the next thing he remembered was taking her to his hotel room. Guilt plagued him the next day and weeks after, so much so that he never returned the woman's phone calls.

The night's chill was evidenced by the frost circling his mouth and nose as he breathed. Dresden's pace was swift, and his mind was absent from his surroundings as he swiftly cut the corner at the start of the park. He circled groups of people, surprised to see them gathered in the streets even on New Year's Eve.

Harper was freezing, but she couldn't stay with Trae and Hasan another second longer in her house. Hasan had been staying with her, and Trae was home for winter break. Her house had always been overrun with testosterone, being that she was the only woman, but she'd forgotten how insane her children were when they lived together consistently. Either Trae was yelling at Hasan for eating his favorite cereal, or Hasan was fussing at Trae for touching his drums.

That night, they'd both lost their minds, directing their wrath toward Harper. It had been over a month since Terrance died, and today was his forty-sixth birthday. The whole house was on edge, but her boys' attitude toward her was downright rude and inappropriate.

Harper reached her tipping point when she cursed at Trae and Hasan like they'd stolen something. She used every single word in her arsenal. After tossing up a hand to stop their rebuttal, she rushed out of the house in haste before she completely lost it. It wasn't until about fifteen minutes into her power walk that she realized how chilly it was outside.

*Boom!*

Turning the corner, they collided like two runaway freight trains.

"Oh, shit," Dresden muttered, grasping the woman by her arms to catch her fall. "Ma'am, are you all right?" he continued, then scrunched his brow.

"Harper?" he said questionably.

"Dresden?" she countered, adjusting the hat on her head to reveal her face.

The shock and serenity of recognition halted them both in their tracks. For a moment, they simply stared at each other as a mix of surprise and an undeniable spark flickered between them.

"You live around here?" he asked, still clutching her arms in his hands.

She nodded, reluctantly backing away from his hold. "A few blocks that way," she said, pointing behind her.

"I'm a few blocks that way," he returned, pointing in the other direction.

"Are you all right? What are you doing out here this late?" he interrogated her.

"Trying not to murder my sons," she chuckled.

"You must have really been fed up. It's freezing out here," he announced.

"Yeah, I am. And it is pretty cold, so I should ask you the same thing. What are you doing out here?"

"Processing," he bantered but was very serious.

"It's New Year's Eve. No hot date with Vivian?" Harper quipped but instantly regretted the joke.

He tilted his head slightly, his brow furrowing in puzzlement as he gazed at her.

Shaking his head, he snickered. "No. No hot date. And no *Vanessa*."

Silence lingered momentarily. Harper's cheeks reddened but not from the cool breeze. She could feel the heat rising to her face, hoping he wouldn't notice. Crowds of neighbors moved around them as they headed into the park.

"Where are all these people going?" he inquired.

"The bonfire. The homeowners' association hosts one every year for the neighborhood. It's pretty fun. The fireworks show is always nice," Harper responded.

"Is that where you were headed?"

She shook her head.

"I honestly forgot." She paused, rubbing her gloved hands together. "Today's been a pretty rough day."

Dresden nodded.

"Yeah. I understand. The holidays are always tough and—"

"It's Terrance's birthday."

"It's Nina's birthday."

Two sets of eyes ballooned in revelation.

"Wow," Harper whispered.

"What are the odds?" he returned in a whisper.

"Were your girls about to kill each other like my crazy kids? Is that why you are *processing*?" Harper laughed.

"Not this year. But that first holiday after Nina passed . . . Murder was definitely on the brain," Dresden snickered.

"For the last few years, we've been able to celebrate. Still a lot of tears but a celebration nonetheless," he continued.

Harper faintly bobbed her head, pondering when they could celebrate Terrance instead of mourn him.

"My kids expect me to not be functional. They accused me of not being sad about their dad's death. But . . . ." Her voice wavered.

"But what?" Dresden probed.

"But . . . I know Terrance is finally resting so I choose to smile . . . Celebrate him. He fought so long and so hard. I'm glad that he's free from that debilitating disease. Of course I'm sad. Of course I cry, but I'm comforted because I'm confident he's at peace." Harper shrugged, swiping an unexpected tear from her face, but they kept falling.

Dresden nudged her chin to lift her face, forcing her eyes to train on him. Her tear-stained face was beautiful as he thumbed away the dewy drops.

"No one can dictate how you grieve, Harper. Your pain is your own, and only you can decide how you cope with it. So, if running away from home for a minute is what you need . . . So be it."

Dresden smiled then mimicked her shoulder shrug.

"Well, to ensure I won't commit a New Year massacre, I will check out the bonfire. At least I can get a good spiked hot chocolate to warm me up," she giggled, adjusting her hat to cover her ears. "Care to join me?" she asked, a faint blush curving her glossed lips.

"You had me at the spiked hot chocolate," Dresden laughed.

Harper waved and spoke to familiar neighbors as they journeyed to the center of the park. Hosts of people surrounded the massive flames from the bonfire. Marshmallows were being roasted, and s'mores were being assembled, and neighbors danced and fellowshipped.

Dresden and Harper perched under a large tree near one of the empty pavilions. They sipped hot cocoa while quietly watching people celebrate. It was about thirty minutes before the new year, but folks were already hugging and kissing with merriment.

"How long were you married?" Harper asked, interrupting the hush.

"Over twenty years."

"I've heard you talk about her, and it sounds like you all had a flawless relationship," she said, blowing to cool the hot liquid.

Dresden pouted his lips, shaking his head.

"Nah. Nina was hell on wheels, and I'm no walk in the park. Sometimes, we collided like a bull in a china shop," he laughed, staring off into nothingness.

"We were both stubborn, but we just committed to communicating. We made a plan. We vowed to listen for the purpose of seeking to understand, not to craft a rebuttal."

"That was rather adult-ish of you both," Harper smiled, pondering on her and Terrance's inability to communicate.

"It's called marriage. She was my wife, so it was my duty to learn and understand her. I was her husband, so she did the same. When you marry as young as we did, you have to expect people to change over the years. Some shit we didn't like, but we learned to love it anyway because the core of who we were remained the same." Dresden shrugged.

A brief hush settled over them until a seemingly drunk and joyful older lady offered them another cup of spiked cocoa. They laughed and chatted with her for a few minutes before she informed them of the time.

*11:35 p.m.*

"Can I ask you a question?" Dresden glanced over to Harper. She nodded.

"What happened with you and your ex?"

*Where do I begin?* she thought, sighing.

"He just stopped seeing me. I wasn't a priority. Terrance was a great provider, hard worker, and an excellent father." She smiled, shaking her head. "But . . . he just stopped seeing me," Harper repeated. "I don't know that he ever did," she whispered, staring at the same nothingness. "I remember once I asked him to hang a painting of my mother that my father gave me. I reminded him over and over. Even went as far as marking the spot where I wanted it. Six months. Six months went by, and the wall was still bare. It wasn't until I hired a handyman that he decided to pay attention. If I heard '*I was going to do it*' one more time, I would scream."

"But you stayed . . . Why?" Dresden boldly asked.

Harper glared at him for a second, unsure if she was angry because he asked the question or pissed because she did not have a good answer.

Sighing, she took another sip before replying.

"My loyalty kept me around some shit when common sense should've slapped the hell out of me," she snickered.

Quiet and contemplation seized the air again. Dresden glanced at his watch. A new year would be upon them in about fifteen minutes.

"Sooo, my daughter is opening a dispensary soon, and she gave me some samples," Dresden said hesitantly, uncertain if Harper indulged.

"Really? That is so cool," she laughed. "That's a serious boss move. Kudos to her."

"You down?" Dresden said, lifting a challenging brow.

"Hell yeah. Let's do it."

Dresden laughed, retrieving the plastic pouch from his pocket. He regurgitated Bryn's explanation of each color gummy before Harper made her selection. Excitedly, she chose the yellow one.

Not even ten minutes after digesting the lemon-flavored goodness, Harper was giddy and borderline goofy.

"What is an auld lang syne?" she chuckled, referencing the song sung on at the strike of the new year.

"A song," he muttered.

"I know that, but what does it say?" she asked but wasn't really seeking an answer.

"For old people we forgot and live a life to sing." Harper slurred the wrong lyrics to the beat of "Auld Lang Syne."

"What the hell did you just say?" Dresden cackled.

Harper continued to sing loud, wrong, and off-key. He laughed so hard he buckled over.

"OK, I have a question for you," he said, still laughing at her silliness.

She tossed up her hand, then gestured a gun and uttered, "Shoot."

"Was there really bacon, hamburger, *and* a hot dog in a bacon burger dog?" he questioned seriously.

Harper eyed him intently for a long minute then belted out a thunderous laugh. Dresden joined the banter. Their intoxicated glee was disrupted by the resounding ring of the crowd's countdown. Dresden stood from the ground, turning to help Harper up.

"*Six, five, four, three, two, one . . . Happy New Year!*" the flock of people roared.

The music blared through the speakers, and Harper looked at Dresden, and he eyed her.

"For old people we forgot and live a life to sing." They sang Harper's bad lyrics harmoniously, then pushed out a resounding chuckle.

The same old lady who offered them hot chocolate floated around, ringing a bell, shouting, "Kiss. Kiss."

Dresden and Harper shook their heads, trying to shoo her away.

No locking of lips at the stroke of midnight leads to a lonely year," the old woman tsked. "Kiss," the lady yelped again.

Harper smiled over at Dresden, shrugging. He hunched his shoulders too. The old lady watched in anticipation. Closing the gap between them, Dresden gently cupped her waist, drawing her closer. Harper placed both hands on his chest, angling her head back to look at him. He rested a soft kiss on her forehead, then slid his lips down the side of her face, pecking her cheek. Dresden gazed into those pretty brown eyes that were heavy from weed and wonderment.

"Happy New Year, Harper," he said, hovering over her lips.

Dresden kissed her softly, and Harper couldn't give a damn about the fireworks lighting the sky. The explosion in her pussy was turbulent and intense.

Breathlessly, she whimpered, "Happy New Year, Dresden."

# Chapter twenty

Harper pulled into the garage of her new home. She could not bring herself to stay in the house where she raised her kids, divorced her husband, nursed him when he was sick, and where he ultimately died. Every direction she turned in the old house, she envisioned Terrance. His spirit was embedded in every square foot of the home. While some would think the memories would help with her grief, they only haunted her.

The quaint, ranch-style home was a big shift from the four thousand square foot Kingsley home but perfect for Harper. Thankfully, she found a place in the neighborhood she loved with all the required essentials: a large owner's suite with an oversized bathtub and closet, an amateur chef's kitchen, a sunporch, and bedrooms for her boys.

She exited the car and walked to the mailbox, waving at a few neighbors working in their yards. She laughed at the Valentine's decorations dressing some of the homes. *Do people really decorate for Valentine's Day?*

Harper was being a Scrooge, or whatever the equivalent would be for the season for lovers. She retrieved her mail and then turned toward her house, but not quick enough to avoid her neighbor, Mario. For some reason, repairing the light in her garage gave him the impression that he could invite himself over for dinner. She'd declined his offer to cook and an invite to breakfast four times. He finally got the hint the fifth time.

*Mario, you're a nice guy, but I'm not interested in a date at all. No breakfast, no lunch, no dinner. I hope you understand.*

Mario waved, then proceeded to his house. *Thank God.* He was a nice guy, but Harper wasn't interested. After New Year's night, the only *interest* she had was Dresden. They hadn't gone on a date or any outing, for that matter, but after nights of captivating conversations and that kiss . . . She was smitten.

Harper had returned to work at the university and the medical trial. After Terrance's funeral, she took time off to settle his business and sell their home. Thankfully, Terrance had already planned his services and his estate. There were no surprises or drama, so Harper could use the time to grieve and start the healing process with her boys.

Most of her work for the trial could be done at home since she primarily analyzed the data submitted through the system. She hadn't been in the office and had not laid eyes on Dresden since their moment on New Year's Eve.

The house was quiet since Hasan had officially returned to his apartment, and Trae stayed in his dorm. Harper picked up Chinese food and planned a relaxing evening while working.

She undressed and quickly showered, opting for only a robe. Walking into her kitchen, Harper plated her food and poured the grape Vess soda over ice. Her mouth was practically salivating in preparation for what she called *ghetto Chinese food*. She ate and watched a few episodes of *First Wives Club* before logging onto her computer.

Harper's eyes widened as she read the exchange between her colleagues referencing a trip to New Orleans for a conference. As she sifted through the messages on their team portal, she was confused about why she was the only team member not invited to attend. Although she had Dresden's phone number and they talked often, she would maintain her professionalism and request a meeting with him to discuss this.

Rapidly clicking the keys, Harper snarkily recited her message aloud as she typed.

> Doctor Xavier, I hope you are doing well. I would like to speak with you as soon as possible about a matter recently brought to my attention. I appreciate your speedy attention to this matter.
>
> Thank you in advance.
>
> Professor Harper Kingsley

Harper lifted her glass to take a gulp of the sugary soda when her computer dinged, indicating an incoming message.

> Professor Kingsley, I'm doing well. It's great to hear from you. We are looking forward to your return to the office. I have some time available tomorrow afternoon if you can come to the office. I'll see you soon.
>
> Dr. Xavier

Dresden pondered over what matter had been brought to Harper's attention. There was no way anyone knew the situation with

Terrance, at least he hoped. So, curiosity ate at him all night after reading her message. He purposely kept his response professional yet vague to see if she would offer some insight. But all he received in response was a Thank you. I'll see you tomorrow.

After his last appointment, Priscilla informed Dr. Xavier that Harper was in the office whenever he was ready. Dresden walked down the hall, which allowed him to see across the shared office space. Harper was talking to another team member with a bowl of something in front of her. She was so damn pretty. The last time he saw her, he could tell that she hadn't been sleeping. But today, she looked rested and lively. The smile brightening her face appeared genuine—no fake show for her colleagues.

He stopped to fill his water bottle and strolled down the hall toward the team's office space. Knocking, he stepped into the room, noticing that she was now alone.

"Professor Kingsley, it's good to see you."

Harper placed a hand to her mouth after scooping a large spoonful of noodles into it. She lifted her pointer finger as she chewed.

"Sorry. I didn't mean to disturb your lunch . . . or dinner," Dresden uttered, glancing at the clock.

It was after three o'clock, and Harper was just getting a chance to eat.

"No worries. I went from not hungry at all to starving in an instant," she said, laughing as she took a few sips of water. "And thank you. It's good to be seen."

"You wanted to talk to me?" Dresden asked, leaning against the small conference table. His eyes were focused on Harper. She stared back, soundless. Being this close to him was still a little unsettling. He pursed his lips and lifted his brow, waiting for her to speak.

"Oh yes. I'm sorry. Um . . . I was wondering why I wasn't considered to attend the conference in a couple of weeks."

Dresden's head reared back in surprise. He was expecting a tough question . . . This was easy.

"I figured that you still needed some time. I did not want to rush you to return."

"Well, with all due respect, Dr. Xavier, you figured wrong. I'm back and ready," she said, nodding with certainty. "For any future opportunities, I would like to be considered. Please," she muttered, clearing her throat once she realized her tone was a bit peppery.

He stared at her, recalling how Terrance described her. *Feisty, and she won't take no for an answer.*

Dresden liked that shit too. Her confidence and assertiveness were sexy.

"I'll have my assistant book your travel," he announced.

"Oh . . . um . . . I don't want to inconvenience anyone. I can go next time."

"No inconvenience. You are right. I should not have assumed your needs. If you say you're ready, who am I to dispute that?"

"Thank you, Dr. Xavier. I greatly appreciate it."

He nodded. "Two weeks. New Orleans," he chimed, strolling out of her office.

Harper rushed through the airport to get to her gate just before they started to board. Everything that could have gone wrong that morning did. The zipper on her luggage broke, so she had to rummage through her new home to find another suitcase. When she hopped into her car, the low tire pressure gauge was flashing. There was no way she could make it to St. Louis with potential tire issues. Thankfully, Hasan had slept at her house the night before so he could drive her to the airport. She would worry about getting back to Monroe City later.

She approached the gate and noticed Dresden standing with headphones draped over his head. He bobbed to whatever music was in his ears when she approached him. She tapped on his shoulder, and he stirred, turning to see her. His smile was wide and bright, warming her insides.

"Good morning," she spoke.

"Good morning," he replied.

"I haven't had my coffee, so forgive my attitude in advance," she warned.

He chuckled. "I haven't either, so we're even," he said, winking playfully.

The gate agent called for all first-class passengers.

"That's us," he said.

"That's you," she uttered. "I'm flying with the common folk."

His brow furrowed. "Hmmm . . . I have a hard time believing that. Check again."

Harper rolled her eyes before she could stop herself. Dresden cocked his head to the side.

"I warned you about my uncaffeinated attitude," she sighed, aggressively swiping her phone screen to retrieve her boarding pass.

"I checked in late last night, and I was in boarding group C, seat 24—" she said, about to thrust the phone toward his face, but she halted, squinting to read the print.

*FC. Preboard.*

"Wait. What? When? . . . How? . . . Who changed this?" Harper interrogated, her forehead scrunched like a wrinkly puppy.

"I wanted you to be comfortable, Professor Kingsley."

She stared at him. "Harper," she whimpered breathily, correcting him. "Th-Thank you, Dresden."

He nodded, then extended his hand for her to walk toward the jet bridge.

Harper didn't allow the flight attendant to ask what she wanted to drink before she blurted *coffee*. She enjoyed coffee and then a glass of mimosa with her breakfast.

"The team is going to be jealous when they see me in first class," she uttered, biting a buttery croissant.

"The rest of the team is either already there or flying in this afternoon." Dresden whispered his last words. "So, no worries about being seen with me."

"So, what's the agenda for the next few days? I saw when you're speaking and other sessions I want to attend, but do we have anything planned as a team?"

"I figured folks would want to chill tonight or see the city, so I didn't plan anything. We have a dinner reservation at Drago's tomorrow." Dresden spoke while focusing on his phone.

"Yum . . . I'm already salivating," Harper teased, rubbing her belly.

"Good. It's one of my favorite spots in New Orleans," he said, smiling at her giddiness.

"After dinner, there's another spot I enjoy with a live band and amazing drinks. If some folks are interested, we can go there. Other than that, people are free to roam about the city."

"Nice. It's been maybe five or six years since I've been to New Orleans."

Harper couldn't contain her excitement. She desperately needed this getaway, even if it was for work.

"Really? Nina and I used to—" His voice waned.

A combination of regret and embarrassment flushed his face.

"No. Tell me. You and Nina visited often?" she queried, flashing him a closed-mouth smile, encouraging him to continue.

He nodded.

"Once a year. Her mom would come and stay with the girls, and we'd have our time in NOLA. Some years, we'd only stay in the hotel and enjoy the spa and food. Other times, we partied like twenty-somethings," he laughed.

"That's cool."

He nodded again, clearing the twinge of emotions brewing. "What about you? What's your favorite city to visit?" he asked, quickly changing the subject.

"Hmm . . . I honestly have never thought about it. But if I had to pick, I would say Las Vegas."

"Vegas . . . Why?"

"I guess because you can get the best of both worlds . . . similar to New Orleans. Great food, good vibes, options to chill or turn up."

"My daughters keep telling me that no one says, 'turn up' anymore," he chuckled, and so did she.

"They sound like my boys. Constantly telling me how lame I am," she giggled. "Can I even say 'lame' anymore? Shit." Harper hurriedly cupped her hand over her mouth as if she was going to be scolded by the principal for cursing.

"My apologies. I didn't mean to get so comfortable with you . . . In a work setting, I mean."

He eyed her warmly. A host of responses were dancing in his head, but he chose the safest retort he could muster.

"I don't mind . . . at all, Harper."

There she went again. Nibbling the inside corner of her lip and swiping across her temple jumpily. Dresden recalled Terrance casually sharing Harper's habits during one of their many conversations while receiving his fake treatments.

*"Harp doesn't have a poker face. She would lose her chips every time," Terrance chuckled.*

*"When she starts to nibble on those lips and fuss with her hair, she's trying her best to prevent blushing. But it doesn't work. The blush reddens the peaks of her cheeks every fucking time."*

The corner of Dresden's mouth lifted in a faint smile. Terrance was right. Her cheeks were beet red against her smooth, honey-hued skin, which was magnificent. *She* was magnificent.

Harper feigned focus on her phone as she retrieved a second mimosa from the attendant. Dresden looked out the window to suppress the desire to stroke the stray curl from her eyes. Instead, he allowed a comfortable hush to overcome them for the duration of the two-hour flight.

The hustle and bustle of a medical conference was no joke. Harper shuffled through the massive convention from session to session to gain knowledge she could take back to her students. While journeying through the space, she laughed at some of the young women attendees who were tiptoeing by the end of the day because their feet were aching in the four-inch stilettos. *They'll learn. Keep it cute and comfy, honey*, she thought, prancing in her animal print flats.

Harper opted for a Kelly-green pantsuit and a sheer black blouse underneath. She swooped her hair into a high bun, allowing some tendrils to fall on each side of her tortoise glasses. A nude lip and light makeup completed the look. She was headed to meet with her team so they could walk to Dr. Xavier's session together. He was one of two doctors on a panel on the main stage of the conference, so it was a pretty big deal.

The entire team was impressed when they entered the hall because the space was already packed with conference attendees. Big screens dropped from the ceiling, giving a better view of the stage for those in the nosebleed seats. One team member spotted Priscilla, and she ushered them to reserved seats in the front row.

Pride and excitement overcame the entire team. If they had not realized it before, they now understood how important Dr. Xavier's work was. And to be a part of his team was an honor.

Harper shook hands and introduced herself to people seated around them who acknowledged the group as a part of Dresden's research team.

Lights began to flash, and the cameraman positioned in the center of the room focused on the podium. The senior vice president and chief diversity officer for the American Cancer Society was introduced as the panel moderator. She then introduced a doctor from Texas known for her research on breast cancer in the African American community.

"Please help me welcome Dr. Dresden Xavier, chief of research at Monroe University Hospital Cancer Center," the moderator announced.

Dresden strolled from behind the curtain, and for Harper, everything paused. It was like he was moving in slow motion. His saunter had so much confidence and swag. But the way the dark blue suit hung from his athletic limbs rendered her weak.

*Damn!*

He wore a crisp white shirt but no tie with a purple ribbon on his jacket lapel in recognition of ovarian cancer victims like his late wife. Harper had just seen the man yesterday, but he appeared extra delectable today for some odd reason. When he smiled, the sparkle in his eyes and gleaming white teeth had all of the ladies swooning. Some of them didn't care to whisper their observations of *Dr. Feelgood*.

"But I could never do this work on my own. I've been blessed with some amazing teams over the years, and that has not changed since I transitioned to Monroe University Hospital. Team, please, stand up. Give them a round of applause, everybody," Dresden declared, clapping with the crowd.

His words barely registered for Harper until her colleague tapped her shoulder, encouraging her to stand. She rose, trying desperately to keep her focus away from Dresden, but her eyes had an agenda of their own. Glancing his way, he was already staring at her. Harper abruptly turned her head. Those damn rosy cheeks told all her secrets.

The team transitioned to the networking reception immediately following the session. Wine, champagne, and hors d'oeuvres were being passed as conference attendees stood in line to ask questions of the panelists.

*Pace yourself, Harp*, she mused, desiring to swallow the champagne in one gulp, but she sipped like a lady instead.

"How'd I do?" a voice sounded from behind her.

She spun around to find Dresden standing before her, looking manly, muscular, and marvelous. *Ugh! Why must this man be so dang fine?*

"Good," she squealed, two octaves too high.

"Just *good* . . .?" he teased.

"Great," she corrected playfully. "No, seriously, you were amazing. It's really an honor to work with you, Dr. Dresden—I mean, Xavier. *Shit!* Dr. Xavier."

Dresden was captivated by her bashfulness yet clueless about why. *Why is she acting so nervous around me now?* Harper's usual cool and collected demeanor became fidgety and a bit unsettled.

"Thank you. I meant what I said. I wouldn't be here without a dynamic team, so cheers to you," he said, raising his champagne flute.

Harper blinked rapidly, lifting her flute to connect with his.

"Aht, aht, Professor Kingsley. You must maintain eye contact when sharing a toast," he instructed teasingly.

"Why?"

"It's a sign of trust. Otherwise, I may think you're a little shady or dishonest," he chuckled.

"Or maybe *you* don't trust *me. Do* you trust me, Harper?" Dresden questioned, staring directly in her pretty brown pupils.

An immediate sense of calm came over her. Previous coyness dissipated with just one gaze from *him*. "Under his spell" could not describe the control he had over her. Dresden's sorcery was deceiving because it was easy and uncomplicated. He held invisible strings and Harper was his puppet.

She nodded. "Yes, I trust you, Dresden," Harper whispered.

"Then no need to look over there or down here," he said, pointing in various directions. "I'm right here," he continued, tapping at the corner of his eye.

These were the same words he had uttered during their first phone call.

Harper concentrated on the specks of gold dancing in the chocolate pools he called eyes. They simultaneously raised their flutes, connecting the crystal until they clinked. Gazes still engrossed in each other, neither of them could contain the desire to glance at the other's lips draping the rim of the glasses. Hers were succulent and plump, while his were smooth and luscious. *Kissable*, they jointly mused.

"Hey, guys. Let's meet in the hotel lobby for dinner in thirty minutes," Priscilla chimed, interrupting their veiled intimacy.

Dresden nodded, gulping down the rest of his champagne.

"Sounds good," Harper sang, walking away from the uneasy moment.

# Chapter twenty-one

The cool night breeze did not deter people from crowding Canal Street. Dresden and his team enjoyed an amazing dinner at Drago's and were now headed to a rooftop lounge. The younger members of the crew decided to barhop while the seasoned members of the team navigated to the lounge.

Harper and Priscilla walked ahead of Dresden and his colleague, Dr. Charles Daniels. Dresden approached a tattered door hinged to what appeared to be an abandoned building. He ushered them inside to an elevator lifting to the third floor. When they stepped off the elevator, everyone was surprised to see a reasonably upscale yet relaxed bar with a live band.

Oversized white leather booths lined the walls, and plush cognac leather chairs circled small bistro tables. Dresden motioned for them to follow him to one of the booths marked reserved. It took no time for a waitress to appear, speaking with the distinctive New Orleans drawl.

"Hey, baby, what you having?" Toya asked, swinging her butt-length box braids. She shot her gaze to the ladies to get their orders first. Various versions of tequila-infused drinks bounced around the table.

"I tell you what, baby. How 'bout you order a bottle? That'll get you two for e'rrbody, baby. Okay?" she said, directing her question at Dresden this time.

"How do you know I'm paying?" he asked teasingly.

"Baby, you look like the moneybag, handsome," she cackled.

Dresden chuckled, nodding.

"Is everybody cool with Clase Azul," he asked, darting his eyes around the table.

Everyone nodded.

"See, you got the money, baby. Which one yo' lady?" Toya inquired, glancing from Harper to Priscilla.

Both ladies shook their heads, laughing at her animation. They remained hushed as Toya put her hands on her hips, demanding an answer.

"We're coworkers," Harper said, dismissing any confusion.

"Well, you're mine tonight, baby." Toya's laughter reverberated over the music.

The group laughed, talked, and enjoyed their drinks as the band played covers of popular nineties music. Harper and Priscilla joined the crowded dance floor of line dancers when Tamia's "Can't Get Enough" sounded. Dresden intently watched her. His eyes traced the gentle curves of her face when she laughed. Harper was brilliant and carefree. Every subtle movement captivated him. A soft smiled danced on his lips as he basked in her joyous beauty.

The band returned from their break and resumed their set when the singer announced, "All the lovers out there, get ready for some slow jams."

One song after another resounded as the crowd crooned and swayed to the mellow beats. The two lead singers rotated through a catalog of songs. When they both stepped to the microphone and began belting out familiar lyrics, Harper mouthed, "*Oh my God.*" She was hit with a lightning bolt of nostalgia.

*The very first time that I saw your brown eyes*
*Your lips said, "Hello," and I said, "Hi."*
*I knew right then you were the one.*

"This was my jam. You couldn't tell me I wasn't in love in high school," Priscilla said, and Harper slapped her hand in agreement.

The band channeled the nineties R&B group Shai as they harmonized about whether they would ever fall in love again. Priscilla yanked Dr. Daniel's hand, pulling him to the dance floor before he could protest. Harper watched them while Dresden watched her.

"Would you like to dance, Harper?" he asked.

"No, it's OK." She shook her head.

"Please," he whispered.

He extended his hand to escort her to the dance floor. Harper floated toward him as though his words invoked an enchanted spell. Harper tried to withdraw. Everything within her that was wholesome and good told her to remove herself from this man.

Settling one hand at the small of her back, Dresden cradled her fingers with his. He rocked her slowly, aimlessly massaging up and down the slope of her back to the harmonious rhythm. Dresden softly clutched her waist, drawing her closer.

*This man has me bewitched.*

Harper's brown sugar vanilla scent invaded his senses. The shit was so damn heavenly. With every deep inhale, his imposing frame melted further into her glorious one. They rocked and swayed, thoughtlessly cradled in each other's caress.

Harper dismissed the ruckus cluttering her head, allowing herself to release. Dresden felt the moment the rigidity escaped her limbs. She crept a soft hand up the nape of his neck, caressing her fingertips against his chocolate skin.

"I love this song too," he uttered.

Dresden's eyes lowered, staring down the bridge of his nose into her big honey-brown eyes.

She nodded, humming, "Mm-hmm. Brings back many memories," her dreamy soft voice whispered.

"Care to share."

She giggled, then said, "I was a freshman in high school, and Leonard Scott asked me to go to the homecoming dance. He was too afraid to dance with me until this song came on."

"Must've been a great dance. You still remember it."

"No. It was awful," she laughed. "Having two left feet was an understatement."

"Well, I hope I'm faring better than Leonard."

"Much better," she said, gazing back into his onyx eyes.

The band had to be clairvoyant because the next several songs were also among their favorites. Dresden and Harper were practically glued to the dance floor and each other. Boyz II Men crooned about being on bended knee while Kelly Price sang the Black women's anthem, encouraging them that "it's gonna rain, but the sun will shine."

Harper sang word for word through every song from her soul. Dresden was mesmerized by the glimmer of gold in her eyes, but he did not miss the hint of affliction. He never did because he recognized the same occasional calamity in himself.

Dresden did not understand what was happening. Touching her in this way was a mistake. The booming sensation he experienced every time he was in her presence had now escalated to a thunderous thud. Harper had resuscitated him in a way that he never could have imagined. Not only was she a beautiful and sexy woman, but she was also witty, astute, and brilliant—the perfect combination to cause his manhood to stir. A slow, steady pulse beat in his heart and his growing member every time she trailed fingers down the slope of his nape.

"Thank you, Harper."

"For what?"

Dresden hesitated, reluctant to speak from his heart. A chilled breeze rippled across the back of his neck in the place that Harper touched.

*"You give the best kisses and hugs and have the biggest heart, Dresden Xavier. It would be a disgrace to keep all of that goodness to yourself,"* he heard Nina whisper.

"Everything, Harper. Thank you for everything," Dresden said, cupping her face.

He didn't care who was watching even once he remembered that Priscilla and Charles were there. Harper shuddered as she slowly retreated from his caress.

Priscilla and Charles were in fact watching when they returned to the table.

Priscilla didn't say a word but the raised brow and smirk curving her lips silently hummed, *"Mmhmm."* The unspoken implication of scandal hanging in the air.

"I think I'm going to head out," Harper said, feeling a little woozy from the Lemon Drops and *him*.

Dancing with Dresden one time would have been fine, but five times had her losing control. She had to find the nearest exit before she kissed that man on the dance floor. Every sultry song was paired with an even more seductive move. His hands caressed her hips as they swayed to everything from Usher singing about seduction to Muni Long crooning about hours and hours.

The desire for distance hurriedly disappeared as the drinks kept flowing. Harper was a little tipsy from the libations, but she was drunk as a skunk off of him. Dresden smelled like tequila and bliss. But her complete undoing came when he nestled one firm hand in her hair, massaging her scalp, while the other rubbed circles at the small of her back. Harper's pussy was wailing . . . wetter than she'd been in a long time.

"You can't walk by yourself," Priscilla announced, but it was clear she wasn't ready to go. She and Dr. Daniels had become just as cozy as Dresden and Harper.

"I'll get an Uber," Harper tried.

"On Canal Street . . ." Priscilla said, glaring at Harper as if she'd lost her mind.

"I'll walk with you. I think the champagne and tequila are getting to me, so I should call it a night too," Dresden exclaimed.

"Dr. Dres . . . Dr. Xavier. I can find my way, I promise," she stammered her words.

"I'm sure you can, but I'm walking with you," he repeated, but this time his tone was more forceful . . . *sexy.*

She nodded, not even bothering to contest.

Canal Street was still crowded with folks drinking, dancing, and collecting beads. They took their time walking back to the hotel. Neither mentioned the electrical currents that bolted through them on the dance floor, but the chatter wasn't minimal. Dresden and Harper gabbed about any and everything until they reached the hotel.

He gently clutched her elbow, ushering her through a mob of drunk partygoers lingering in the lobby. Dresden released her once they reached the elevator. The elevator doors creaked open. Moving to the side, they opened a path for a few people to exit. He nodded for Harper to enter the empty car first.

Dresden swiped his key card and pressed the illuminated seventeen. Turning to Harper, who had posted up against the farthest wall, he asked, "What floor?"

"Seventeen," she whispered.

When they exited the elevator, the guests' floor layout was a complete maze in Harper's tipsy state. She recalled navigating two hallways just to get to her room.

"What room number are you?" Dresden asked.

"Seventeen-thirty," she responded. "It's down one of these hallways," she giggled through a yawn.

"I'm right here," he said, pointing to room seventeen-zero-five, a few doors from the elevators.

The elevator dinged, startling them both. A boisterous group exited, belting apologies as they bumped into Dresden and Harper.

"Good night, Dresden," she sang, starting to walk in the same direction as the rowdy bunch.

"Nah, I'll walk you," he said, hovering protectively.

"They're harmless. I don't think anyone is lurking around the corner." Harper tilted her head to the side, lifting her eyebrows.

"It's New Orleans. Anything is possible," he declared, nudging her to proceed down the hall.

Harper retrieved her key from the clutch purse as they approached her room. She paused, then sucked in a breath of composure before shifting to face him.

"This is me."

He nodded, waiting for her to unlock the door. Instead, Harper rested her back against the door, staring down at her shoes.

"Thank you for everything," she whispered.

Dresden fingered her chin, lifting her head to look at him. "Now, what were you saying?" He blushed.

Harper pursed her lips, faking irritation. "Thank you for dinner, walking with me from the club, and to my room. Thank you for everything, Dresden," she said, parroting his sentiment from earlier.

"Don't forget my stellar dancing abilities," he teased, and they chuckled.

"You're welcome, Harper."

"Good night," she whispered.

Dresden eyed her. Desire, desperation, and distress frolicked in his eyes. That damn stray curl was calling for him again. He sought to cease his pursuit, but the yearning to touch her was too potent. He swiped a finger across her brow, sweeping her tendrils behind her ear. Cupping the curve of her face, he smiled. The crimson cheeks he was growing to adore had returned. Begrudgingly, he released her face, and instantly, her eyes fell to an unknown place.

"I'm right here," he whispered.

Just as quickly as they plummeted, her eyes reconnected at his command.

*Fucking bewitchery!* she pondered.

"Good night, Harper," he uttered, planting a kiss on the back of her hand.

Harper couldn't move. She just stood there like an idiot, watching him walk down the hallway.

He turned around midstride and muttered, "Go inside. There still may be someone lurking around the corner."

A spirited smile graced his face. Her center was doused and discombobulated. But what was most terrifying was how Dr. Xavier permeated her mind. No topic was off-limits during their conversations. Anything from medical miracles to politics to their desire to visit The Book of HOV exhibit at the Brooklyn Library. *I'm being mind-fucked and I think I like it.*

Harper hopped in the shower and allowed *Midnight* to quickly relieve the strain on her kitty so she could have a good night's sleep. Remembering Joya's earlier text message with instructions to call her no matter how late it was, Harper curled up in bed. Dressed in pajama shorts and tank top, she texted Joya, *'You up'* before calling. Harper laughed when her phone instantly rang.

"Hey, Joy," she answered.

"Hey, friend. How was everything today?"

"It was good. The sessions were very informative. I can't wait to share what I learned with my students."

"OK, heffa, cut the crap. The real question is, how is *Dr. Feelgood*?"

"Joy," Harper whined.

"Harp," Joya mimicked.

"He's. He's. I don't know," Harper whined again, covering her face with a pillow. "I don't even know how to describe that man."

"Fine. Sexy. And more fine," Joya quipped.

"I wish that was all, Joy. If he were just fine, I wouldn't feel like this," Harper announced.

"Like what?" her friend probed.

"Giddy like a damn teenager. Excited in anticipation of seeing him. Eager to hear his voice while he entices my mind." Harper paused, allowing her admittance to absorb for a second. "I like him, Joy."

"It's OK to like him, Harper. You're single. He's single. Make it happen," Joya said, clapping her hands.

"Is he, though? Sometimes, he speaks about his wife as if she were still alive. The love he has for her . . ." Harper wavered, shaking her head as if Joya could see. "It's beautiful, but I don't know if any woman could compete. Even with a ghost."

Dresden paced the carpeted floor of his hotel suite. At least an hour had passed since he walked Harper to her room. Their time on the dance floor pranced in his mind far too many times. Her scent, the way she felt in his arms, and the need in her eyes all had him dazed, but he wasn't confused.

"I want her," he whispered, momentarily halting his stride.

He glanced at his reflection in the full-length mirror mounted on the wall. His expression was . . . anticipatory . . . happy for the first time in a long time. And terrified.

Dresden searched for his phone and pressed a few buttons to make a call.

"Dre, is everything all right?" Adriana growled sleepily.

"I want her," he exclaimed.

Adriana smiled, although her eyes were still closed. She knew her brother had feelings for the woman he spoke of often. *Harper is brilliant. Harper is so funny. Should I go to her ex's service? I'm giving Harper time.* Dresden had mentioned her on more than a few occasions, and that had not happened since Nina.

"Tell me something I don't know," Adriana chuckled. "Talk to her, Dre."

Dresden's silence always indicated he was processing strong emotions without saying a word. His sister respected his process, his need to think.

"Are we just swapping grief though? Bonded by our trauma. I've lost; she's lost. Her grief is so new."

"I hear you, Dre, but wasn't she divorced *before* her ex got sick?" Adriana asked but did not expect an answer because she knew she was right. "Yes, she's grieving a loss, but not the loss of her *husband*, Dresden. As you said, they were still *friends*. She's grieving the loss of her kids' father and her friend, bro."

"Yeah," Dresden groaned, sitting on the edge of the bed.

"What is this really about?" Adriana probed, sensing that there was more to his uncertainty.

"We work together. What will people think?"

"People will think that you're grown, and they should mind their own business," Adriana blurted with a heap of attitude. "Now, stop bullshitting me. I'm sleepy. You've never cared about other people's judgment. So what's the problem?"

The stillness lingered again for a prolonged heartbeat.

"It's less about other people and more about me. I'm judging me," he admitted.

Adriana did not respond, but Dresden knew that she was listening.

"Will loving her diminish my love for Nina? If I smile too much or feel too happy, does that mean I am not heartbroken over my Rosie anymore? Does God grant us the type of love I've experienced only once in a lifetime? Do I even *deserve* to be happy again?"

Dresden's words tumbled out in a rush. A storm of emotions and confessions that left him breathless.

"Brother, I love you and know you miss Nina more than anything. But you can still love her just as deeply and unconditionally as you always have while loving someone else."

"What woman would accept that?" Dresden questioned doubtfully.

"The right woman," Adriana said definitively, momentarily quelling his doubt.

Harper riled at the sound of a light knocking against her door. Staring at the door, she didn't move, assuming maybe someone made a mistake . . . until another knock startled her. She placed her tablet on the nightstand before tiptoeing to the door as if *she* were the late-night intruder. Placing her eye on the peephole, she audibly gasped at the sight of *him*.

*What the hell is he doing here?*

"Harper. I can hear you breathing," Dresden said, seriousness lacing his tone and expression.

Harper opened the door but kept the security latch on.

"Dresden. Hi. Wh - what are you doing here? Is everything OK?" She stumbled over her words.

"I-I know it's late. I'm sorry, but . . ." His voice trailed off.

"But what?" she asked, nervously clutching the thin shirt closer to her body.

"I shouldn't have come," he said, his eyes wandering everywhere but on her.

"I'm not down there. I'm right here," she whispered, echoing his usual words back to him.

He lifted his eyes and Harper was weakened by the obvious signs of distress.

"I can't sleep." His husky baritone, usually strong and warm, was now tinged with a note of strain trembling every syllable.

They exchanged stares for an extended heartbeat, weighing the risks and rewards of what the night may bring. Harper released the security latch, terrified yet exhilarated in knowing that her decision to open the door could change everything.

"Come in."

Dresden stepped into her room, which resembled his. The curtains were opened wide, allowing the sparkle of the city lights to illuminate the room. He'd changed into a Nike jogging set and slides. This was likely the most dressed down she'd ever seen him. And he looked *good*.

Harper crossed her arms over her chest just in case her unruly nipples were acting up. "Why can't you sleep?" she asked, hoping to disrupt the awkward silence.

He shook his head, running a hand down his gorgeous face. "My head's all fucked up," he said, pacing the floor slowly.

"About what?"

Harper's eyes darted back and forth to the rhythm of his pacing until he paused abruptly. Unmoved, she stared at him, anticipating his answer.

Dresden hesitated, uncertain of how his disclosure may land. He took a few steps, shrinking the distance between them. With barely an inch of separation, his eyes locked on her but she diverted his stare.

"You!" he blurted.

Their breaths mingled with intensity as Harper processed the one simple word. She had no issue finding his eyes this time. Her gaze bore into him, searching for anything to help her determine their next step. Dresden's demeanor battled between gloom and gladness, so Harper approached him with gentle caution.

"What do you need, Dresden?"

Pressing his forehead against hers, he closed his eyes to clear the tangled mess of emotions. Dresden was unsure how to unravel the inner chaos but was certain that he needed her at that moment. Shit, in his life.

"I just want to sleep. Can you help me sleep, Harper? Please."

Doubt and desperation misted the whites of his eyes. Harper did not speak. She simply turned to walk toward the bed but realized that he hadn't moved. Reaching to grab his hand, she motioned her head and whispered, "Come on," giving his hand a reassuring squeeze.

He followed, now yielding to her sorcerous demand. Dresden pulled off his sweatshirt to reveal a white tank top. Harper gasped in response to his corded upper arms painted with tattoos. His rolling abs had her dizzy. Dresden's sweatpants weren't gray, but they still revealed the bulky package he was handling.

He climbed into her bed, and she regarded him in awe. Simply put, Dresden was a beautiful man. God cooked up the perfect remedy to cure all ailments when He created that man. The optimistic sorrow that lowered his eyes was captivating, and she could not stop staring.

*What made him come to me?* she thought, astounded but amiable to his needs

Harper lay next to him, hugging the edge of the bed. *If I get too close, I'm going to fuck this man.*

"Can I hold you, Harper?" Dresden requested, his baritone low and pleading.

She nodded.

Scooting back toward him, she still endeavored to leave a little room. Even with the distance, his steeliness was apparent. Harper was stupefied about why she was so comfortable with this man, opening her door in the middle of the night and offering her bed like they were commonplace acquaintances. Unforeseen emotions overwhelmed her. Harper had been a caretaker for so long she'd forgotten how it felt to be cared for. His embrace was nurturing . . . secure. Burying her face in the pillow, she attempted to hide her tears. *Epic failure.*

Dresden snaked his arms around her waist and pulled her taut waist into his body, spooning her like they were familiar lovers. She smelled of honey and happiness. They cuddled closer and closer, unable to decipher her start from his finish. Her beginning was his end. Inadvertently, he stroked his fingertips up and down the arc of her hip. It wasn't sexual or sensual; it was . . . passion.

Burrowing his face in her neck, they released unison exhales.

Solace. That is what they'd both been seeking and somehow found it in each other. Sleep came in a flood as Dresden's eyes sluggishly narrowed to a close. Harper listened as his breathing steadied. She smiled when the faint huffs of his snores tickled her ear. As her eyes became heavy, she finally found the word to describe Dr. Dresden Xavier . . . *Everything.*

# Chapter twenty-two

Dresden awakened disoriented as he peered around the dark room. It didn't take long for his memory of the past few hours to return once he eyed the gorgeous figure sound asleep next to him. She was curled in the fetal position, with her face partially masked by the plush pillow.

Her body's curled manner did not conceal the curve of round, perky breasts with taut nipples distended against the silk fabric of the pajama top. Probing eyes danced up thick, bent legs trailing a path to her ass cheeks playing peek-a-boo in the coordinating pajama shorts.

Dresden fought to tear away his ogle from her beautiful body. His eye landed on an even more beautiful face, clear of any traces of makeup. She stirred a little with puckered lips when he straightened the silk bonnet protecting her hair.

A wide smile decorated his face, loving Harper's confidence. Bonnet-wearing, shea butter-coated, fresh-faced Black woman was all he ever desired. Plenty of women would forgo the bonnet and risk a good silk press to impress a man—especially one who randomly knocked on her door and asked for help falling asleep.

At some point during the night, she must have closed the blackout curtains, which caused confusion about the time of day. Dresden glanced over her shoulder at the clock on the nightstand. It was almost eight o'clock in the morning. He hated to leave but was scheduled to attend a physicians' breakfast in an hour.

He cradled her, settling back into her soft, cozy frame. The warmth from her body and the soft buzz of her snore almost rocked him back to sleep. Dresden found comfort in her caress for a few minutes longer, but he had to go.

Carefully easing out of the bed, he slipped into his slides and circled the bed to stand before her. Dresden couldn't prevent his snicker. Harper was knocked out. Her mouth slightly opened, and her body was lax. *I guess she needed help sleeping too.*

At that moment, he decided not to disturb her slumber. Dresden left a written note on the nightstand, kissed her forehead, and reluctantly left her room.

Harper woke from her sleep in a daze. She peered around the dusky room, expecting to get a visual of the six-foot, peanut butter-brown hunk of a man, but he wasn't there. Her brows furrowed, wondering if it was all a dream or a vicious nightmare since he was gone. Harper recalled reading a book on her tablet and then hearing the knock on her door. She wanted to be ashamed of effortlessly escorting Dresden to her bed, but she wasn't.

*Did we have sex?*

A thunderous gasp escaped her lungs. She shot up in bed to determine if her kitty had been penetrated, but to her dismay, it was still intact. Harper switched on the lamp and continued to sit there pondering about what happened last night.

*Maybe I was dreaming.* It wouldn't have been the first time Dr. Xavier inundated her fantasies. Images of the good doctor wantonly compromising her pussy until she was comatose danced around in her head nightly. She reached for her phone on the nightstand and noticed words scribbled on the hotel-branded notepad.

> *Good morning, Harper,*
> *I didn't want to leave, but I had a breakfast meeting at nine.*
> *You were sound asleep, and I refused to disturb you.*
> *I can't put into words what I needed last night, but you provided it and more.*
> *Thank you, Harper, for being everything I didn't know I needed.*
> *—D*

All Harper could do was smile because, unlike Dresden, she could clearly articulate what she needed, and it was *him*. His towering frame and brawny arms welcomed her, providing the safe and satisfying solace she needed to rest.

A good night's sleep hadn't come since Terrance required round-the-clock care. Nights were spent either worrying or caretaking. Either way, sleep was often an illusion.

Harper squealed through an audible stretch, wishing she could get another hour of slumber. The phone buzzed a few times before she shifted her focus away from the note she'd already read too many times. She stared at it for another minute, desiring to delay the real world for a bit longer. But duty called.

Checking her phone, Harper read the message in the group text from Priscilla.

> Hey, All. Team lunch at noon if you're interested.

Was she interested? Could she engage with Dresden so soon after . . . *So soon after what?* Harper mused. Two lonely people needing a little company, that's all she continued her pondering as she brushed her teeth.

But was that all? The ease of last night felt cozy as if it was their regular routine. Harper needed answers, but lunch was not the time or the place. She texted him to determine if they could find time to chat.

> **Professor Kingsley:** Good morning, Dr. Xavier. I hope your breakfast meeting went well. Can we find some time to talk at some point today? Thanks.

Harper halted her morning routine, expecting Dresden to respond immediately. Crickets. No dancing dots, nothing. By the time she was dressed and ready to walk out the door, he still hadn't responded. She went to the elevator and watched her phone the whole ride down to the lobby. Deliberating, she considered playing hooky from the team lunch.

"Harp, you headed to the restaurant?" Dr. Charles said, stepping off the elevator.

Clearly, her deliberating had been in vain. She nodded, a wry smile curving the corners of her mouth.

Dresden was already seated at the table when Harper and Dr. Charles arrived. He lifted his onyx orbs from his phone and offered her a slight head nod. She smirked sarcastically, trying not to roll her eyes. Quickly observing the seating options, she selected the chair at the end of the long table, farthest from *him*.

The team lunch had been in a word . . . awkward. They sat on opposite ends of the table, and their eyes capered in a game of hide . . . There was no seek because they both avoided each other's gaze. If Dresden looked to the right, Harper peered left. The only time they engaged directly was when absolutely necessary. The team seemed none the wiser regarding the change in their dynamics. But Harper and Dresden were very cognizant that the pendulum swung from work friends to something very different, yet undefined, overnight.

Harper arrived at the New Orleans airport several hours before her flight departed. Mentally, she'd mapped out what she needed to do once she landed in St. Louis, then suddenly remembered that Hasan was supposed to pick her up. She had not heard from her son since he dropped her off four days ago. She shook her head, preparing for the bullshit that often accompanied him. Although Hasan lacked any of Terrance's features since they did not share DNA, he absolutely inherited his sometimes dismissive and selfish personality.

> **Ma:** Hey, San. Don't forget that my flight lands at 5:40.
>
> **Ma:** Hello?
>
> **Ma:** Hasan Kingsley, I am boarding my flight. Are you getting my messages?
>
> **Ma:** Trae, have you talked to your brother?
>
> **Trae:** No. I texted him before I left for track camp. What's wrong?
>
> **Ma:** Nothing. I'm fine. He's supposed to pick me up from the airport tonight.
>
> **Trae:** Oh. OK. Text me when you make it home.
>
> **Ma:** OK. Love you.
>
> **Trae:** LU2

Harper shook her head. Trae had always been protective of her, but his territorial nature had multiplied tenfold since Terrance's death. But at that moment, Trae was the least of her worries.

*Where the hell is Hasan?*

"Harper. Is everything OK?" Dresden asked.

He immediately noticed her when he made it to the gate. But he also detected tension, as evidenced by the lines wrinkling her forehead.

Tapping away on her phone, she startled, flickering wide eyes in his direction. She was unsure if they were on the same return flight and didn't bother to ask. After lunch, Harper grabbed her luggage and dashed off to the airport quickly, trying to avoid him.

"Um, yes. Thank you. I'm trying to get in touch with my son. He's picking me up from the airport," she said, concentrating on the unanswered text messages on her phone—anything to avert his stare.

"I can take you home, Harper."

She could feel Dresden coming closer as passengers began to line up to board the flight.

"That's not necessary."

"It's no problem. Honestly, it doesn't make sense for him to make the drive from Monroe when I have to go that way," he said, chuckling.

Harper huffed, irritated that he thought this shit was funny. She knew how ridiculous it was to have Hasan pick her up, but at that moment, stubbornness was her primary goal.

"I'm good, Dr. Dresden . . . Xavier," she corrected.

He smiled, loving every time she called him Dr. Dresden instead of Dr. Xavier.

"We are now boarding first-class passengers," the gate agent announced.

"Come on, that's us," he instructed.

Harper rolled her eyes, grudgingly stomping ahead of him. Here he was again, being all sexy, chivalrous, and commanding. Dropping down in her window seat, Harper shot one last text message to Hasan. Waiting a minute for a response and receiving none, she secured the earbuds in her ears and closed her eyes.

"Would you like me to order you something to drink?" he inquired.

She shook her head.

Dresden regarded her demeanor. She was upset. He knew her anger was merited because he had acted like an ass the entire day after a night of bliss. While he could articulately pour out his feelings to his sister, Dresden wanted to navigate the conversation with Harper carefully. This was new for him. Butterflies . . . that *Boom* . . . feelings . . . for a woman that didn't carry the name Nina Rose Kingsley. *I better shut up for now before I fuck this up.*

Harper slept the entire flight while Dresden worked on his laptop. She jerked when the flight attendant announced the descent into St. Louis. She inhaled deeply, blinking her eyes until she became oriented to her surroundings. A bottle of water and a snack pack sat on the table before her. There was no question that it was Dresden's doing. She'd stubbornly declined any refreshments but was thankful for them now.

"Thank you," she muttered.

"No problem."

Checking her phone, Harper audibly sighed. Hasan finally replied to her countless messages, but his response wasn't what she wanted to see.

> **San:** Ma, I am so sorry. My phone died while we were rehearsing, and I completely forgot. I can leave now and be there in several hours.

Harper looked at the time. He had just responded twenty minutes ago. She quickly shot back a message to him.

> **Ma:** Don't worry about it. I'll figure it out.

**San:** Ma, I'm on my way. I'm sorry.

**Ma:** I said don't worry about it. I can get a ride with a co-worker. We'll talk tomorrow.

The whole exchange felt like déjà vu, except Terrance was usually on the other end of the apology message.

Harper and Dresden deplaned together but walked in silence. When she stopped at the restroom, he waited. He waited for her when she had to pick up her luggage at baggage claim, although he had not checked a bag. If she decided to wait for her son, he would have delayed his drive until he knew she was safe.

"What's the verdict?" he said, breaking the uncomfortable quietude.

"I don't want to inconvenience you, Dr. Xavier."

Dresden snickered, shaking his head. He'd forgotten about this part of courting a woman . . . them being difficult for no damn reason.

"Let's go," he instructed, retrieving the luggage from her hand.

Harper followed him into the parking garage and down the aisle until he stopped at a white Range Rover. Dresden opened the passenger-side door and motioned for her to get in. He loaded the luggage in the trunk, then rounded the truck to slide into the driver's seat.

"Are you hungry or anything before we get on the road?"

"You're one of those guys, huh? Refusing to stop during a road trip unless the woman is threatening to pee all over this beautiful supple leather," she quipped. '

As much as he wanted to, Dresden couldn't suppress his laugh. *This damn woman.* While there were countless differences between Harper and Nina, their witty sense of humor was identical.

"Pretty much. Especially for a less-than-two-hour drive. So you better drop the bat signal if you need to stop. Otherwise, I'm rolling until we get to our destination."

Harper pinched her lips, struggling not to laugh. Dresden pulled out of the garage and onto the highway headed to Monroe City. Shuffling through Sirius XM channels, he stopped at the Rock the Bells Radio channel.

Dresden and Harper nodded their heads, mouthing the lyrics to a few songs until Notorious BIG blasted through the speakers, rapping about how it was all a dream. Their previous rap battle in his office resumed. Harper matched him word for word as they both did a horrible job suppressing their blush.

The tempo and mood in the truck shifted when LL Cool J voiced that he needed love.

"Dresden . . . I am the type of woman who thrives on communication. When I am left to my devices in silence, my vivid imagination reigns supreme, and I begin to believe the stories in my head," Harper blurted. "So, with that said . . . about last night—"

"Harper," he interrupted, his eyes fixed on the highway.

"I am the type of man who is an analytical thinker about everything. I calculate a million scenarios before landing on a decision. I'm a practical processor who needs time. It takes me a minute to formulate my words to express my thoughts," he retorted.

"What are you saying, Dresden?"

"I'm saying I need a minute before I can discuss what happened last night."

Harper involuntarily nodded, staying quiet for a second because she had to *practically process* how *not* to curse him out. Her forehead scrunched as she fixated on the passing pastures from the window.

"So, when you say, 'a minute,' do you mean a literal minute or like a Black person's minute?" she asked.

Dresden now wore a wrinkled face. "I'm not sure if I know what you mean," he chuckled.

"You know how Black people say, '*I'll call you back in a minute*,' but they call you back like two days later. Or do you mean a minute as in sixty seconds?"

Dresden stammered, actually contemplating her differentiation.

"More like a Black person's minute," he said, trying to hold in his laughter because he'd never heard time explained quite that way.

She nodded.

An hour later, Dresden pulled into her driveway. Harper disarmed her house and opened the garage using the app on her phone. He crawled out of the truck to retrieve her luggage from the trunk. She slithered out and waited for him to get her bag. They were exhausted, and it showed in their temperament . . . muted, dry, and maybe even a little aggravated.

Harper reached for her luggage, and he jerked away, preventing her from reaching it. Then Dresden walked toward the garage as if he'd been there before. Unlocking the door to enter her home, Harper turned around and grabbed her bag, placing it in the mudroom.

He towered over her even though she stood on the step leading into her house. His eyes brushed through a flutter of lashes as big, beautiful, bemused eyes gazed at him. Dresden could not resist swiping that loose curl behind her ear that was dangling in her face. He bit his lip to prevent kissing her. Erratic emotions short-circuited in his brain, creating a clash of mournfulness and magnificence, blues and bliss.

Dresden was losing his mind. With every stride forward, his heart, the place where Nina lived, was screaming for him to retreat, while his head, the place Harper was steadily residing, instructed him to advance . . . move on. Harper remained motionless while Dresden took another step forward, minimizing the space between them. One sniffle, a simple clearing of the throat, would thrust their lips into a carnal collision.

"Dresden." Harper quivered in a whisper.

He rested his lips on her temple for what seemed like an eternity. Coupling their foreheads, he whimpered, "Good night, Harper."

Dresden was thankful for the weekend. It allowed him to think through the processing he had told Harper about. His brain was like a twisted ball of yarn tossed around by a cat. He needed this time to unravel the threads holding him back.

The house was quiet as he perched in the egg-shaped swing chair on the back patio. He hated these chairs when he first looked at the house, wondering why someone would bolt two egg-shaped chairs from the ceiling of their patio. Now that he'd been in the house for a few months, it was his favorite place to *process*.

Dresden stared at his phone, hesitant about making a much-needed phone call. He'd contemplated over several glasses of Macallan for hours. *Get it over with, Dres*, he thought, hearing Nina's voice as if she were swinging in the chair beside him.

He stood up from the chair and walked to lean against the patio railing. His backyard was large, almost too big for him to maintain. Rabbits scurried through the grass as the sun moved over to make space for the moon. Dresden gazed at the yellow rose garden he planted in honor of his Rosie while the video call rang.

"Well, hello, stranger," Patricia Hanover, his mother-in-law, rang.

"Hey, Miss Pat. It's definitely been too long. My apologies."

"No worries at all, son. How are you doing? How are Marcella and Dresden Senior?" she asked.

"I'm good. My parents are great. You know them, living their best lives," Dresden chuckled.

"How are you?" he asked.

"Hanging in there. Still working at the church. Just trying to keep busy," Miss Pat uttered.

Dresden gazed at her because she was exactly how he imagined Nina would be at seventy. Short salt-and-pepper hair, bright hazel eyes, smooth milky skin, and a smile that brightened any dreary day.

Patricia Hanover had experienced a world of loss over the past ten years. First her husband of forty years and then her youngest daughter. But through all of her sorrow, she always had a positive disposition, citing that *God provides*.

"That's good. Have you talked to the girls lately?"

She nodded. "I talked to them a few days ago. Bella showed me some updates she made to her dorm room. That girl gets more and more like Nina every time I see her."

Dresden nodded. "They were more twins than Bryn and Bella," he laughed.

An easy silence wafted through the air on both sides of the call. Without saying it, both Miss Pat and Dresden were reminiscing about Nina.

She eyed him searchingly. There was a reason for this call. "What's her name?" Miss Pat asked, a sweet softness dripping from her tone.

"Huh? Whose name?"

"The woman who has caught your eye," Ms. Pat said, as a pained smile laced her face.

Dresden's mouth fell agape, and his eyes bloomed, then pinched to mere slits.

"How . . . Why would you say that?"

"My Nina told me that whenever you call with a pained and confused expression, you are calling for permission," she uttered, smiling at her disclosure.

"Permission for what?" Dresden croaked, clearing the swell of emotions from his throat.

"To love again. So, I'll ask you again . . . What's her name?" she queried with that glimmering beam that matched her daughter's.

A whiff of air capered across the roses just as Dresden thumbed away a lone tear.

"Harper."

# Chapter twenty-three

Dresden clearly required more than a *Black people minute* because he had not uttered a word about what happened in New Orleans. They'd been back for about a week, and Harper assumed he was still *processing*. She, on the other hand, was done pondering. It was apparent that she misunderstood . . . *everything*. The playful eye contact, the flirtatious bite of the lips, and the snug cuddling all night long must have been a figment of her imagination.

Since the new semester started, Harper split her time between the medical center and campus. Spending only two days at the clinic, she would often miss Dresden in the office. Honestly, she tried to make every concession to avoid him if possible.

Harper worked late to get a head start on the latest data Priscilla uploaded onto the portal earlier that morning. She could have reviewed the information at home, but Harper preferred the visibility of the large interactive touch screen mounted in the staff office. Line after line of quantitative and qualitative details had her seeing double, a clear sign that it was time for her to go home.

Once again, she'd averted Dresden for the third day in a row. The last time she had a visual of him was earlier in the week when he called a staff meeting. Harper hated that he looked so damn good in the most basic gear. The man literally wore black slacks with a gray dress shirt and looked good enough to devour. After the meeting, Harper channeled her inner Sha'Carri Richardson and bolted out of the office.

Harper stretched, yawning as she carefully rubbed her eyes to avoid disturbing her lashes. Glancing at the clock on the wall, she shook her head, realizing it was almost seven o'clock at night. She packed up her laptop, shut off the lights, and headed toward the garage exit.

*Dresden.* Harper smelled him before she could see him. He rounded the corner, the scent of summer rain and seduction wafting in the air.

"Harper. Hey," he said, surprised to see her there.

*Hey? Is* all *he has to say is, "Hey?"* Harper pondered irritably. She narrowed her eyes, wishing she could walk through a wall right now.

"Dr. Xavier. Hello. I was the last person in the office, so you'll have to reboot everything," she instructed. "Excuse me." Harper attempted to walk around him, but his stately frame was like a brick wall.

Dresden tenderly gripped her arm, ceasing her motion.

"Harper, can we talk?" Dresden's baritone was heavy.

She shook her head. "No, Dresden. There's nothing to talk about. I need to go." She slipped by him, speed walking to her car.

Dresden ogled her, not immediately recognizing that he was moving in her direction. His long strides had him on her heels. Harper clicked the button to unlock her car, but she spun around instead of opening the door. Anger, hurt, and embarrassment lived in the faint lines creasing her face. He was so close that they battled for space to exhale.

"Dresden, don't. You don't need to say anything. I misinterpreted what we shared. That's on me. It will not impact our working relationship—"

He snatched the words from her lips, kissing her with a fervor that rendered her speechless. Their mouths crashed together in a kiss that was both fierce and tender. Every motion was a desperate dance of passion and longing.

Harper moaned from the delicious tongue-lashing. She inhaled deeply and unclenched her thighs because a fainting spell was upon her. The deep, all-consuming kiss began to wane as Dresden pecked her softly. Raw emotions stained his handsome face.

"One thing Nina taught me is women don't tolerate bullshit. So, I don't want to bullshit you, Harper," Dresden whispered against her lips.

Harper choked on a breath, anticipating a *it's-me-not-you* type of conversation. Or *I'll never want anyone like I loved my wife.* She released an exasperated breath, praying that the tears stayed hidden behind the lids of her misty eyes.

"Harper, look at me. I'm right here. Please, look at me."

Lazily opening her eyes, Harper surveyed him tentatively.

"I want you. I have wanted you more than I've desired anything in a long time, and it's scaring the shit out of me," Dresden admitted.

Coupling his head to hers, he sighed. "I crave you, Harper Kingsley. I haven't slept in three years, and I rested for the first time with you."

"Dresden," she whispered, cupping the curve of his face.

Their lips hovered, fighting for the moment to get reacquainted. Harper pouted her lips, shrugging innocently before resting her head against his chest. Dresden towered over her, burrowing his chin into her springy curls. He trailed a hand from her back, then up the slope of her neck, nestling his fingers in her hair.

Kissing her temple, he whispered, "Say something."

He felt her shift side to side against his chest.

"Please," he mumbled.

Harper lifted her head, gazing directly into those onyx eyes that cast spells daily. "I feel safe and seen with you, Dr. Dresden Xavier, and it scares the shit out of me," she admitted, chuckling nervously.

Dresden seized her, capturing her quivering frame in his arms. He'd spent enough time listening to Terrance's tales about his and Harper's relationship, so it was no secret that she'd been overlooked in her marriage. While he had no clue what was next for them, he knew he had to navigate his steps carefully with her.

"I only know how to do this one way, Harper, because I've only done this once," he whimpered, whispering in her ear.

"What is *this*?" she questioned.

"*Love*. I only know one way to love."

Their eyes dotingly danced, quietly narrating their unvoiced yearnings. Dresden couldn't close his eyes because he wanted to see her when he coupled his lips to hers.

Soft, dainty, impassioned kisses sprinkled with a hint of eagerness. Connected, their lips were a powerful surge of electricity, leaving them dizzy. Heatwaves shot to Harper's center the moment his steeliness pressed against her stomach. One thing was for sure: they both wanted this . . . bad.

Harper panted, her breaths dripped with need. She pushed him away, endeavoring to stop the carnal chaos lingering between them.

"Dr. Dresden, please step away before I fuck you in my car," Harper begged.

Dresden expelled a lively chuckle. His bass-filled tone echoed throughout the garage. It wasn't until that moment that they realized they were out in the open. In public and unapologetic.

"I'm sorry. I'm sorry," he whispered, his lips still bonded to hers.

"Maybe we can get away this weekend? Only if you—"

"Yes," she piped, interjecting before he could retract the offer.

"It's a date," he said, smiling as he kissed her again.

Dresden tucked Harper safely away in her car. As she pulled off, he swiped two fingers down his lips, tasting the remnants of her on his tongue. He glanced down and saw his manliness was on full display for the world to see, and *she* was the culprit.

"Damn. Harper *mutherfucking* Kingsley."

# Chapter twenty-four

Five inches of snow fell overnight, creating the perfect winter wonderland in Monroe City. Snow-covered branches bowed at the weight of the crystal icicles while a bevy of deer pranced in the patches of now-milky-white grass. The city was no stranger to an occasional winter blitz, clearing the roadways at a record pace just in time for the Friday morning commuters.

Dresden and Harper were a little disheartened once they saw the snow plummeting heavily the day before. If the city accumulated just a few more inches, their weekend getaway would have been ruined. Thankfully, aside from a few flurries, the forecast was clear for the next few days.

They both navigated the frigid chill on a Friday afternoon to complete some errands before Dresden was scheduled to arrive at her house. Harper Facetimed Joya the night before to get a second opinion on some of the nighttime attire she selected. This was a newfound adventure for her since she hadn't had an actual date in years, let alone a weekend getaway.

"Do I go straight hoeish or ease into my ho wardrobe," Harper teased.

"Be easy, sis. It's been a minute for both of y'all. You may combust before he even gets started good," Joya bantered, but she wasn't wrong.

The thump pulsating through Harper's yoni had her wondering what things went bump in the night. *Heffa, your pussy.* She ached for him to grant her access to what she believed were countless inches of girth and goodness.

"Do you have everything?" Joya asked.

Harper nodded.

"Sexy lingerie?" Joya inquired.

"Check."

"Granny panties and a housedress . . . just in case he *ain't* working with a monster?" she continued.

"Check," Harper giggled.

"Condoms?"

"Check, check. Standard and Magnum," Harper countered.

"Lubrication?"

"Check. Liquibeads and a bottle," she confirmed.

"Liquibeads? What's that?" Joya's brow furrowed.

"My gynecologist recommended them for occasional dryness. Just pop in a bead, and ta-da, the kitty cat is wet."

"Are you keeping secrets, friend? You know us menopausal girlies gotta stick together. I need all of the pussy-wetting tricks."

Harper hollered but there was silence on the other end.

"Joy? Did I lose you?" Harper popped back into the camera screen.

"Nope. I was just adding Liquibeads to my Amazon cart. They'll be here tomorrow."

Harper shook her head at her crazy friend as they laughed.

Dresden packed light since he did not believe they would leave the cabin until it was time to return home on Sunday. His errands consisted of the grocery store, barbershop, and a condom run at Maurice's recommendation. After more than twenty years without condoms and more than a year without sex, Dresden needed a coach to make it through this weekend.

Maurice recommended a few bourbons and wines that Harper may enjoy and a menu they could prepare together. A few samples of Bryn's edibles also made their way into his bag. Dresden did not need to be instructed to bear gifts for her this weekend. Giving was just a part of his nature. The service that his parents hired to maintain the cabin notified him that the house had been cleaned and cabinets stocked with other nonperishable items for their convenience.

Dresden and Harper turned into the long driveway of his family's cabin close to six o'clock due to traffic from the storm. The house was in a small town about an hour outside Monroe City called Clearview Lake. It was less than thirty minutes from the beautiful wine country in Brighton Falls, making it the perfect location for a getaway.

The grandeur of the quaint and cozy log cabin nestled in the picturesque hills of the Vista View neighborhood could be seen as soon as they arrived. The reddish-brown exterior adorned with a wraparound porch provided breathtaking views of the now-frozen lake. The oversized crimson entry door led into the gorgeous modern interior, offering three bedrooms, three baths, and a chef's kitchen.

Harper was in awe of the open-concept living area featuring high-vaulted ceilings, rustic wooden beams, and large picture windows that allowed them to enjoy the stunning vistas from every corner of the cabin. There were three fireplaces, one electric, one gas, and one wood burning just in case they lost power. There was even a hot tub on the Four Seasons patio. The house was perfect for what Dresden promised her.

"*A little serenity and relaxation just for me and you,*" he assured her.

"My parents have certainly done some upgrades since the last time I've been here," Dresden uttered, looking around in just as much amazement as Harper.

"Do they come here often?" she asked, opening the blinds to welcome in the natural light.

"In the summers and usually for Thanksgiving. They rent it out mostly, though," he responded, flipping the switch to ignite the gas fireplace.

"This place is beautiful, Dresden. Thank you."

He nodded. "I put your bags in the bedroom at the end of the hall if you want to get comfortable. This thing should heat up pretty fast," he said, pointing to the flames beginning to swell.

"If you're hungry, I can throw something on the grill."

"OK. Give me a few minutes to get changed," she said, blushing.

Harper walked into the massive suite and was struck by yet another beautiful space. Mr. and Mrs. Xavier spared no expense with this place. The king-size bed was dressed in the plushest ivory comforter with a velvet bench positioned at the foot of the bed. The room was like a small studio with the Jacuzzi planted right in front of the floor-to-ceiling window. Her brows perked up, thinking about what they could do in that tub.

Stepping out of the equally magnificent bathroom after washing her face and freshening up the "downtown," Harper noticed that Dresden had only placed her bags in the bedroom. Her face scrunched, wondering if Dresden was that damn chivalrous. Changing into lounge pants and a coordinating shirt, Harper covered her feet with socks and pulled her hair into a high bun before going into the great room.

The smell of fresh seasonings circulated the room as he dressed the steaks for dinner. Dresden heard her feet pattering against the heated hardwood floor. He peered over his shoulder, flashing a slight smile.

"You good?" he said.

She nodded. "Yes. I may have to take a swim in that Jacuzzi and then run through the multijet shower just for fun," she winked, causing him to chuckle.

"Can I help?" she asked, motioning to the clutter he created on the counter.

"Yes, please. The veggies need to be sliced, and the twice-baked potatoes warmed. I picked them up from Ethos, but that was earlier today."

"Got it."

Dresden shouted for Google to play nineties R&B, and they cooked, danced, and swayed, similar to that night in New Orleans. Delicate touches and tender kisses came instinctively. While Dresden preferred to nibble at the base of her neck, Harper enjoyed the strength of his arms around her waist. The spirited exchange was captivating . . . maybe even a bit liberating. Their friendship had been slowly ascending to ten thousand feet for several months, and now, they'd reached the desired altitude. They were free to move about in a relationship like old familiar friends.

The view from the dining room was spectacular. The snowcapped mountains appeared to be within reach as the sun began to set, permitting the moon and stars to have a chance to shine. They ate in comfortable silence as the once-pristine view became pitch-black dark. The sounds of the wilderness filled the hush. Dresden snickered as Harper's eyes widened in response to what she thought was a wolf.

"Was that what I think it was?" she asked.

"If you're thinking it's a wolf, then yes. There is some of everything up here," he said casually. "We're good, though," he assured her.

Harper slanted her head skeptically. "I trust you, Dr. Dresden," she uttered.

"Do you do that on purpose, or is it just a slip of the tongue?" he interrogated her, his eyes sexily pierced, awaiting a response.

"A slip at first, but now, I kinda like it," she muttered, licking her lips before she took a sip of wine.

He eyed her for a long minute, then stood to clear their plates. She followed behind him with the water glasses and salad bowls.

"You ready for dessert and champagne on the patio?"

She nodded.

"I need to ask my dad when they installed the Jacuzzi. It wasn't here when my sister and I were growing up."

"Your parents are retired and living their best lives. I love it."

"If I would've known, we could have brought suits."

"Maybe we don't need them," Harper blurted, allowing a coy yet lustful smirk to grace her face.

Dresden flicked his gaze over to her. He'd wondered what was underneath the black, silky lounge pants all night.

"Maybe you're right," he returned with a wink.

Standing from the couch, he walked over to the thermostat, adjusting the heat before he activated the Jacuzzi. Harper watched him, and to her surprise, he peeled off his hoodie and T-shirt, unwrapping dark chocolate abs created by the hands of God Himself. Or maybe God was a woman because only a woman would grant her the blessing of this fudge-colored man.

Dresden stepped out of his sweatpants, and the black boxer briefs hugged him like skin. They hung low on his waist, forcing her eyes to follow the trail of fine hairs leading to his weightiness.

The tent pitching in his boxers confirmed it . . . He was working with a monster.

Harper quietly practiced her Kegel exercises because she needed every pelvic floor muscle to withstand that anaconda. He gazed at her with a suggestive smile before he crooked his finger, demanding her presence. She obliged. Rising from the couch, she slowly walked toward him, never disconnecting her gaze from his gorgeous body.

While Dresden gave her a bit of a striptease, he decided that he preferred to rid her of her clothing himself. Kissing her temple, he unlatched each button on her shirt individually. Happily undressing her, he revealed caramel-dipped areolas pressing against the sheer black bra. He trailed kisses from her nose to her lips and down the arc of her neck before landing between her breasts. Dresden inhaled, and she carried an alluring fragrance of sugar and spice. The delectable mix of caramel sweetness and peppery warmth made him drool. He grazed his mouth over her nipple, desperate for the saccharine good.

Fingering the elastic waistband on her pants, he eased them over her ass and down her thighs. The matching panties made him smile. Beautiful curves delighted his eyes. Harper was curvy with just enough breasts to devour and enough ass to palm. Undeniably sexy, he wanted to smell more of her—shit—taste all of her, but he was sure that if he got a whiff of her sugary center, they would never make it into the Jacuzzi.

She stepped over the pants pooling at her feet before grabbing the champagne bottle from the table. Dresden clutched her hand in his, ushering her into the bubbling, steamy water.

"Mmm," she hummed, enjoying the force of the jets against her back.

Harper perched on one side while Dresden settled on the other. They stared, sharing a hushed dialogue of *Do we or don't we? Who should make the next move?*

Harper recalled his lips grazing her nipples, and she wanted more. *Fuck it*, she mused.

Floating through the water, she faced him, wrapping her arms around his neck, daring him to kiss her. Dresden slid a finger down the curve of her face, against her neck and heated goose bump-covered chest. Harper's breathing was shallow but controlled. She wanted him. The melodic rise and fall of his chest was hypnotizing, indicating that he craved her too.

Gliding her tongue against the seam of his lips, she slipped into his mouth, circling at a slow, dallying pace. Desperation and urgency lingered in their loins, but the kiss was unhurried and deliberate. They moaned as harmonious bliss reverberated throughout the space.

Dresden nipped her lips as their tongues collided in the most passionate exchange. He fisted handfuls of the curls he adored, dismantling the loose bun, allowing the tendrils to halo around her face. Tugging gently, he drew her nearer until her legs locked around his waist.

Harper was exquisite, and he wanted all of her. She grinded against his weighty member, the delicate fabric of their garments creating a temporary barrier for what was inevitable. There would be no ceasefire now.

"Harper, baby, slow down," he chuckled. "It's been a long time for me, and I don't want it to end before it gets started," he panted, capturing her face in the U of his hand.

"I think I can take care of that."

Harper did not wait for a reaction. She snaked her hand down into his boxers and proceeded with a slow, languid stroke. The head of his girth rested idly in the palm of her hand. Sluggish oscillations from the tip to the base and back up again were about to make Dresden combust with need.

"Shit, Harper," he groaned, tossing his head back to rest against the railing of the Jacuzzi.

The experience was intimate and intentional. Harper's hand wrapped around Dresden's dick created a seamless flow. Every stroke, twist and turn were executed with effortless precision. The heated, soothing currents of the water pulsed against his skin in a steady cadence.

Dresden's expressions became more intense as his erection grew thick with anticipation.

"Ahh. Ahh," he hissed.

Harper did not leave him stranded, stroking the length of his pole while fondling his family jewels simultaneously. Tension creased his brow as the pace quickened, pulling him to the edge. Relentless, she directed him through a mind-blowing orgasm.

"Harper. Harper, fuck," Dresden groaned through a heart-stopping climax.

Swallowing hard, he fought to catch his breath. He slightly felt like a punk after his one-minute-man performance, but he was optimistic that he would rebound quickly.

Kissing and licking behind her ear, he whispered, "Can I take you to bed?"

Harper nodded.

Dresden exited the Jacuzzi first and grabbed a towel for both of them. She quickly followed once the cool air hit her body. Wrapping her in the cloth, he scooped her up as if she were weightless. They trekked water through the house but didn't care.

Entering the bedroom suite, Dresden kissed her until they were both delirious. He removed her bra and then slid down the length of her body to remove her panties. They were soaked for more reasons than the Jacuzzi.

Sprinkling kisses up her inner thighs, he reached her hidden treasure and deeply inhaled. He kissed against the smooth, bare skin, peeling back her folds to swipe his tongue against her clit. Harper's knees almost buckled. Dresden glided up her body, soaring over her shorter frame. Gazing down at her, he noticed a slight shiver.

"Are you nervous?"

She nodded. "Yes," Harper murmured.

"Me too," he admitted, chuckling.

Dresden kissed the tip of her nose, then gently swiped against her brow as if the action would quell her anxiety. It did. Grounded by the warmth of his touch, a wave of calm brushed over her the moment his fingers intertwined with hers.

"Like I told you the other day, I only know one way to do this, beautiful," he whispered.

"What does that mean?" she probed, not making any assumptions about his intentions.

"I want to learn you, Harper. And you learn me. I want to know every door to unlock to unleash a heightened experience that neither of us will forget. Where you go, I will follow."

Harper's eyes widened, then narrowed to slits as she erratically panted. She was almost at the pinnacle, and this man had not done a thing other than penetrate her mind. *Mind-fuckery*.

"Can I take my time with you, gorgeous?" Dresden requested.

She wanted to scream, "*Boy, shut up and lick my pussy*," but she acquiesced, answering, "Yes. Please."

Dresden laid a towel on the mattress, then settled Harper on the bed. He hovered over her, still wearing his damp boxers, while he dried every inch of her shapely physique. Paying special attention to the absolute perfection between her thighs, Dresden dallied at her clit, parting the seam of her delicacy with two fingers.

Tight could not describe Harper's insides. Her walls were a narrow alleyway closing in on his long fingers. There was just enough room to slowly slip in and out and in and out. A low, guttural moan escaped her lips as she battled through every ardently agonizing swipe. Gooey, warm juices saturated his fingers as they plunged faster and deeper, deeper and faster, with every glide.

"Oh my Jesus. Ahh . . ." Harper moaned, her back arching off the bed.

Dresden continued his merciless pursuit. With every shift of his wrist or repositioning of his fingers, he carefully noted any subtle cues of joy or pain, desperate to unlock the secret to pleasing her. Dresden was not bullshitting when he said he wanted to learn everything about her. Her body, mind, and soul were his for the taking.

Leaning down to kiss her nipple with his fingers still lodged inside her essence, Harper released a strident outcry. Dresden smiled, noting the wanton response.

"Aaahh, *sssss*," Harper hissed when he kneaded the tip of her jewel with the palm of his hand.

*Another one*, Dresden thought, calculating every possibility like a skillful surgeon.

"Dresden, I need to feel you inside of me. *Please*," she begged, feeling absolutely zero shame.

"Not yet. Be patient, beautiful," he said, the gruff lacing his voice causing her head to spin.

Harper slightly regretted taking the edge off for this man. She kindled the intense desire glowing in his eyes, and now was certain she would struggle to extinguish the very fire she set aflame.

"Siri, play the Winter Wonderland playlist," Dresden uttered to activate the music.

The familiar tune of Shai singing "If I Ever Fall in Love" resounded lowly throughout the room. Harper opened her eyes briefly to see him staring at her. He studied her face, regarding her unassuming beauty. This man had her all discombobulated. Dresden's gaze was fixed on her while his sturdy hand continued to massage her pussy in gradual, dragging, painfully delicious motions.

"I remember the day you walked into that conference room. Harper, I lost my damn breath. I hadn't felt anything like that in a long time."

"Like what?" she gasped through her words.

"A boom in my chest. Like my heart was slowly being resuscitated, and every day since then, that boom . . . The beating in my chest pounded." He shook his head, never ceasing the circular movements right above her clit.

"Growing louder and louder with every one of your smiles, your laugh, the way your brow pinches tight when you're deep in thought. When those damn auburn curls bounce and sway across the bend of your shoulders. It sounds so cliché, but you had me at hello," Dresden declared, softly kissing her lips.

Harper snapped her eyes shut because a bubble of tears was building, and she did not want to cry.

"Sweetie, look at me."

She vigorously shook her head, sheathing her face with both hands. The deep, guttural inhale did nothing to suppress the waterworks streaming down her face onto the pillow. A commotion was disturbing all of her senses. He already had her mind and body under a trance. Now, he'd taken dominion over her heart.

Harper finally did as she was told and parted puffy eyes to gaze at him. The reddened dewiness gracing his eyes was beautiful.

"I saw your pain, Harper, because it mirrored mine. The same hurt and sadness resided in the depths of our eyes. I wanted to erase any and everything that was troubling you, even though I didn't know the cause or extent of your pain. Maybe I was being selfish," he chuckled.

"How?" she croaked, lazily scraping her nails up and down his back.

"Because I hoped that if I could erase your pain, you could do the same for me. Eliminate all of the noise and confusion rattling in my head," he said, crashing his lids closed as if he were dismissing the clatter he spoke about.

Harper swiped a thumb across his lips to catch the tears he didn't realize tumbled from his eyes. Dampness coated her skin, and she welcomed his tears, wearing them like a badge of honor.

"I can, Dresden. I will," she whined.

Never had she ever experienced intimacy and passion like this before. Just minutes ago, she was so close to her pinnacle, and now, they were engaging in a heartfelt conversation while still carnally connected. Miraculously, her orgasm loomed at the brink of erupting, but only at his command.

His hand continued to navigate her sodden center, whirling his thumb around her swollen bulb. Harper bucked and jerked at the slightest touch. She was so damn sensitive and soaking wet.

Dresden kissed her, allowing their tongues to twist and tangle to the rhythm of their synchronized moans. Returning to his previous cadence, he relentlessly drove one, then two, then *three* fingers in and out of her ocean. Harper fisted the sheets. She was almost there. Then . . .

"Huuhh," she hiccupped breathlessly, reacting to the abrupt vacancy.

Harper widened her eyes, and the sockets practically levitated above her face. They lowered when she saw the serious expression on his face. Dresden was such a clever and calculated man, but he was also a mystery. Positioned directly above her, he scanned her eyes, gazing at her teeth biting those puffy lips.

"I don't want to use a condom," he spouted, whimpering with apprehension. "I swear I'm clean. It's been almost two years," Dresden announced.

"I'm not on birth control," Harper replied.

She honestly wasn't concerned about his STI status, but a love child at forty-two years old with her boss was the last thing she needed in her already complicated life.

"Vasectomy," he groaned.

"Oh, thank God," she exclaimed, ready to concede to his request.

His dick entering her essence unsheathed was everything her dreams were made of. Reaching between them, Harper curled her tiny hand around his wideness and slowly, carefully guided him into her core. They both released a cleansing, long overdue exhale.

"Look at me, baby," Dresden uttered. A sensuous strain coated his voice.

She did. His onyx eyes were beautiful and burdened.

"One way. This is all I know. Slow and steady," he whispered.

Gradually, Dresden inched through every complicated layer until his dick was burrowed to the hilt. He paused, reveling in her wonder while she basked in his glory.

"Shit," they moaned in the same breath.

As he pressed against her, Harper felt it. That thump. The boom in the center of his chest. It was choppy and unsteady, although his strokes were rhythmic and controlled. She kissed his lips. An abundance of soft, sprinkled pecks quickly escalated to a hungry, greedy surrender. But in their ravenous, eager exchange, suddenly, the boom settled in his center, stabilizing under her authority.

# Chapter twenty-five

Early the following day, Harper stirred, and a heated sensation excited her center. She shifted to see Dresden still asleep. Glancing down at her naked frame, the evidence of his need was still dripping from her essence. She chuckled, thinking back over last night. Dresden was insatiable after releasing the initial pressure for him in the Jacuzzi. He fondled, lapped, and thrilled her pussy until they both tapped out. So listless and lethargic, they could not even move to clean up the sensual mess.

*5:32 a.m.*

Harper eased out of bed and quickly crept to the bathroom. She couldn't remember the last time she peed. Flopping onto the toilet, she surveyed her body, noticing a trail of small dark marks on the center of her thighs. She jerked a little, reminiscing about Dresden's mouth all over her kitty.

He positioned his lips right at her glazed, blossoming opening, eye-waring with her pussy, seemingly preparing for a battle. Licking along the plump folds of her private lips, Dresden siphoned, sucked, and tongue-kissed her kitty until she was unconscious.

The sound of his slurps guzzling her sweet nectar was the sweetest lullaby, rocking Harper into a deep sleep right after she frantically bellowed, "Doctor. Xavier. Dresden." Then, finally, she screamed, "Dre," uttering her last words before she said hello to the Sandman.

Harper wet a towel in the sink to wash her face and then attempted to cleanse away the remnants of their lovemaking. Dresden was everywhere: on her legs, breasts, stomach, and even a tiny mark behind her ear. She hopped in the shower, desiring to get clean while also yearning for him to consume her all over again.

Harper traipsed through the dusky house to the kitchen, draped in a white robe. She prepared a cup of tea and grabbed a few bottles of water before returning to the bedroom. Dresden was still dormant, unmoved by her scampering.

Light snow flurries sailed through the early-morning darkness, brightening the stark white snow. Harper perched in the gigantic bay window, extending her legs to lean against the seal. She sipped the hot peppermint tea, peering out the window. Her eyes followed the tracks of a fluffle of bunnies playing in the snow. Harper smiled because she felt as cheerful and carefree as those bunnies. If it weren't deathly cold outside, she would hop, dance, and frolic right alongside them. She didn't completely understand why this felt so easy with Dresden, but she refused to complain.

On the other hand, Dresden seemed to be battling enough for both of them. While Harper did not doubt that he was a willing and forbearing participant in last night's festivities, she saw the burdensome blur occasionally darken his eyes.

*I only know how to do this one way.* She pondered his words. She tried to make sense of his words, permitting them to mingle in her dreams all night until the realization shook her awake.

Nina . . . *His Rosie* . . . She was his one. The only way he knew how to love was to love her. And then he lost her.

Harper cried. Although her bereavement was different from his, she understood the gravity of his loss.

Without ever meeting Nina or experiencing Dresden with her, Harper mourned and longed for that kind of love story.

A faint rumbling in her background jerked her from her reverie. She turned to see Dresden sitting in bed, staring at her. Those eyes. Those beautiful onyx eyes bore into her. Harper became lost in them as they mutedly narrated a story.

"Hey," she said.

"Hey," he croaked. "You okay?" he continued.

She nodded.

Dresden exited the bed in all of his naked glory.

"Can I join you?" he asked, his morning masculinity fully displayed.

Harper blushed, then nodded.

"Please, be my guest," she said, smirking as she motioned for him to come closer.

"Give me a minute."

Dresden disappeared into the bathroom, and Harper could not pull her stare away. He quickly reappeared, draped in the other white robe. Harper lifted up, giving him room to sit behind her. Dresden wrapped his long legs around her body, nuzzling his nose into her neck. They lazed in silence, watching the same colony of bunnies continue their undisturbed, cheerful day.

"Can I ask you a question?" she said, breaking the hush.

"Anything," he responded.

"Last night. You kept repeating that you only know how to do this 'one way.' I still don't understand what that means."

Dresden sighed, cradling her closer to him as he leaned back. Resting the side of his face against hers, he kissed her cheek. Cool mint chilled her skin.

"It's the story of a man who loved a woman immensely, believing that she would be his one and only true love . . . until he suffered a loss so great, he could hardly breathe. Shit, there were moments when he did not want to take another breath. But then one day, a familiar feeling returned. A thud right here," he said, guiding her hand to her chest, covering her heart.

"A spark that set his damn soul on fire. But he played around in his head instead of following the beating of his heart . . . until one day the man realized that it was OK to mourn *and* reach for a new day at the same time."

Dresden kissed her cheek again. "I truly believe that you are my new day, Harper."

Her majestic face was flooded with thunderous tears. She cocked her head back regarding his handsome features. The generosity of his heart had been evident from the first day they met. But Harper saw something unconditional exuding from his soul. She felt it too. Could it be adoration? Maybe love? She wasn't sure, but whatever it was felt damn good.

She deeply exhaled as Dresden brushed away the tears, enclosing her in his endearing embrace. Harper smiled, reciprocating his steadfast, enthusiastic caress. She closed her eyes, lingering in the stillness for a brief moment before she spoke.

"And when great souls die, after a period, peace blooms, slowly and always irregularly. Spaces fill with a kind of soothing electric vibration. Our senses restored, never to be the same, whisper to us . . . They existed. They existed. We can be. Be and be better. For they existed."

"Mmm," he hummed, eyes sealed tight. "Maya Angelou," he uttered.

She nodded. "When Great Trees Fall," she said, offering the poem's title.

"My father would read it to me after my mother died. I was eight. She got really sick one day and seemed to be gone the next. I don't remember much about her other than her love for Maya Angelou."

"It's beautiful. You're beautiful," he declared, hugging her tighter into his frame.

The newly minted pair observed as the snowflakes danced in the glimmer of sunlight. The rest of their morning was spent in complete stillness as they napped. She wrapped in his peace, and he draped in her tranquility.


Harper and Dresden blinked, and it was already Sunday afternoon. The cabin offered an amazing backdrop for the perfect weekend. They barely stepped foot out of the house other than when Harper suggested they play in the snow. She'd spent too much time watching those bunnies have a good time and wanted in on the fun. After about five minutes spent in 11-degree weather, she dashed into the house, leaving Dresden out in the cold . . . *literally*.

They pulled into her driveway around three o'clock that afternoon. To her dismay, her driveway was covered in snow, although Hasan said he and Trae would clear it before she returned. Harper did not disclose her whereabouts because she was not ready to share anything with her boys until there was actually something to share. The weekend was technically Dresden's and her first date, so there *was* nothing to tell.

Harper opened the garage and plowed toward her house through the small hill of snow to escape the cold. Dresden retrieved her bag from the trunk, then schlepped into the garage, stomping the debris from his Timberland boots.

"Where's the shovel?"

"Dresden, don't worry about it. I'll call someone to come."

"You need to go in the morning, right?"

She nodded.

"Shovel . . . Please," he said, softening his tone.

Thirty minutes later, Harper's driveway was clear. She watched him from the living room window, mesmerized by this . . . . this . . . *man.* He knocked on the door in the garage leading into her house before he stepped in.

"Hey," she whispered. "Thanks again."

"No problem."

"You want some coffee or tea to help you warm up?"

He shook his head. "I need to head home."

She nodded. "Oh. Okay."

Dresden advanced toward her, diminishing the gap between them. He pulled her into his body by her waist. She jerked in response to his cold hands.

"Sorry," he chuckled.

Cupping his chin, she warmed his frosted cheeks with her hands. He leaned down and kissed her lips. One peck, then another, then another. Dresden placed his cool hands atop her and draped her arms around his neck. Deepening the kiss, he rested his hands on her ass, caressing and rubbing, dispatching some well-needed heat through his core.

Dresden needed to get the hell out of there before he wouldn't want to leave. He gazed into her mesmerizing honey-brown orbs that were wide, woozy, and exhilarating.

"Good night," he muttered against her mouth.

"Good night."

Reluctantly, Dresden backed away from the kiss. He spun around, headed for the garage, pulling Harper behind him. He sprinkled her face with three kisses to her forehead, behind her ear, and finally, her lips.

"Be careful, Dresden," Harper said, quivering as she stood in the doorway.

He nodded, then opened the door to his truck. "Hey, Harper,"

She perked her brows.

"I like it when you call me Dre," he snickered.

She blushed, gnawing on her inner cheek as a rush of warmth covered her skin. Harper could not recall if she actually audibly verbalized the name *Dre* or if it was in her fantasy. She hoped for the latter, but no such luck. Winking, he sexily licked his lips before dropping into the driver's seat.

Harper happily hopped through her mudroom and into the kitchen like she was a damn rabbit. She had not felt so rested in years. Grabbing her suitcase, she sauntered to her bedroom and immediately changed into a nightgown. She was in for the night.

Just when she climbed into bed, her phone rang.

"Heffa, do you have a spy cam hovering over my house or something?" Harper fussed, seeing Joya's name on her screen.

"You better be lucky I didn't trample down the street like Sophia stomping through that field. She was going to whoop Harpo's ass," Joya ranted.

"Joy, focus. What do you want, friend?" Harper teased, knowing damn well that her friend wanted the entire dissertation, not the CliffsNotes, detailing her weekend.

"Bitch, do not play with me. I'm mad it's cold as shit outside. Otherwise, I would be coming around the corner for this tea. Spill it," she demanded.

"Friend, I'm in trouble," Harper snickered, collapsing onto her bed.

"Did Dr. Feelgood not . . . *feel good*? Aww, or was he itty-bitty? Or even worse . . . gigantic? You know these young bitches out here talking about they want ten or eleven inches. Girl, bye. I want to keep my uterus, please, and thank you."

"Joya! What the hell are you talking about?" Harper quipped, releasing a thunderous question.

"Oh, shit. I'm sorry. You know how I get when I'm excited. OK, friend. What's the problem?"

"He was amazing. Not just the sex . . . which was *spectacular*," Harper stressed.

"But everything. He was patient, kind, and gentle. We talked and laughed and danced," she giggled, recalling when she taught him the line dance to the Tamia song, "Can't Get Enough."

"It sounds like a remarkable weekend. Better than you hoped for. So, why are you in trouble?" Joya probed.

"Because my name is not Nina Xavier. Joy, I believe I'm competing with a ghost."

# Chapter twenty-six

H arper was on campus to join the last day of Black History Month celebration. The quad was packed even with the frosty chill in the air. Food trucks blocked the streets while the band played, and the Black Greek organizations were preparing to host a unity step show later in the day.

Every school hosted different festivities aligned with their school's focus area. The Regina M. Benjamin School of Nursing was honoring Black doctors, nurses, and medical staff from the Monroe University Hospital during a luncheon as their contribution to the campuswide Black History Celebration.

Harper's ass collapsed to her toes when Dr. Hurts provided the list of awardees.

*Dr. Dresden Xavier Jr.*

Her lungs quickly followed when Dr. Hurts asked her to introduce this year's honoree. Dresden and Harper were doing a pretty good job of keeping their budding romance under wraps while at the cancer center. She was only there a few days a week now, so she welcomed the reprieve from holding her breath in his presence during staff meetings or a leisurely chat at the coffee machine.

They did flounder on their unspoken oath of professionalism while in the office a few times. There was one day when Harper wore a black sweater dress with knee-high boots and Dresden could not resist her. He yanked her into the janitor's closet, drawing her dress up to her waist and plowing into her ocean.

There was also the time when she was simply horny and needed a release. Harper scheduled a private appointment on his calendar in exam room nine, the farthest away from the patient therapy room. When he walked in wearing his serious, astute physician's scowl, his face instantly heated at seeing her perched on the exam table.

Now, she would have to introduce this fine-ass, chocolate-ass, powerful-ass man . . . in front of her university colleagues. *Lord. Get it all the way together, Harp.*

Dresden had been traveling for the past week so they had not connected beyond a few text messages and one Facetime call. Her body was aching for him. Between both of their crazy schedules at the clinic, his hospital administrator duties, and her increased responsibilities on campus now that she was seeking tenure, life was undeniably getting in the way of them being able to live a life. They had not really had an opportunity to truly couple since the cabin.

Harper's office phone rang. She pressed the button, and her student worker, Kyra, spoke through the speaker.

"Professor Kingsley, you have a visitor," Kyra's squeaky voice sang.

"Send them back," Harper instructed.

She was in the middle of freshening her makeup before it was time to head to the auditorium for the ceremony and luncheon. Putting away her cosmetics, she heard heavy feet hit the floor approaching her office. *Dresden.* She could identify his scent amid a five-alarm fire.

"*Knock, knock,*" he said, entering her office.

His rich baritone incited the biggest smile to coat her face.

Dresden's imposing frame filled the doorway to her office. She eyed him from his bald head all the way down to his shiny cognac shoes. He wore a deep burgundy-colored suit with a crisp white dress shirt opened at the collar. His beard was freshly tamed, and the tiny diamond earrings sparkled. *Good Lord.*

He stirred up all types of commotion in Harper's middle. Her kitty was going haywire. Dresden closed the door, and the thump that had been pulsating in her yoni all week was loud, deep, and resounding. Harper wouldn't have minded being slung across her desk, but . . . the oath. *You will not fuck that man every time you see him. You will not drop to your knees on every occasion just to feel his heaviness against your tongue. Harper Paloma Kingsley, you will not fall head over heels for Dr. Dresden Xavier.*

Harper feared that it was too damn late. Dresden circled her desk, extending his hands to clutch her. He lifted her from the chair, and she immediately melted into him. He nudged her chin, lifting her head to look at him. Then she tossed her head back between her shoulder blades, endeavoring to see every crook and crevice of his face, and smiled.

Feathering the curves of her face, he snuggled her into a delicate embrace and planted a guiltless kiss on her temple. His nose lightly brushing against her ear, he whispered, "Did you miss me?"

Harper nodded.

They settled in agreeable silence for several moments, intently surveying each other, calculating the possibility of a mutiny. *The hell with the oath*, they mused. Their eyes coupled, then closed in unison before they shared a sweet kiss. The pecks were quick yet passionate.

Chuckling, Harper shook her head, compelling him to stand down. One of them had to be the responsible party in this thing . . . Whatever *it* was.

His deep murmur broke the stillness. "So, I heard you are introducing me when I receive my award today."

"Yes, unfortunately."

"Damn, it's like that?" He laughed.

"No. I mean, yes. I will probably bobble my words and call you Dr. Dre or something. Shit, maybe even DMX."

Dresden hollered. Harper quickly cupped her hand over his mouth to muffle his titter. He kissed her palm before guiding her hands around his neck.

"You'll be fine. Speaking of fine, you look amazing," he said, ogling her in the fitted black dress and red stiletto heels.

"Thank you."

Harper glanced over his shoulder at the clock on the wall.

"You better get going. We probably should not arrive together." She playfully pushed his chest.

"Harper, we work together."

She nodded. "True. I'm doing too much aren't I?"

He nodded. Laughing, Dresden pulled her into a warm comforting connection.

"We're good Harper, OK?"

"OK."

Hey, before we go, I have something to ask you," Dresden said.

Harper pursed her lips, always anticipating the other shoe to drop.

"My birthday is in two weeks, and my daughters talked me into having a celebration. It's just a dinner party with family and a few friends at my house. I would like for you to come."

She knew his birthday was March 13. His forty-fifth. Priscilla had collected money from the team to get him a gift. She also mentioned that the staff was invited to a dinner party at his home. Harper had not submitted a response to Priscilla, but she planned on going and adding Joya as her plus one.

"I was planning on coming. Priscilla shared the invitation with the team."

"I know. But I'm asking you to come as my date. As my lady, Harper," Dresden uttered, fixated on her eyes.

"Does that work for you?" he asked, trying to gauge what her audible sigh meant.

She nodded. "Yes, Dre. That works for me," she said, smiling teasingly.

He snuck in one last kiss before they crossed the threshold into the hallway, resuming their professional personas.

Dresden climbed the steps of his house to find Bryn. He'd needed to talk to her for a week but never could muster up the nerve to have the long, overdue conversation. He really needed to speak with both of his girls, but he knew Bryn would be the hardest nut to crack.

Walking down the hallway, he knocked on the door with a green B hanging from a hook. The door immediately across the hall wore a red B, which was Bella's room.

"Bryn, can I come in?" he asked, knocking on the door.

"Yeah, Dad," she yelled.

She sat with her legs crisscrossed and a laptop rested on her thighs. To his surprise, Bella was sprawled across the foot of her sister's bed.

"Hey, Bell. What are you doing here on a Thursday night?" he said, leaning down to kiss his girls.

Bella stood to hug him, whereas Bryn kissed him back and then extended her fist to bump his.

"I only have one class on Fridays, and it was canceled. Me and Bryn are putting the final touches on the par-tay," she jeered.

"Are you excited about your party, Daddy?" Bryn inquired, focused on her laptop screen.

"You mean the party you both forced me to have?" he scoffed. "Yeah, I am looking forward to it. How much did it cost me?" he chuckled.

"Details, details. Don't worry about that. It's going to be fire," Bella sang.

"So, people still say fire?" Dresden asked sarcastically.

"She does," Bryn joked, and they all laughed.

"I am glad you both are here. I need to talk to you about the party."

"Daddy, we are not canceling. It's on Saturday. Everything is already set," Bella whined.

Dresden shook his head. "No. I don't want to cancel. Like I said, I'm pretty excited about it."

"Uh-oh," Bryn mumbled, taking her stare away from the computer screen for the first time since her dad entered the room.

"Uh-oh," he mocked. "It's nothing bad."

"Let us be the judge of that," Bella teased, but Bryn's face remained stoic.

Dresden pulled the chair from the desk and moved it to the bed. He rolled his eyes as he carefully perched his monstrous frame in the dainty green chair. Bryn and Bella snickered a little, observing how uncomfortable he looked.

"I've invited somebody to the dinner party," Dresden confessed.

"You gave us your list already. We sent the invitation to your high school friends and the people at work," Bryn announced.

He nodded. "Thank you. I know, but this is a *special* friend," he stammered.

Two sets of matching eyes looked at him, one filled with elation, the other burning with exasperation.

The boulder lodged in his throat, anticipating this conversation had started to crumble a little. Dresden was honestly afraid of their reactions, but he needed to get it out in the open. He never lied to his daughters, even through omission, and he was not planning on starting. That wouldn't be fair to them or Harper.

When he spoke to his sister about being judged by others, he was really referring to his girls. Not that they would judge him per se, but they might also question if his love remained for their mother. The answer was a resounding *yes*, but he was ready to make room for someone else.

Bryn, his protector, was Dresden's primary concern. Her jaw was locked tight, and he did not miss the taut lines creasing around her eyes. She wanted to cry, and he was going to comfort her.

"*Special?*" the twins blurted simultaneously, speaking in two distinct intonations.

Dresden nodded. "Yes, special. Harper and I have been—"

"Harper, as in *Professor Harper Kingsley?*" Bella squealed, interrupting him.

He flashed a small, closed-mouth smile. "The one and only," he uttered.

Bryn's eyes reddened, fire blazing behind those beautiful hazel irises. The grin on Bella's face was not helping at all. She was giddy with excitement, recalling when she saw them together the day of the new student orientation. The glint in their eyes was mutual, and now her dad was dating the woman responsible for his *genuine* smile.

"Since working together, she's become a good friend. I was immediately attracted to her, which has now turned into something else," he explained.

"Something else like *what?*" Bryn thundered.

Dresden cocked his head to the side, begging her pardon. Bryn instantly straightened up, but the wrath she was experiencing had not diminished.

"I don't know. *We* don't know. We're taking things one day at a time. The bottom line is that I like her . . . *a lot*. And I've invited her to my birthday celebration as my date. My lady."

"Your lady? As in *girlfriend*?" Bryn angled her head, seeking clarity. He provided none.

"I don't know about this, Daddy," Bryn mumbled through a huff.

"I'm not seeking permission, Bryn. From either of you." Dresden's booming baritone was firm and resolute.

Bryn blinked rapidly; her top lip quivered in an attempt to suppress the tsunami of tears. Dresden knew her anger was less about Harper and more about her mom. He also had to rifle through the baffling emotions so he understood her apprehension.

"I didn't want either of you to be surprised. Harper will be my guest, and I expect you to treat her respectfully. Understood?" He darted his eyes from Bella to Bryn.

She remained hushed.

Dresden stood and sat on the edge of the bed with the twins.

"Bryn. Understood?" he parroted.

She nodded. Dresden kissed each of them on the forehead, then turned to leave the room.

"I'm happy for you, Daddy," Bella said, a misty-eyed smile gracing her face.

He turned, smiling at his baby girl, who was just good for the soul. Bella's spirit was just as pure as her mother's.

Dresden darted his eyes to Bryn and flashed her a faint smile. He winked at her, and she hesitated momentarily but winked back.

*I'll take it*, he thought, understanding that he'd have to give her some time.

# Chapter twenty-seven

The backyard at the Xavier house was transformed into an elegant, intimate extravaganza to celebrate Dresden's forty-fifth birthday. He and Nina planned to go to Johannesburg for the milestone birthday, but life quickly altered those plans. That is the reason Dresden did not put up much of a fight when his girls proposed a party for his birthday.

If nothing else, the last several years taught him to live life while you still can. He'd spent a lot of time wondering about the what-ifs, questioning God's plan, but now, he was finally ready to submit to whatever cards life dealt him.

The twins, their grandmother, and their aunt dashed through the house, spitting instructions to the decorators and caterers. They'd order their dad's favorite dishes from Ethos and even hired a cigar roller since he only indulged on special occasions. A full bar was positioned under the heated tent in the backyard, where long tables were meticulously decorated in black and white with hints of gold.

Draped in beautiful white dresses that Dresden would swear were too short, Bryn and Bella looked gorgeous. The ladies were asked to wear white, and the men would dress in black, coordinating with the color scheme.

Dresden stood in front of the full-length mirror built into his custom closet. Tailored black suit, with a coordinating black dress shirt and bow tie hugged his athletic six-foot frame. He fixed his lapel, that was sprinkled with glints of gold. A gold link bracelet and stud diamond earrings were his only jewelry. He finally tucked away his wedding ring in the box on his dresser next to the space where Nina's picture resided.

"Forty-five. You're looking good, young man," he uttered to himself.

Dresden glanced over at the picture of his Rosie. It was his favorite. They had taken some professional photos one year for their anniversary, and the photographer allowed him to toy with the camera. He caught her in a moment of reflection. What others thought was a blank expression, he knew was her ruminating. Nina had just been diagnosed with cancer and was given some good odds. The picture was his favorite because the camera captured her just as she gazed directly into his eyes.

"You're probably mad, Rosie, but she's pretty cute," he chuckled. "I believe the two of you would have been friends in another lifetime. Not in a sister-wives kind of way, but she's cool. Good people. A witty sense of humor, just like you. I can't say that it's love or anything, but you were right. It feels good to share myself with someone." Dresden spoke effortlessly as if she was standing next to him. He took a deep breath, closing his eyes just for a moment. Nina lived behind those eyes.

*"Finding someone is a part of the healing process, Dres. When you are ready, you'll want companionship and connection. Baby, it will be critical for your survival,"* Nina encouraged him.

Dresden sent a car for Harper, which was scheduled to arrive in less than an hour. She bought three different dresses, unsure of the look she was going for. Since this was an intimate setting with a small group of his family and friends, Harper did not want to be too hoochiefied. However, it was his birthday, and she wanted him to swoon a little, so the matronly look was a no.

After hours of deliberation, she decided on the white, long-sleeved, off-the-shoulder ruched bandage dress that accentuated her curves perfectly. She paired it with nude, studded Louboutins and a matching clutch purse.

Harper visited her favorite stylist and makeup artist earlier in the day. She'd trimmed her hair, allowing it to hang in loose waves. Her face was beat for days, giving her a natural look to complement the stark white dress.

A flock of butterflies flitted inside her stomach as the car arrived in front of his house. Harper texted Dresden to let him know she was on her way. He only lived less than ten minutes from her, so she did not have long to quiet the rumblings in her belly. The driver must have notified him of their arrival because Dresden stood at the top of his steps when they pulled up.

He looked like a Hershey's chocolate bar. No, correction. A *Ghirardelli* chocolate bar. The intense dark with over 70 percent cacao. Harper pursed her lips, slowing her breathing as she quietly meditated. Dresden approached the back door, opening it. He gasped, breathless before she even stepped out of the car.

"Harper. Damn."

That was all he had. She literally had him speechless. Her body in that dress was all the birthday gift he needed. *Swoon. Mission accomplished*, she thought.

"Dresden. Damn," she countered, snickering with a sexy grin curving her nude-painted lips.

He kissed the back of her hand, then nudged her arms to cradle his neck. Kissing behind her ear, they shared an intimate caress.

"Happy birthday," she said, planting one delicate kiss on his lips, then wiping away the faint trace of her lipstick.

"Thank you. You ready?"

"Are *you* ready?" she echoed with a smile.

This was his party. His family. His friends. These people had loved Nina and mourned the loss of his late wife right alongside him and his daughters. Dresden had not dated, let alone introduced a woman to anyone connected to him.

Harper was prepared for the strange looks and questioning whispers. Tonight would either be a beautiful rite of passage or a ghastly recipe for disaster. Walking into his home, she expected it to be filled with partygoers. Instead, it was fairly empty aside from the caterers in the kitchen and a few people seated in a small sitting room.

A man rose from the brown leather couch, standing as tall as Dresden with a matching face. Harper figured it had to be his father. The woman next to him with the gorgeous salt-and-pepper curls wearing a smile that mirrored his had to be his mother.

Dresden rested his hand on the small of her back, ushering her into the room.

"Ma, Dad, Adriana, this is Professor Harper Kingsley," Dresden introduced.

"Harper, this is my mother, Marcella, my father, Dresden Senior, and my sister, Adriana."

"You can call me, Dri," his sister said, waving her hand.

"Nice to meet you, Dri," she said, then turned to his parents. "Nice to meet you as well, Mr. and Mrs. Xavier."

"Please, call me Marcella," his mother said, clasping Harper's hand with a tender shake.

She nodded.

"And you can call me Senior," his dad said, nodding.

The silence was only momentary when Bella and Bryn's voices chimed from the hallway.

"Dad, it's time," one of the twins yelled.

The girls bent the corner and paused midstride when they eyed the woman beside him. Bella was familiar and immediately greeted her.

"Hi, Professor Kingsley. It's nice to see you again."

"You as well, Bella. I hope you're enjoying Monroe University," Harper smiled.

Bella nodded. Meanwhile, Bryn just glared at Harper, scowling. She scanned from her hair to the points of her shoes. Dresden shot Bryn a death stare while, at the same time, his mother cleared her throat and raised brows directed at Bryn.

"It's nice to meet you," Bryn muttered dryly.

Harper smiled and returned her sentiment. *Recipe for disaster*, she sang mutely.

The twins directed the family down the hall toward the backyard. Harper was clueless about what was happening until she heard Bella mention walking a red carpet.

*What the hell?*

Dresden could sense her anxiety. He stole a quick moment alone, and his narrowed eyes ogled her. He'd already complimented her outside, but after journeying his gaze from the crown of wavy hair to the point of the four-inch red bottoms, he had to sing her praises once again.

"You are absolutely stunning." He sexily smiled, and she returned the favor.

Dresden's bold baritone, coupled with the facets of fresh, earthy, and ambery aroma, dispatched a blissful caper through her center.

"The girls want to walk me out and be celebrated," he said, rolling his eyes.

"That's so sweet. You deserve it," she exclaimed, tweaking the tip of his nose as he often did to her. "I'll go find a seat."

"You're at my table, next to me. Go with Dri, and she'll show you the way," he instructed.

Harper nodded.

"I'll see you out there, birthday boy." She winked, then exited through the sliding patio doors leading to the backyard.

The space was gorgeous. Immaculate even. Harper loved the way his girls doted over him. Dresden deserved to be celebrated and applauded as much as he hated it.

When Harper walked with Dresden's sister to a reserved seat, curious eyes landed on her from his family, friends, and especially the folks from the center. Priscilla stared right along with the thousand other eyes fixated on her. Harper connected with Priscilla's widened eyes, and they screamed, "*Bitch, you fucking Dr. Feelgood.*"

Harper tucked her lips, averting her gaze, and that was all Priscilla needed to confirm her suspicions. Priscilla pursed her lips and did a little happy dance in the gold Chiavari chair while lightly tapping her fingertips. Harper snickered, shaking her head.

Adriana announced the Xavier family, reading sweet sentiments written to Dresden by his daughters. He strolled out of the patio and onto the gold carpet, not red, looking like a fine bottle of wine aged to perfection. With his daughters by his side, Dresden nodded his thanks to the small crowd as they clapped and hooted in celebration. Bella and Bryn beamed as they escorted their father to the round table reserved for the immediate family and Dresden's *special guest*.

The dinner and alcoholic beverages provided by Ethos were terrific. The dinner atmosphere was quickly transitioning to a party scene. Dresden introduced Harper to other members of his family and a few more of his friends with whom he'd recently become reacquainted. Surprisingly, Joya's brother-in-law, Matthew, was at the party. He played basketball with Dresden in high school. Monroe City was the smallest city in the world. Everybody was connected in some fashion.

Harper excused herself from the conversation with Dresden and his friends, opting to find some solitude at the empty table where they dined. However, the privacy was short-lived as Dresden's mother sauntered toward the table.

"May I?" she said, pointing to the vacant chair beside Harper.

"Of course."

"Junior tells me that you are kin to Herlon Boyd," she said.

"Yes, ma'am. She's my aunt. My father's sister."

"Herlon is a mess. Me and her cut up at church," Marcella chuckled.

Harper laughed. "That sounds like my auntie."

The chatting took a momentary hiatus as they nodded their heads to the music. Harper blushed when Dresden's searching gaze landed on her. Marcella faintly smiled, witnessing cheerful features brightening her son's face.

Dresden lifted his head, ensuring that Harper was okay. She discreetly nodded. Bryn was on the opposite side of the dance floor, eyeing the flirtatious exchange.

"My Bryn is a feisty one, much like me," Marcella laughed. "It's going to take her some time to adjust. But she really won't have any other choice, will she?"

Harper's beautifully arched brows furrowed. "What do you mean?"

"I have a feeling you're going to be around longer than either of you care to admit," Marcella exclaimed.

"Why do you say that? Dresden and I are very new. Undefined," she declared.

"Chile, longevity don't mean a thing when it comes to matters of the heart. I know my son, and when he wants something, he pursues it fearlessly. Academics, football, medical school, cancer research, Nina, and now you. He's never been the type of man to fool around with a flock of women. They love him now, don't get me wrong," she snickered.

"But he never toyed with women in that way. Dresden is built to be a father and a husband. Unfortunate circumstances halted the ladder. But now that I've met you . . . seen him with you, I believe it's just a temporary pause."

Harper was floored. His mother painted the picture so clearly she could almost see it too. She shook her head, clearing it of the implausible fascination. Mrs. Xavier had excused herself from the table when her husband summoned her to the dance floor.

Finding Dresden's stare on her again, she smiled. They could not take their eyes off each other, afraid that with any delayed blink, they would awake from the dream, and the feeling would be gone. But it wasn't a hallucination. It was genuine, and their feelings were real.

"Bitch, are you fucking Dr. Feelgood?" Priscilla appeared out of nowhere, holding a glass of red wine.

"Priscilla, *really*? Announce it to the world, why don't you?" Harper said, gritting through her teeth.

"I don't need to announce it. You in that dress, and his eyes on your ass all night is announcement enough, honey," she whisper-yelled.

Harper rolled her eyes.

"Now you know we're going to lunch next week, and you *will* tell me *everything*," Priscilla demanded.

"Yeah, yeah, yeah. I have to pee. Move," Harper cackled, playfully pushing her out of the way.

Dresden caught Harper's arm as she walked by him. He was speaking with a few people that he identified as his cousins.

"You okay?" he inquired.

"Dresden, I'm fine. I'm going to the restroom. Enjoy your party," she fussed.

He nodded.

Harper stepped into the house, and for the first time, she noticed how beautiful his home was. Vaulted ceiling and large, open spaces painted in hues of brown, blue, and ivory. While the decor was fairly masculine, you could see some feminine touches.

She wandered down the hallway, searching for the restroom, coming across a painted portrait hanging on the wall. It was beautiful. *She* was beautiful. Damn near angelic. Short ringlets framed her pretty face. The dimpled smile was immediately captivating. Golden, hazel eyes practically leaped from the canvas. The script in the bottom corner read *Nina Rose*.

Other pictures of the Xavier family lined the wall, but there was something about those eyes. They seemed to pierce into Harper as she continued to hunt for the bathroom.

Flushing the toilet, then washing her hands, Harper paused, taking a moment to retreat. She rested her hands on the edge of the countertop, rocking back and forth and back and forth as she looked at her reflection in the mirror. Tears fought to cloud her eyes, but she refused to allow them to topple. *This house is a shrine. A memorial for Nina*, she thought, wondering just how many memoirs of his deceased wife were on display.

"Stop, Harper," she chastised herself.

*I will not compete with a ghost*, she quietly admitted.

After several extended minutes, she walked out of the bathroom, deciding to go in the opposite direction to avoid the tributes to Nina. Elevated voices could be heard coming from the first room that Harper entered when she arrived at the house.

"Bryn, Bella, stop it. What are you arguing about?" Adriana said.

"Bryn is being a bitch, Aunt Dri," Bella cried.

Adriana's eyes bucked. "Bella," she fussed.

"Fu—" Bryn ceased the word that was sure to get her slapped by her aunt *and* grandmother.

"Screw you, Bella. You mad because I am not hopping up that professor's ass like you."

"No, Bryn. I'm mad because you are ruining everything," Bella wailed, crashing to the couch.

"B, what am I ruining? Daddy is not ready for a relationship. He does not need a girlfriend right now," Bryn shouted.

"Then when? Huh, B? When?" Bella inquired.

Bryn shook her head. "I don't know, OK? Maybe never. If she's not Nina Xavier, then *never*," Bryn screamed, weeping as she dropped onto the couch beside her sister.

Bryn laid her head in Bella's lap. Adriana watched with tears streaming down her face. Harper wanted to walk away, but she could not move. Her Louboutins had suddenly filled with cement, rendering her motionless.

"I promised Mommy, Bryn," Bella whispered.

Bryn's head shot up. "Promised her what?"

Bella's beautiful brown eyes which matched their mother's, shifted to avoid her sister's stare. She slightly repositioned on the couch to peer out the window in the sitting room.

"No secrets, no lies, remember?" Bryn said, lifting her pinkie finger, waiting for Bella to link hers.

She shook her head. "No secrets, no lies," Bella echoed.

"I promised Mommy I would do everything possible to bring Daddy back to Monroe. Closer to family. That is why I chose

Monroe University. It was the only way he was going to take the job."

Bryn jabbed her with a puzzled glare but did not say a word.

"Ma said I needed to help him when she was gone. Help him get out and meet new people. He was never going to do that in Maryland. There were too many memories," Bella exclaimed.

"She said I would know he was ready when Daddy stopped with that goofy, fake smile, when he smiled his real smile. The one that he gives us every morning. The one he gave to Mommy. The smile that brightens his eyes, causing that cute wrinkle on his forehead." They chuckled, swiping away each other's tears.

"Daddy smiles with Harper, Bryn. I've seen it with my own eyes. He looks at her like he looked at Mom. Like she manufactured the sun," Bella giggled.

"He's ready, Bryn. And we shouldn't stop that," Bella uttered confidently.

Harper quickly shifted so that she could get the hell out of that house. She spun, running directly into a table and knocking over a candleholder.

*Shit.*

Three sets of curious eyes darted over to the foyer.

"I'm sorry. I got turned around coming from the bathroom," she sorta lied.

The silence was thick, too heavy for Harper to withstand. Just as she was about to walk away, a picture of Dresden with his daughters came into view on the table she just bumped into. That thud in her heart started drumming, beating for him. For what they could be.

Turning back around to face them, she slowly walked into the sitting room where emotions were high. Her eyes focused on Bryn.

"I can't imagine how hard this must be for you, Bryn. Either of you. I lost my mother really young, so I don't have the memories you two have of your mom. But I do remember putting peanut butter in the shoes of the first woman my dad introduced me to after my mother passed," she tittered, recalling the look on *Miss Theresa's* face when she slipped her stinky feet into those ugly shoes.

"I resented my dad when he started dating. I didn't want him to stop loving my mom. I was maybe even afraid that his love for me would change. But I remember when he introduced me to the woman who became my bonus mom and said something I'll never forget. He said, '*Pudge, your mother is with me when I greet each day and every time the sun rises and sets. She's everywhere I go.*'" Harper dapped at the corner of her misty eyes.

Adriana smiled at her, nodding, seemingly gesturing her approval. Bryn and Bella could not stop their tears because those were almost the exact words Dresden would tell them about Nina.

"*Your mom is the sun, the moon, and the stars. She's everywhere we are.*"

Harper returned the smile, nodding as she whirled around to walk away.

"Professor Kingsley," someone called out. Bryn and Bella sounded so much alike that she could not decipher their tones.

Glancing over her shoulder, she saw that it was Bryn who summoned her. She perked her brows.

"Thank you," Bryn croaked.

Harper nodded. "Anytime."

She started her pursuit toward him when Bryn beckoned her again.

"Oh, and Miss Harper. We'll talk about the name *Pudge* later." She laughed. Not too loud or too jovial. Just the right pace for their current status.

Harper perched at the table, watching Dresden say goodbye to the last guest. She sipped champagne with her feet propped in an empty chair. His parents left over an hour ago, and his sister followed shortly after. After the emotional roller-coaster conversation, Bryn and Bella were exhausted, retiring to their rooms.

Dresden loosened his bow tie, allowing it to hang around his neck. He'd lost the suit jacket several hours ago. Carrying his own bottle of champagne, he closed the distance between them, drinking directly from the bottle.

Harper liked this Dresden. He was so relaxed and untroubled. Harper, his sister, and his daughters did not discuss their "moment" with him. He did not need anything to taint his flawless birthday.

"Did you have a good time?" he asked, gazing down at her from his standing position.

"A wonderful time," she uttered, peering up at him.

Dresden set the champagne bottle on the table, then extended his hand toward her. She clasped her hand in his, standing as he pulled her into his body.

"We didn't dance at all tonight."

"Hmm . . . I wonder why," she teased, placing a finger to her chin questioningly.

"Because you were hiding from me."

"Were you trying to find me?" She tucked her lips, shyly blushing.

He nodded.

Dresden rocked from left to right. They did not need any music because the Winter Wonderland playlist would always score their relationship. Every rhythm and blues song strummed in their psyche, directing their leisurely sway.

"I have a present for you," she whispered in his ear but never ceased their motion.

Dresden hummed, hugging her tightly against him. They stayed in that stance for at least another fifteen minutes as Harper sweetly sang in a lazy drawl.

*"Happy birthday to you. Happy birthday to you. Happy birthday, Dr. Dresden. Happy birthday to you."*

Kissing him, she gently caressed the curves of his face. "Do you want to open your present?"

He nodded. "If you insist."

Harper retrieved a small box wrapped in black and gold paper from her clutch purse. Handing him the box, he playfully shook it. She nudged his shoulder, encouraging him to open it. Tearing through the paper, he lifted the top of the box to reveal a black onyx and gold bracelet with a sculpted lion's head positioned in the center.

"Harper . . . It's amazing."

She smiled. "I thought it was fitting for you. Not too dainty but not too flashy either."

"Why the lion's head?" he asked.

"Lions symbolize courage, strength, and nobility, among other things," she said, lowering her head. He cupped her chin, and she did not need any influence to continue speaking.

"That's what I think of when I think of you. And . . ." Her voice waned playfully.

"And what?"

"And you're a beast," she giggled.

Dresden scooped her up into his arms and kissed her with a fervor he had not felt in years. Slowly, passionately, lovingly, that kiss was equally hopeful and hopeless. Harper carried the heaviness of the ghost of Nina in her heart, but she couldn't, wouldn't articulate it to him today. There was no one in the tent but them, and they were lost and disoriented, falling into the abyss of Dresden and Harper-land.

"Stay," he exclaimed, his lips still conjoined to hers.

She shook her head, releasing from his comforting hold. "Your daughters. This is all so new for them. Shit, for us. I want to be respectful of that."

Dresden nodded, but he sensed caution . . . unease in her beautiful eyes.

"What are you *not* saying, Harper?" He interrogated her, knuckling her chin, pressing her to look at him.

"No secrets. No lies," he said, uttering words he used with his daughters.

She shook her head. She hated this feeling of being tormented by the supernatural. "I feel like I'm being inconsiderate and childish if I say this," she mumbled coyly.

"Talk to me," he demanded.

Harper drew in a long, deep breath, gathering the courage to unshackle from the weight of the truth hidden in her heart.

"Your home. It's so beautiful . . . and a shrine. It's a monument . . . *for your Rosie*," her voice waned, spewing nauseating words.

Dresden slowly lowered his eyes. Regret loomed over him. He hadn't even considered Harper's feelings about the countless artifacts representing Nina spread throughout his house. His mind played back to his chat just a few hours ago with the picture prominently positioned on his dresser.

"She's everywhere, Dresden," Harper croaked, despising the jealousy burdening in her tone.

"Our situation is complex. And I am prepared for a demanding, even grueling bout if we decide an *us* is what we want. But I can't . . . I won't compete with a ghost, Dre. Please don't ask me to fight a battle if I have no chance to win."

Dresden nodded, unable to identify a counter because there was none. Before moving to Monroe City, his mother, sister, and therapist had encouraged him to, slowly but surely, eliminate some of the remembrances he reserved of his late wife. Even Nina urged him to relinquish her.

"Dres, I know you. You'll keep the straw I drank from on our first date," she chuckled. "Let that shit go. Pack them away for the twins to decide what they want to keep."

"Not even a picture, Rosie?" Dresden asked.

"OK, just one picture, Dres. A really cute one. Maybe with me and the girls," she suggested.

"I am so sorry. Harper, sweetheart, I didn't think this through when I invited you. The only thing I knew is that I wanted you here."

Harper shook her head. Cupping his face in her hands, she speckled tiny kisses against his lips.

"Stop. No need for apologies. Thank you for listening and understanding, Dresden. I'll move at your pace . . . when you're ready," she uttered.

Dresden released a cleansing breath. He kissed her forehead, nibbled the meaty part of her earlobe, and a delicate peck to her lips.

"Thank you," he whispered. "I hear you and I respect your position. We'll find *our* pace. Hmm," he hummed, seeking her agreement.

She nodded, allowing him to rest his lips against hers. The kiss was slow and tender at first, a gentle reminder of the delicate nature of their relationship. It was like a fragile rose bud, just beginning to bloom. While patience and nurturing would be required for love to take root, the undeniable desire between them grew wild and untamed, like weeds.

Dialogue of this nature should normally dampen a mood, but for Harper and Dresden, it caused a lascivious stir in their libidos. As their lips lingered, a rush of passion deepened the kiss.

Breathless, Harper said. "Um, my house is always an option, though." He adored the sexy smirk that reddened her cheeks.

"And there may be a birthday cake made special for the birthday boy." She winked, and his eyes beamed.

"You planned this?" he inquired quizzically.

She nodded. "I hoped for it," she whimpered, grinning.

Dresden grasped her hand, kissing her palm before trailing kisses down her forearm.

"I'm ready to get the real party started."

# Chapter twenty-eight

Serene mornings filled with profound and meaningless chatter with their limbs lovingly tangled were becoming commonplace for Harper and Dresden. After the night of his birthday, they'd been entwined, utterly ravenous for each other. Oddly enough, sex was not always on the agenda. Conversations, laughter, sweet kisses, and tender embraces were the only orgasmic climax they needed.

Harper still had not stayed at his home, so Dresden found himself packing a bag on most weekends. In the midst of their dialogue day and night, he never asked why. His primary focus was falling into a deep slumber with her by his side, wherever that may be.

He loved waking up to the fragrance of *her*. He tried to define the aroma but quickly realized the honey-glazed scent was just *her*. After a night of exploring Harper's beautiful mind and bodacious frame, falling asleep wrapped in those mocha thighs was the best place on earth.

Awakened by heated sensations sheathing his body, Dresden slowly opened his eyes and smiled. He was caressed by her unyielding grasp and loved every minute of it. With her face nestled into his neck and a bouquet of big curls sprawled against his chest, she swirled gentle strokes up and down his stomach, tickling the fine hairs surrounding his navel. The velvety smooth skin of curvy legs brushing against him had his manhood standing at attention.

"Good morning." His voice was gruff and sexy.

"Good morning," she rasped.

"You need to get up if you're going to make it to brunch with your girls," Harper advised.

As always, Sunday afternoons were reserved for his daughters. They would sometimes attend church with his parents, then explore a new restaurant in midtown. Dresden skipped church this morning but promised the twins he would make it to brunch.

"I know, but this bed *and you* are holding me hostage," Dresden drawled, massaging his fingers through her hair.

"You would know if I was holding you hostage, sir," she bantered.

"Oh really?" he said, his brow piqued with curiosity.

"Mm-hmm," she hummed.

Gliding her tongue down the length of his body, Harper kissed his nipples, circling her tongue in slow, firm strikes.

"Did you know that the tongue is made up of eight different muscles that intertwine with one another to create flexibility?" Dresden said, groaning.

Harper nodded. "Is this a test, Dr. Dresden?" she asked, grinning against his skin as she continued her pursuit.

He shook his head.

"Did you know," she said, sprinkling pecks down his stomach, ". . . that the average human tongue is about four inches long and has thousands of taste buds and performs many important functions?"

Dresden nodded his head, his eyes rolling uncontrollably. Her balmy touch was so tender.

Harper paused, lifting her head to gaze at him. "Dre, look at me," she commanded.

He complied, staring down the length of his body. She was so damn sexy with her sultry eyes concentrated on him. Her mouth lingered right above his fully erect dick.

"My tongue ain't average," she said assuredly, then ushered his manliness into her mouth.

"Oh shit."

Dresden's pants were spasmodic. Harper was causing all kinds of disorder and disarray. She sucked him like a woman possessed. A reckless, unwavering frequency was her preferred pace.

Dresden strained to whimper lowly, but he uncaged a resounding grunt.

"Honey . . ." Dresden growled when the orgasm ripped through his center.

Harper giggled, loving the nickname he coined for her one night over dinner at her aunt's restaurant.

"*Why does she call you 'pudge'?" Dresden asked.*

*Harper rolled her eyes, laughing. "When I was a baby, I was a little chubby. My dad says my mom would tickle my belly and sing, 'my sweet pudge,' and I would burst out in a fit of giggles," Harper chuckled, reminiscing on the few vivid memories of her mother.*

*"Tickling while calling you pudge makes you laugh. Noted," Dresden quipped.*

*"That nickname is reserved for my dad and aunt. No one else calls me that . . . including you, sir," she chuckled, chewing on a piece of her aunt's famous fudge brownie.*

*"I already have a nickname for you,"* Dresden announced, nibbling his lip with a sneaky smile.

Harper tilted her head, curious about his secret moniker for her.

*"You care to share?"*

*"Honey,"* he said expectantly, anticipating her response.

*"You need more honey for the biscuits?"* she asked, referring to the flaky biscuit that accompanied the honey-fried chicken.

Dresden snorted through a laugh. *"No, Harper. That's the name."*

Her brows hiked, delighted but interested in understanding his reason why.

*"Because you are one of the sweetest people I know,"* he uttered, answering her voiceless musing.

*"The dark golden hue of your skin has always reminded me of honey. And your natural aroma . . ."* Dresden paused, drawing in a deep breath, shaking his head.

*"Breathtaking."*

Crooking his finger for her to come closer, Dresden leaned in, swiveling his head left and right as if he were about to reveal top-secret information. Harper's eyes perked in suspense.

*"And the gooeyness between those thick thighs . . . just like honey,"* he winked.

Harper squirmed to extinguish the flame he ignited in her treasure.

"You better get moving. You're going to be late," Harper said, grinning like she should be awarded a prize.

Dresden was immobile, staring blankly at the ceiling.

"OK. I'll hop in the shower in a minute."

She nodded, kissing the tip of his limpness. "I'll be in the kitchen."

Harper put on her robe and leisurely strolled into the kitchen. She may as well have been skipping, she was so bubbly and carefree. Opening the refrigerator, she retrieved eggs, turkey sausage, and vegetables to prepare a crustless quiche. Her favorite specialty coffee brewed while Harper downed a mix of vitamins.

Leaning against the counter, she swayed her nose above the steaming coffee, blowing to cool it a bit before taking a sip. The quiche was in the oven, and the salmon she would cook later was thawing. Harper halted, listening carefully to confirm she heard a noise.

Dresden was in the shower, but the sound was coming from the entry door in the garage. After contemplating for a second, she quickly realized that one of her sons was the culprit on the other side of the door. They both had the garage code, but not a key to the deadbolt ... purposely.

*These kids are going to get enough of dropping by my house unannounced. Don't catch Mama in a compromising position*, she mused.

Harper peeped down the hallway, and the shower was still running. Marching to the door, she mumbled a few choice words that she would direct at whoever was banging on her door.

Aggressively swinging open the door, she whisper-yelled, "What are you doing here?"

Her eyes widened at the sight of Bella standing next to Hasan. Trae's big box of curls spiked above his brother's shorter frame.

*What the hell is this? A family affair?*

"Ma, why is the door locked?" Hasan probed, attempting to step around his mother.

"Professor Kingsley is your mother?" Bella chimed questioningly, her big eyes peering at Harper.

It did not take Bella long to figure out that Harper had not mentioned to her sons that she was dating ... *her dad.*

"San. Trae. What are you doing here with—"

"Bella?!" Dresden's baritone thundered behind her. His brow was pinched so tight that strained lines bubbled on his face.

Harper twisted around, and her hardened gaze instantly softened at seeing Dresden in gray sweatpants and no shirt. *Good Lord.*

"Who the hell is this?" Hasan screeched, slithering past his mother to enter the house.

"Daddy," Bella blurted, her eyes still bulged, darting from her dad to Harper, then over to Hasan.

"Daddy?" Hasan repeated, confused.

Hasan warily eyed Dresden's half-naked frame, then shot fiery eyes to his mom, tightening her robe.

"What the hell is going on?" Hasan shouted.

"First of all, boy, fix your tone." Harper popped his arm. Her shout matched her son's. "The last time I checked, *I* paid the mortgage up in here. So do *not* come into *my* house asking questions," she schooled.

Trae's narrowed glare was trained on Dresden standing behind his mom, but he did not say anything.

"San, Trae, this is Dr. Dresden Xavier," Harper introduced, looking at Dresden like he was the sunrise and sunset.

"Dude from the cancer center?" Trae finally spoke, his pitch questioning.

"I thought he was your boss," Hasan followed.

"He's my friend, Hasan," she whispered, feeling Dresden's imposing yet protective frame approach from behind her.

"Your *boyfriend*?" Trae probed.

"I said what I said, Trae. Dresden and I are friends." Harper ripped a daring stare through her son, begging him to say something else.

"Friends that fuck," Hasan blurted, advancing.

Dresden's head reared back, praying that he wouldn't have to put hands on this young man. He shifted to move in front of

Harper, but her hands whirled toward Hasan's face as fast as Bruce Lee. She slapped him hard.

"Hasan Terrance Kingsley," she uttered. "You will either show me some respect or get out of my house!"

Harper and Hasan had their differences over the years. He was unquestionably the child that tested her patience, but he'd never disrespected her. Her lip quivered as tears welled in her eyes. Harper thought Dresden's birthday dinner would be a recipe for disaster, but the debacle was cooking up right in her kitchen.

"Why don't we all take a breath, calm down, and have a conversation?" Dresden advised. "We've determined how I know your mother, but how do you know my daughter?" he asked, swiveling a firm fatherly finger toward Hasan and Bella.

"Daddy, Hasan is my friend. We met at the festival, and we've been hanging out," Bella answered.

"Why wouldn't you tell me your father is my mama's *friend*?" he said, pursing his lips skeptically.

"I thought your name was Hasan *Love*. If you would've told me it was Kingsley, I could have made the connection," she countered.

"That's just a stage name," Hasan clarified.

The hush that hovered over the room was so robust a bullet couldn't penetrate.

"Can we talk to our mom? Alone, please," Trae mumbled, angst living in his glossed eyes.

Dresden flitted his stare to Harper, and she nodded.

"Bella, I need to grab my things. Wait for me in the car," Dresden demanded, and she wouldn't dare challenge him.

"Can we talk for a second?" he asked, gently clasping Harper's hand and pulling her toward the bedroom.

She nodded, expelling an incensed breath. At this point, she was overwhelmed, exhausted, and starving, but amid the chaos, the damn quiche burned.

"Dre, I'm so sorry—" she tried.

Dresden quickly put one finger to her lips. "Honey, babe, why are you apologizing? Neither of us is doing anything wrong. We are consenting adults navigating a very sensitive situation with our kids."

"They've never seen me with anyone other than Terrance, although we were divorced," Harper announced.

Dresden nodded. "Neither have my girls." He bent to join his forehead to hers. "We knew this wasn't going to be easy, right?"

She nodded, poking her lips into a pout.

"Talk to your sons. Settle their hearts and minds . . . *and yours*, beautiful. Okay?"

She nodded again, puckering her lips to accept his kiss.

"Call me later."

Shortly after the collision at Harper's house, Dresden and Bella entered the restaurant where Bryn was waiting.

"Um, Dad, did you just go running? Why are you dressed like that?" Bryn asked, tilting her head from her seated position so he could kiss her cheek.

Dresden did not have a chance to go home to change clothes. He was dressed in a charcoal gray Polo sweat suit and black patent leather Jordans. The twins were not used to seeing their dad dressed so casually. Harper was bringing out an uninhibited version of Dresden that his family hadn't experienced in a long while.

"No. Do I look OK?" he said, glancing down at his attire before he sat down.

"You look fine, Dad," Bryn confirmed.

"Why are you two together? I thought you were with *li'l drummer boy*," she continued, teasing Bella.

"Who?" Dresden chirped.

He signaled the waitress for a cup of coffee and water as he examined the menu.

"Her boyfriend," Bryn sang.

"He's *not* my boyfriend," Bella said, grunting through gritted teeth.

"So you've met Harper's son too, and nobody told me?" Dresden's narrowed eyes sprinted back and forth between his daughters.

"Harper's son? What are you talking about?" Bryn furrowed, confused by his interrogation.

"Hasan is Professor Kingsley's son." Bella shrugged, looking at her sister, and then shifted her eyes to Dresden. "Daddy, I didn't know. I swear."

"Can someone please explain to me what is going on?" Bryn begged.

Bella, more than Dresden, recapped the events from earlier while Bryn's eyes bucked with her mouth fixed in an *O*.

"Dad, are you and Miss Harper serious? Is she your girlfriend?"

Dresden dove deep into Bryn's pretty hazel eyes, trying to decode her stare. The sorrow and angst she felt the night of his birthday had since drifted away. Today, her eyes divulged something different. Maybe a hint of gladness sprinkled with a bit of hope.

"I think we are too grown for the *girlfriend-boyfriend* label," he chuckled. "But Harper is very special to me. So, yeah, she's my lady," he announced.

"Soo . . . Does she know that, because she called you her 'friend.' And I have a feeling that description is coming directly from *you*, Dr. Xavier," Bella quipped.

Dresden scoffed, lowering his head because his daughter was right. The women in his life were schooling him and giving him hell. Shit, even the woman floating in the afterlife was a spitfire, scolding him in his dreams.

"Daddy, if I know you as well as I think I do, I know your actions speak volumes about your feelings for her. I have no doubt that if you care for Miss Harper, you are catering to her every need. That's just who you are. But . . ." Bryn's voice trailed off, darting her dewy eyes to her sister.

"But sometimes actions absent of words can be contradictory," Bella finished.

"Daddy, you show us how much you love us every day, but when you speak it, it's . . ." Bryn halted again.

"It's intentional," the twins chimed together.

The thud in Dresden's heart was beating out of control. Pride was not enough to describe his feelings. Dresden always praised Nina for raising two amazing daughters, and he wasn't wrong. But in that moment, his chest swelled a bit at the realization that his acts of affection through hugs, kisses, and special yet distinctive bonds taught them how they should be treated.

Dresden thought about Harper. Since the weekend at the cabin, they'd spent countless days and nights together. He treated her like a queen. Flowers, candy, impromptu lunches on the roof . . . No stone was left unturned. But after the conversation with his daughters, Dresden was committed to ensuring that the impact of his actions aligned with the intent of his words.

Harper sat on the mustard-yellow couch across from her sons perched on a matching couch. They stared at her like she was the primary suspect in a murder. She wasn't sure, but she believed they thought their narrow-eyed leers were supposed to scare her.

*In the words of Bernie Mac, I ain't scared of you mutherfuckas*, Harper thought, snickering at her silliness when her boys were so serious.

"What's funny?" Trae asked.

"You. Y'all."

"How?" he continued.

"Uh-uh," Harper shook her head. "No small talk. Let's get to the point."

"You're not ready for a boyfriend, Ma. Dad just died months ago," Hasan declared.

"And as much as I miss your father, he was *not* my husband. Our marriage was over long before he got sick. I'm confused by this reaction from you—both of you."

"Yeah, y'all were divorced, but while Dad was living with us, it seemed like y'all were back together. You took the best care of him, Ma," Trae offered.

Harper shook her head. "Because Terrance was my friend. I loved my friend," she said, wiping away the lone tear. "But we relinquished a marital relationship a long time ago. I've dated other men," she announced.

"Yeah, but not like this," Hasan shouted.

Harper angled her head to the side, darting a vicious glare his way. "We agreed that you would maintain some respect when you're speaking to me. Otherwise, this conversation is over, and you can leave," Harper muttered. Her drawl was so low and emphatic it was eerie.

"I'm sorry," Hasan whispered.

"We just—" he halted, squinting his eyes as his head swiveled from side to side.

"We haven't seen you like this in a long time," Trae said, uttering his brother's unspoken thoughts.

"Like what, baby boy?" she asked, leaning on the arm of the couch.

"Happy," Trae blurted.

Harper's guise did not change. She gazed at her handsome son, who looked just like his father. Tall, thickset, with a gorgeous smile. Even his scowl was striking.

"You don't want me to be happy?" she questioned, bracing a bit for an answer.

Trae nodded, and so did Hasan.

"Of course, Ma. We want the best for you every time," Hasan said.

"We just . . ." Trae's eyes faltered, freeing the tears he tried to hold captive.

Harper rose from her seat, walking over to sit between her sons. "You miss your dad."

Her boys nodded. Lying against her shoulder, they crumbled to pieces. Harper pondered what comforting words she could provide or Bible scripture she could quote, but instead, she silently permitted them to break.

Deafening wails filled the living room. Several hours passed as Harper and her boys lazed in the same position on the couch. Their tears ceased, but they refused to surrender from their mother's heartwarming, tender caress. A hush suspended in the air. Private reminiscences of what they loved and lost lingered between them.

"How lucky we are to have something that makes saying goodbye so hard," Trae whispered. His head rested on Harper's lap. She smiled, allowing his words to resonate.

"Did you *really* just quote Winnie the Pooh, bro?" Hasan said, looking at his brother.

Trae lifted his head, and their matching eyes flitted until they all burst out in laughter.

# Chapter twenty-nine

Harper enjoyed the evening with her sons. At Trae's request, she cooked her famous honey hot wings and homemade french fries. They talked and laughed for hours until the boys fell asleep on the couch. Harper leaned against the wall, staring at them after covering them with blankets. There would be more bumps in the road as they continued to navigate their grief, but after the revelations shared today, Harper was hopeful.

Settling in the lounge chair in her bedroom, she called Dresden. He texted several times throughout the evening to check on her, but she was committed to focusing on Hasan and Trae.

"Hey," he answered the video call after the first ring.

"Hey," she sang.

"You good?"

She nodded. "Are you good?" she returned.

He nodded.

"I want to see you, babe."

"Hasan and Trae are asleep in the living room. We talked, but I don't think right now—"

"Then come here. I'll pick you up."

"Dre, it's late."

"And?" he said expectantly.

"And . . . Isn't Bryn home?" Harper asked.

"Yes. And . . .?" he countered. Dresden shuffled around his bedroom, seemingly putting on a hoodie and shoes.

"Be ready in ten. I'm on my way," he ordered.

Harper was reluctant, but she smiled, nodding her agreement.

Twenty minutes later, they were walking into Dresden's home. Harper swallowed hard, bracing for Nina's piercing eyes to follow her throughout the house. Strolling into the kitchen from the garage, Dresden asked if she wanted a drink. She opted for water and wine. He retrieved a tray from the pantry and placed a wineglass, a bottle of red blend, a glass filled with cognac, and two bottles of water on the tray.

Dresden motioned his head for her to follow him. She had only been in his home once and could not vividly recall the layout, but she remembered every location that Nina's photos occupied. They walked through the great room—no Nina. The picture is the foyer . . . gone. Trekking down the same hallway toward his bedroom . . . nothing.

With her forehead scrunched in disbelief, she stayed silent. They crossed into his bedroom, where she was certain a picture was displayed. The night of his birthday party, the spirit of nosiness ordered her steps toward his bedroom. She peeped into the massive suite decorated with hues of soft gray, white, and navy blue . . . and there were those hazel eyes again. A beautiful portrait of *his Rosie* sat on a tall, mahogany dresser. Her eyes were trained on something unseen. By the devoted, amorous glimmer in her eyes, Nina was gazing at *him*. Harper was positive because she was familiar with the admiring stare. It mirrored her.

"Honey," Dresden said, looking at her like he'd been calling her name.

She stirred from her reverie, flashing him a pseudo smile. Dresden placed the tray on the table in the small sitting area in his bedroom. Extending his hand, he encouraged her to join him on the couch. Dresden lumbered one long leg onto the sofa, making an opening for her to settle into. Harper practically collapsed into him. Her soft backside melted into his firm chest. He kissed her neck, and they both released a purifying breath.

"Today was tough," Harper said, breaking the silent barrier.

He nodded. "Yeah, but necessary," he responded.

She nodded in agreement. "Dresden ... Nina ... the pictures," she stammered.

"Are packed away in a keepsake box for the twins. They picked one family picture to sit on the mantle, but the rest are for them when they have their own homes and families," he pronounced.

"I didn't mean for you to erase her."

Dresden shook his head. "That's impossible. Nina lives on through my girls. Through me. Little by little, I let go of the loss, but never the love I had for her," he uttered confidently.

Dresden tilted her head toward him to look into her eyes. He needed her to understand that while his first love was no longer navigating this earth, she would never stop roaming around in his heart. Harper did not flinch. While she and Terrance did not have the traditional *until death do us part* ending, her love for her friend would never fade.

"I guess they're both a part of our story," Harper whispered.

"Who?" Dresden said, unconsciously rubbing a finger up and down the arc of her face.

"Nina and Terrance," she replied. "Without them, we wouldn't be the man and woman we are today who somehow found each other. Whatever this is, they are knitted in threads of it."

*Whatever this is*, he repeated silently, pondering his daughters' advice. *Tell her, Dad.*

"This," he stressed, "is *us*—a relationship. The start of something I want to see to the end," Dresden declared, nestling his nose into her cheek.

"I believe the same God that took away a love I never fathomed I could live without is the same power that will bless me with another love that I could never visualize, even in my dreams."

Dresden gazed through a flutter of lashes as he kissed the tip of her nose.

"I think I always knew, Dre," Harper stated.

"Knew what, baby?"

"That you were . . ." She paused, recalling how she described him to Joya after their time in New Orleans.

"Everything," she uttered. "Those damn onyx eyes. *Jesus* . . . They had me in a trance," she said, her eyes beaming up at him. "The more we talked about work, everything, and nothing at all, the closer we became as friends. And the more I wanted to be everywhere you were."

Dresden regarded her, looking into glazed eyes that just put her feelings out on the table. Raw and exposed, she was brave enough to take a chance even after a marriage she termed "*lax love*," she still allowed her heart to take the lead.

Dresden contemplated verbally responding but permitted his actions to speak this time. He captured her lips with a delicate and tender kiss, momentarily withdrawing to search her face. Dresden was enamored by this woman. *A fucking wonder*, he thought. Parting her lips with his tongue, he slowly, tenderly, made love to her mouth. Harper slithered her body around until she was straddling him on the couch. He stroked the curves of her face with one hand while fisting handfuls of her curls. They were disoriented, lost in the depths of a sensual kiss.

Countless inches of heaviness pressed against her center. Harper grinded on him, swaying back and forth and forth and back. She wanted to strip them out of their clothes, but the wanton friction felt so damn good. Her strong legs locked around his waist like vise grips.

Instantly, Dresden lifted her from her straddle position to stand in front of him. He nuzzled his face into her belly button. Pudge was her nickname because she was chubby as a child, but now, Harper was thick and curvy in all the right places.

Stripping one piece of clothing at a time, he ogled her naked frame.

"Damn, you're beautiful," he whispered.

Kissing down her stomach, he softly trailed his tongue to her private lips. Dresden inhaled, smelling the scent of honey and succulence, everything he yearned to steep on his tongue. Harper released an audible gasp when he circled his tongue, then kissed, circled his tongue, then kissed, on repeat.

"Ahh," she moaned.

Dresden was like a man possessed. He clutched her ass and ate her pussy like a starving man, and her womanhood was the only sustenance to sustain him. Standing from the couch, he kissed her, permitting her to indulge in her sweet essence. He spun her around, his hard places cuddled her soft ones. Climbing onto her knees on the couch, Harper did not wait to be instructed. She arched her back to lift her ass, welcoming him to come in.

Clutching her waist, Dresden passionately guided his dick into her slick, heated folds. He melted at the hands of her plump, enticing pussy. Closing his eyes, he slithered in and out at a sluggish pace. He required no visibility because every crook, crevice, and curve of her body was tattooed in his brain.

Dresden guided his manhood left, knowing that it would summon a soft moan. Steering to the right was guaranteed to spark a hiss. Extracting his length all the way out to the mushroomed tip, then one pounding thrust, and then again, secured his favorite reaction.

"Doctor. Dresden. Xavier. Dre, Dre." Harper reached a gratifying, thunderous climax.

The following day, Harper awakened in the comforts of Dresden's bed with his steely member arrested between her thighs. He was still asleep after they decided to play hooky from work today. She was sure he would not be idle for long because working was a part of his nature.

Harper slithered from under his grasp, and he did not move a muscle. After showering, she settled on the couch in his room with her laptop on her thighs. Priscilla texted, informing Harper that a new data file was available for her to review. She sipped her bottled water, hoping that Dresden would wake up soon. She was craving coffee and did not want to rummage around his kitchen, especially with his daughter upstairs.

Opening the file, Harper walked through her routine to organize the data into a filtered spreadsheet before starting the analysis. She sorted the document, and a row of data highlighted in red caught her attention. In previous data files, green and yellow were the only colors signifying the stages of a patient's treatments—never any red data sets.

She scrolled across the page to determine the status. The file was marked "*placebo*" in the control group column and "*deceased*" in the status column. Harper was confused yet intrigued. She continued to shuffle through the lines of data but could not understand it. That file was the only record marked deceased. Although the name and other demographics were kept confidential, the trial only included Black men, and their ages were visible in this file.

Harper texted Priscilla to get some clarity.

> **Harper:** Hey. Did you send me the wrong file?
>
> **Priscilla:** I don't think so. Let me check.

While she waited for Priscilla to verify, Harper investigated further. The record was for a forty-five-year-old placebo volunteer.

> **Priscilla:** It's the right one.
>
> **Harper:** There is a file for a placebo volunteer who died.
>
> **Priscilla:** Yes. You'll have to ask Dr. Xavier about that. I rejected the application, but he accepted it at the last minute.

Harper gasped, dropping her phone. She heard movement behind her. The loud clunk of her phone hitting the floor must have roused him awake. He climbed out of bed and walked directly to the bathroom. Harper was thankful for the momentary reprieve. She had to breathe.

*Is this Terrance? Why would he be in the placebo group? If Priscilla rejected the application, there was something wrong with the patient.* Harper deliberated through sane and insane possibilities.

Dresden strolled out of the bathroom wearing nothing but boxer briefs. He bent over the back of the couch to kiss the nape of her neck before circling to sit down. He immediately noticed agitation stressing her face.

"Honey, what's wrong?" he asked, his forehead crumpled with worry.

"Had Terrance's disease advanced when you examined him?" she blurted.

"What?" Dresden was honestly confused by her question. *Where's this shit coming from?* he thought.

Harper turned her laptop around so that he could see the screen.

"Forty-five-years-old. Placebo. Deceased. Is this Terrance?" she demanded.

Dresden swallowed hard, hoping he could find some lubrication for his throat.

"Yes," he croaked.

Harper lost her breath. She abruptly rose from her seat, causing the laptop to topple over. "Why didn't you tell me? You lied. Through omission, you lied."

"When he came to me, he had already been told by his physician that the cancer had metastasized. He knew that he was terminal when he applied. But he begged, *pleaded* with me to accept him. And against my better judgment, I did."

"Why?" Harper screamed.

"For you. I did it for you." Dresden stood to his full height and began pacing the floor.

"Why?" she whimpered, tears streaming down her face.

"Terrance didn't believe that you or his sons were ready. He wanted you to know that he fought right up until the end. He knew he was dying, Harper. He knew he only had a few months to live."

She vigorously shook her head. "You're lying. Terrance wouldn't keep that from me."

"I swear to you . . . *on Nina*, I swear to you that I am telling you the truth."

Harper's body trembled. She could not believe this was happening. She refused to believe that Terrance would withhold information as critical as a terminal diagnosis.

"I can't be here. I have to go," she said, scampering through the room to gather her belongings.

"Harper. Baby, please don't go. Let's talk about this," Dresden begged.

He advanced on her, clutching his arm around her waist, but she jerked, pushing him away. Slinging her bag over her shoulder, she snatched her phone from the couch and the laptop from the floor. Then she stormed toward the bedroom door.

"Harper. Please. Just talk to me. We can figure this out. It doesn't have to change this between us." Dresden's demeanor was crushed and broken. He would have rather lost his medical license than lose her before they really got started.

Harper halted, her hand on the doorknob, prepared to depart. She peered over her shoulder at him. Her face was drenched with tears.

"This changes everything."

# Chapter thirty

Harper found herself pulling into Joya's driveway. She did not want to go home. Hasan and Trae would have too many questions that she was unprepared to answer. Shit, she couldn't answer them because dazed and bemused were her only certainty at the moment.

Joya yanked open the door expectantly. The first person Harper thought to call was her best friend. She was confident that Joya would help her either rationally navigate the situation or help her key his car and trash his office. Either way, Harper knew Joya was down for whatever reason.

"Friend, what happened? Come in. Come in," she said, tightening her robe as she moved aside to allow her to enter the house.

Harper was so distraught she could not speak. Her face was red and puffy, and the tears would not cease. Joya clutched her hand, ushering her into the kitchen. The house was quiet aside from the drip of the coffee machine. Joya knew what her friend needed.

"Are you here alone?" Harper asked.

"Mason is asleep. The kids are off doing their own thing." Joya rolled her eyes. "Now talk," she commanded.

Harper dropped her face into her hands, firmly caressing her temples.

"Dresden knew that Terrance was dying. He knew that the cancer had spread and no treatment would work. He *knew* and did not tell me."

Joya huffed, shaking her head. "I'm sorry, Harper. How did you find out?" She gently stroked Harper's back.

"The case files. Priscilla sent me new data files, and I saw a record for a deceased patient. I put two and two together."

"Have you talked to him?" Joya continued to probe, never ceasing her strokes to help calm down her friend.

Harper nodded. "I was at his house. I stayed there last night after dinner with San and Trae."

Joya's eyes bucked in surprise. She was well aware of Harper's hesitance about being at Dresden's home.

"Whoa ..." She croaked curiously. "You stayed in the *sanctuary of Nina?*"

Harper shot a glare at Joya, nudging her shoulder. "You wrong, Joy," she snickered.

"I'm only saying what you wanted to say, so you wrong too, friend," Joya shot back.

Harped concurred with a weak head nod.

"Dre packed up everything. No visible traces of her except for one family portrait that he and the twins agreed to keep on the mantle."

"Whoa," Joya echoed.

"Why do you keep saying that?" Harper questioned irritably.

"That's a huge move for a man you thought would try to get you to sleep in a room with pictures of his dead wife staring at you.

Dresden got rid of the pictures because he's ready to make room . . . for you, Harper," Joya declared, peering directly into puffy eyes.

The tears had begun to ceasefire, but Joya's declaration riddled shots into her heart. Harper shook her head, sobbing. "It doesn't matter anymore. He's not what I thought he was. He's a liar."

"Friend, what did he lie about really?" Joya probed, holding up a hand to pause Harper's retort. "Yes, he kept some critical information confidential about a patient, but what did he lie about?"

"Joy, *really*? Terrance would not have kept something like that from me. I don't believe he asked Dresden to do something like this."

Both Joya and Harper jumped when Mason cleared his throat, standing under the archway leading into the kitchen.

"Mason, shit. What are you doing?" Joya fussed.

"Good morning, wife," he said to Joya, slapping her butt when he walked by.

"I believe there is something Harper needs to see," Mason muttered, his voice still gritty and sleepy.

Mason stood in front of the Google Home device on the kitchen counter and tapped on the screen for a few seconds before bringing the tablet to the island where Harper was seated. Mason clicked a button, and a video of Terrance was paused on the screen. She gasped.

"Babe, what is this?" Joya asked. Her expression was just as confused as Harper's.

Mason did not speak a word. He hit play and stepped back to lean against the wall. Terrance was in his bedroom, seated in his favorite position by the window.

*"Hey, Harp. If you are looking at this video, then two things are true. One, I've passed on to another dimension. And, two, you have found love, and you're running scared."*

Harper was holding her breath. She had so many questions. *When did he do this? Why did he do this?* But she stayed silent.

"*It's true, Harper. I asked Dr. Xavier to accept me into the trial under any circumstance. That night on the patio, you told me the only thing Trae wanted for graduation was for me to apply for the clinical trial. That was the day my doctor confirmed that the cancer was everywhere, and there was nothing else they could do. I came outside to tell you that night, but when you told me what my baby boy wanted . . .*" Terrance paused, fighting back tears.

"*What else could I do? I had to show the boys . . . and you that I was going to fight until the end, although I already knew the end was near.*" Terrance looked away, preoccupied with something out of the window.

"*Doctor Xavier accepted me because I begged him, guilted him into it. So, don't blame him, Harp. He fought me tooth and nail, but you know how convincing I can be,*" Terrance chuckled.

"*He's a good dude, Harper. I've seen the two of you together . . . moments when neither of you realized anyone was watching. How you laughed at his jokes and fluffed your hair whenever he was around. The enamored spike in your voice when you called him brilliant. The Doc listens to you like somebody's husband is supposed to do. I fumbled on that, Harp, and I'm so fucking sorry.*" Terrance sighed, his eyes finally focused back on the camera.

"*But Dr. Xavier seems like he may be interested in recovering what I dropped the ball on years ago.*"

Mind-blown was an understatement. Harper was discombobulated, stunned to sickness. Drowning in a tsunami of emotions, she clenched her stomach, gasping for air. Mason was about to pause the video, but she slowly shook her head.

"Don't. I'm fine," she whimpered.

"*I read somewhere that death is only tragic if you haven't lived. So, don't cry any more tears for me because I lived. We lived, Harp. Even at the end when cancer infiltrated my body . . . We lived. Laughing so hard at the dumbest things until we cried. Playing spades with the boys and whooping their asses every time. Smoking on the patio with Joy and Mace. I lived." Terrance released an audible breath.*

*"I'm getting tired, so let me wrap this up. I know it's chaotic right now, and you're confused, but you'll find peace and purpose amid the clutter. You always do. It's your superpower," he laughed.*

*"Harper Paloma Kingsley, thank you for loving me without conditions and sacrificing the last year of your life to care for me. You are my best friend, and I will love you in this life and the next. Go live, Harp. Go love. You deserve it. Kiss the boys for me, OK? Until we meet again." Terrance tossed up a two-finger salute, and the video ended.*

Hush and heartbreak loomed like a murky cloud primed to downpour over everything. Mason and Joya looked back and forth between each other and then over to Harper.

"When did he do this?" Harper's voice resonated with nothing but affliction.

"A couple of weeks before he died. He asked me to do him a favor and keep it until I thought you needed it. I heard part of the conversation just now, and I figured . . . You needed to hear the truth from Terrance," Mason explained.

Joya's eyes were drenched with tears too as she listened to her husband solemnly explain the last request from his friend.

Harper fisted her hair while exhaling a weary breath. Dresden was telling the truth. She should have known he wasn't lying. He swore on his deceased wife's name. And one thing Harper knew for sure: Nina was his pride and joy, and he would *never* shame his Rosie.

"I have to clear my head," Harper blurted.

"OK, but first things first . . . You have to go apologize to that man," Joya demanded with her hand propped on an ample hip.

"Facts," Mason seconded his wife.

Harper puffed out a breath. Her glazed, reddened eyes were keenly fixed on nothing at all, but she knew what she had to do.

*Knock. Knock. Knock.*

Dead silence. Nothing.

*Knock. Knock. Knock.*

The front door jerked open. Bella and Bryn's hardened faces feigned irritation at the person knocking on the door like the police. Their twin orbs immediately softened when they saw Harper.

"Hi, Bryn, Bella. Is your dad here?" she stammered.

Bella shook her head. "No. He's not," Bryn said harshly.

Instantly, Harper knew that his daughter likely overheard their conversation this morning and the door slam when she stormed out.

"My daddy is *not* a liar," she continued.

Harper nodded, blinking tired and weary eyes. "I know he's not. And I am so sorry about whatever it is you heard. I was wrong. And I am truly sorry," Harper rasped, clutching praying hands to her chest, gesturing for forgiveness.

Bella and Bryn stared at her, searching her eyes for sincerity. They found so much more. The twins recognized love dangling in the center of Harper's eyes.

"He went for a run," they responded simultaneously.

"Thank you," Harper whispered.

She hopped in her car and sped off down the street. If he was out for a run, he was *processing*, and she knew exactly where he would go.

Dresden was perched under the old oak tree where he and Harper brought in the new year. He was dressed for a run but lacked energy and motivation. Dresden called and texted Harper several times with no answer. He simply wanted to ensure that she was safe.

He gazed into the heavens with his head leaned back on the tree stump. Usually, when he needed a sign, Nina would send a gust of wind or a flashing light to let him know she was there, and everything would work out just fine. But this time, the air was still, unmoved. He guessed shit wasn't going to be resolved this time.

Leaves shuffled in the background, but Dresden did not stir. He simply closed his eyes because he felt *her*. Harper's energy caused a magnetic force, and he was prepared to succumb to her power willingly.

"Hey," she whispered, rounding the tree to stand before him.

"Hey," he responded, gazing up into beautiful, burdened eyes.

Dresden patted the grassy plot beside him, convincing her to sit down. She obliged. Staring out into the open field, they did not look at each other. Dresden clasped her hand, lifting it to kiss the center of her palm before guiding her hand to cup his face.

Shifting, he examined her. A pile of wild curls settled on her head, cherry-red eyes and rosy cheeks plagued her face, and apology danced in the apex of those pretty brown orbs.

"Dre, I am sorry. I was wrong. So fucking wrong," she cried.

"I would never lie to you, Harper. I just . . . I tried . . . I didn't know what else to do. I asked Terrance to talk to you. To prepare his family for the inevitable. I thought he did until today. Until your reaction. But his truth was not my story to tell."

Harper nodded. "Deep down, I knew. I ignored all of my medical training and education because I did not want it to be true. I didn't want my kids to lose their dad. So I ignored the signs."

She turned to face him, enfolding the curves of his powerful face in her hands.

"Dre, please forgive me."

He shook his head. "There's nothing to forgive, honey."

Their foreheads gently collided. Adjoined so intimately, his exhales supplemented her inhales. Dresden charitably fed her his tongue, and Harper greedily feasted. He gently kissed and caressed her as he parted her pouty lips with his tongue. Harper's sweet savor mingled in his nose as their tongues entangled in a delicious dance. The pace was sluggish, leaden as if the park wasn't filled with onlookers. It did not matter. The couple cherished the sensuality, the passion, and the wanton lustfulness they shared.

A flurry of wind ruffled the leaves, lifting them from the ground. Dresden momentarily retreated from the kiss, watching the leaves flitter in an organized dance. That thud, the pounding in his chest, amplified at a rapid, resounding frequency. Harper rested her hands against his chest. The thump continued to hammer, but it capered to a different beat. It drummed at Harper's control because she possessed ownership of his heart. He smiled, one of those big, beautiful, *real* smiles that Nina adored.

"Harper Kingsley, my honey, my best friend, I love you," Dresden declared.

Harper giggled, blushing. "Dr. Dresden, I've loved you since our first hello."

## THREE YEARS LATER . . .

"Dre, are you sure about this?" Harper asked as they navigated through the airport.

"Yes, honey, it will be fine. Everyone will be on their best behavior. Right?" he shouted over his shoulder at the mass of people following behind them.

This was the first family trip with the entire Xavier and Kingsley crew. This also included Joya and Mason's family and Annette and her kids, so it was truly a family affair. Harper's forty-fifth birthday was in a few days, and they were celebrating in Turks and Caicos.

"Right," their kids drawled.

"This should be interesting," Harper moaned.

Harper and Dresden had been exclusively enraptured long before the day at the oak tree, but the confessions of *I love you* sealed their fate. They certainly navigated some rough terrain with their kids still grieving from the loss of a parent and accepting that their living parent has found new love.

Bella and Harper immediately connected like kindred spirits. While Harper never attempted to play a motherly role, she helped Bella navigate life situations like a best friend. Bryn was a harder nut to crack, but eventually, she loosened her reins over her father.

While Trae was slowly building a relationship with Dresden, Hasan was another story. The first two years after Terrance's death, Hasan spiraled out of control. Drinking heavily and even experimented with more than just weed. Harper threatened to sell the family business if her son was not going to honor the promise he made to his father. Her final straw was when Hasan was arrested for fighting after a performance with his band.

Harper was so devastated she could not bring herself to see her son in a jail cell. After cursing that she would '*leave his ass there to rot,*' Dresden convinced her to let him handle it. Harper never asked her man or her son what happened between them the night Dresden posted bail, but Hasan's behavior drastically changed.

A little birdie named Bella told Harper that after Hasan's release, her dad may or may not have pinned him against the car, barking that he would '*whoop his ass if he continued to hurt his future wife.*'

Bella supported Hasan through his sobriety and even convinced him to attend grief counseling. To his dismay, Bella only wanted a friendship, and he obliged. But everyone could see the amorous glint brightening his eyes every time she entered a room.

The oceanfront cottage was divine. It was quiet and secluded with a private beach, yet accessible to everything the island offered.

The seasoned adults of the group decided to rest by the beach while the young folks explored the nearby shops and restaurants.

The next day was Harper's birthday. Dresden hired a chef to cater a private dinner on the beach and secured a masseuse and makeup artist to pamper her and the other ladies for the day. Harper was dressed in an ivory spaghetti-strap silk dress that dipped almost to her waist in the back. Sparkling red bottom shoes graced her feet. Her throng of curls was swooped to one side, secured by a diamond-studded comb. And her makeup was flawless.

"Damn, honey. You are absolutely stunning," Dresden whispered, love and lust prancing in his eyes.

Harper could not ignore how damn good Dresden looked. He was gorgeous in an ivory-tailored suit with a coordinating shirt open at the collar. He wore ivory and gold Versace sneakers to match the gold accents on his lapel.

"Mmm, Dre. You look tasty enough to eat, baby," Harper winked.

"Later," he promised.

At six o'clock in the evening, Dresden escorted Harper to the beach just before sunset. She gasped at the sight. Candles illuminated the pavilion draped in satin. Two long tables were beautifully decorated with gold vases filled with sprays of white roses. The white and gold place settings complemented the golden wineglasses. It was the most glorious and intimate setting she'd ever seen.

Harper's family and friends looked fabulous dressed in white as they sang Happy Birthday. She slowly strolled down the planked walkway, laughing and crying. Dresden followed closely behind her. As they got closer, she was in awe of the magnificent display. He'd outdone himself, and once they entered the pavilion, she spun on her heels to tell him so.

Another audible gasp escaped her lungs. Dresden was on one knee holding a stunning three-carat solitaire platinum ring.

Harper rested a hand on her chest with her mouth hung open in an *O*.

"Harper, I thought I would never find love again. I didn't believe that anything was waiting for me on the other side of grief. But the day you walked into my life, you made me feel again. You made things feel like forever. Harper, the way you love has no limit. It's unconditional, free, and uncomplicated. Now I know that the tears I cried over the years were just water to help the seeds of happiness grow. I did not know where they were planted or when it would bloom . . . until I found you."

Harper dapped the corners of her eyes and vainly attempted to preserve her flawless face.

"I love you, Harper, because my whole family rearranged their plans to help me find you. My mother told you that I was built to be somebody's husband. And I want to be that for you." He clasped her hand, kissing it before proceeding.

"Harper Paloma 'Pudge' 'Honey' Kingsley," he snickered, "will you marry me?"

She did not require a moment to pause or hesitate. Harper cupped his face and yelped, "Yes, Dresden. Yes. Yes. Yes!"

Dresden stood, then slid the ring on her finger. "Tonight," he said. "Right now. In front of all of our important people."

Her eyes widened, but she nodded vigorously.

The officiant stood at the top of the pavilion, waiting for the couple to arrive. Hasan and Trae walked their mother down the aisle. She kissed each of them on the cheeks, thumbing away their tears.

"We love you, Ma," her boys uttered unanimously.

"I love you most," she responded.

Bella and Bryn were flanked on each side of their dad. They escorted him down the aisle to greet his future wife. Dresden kissed their forehead before enclosing them in a firm hug.

"Congratulations, Daddy," Bryn cried. "I miss Mom like crazy, but I am happy you found love again."

"She's here, B. Remember, she's the sun and moon," Bella chimed, kissing her dad's cheek.

Just as Harper and Dresden exchanged their vows, the majestic sun began to dip below the horizon, splashing rays of orange and white against the rippling waves of the ocean.

Dresden gazed into Harper's pretty brown eyes as she reveled in his onyx orbs.

Harmoniously, they sang, *"To love and to cherish, till death do us part."*

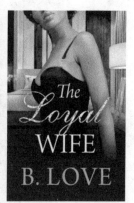

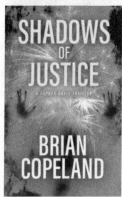

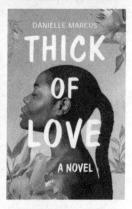